**l**

**(Book 3 of tl**

**By:**

**A.M. Madden**

Dear Karen

Wishing you a fantastic HEA.

♡

A.M. Madden

Encore

A.M. Madden

Published by A.M. Madden



First Edition, eBook-published 2014

ISBN: 1500167886



This book is a work of fiction. Names, characters and incidents are products of the author's imagination or are used fictitiously. Any resemblance to actual persons, living or dead, events or locales is entirely coincidental.

The use of artist and song titles, locations, and products throughout this book are done so for storytelling purposes and should in no way been seen as advertisement. Trademark names are used in an editorial fashion, with no intention of infringement of the respective owner's trademark.



www.ammadden.com

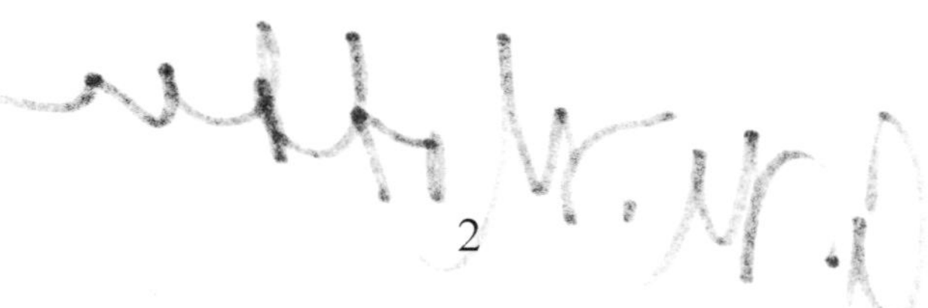

To my three kings, you rule my world.

## Table of Contents

Meeting you was ***fate***, becoming your friend was choice, but falling in ***love*** with you was ***destiny***.

~Unknown.

You don't find ***love***, it finds you. It's got a little bit to do with ***destiny***, ***fate***, and what's written in the stars.

~ Anais Nin

***Fate*** had you walking into that studio two years ago. I had no idea what ***love*** was, what love was capable of doing. It suffocates and debilitates and strips you raw, and I would do it all over again. You rocked my world to the core, you've altered every cell in my body, and you have secured my ***destiny***.

~ A.M. Madden

## Leila's Prologue

Antigua ~ June 22, 2014

When we arrived, I couldn't contain my happiness. I bounced on my toes while clutching his hand tightly between both of mine. He squeezed my hand in return and smiled wide at my enthusiasm. Our private butler, Jensen, showed us our cottage. As we moved from room to room, all I saw were the many places we could have sex. The huge Jacuzzi tub, the four different couches, the king size bed, the chaise lounges on the patio, the private pool, the private beach, the ocean…just to name a few.

I am not a shallow sex fiend who's only interested in getting some. I love my husband with all my heart. Our connection goes way beyond the physical. Our connection is emotional and consuming. Our connection is perfect. The frosting on my cake is that the sex *is* also perfection.

The notion, that this flawless specimen of a man loves me beyond reason and adores me beyond compare, is an aphrodisiac of the most potent kind.

At the end of our tour, Jensen explained we were stocked with supplies and a phone call could get us anything we desired. He reminded us housekeeping would be by every morning unless we hung a "Do not Disturb" sign on the door. Jack tipped the kind man and closed the door behind him.

When Jack turned to face me, his gaze could literally incinerate the clothes I was wearing.

"For the record, we aren't leaving this cottage. So I hope you like this place, because you and I are staying put for fourteen days."

"Sounds like a plan." My panting made me sound as winded as if I ran a few laps around the island.

He stalked over to me, lifted me in his arms, and asked, "Where first?"

True to his word, we never left. We've christened every surface, both inside and out. We barely saw other humans. Our only contact with the outside world was our sweet housekeeper named Rosa, and when Jensen delivered our meals at random times of the day, when we decided we needed fuel to continue our physical activity.

I was in a constant state of ecstasy and not just from his physical love. Yes, we barely wore clothes and couldn't go an hour without foaming at the mouth. More importantly, we talked about everything. We celebrated our birthdays wrapped in each other's arms. He serenaded me on the beach with his guitar. As his fingers moved over the strings, all I could focus on was how sexy his hand looked while sporting his new wedding band.

This man, who is now my husband, who I adore and love more than anything on this planet, attended to my every need: emotionally, physically, and sexually.

In spite of the fact I've been in a state of complete and utter bliss since arriving two weeks ago, I'm now in a horrible mood. I am feeling melancholy that our honeymoon is over. I'm feeling grumpy that Jack has to start wearing clothes again. I don't want to leave. I don't want to share him. I want to stay right here forever. How am I handling it? I am sulking and brooding and acting like a spoiled brat.

Even I am aware my behavior is ridiculous. I'm going back home as Mrs. Jack Lair. I will be living with him daily and working by his side…not exactly hell, but I love naked Jack. I love the feel of the warm Caribbean Ocean between my legs when he takes me, or the rough sand beneath my back when he devours me. I love the feel of cool marble as I consume him on the steps of the pool while on my hands and knees.

Which brings me to my second issue, I am completely out of control. This loss of control isn't like anything I've ever felt before. The best way I can describe it is as if we unleashed a beast. When we were on tour, in constant company with our band mates on a crowded bus, we had to behave. We had to act like civilized people. *I* had to act like a civilized person. I wasn't aware this sexual barbarian even lived inside of me. It was contained, controlled for my entire adult life. I am a completely rational human being. I understand the ramifications that would occur, if I weren't able to control my Jack Lair appetite out in public…mainly being arrested for lewd conduct. But, being here without witnesses or law enforcement to keep me in check has severed the restraints that contained the beast…and now it's out.

"Baby, do you have everything?" He calls out to me from the bathroom. When he's met with silence, he steps into the doorway, waiting for my response. "Babe?"

"Hmm?" I ask distractedly. He isn't wearing a shirt, again. His jeans are hanging low on his hips and my girly parts start to pulse.

What the *fuck*?

I just had him seven minutes ago. How can I be so completely turned on by my husband standing in a doorway, asking me a simple question?

He walks over with concern etched on his face and asks, "What's wrong now?"

"Everything."

"Lei, you're scaring me." He sits next to me on the bed, taking my hand in his. "You've been acting strange all day."

"No, no…not bad wrong. Good wrong."

"What are you *talking* about?" His confusion is clear in his exasperated tone. "How can something be good wrong?"

"I want to stay here, forever."

"I know, me, too. But we can't, Babe. We need to get back. We have the Casiano wedding and the benefit concert and studio time…"

"I know." I cut him off mid-sentence. "I am quite aware of ALL the adult responsibilities that face us when we get home. It doesn't mean I want to be a responsible adult. I like being carefree and naked. And…"

"And what?"

"I want you naked all the time," I fold my arms determinedly, and he laughs. "Stop laughing. It's. All. Your. Fault."

"What's my fault?"

"You've given me the best honeymoon, but you've also created a monster. You've made me an insatiable sex-maniac, and I'm not so sure I'll be able to function outside of these walls among society. I can't be held responsible for my behavior, if you so much as show me your dimples. It's all your fault."

He gives me a lop-sided grin and says, "You are one to talk." He takes my hand and places it on his arousal. "This is just from seeing you sitting on this bed in a string bikini, acting like a brat. Not exactly normal, is it?"

I thrust my tongue out at him, and he captures it between his fingers and tugs.

"How are we going to behave?"

"Not sure it's possible." He moves my hair off my shoulder and nibbles on my earlobe. "We have time for another round. Would that help?"

"No, but I'll take it."

He moves his lips over a few of my erogenous zones, driving me insane in the process. I take hold of his head and force him to look into my eyes. "Thank you. You *have* given me the best honeymoon a girl could ask for. I love you so much. Thank you."

"You're welcome." He leans in and kisses my lips softly. "I love you, too."

We end our honeymoon the way it started. He worships my body on this huge comfortable bed, and makes love to me as if it's the first time. While Jack sinks into me slowly, tears fill my eyes as I stare into his. A flash of our future helps my mood. Slowly, rationality seeps back into my subconscious, allowing me to think clearly. Today is just the beginning. Today is truly the first day of the rest of our lives. We have so much to accomplish, together…and we are just getting started.

## PART ONE - FATE

# Chapter 1- Leila

Just kill me.

Smother my face with a pillow and put me out of my misery. The tightening in the pit of my stomach starts up another round of dry heaving. The vomiting has stopped, only because I haven't had any food or drink in two days. There's nothing left in me. But each bout still sends me to the toilet, just in case. My head pounds in pain from being dehydrated.

Just kill me.

"Babe?" Jack calls out to me from the living room.

The only form of communication I can muster is to grunt. He walks into our bedroom, immediately coming over to where my listless, drained body is lying in a lump on our bedroom floor.

"Holy shit, Baby! What's wrong?"

"It was easier to get to the bathroom each time, if I just lay right outside of it."

"You scared the fuck out of me!"

"Ugh. Please don't yell. It'll make me throw up again."

He palms my forehead, my cheek, my chest, checking for my temperature. "You're not hot. When did this start up again?"

"A hundred hours ago."

He chuckles and lifts me off the ground. "I've been gone less than an hour."

"Jack…hurry…bathroom."

He does an about-face and carries me into the bathroom.

"Get out." I manage to say, right before I commence another round of dry heaving.

He squats beside me, holding my hair. "I'm not going anywhere. Why didn't you call me?"

"The phone was too far way." I heave repeatedly, staring into the bottom of the toilet, wishing something would finally come up.

"You need to see a doctor. This is the third time in two days. I no longer think it's food poisoning. It must be a bug." His tone is angry. He's been hounding me to call the doctor since I first tossed my cookies two days ago. I told him he was, once again, overreacting, and it would pass. I hate being wrong. I especially hate when he's right. He first becomes indignant, and then he gloats annoyingly.

"Ok," I concede. I don't have the energy to fight or argue any more. I'm exhausted. Just as I feel better for a few hours, bam, it hits me again.

I can feel his warm hand rubbing soothing circles on my back. Normally, his touch would rile me up. There must be something seriously wrong with me.

After a few minutes pass, he asks, "Done?"

I nod weakly, afraid that speaking at this moment will trigger my gag reflex. He bends and lifts me again, carrying me toward the bed. He securely tucks me in and commands, "Don't move."

He leaves me for a few seconds, returning with a bottle of water and a large pot. I barely lift my head to acknowledge.

"Why the pot?"

"If you need to get sick, use this," he says in all seriousness. I gawk at him in a very unflattering way. "What?"

"I'm not going to puke in front of you and I'm not using a pot."

"I couldn't find a bucket."

"Jack, that's disgusting."

"I don't give a damn. I don't want you laying on the floor anymore," he barks. When I roll my eyes, he shakes his head. He reaches for my cell phone and scrolls through contacts until he finds the person he needs, as he mumbles under his breath, "You're so stubborn."

I won't admit this to him, but it does feel good to be under the covers. I settle into the coziness and warmth, not missing the hard cold floor. My eyes drift drowsily as I listen to Jack speaking to the receptionist at my doctor's office. After a round of questions regarding my symptoms, his next comment jolts me awake.

"*Pregnancy* test?"

It's as if a light bulb goes off in his brain. A smile slowly spreads across his face. He answers a few more questions, asks some of his own, and then disconnects the call while grinning like a fool.

"So, um…they think your symptoms could be morning sickness."

"It's nighttime."

"It can happen any time of day."

"*Pregnant*?"

Can that be? Crap…I instantly remember the two days I forgot to take my pill. I was supposed to cut him off, and the beast wouldn't allow it. But come on, pregnant? It fucking figures that Jack Lair's sperm is as tenacious as he is.

"Pregnant?" I question again.

He gives me a dazzling smile and skims his thumb along my bottom lip. "You're going to be an amazing mother, my very own MILF."

"Damn it," what I'm thinking slips out of my stupid mouth. My comment causes him to stop his motion and frown.

"Really? It would upset you to be pregnant?"

"We have a tour we are leaving on in a few weeks. How is this going to pan out?"

Jack takes hold of my chin and lifts until I am staring back at him. "I don't give a fuck about the tour. We'll cancel it. It can wait."

"We will do no such thing! Jack, don't start and do not test me on this..." I jerk out of his hold, folding my arms in defiance. He mimics my stance, smirking, and quirking a brow in a challenge.

"OR?" he asks mockingly.

"Or I'll…" I come up empty, not able to think of one suitable threat. I can't threaten to withhold sex, because that simply ain't happening!

When I pout from my frustrations, he kisses me chastely and shakes his head.

"Yeah, hot shot, you got nothing. The tour should be the last thing you worry about."

"I can't help it," I respond petulantly.

This tour was going to be such a pivotal event in our lives. Not having the stress from the last one following us this time, being more comfortable in our rock star skin, having found fame and becoming more popular every day, all make for the ingredients of an epic tour. Pregnancy does not fit well in this recipe and is the last thing I want to happen while we cross the country. On the contrary, there is no way in hell I'm canceling.

Damn it!

"We leave in a month," he counters. "You can still have this morning sickness."

"I'll eat a lot of crackers."

"Lei, it's a short tour."

"Exactly…it's a short tour."

"We can postpone it," his tone becoming short and annoyed.

"No way! I'll go without you." I finally think of a rebuttal, although a lame one.

"Really?" he smirks.

"Yep." He openly laughs at me, spurring me on further. "I'm serious."

"How about we see if you are pregnant first, before you start one of your typical freak-outs?" I stick my tongue out, which he grabs it in between his fingers and tugs.

"Will you be ok here while I run to the drug store?"

I nod distractedly, consumed with the possibility that I could be pregnant.

"I'll be right back."

"Be careful."

"I'm only going up the block. I'm fine." After a kiss on my forehead, my husband practically skips through the door, leaving me alone with my thoughts.

I'm torn. Of course I want kids with Jack, but is this a good time? We're still newlyweds. Next week is our first anniversary. We've been so busy, the last year has been a blur.

We were all exhausted, when we got home from touring. For me, it was more of a mental exhaustion than a physical one. The whole Danny and Jessa debacle wiped me out. Once home, I couldn't get past the "what ifs." What if Jessa had succeeded in ruining Jack's career? What if the baby had been his? What if Danny had succeeded in harming me or killing me? What if Danny had been successful in getting to Jack instead?

I forced myself to stop that line of thinking. I forced myself to enjoy every minute of my life, because I had so much to be grateful for. Between my marriage, my career, and my success, I refused to give that fucker any more power. He tried and failed. He wasn't going to seize my happiness. Our success has been great, and I refuse to be neurotically worried, forever looking over my shoulder. He's in jail, and we need to move on. Jack and I do not agree on this subject. He says security is a must and will do everything in his power to ensure we are safe.

A few weeks after our return, Bayou Stix invited us to guest appear during their concert at *Madison Square Garden* in New York City. We were blown away. Bayou Stix, one of the hottest rock bands ever created, wanted *us* to perform at their show. They caught our show at *The House of Blues* in Baton Rouge last fall. They were impressed and invited us to share the stage with them. We even hung out afterwards and partied until dawn. During the after party, Oscar made friends with their security team. He now runs his own company and is always looking for ways to improve. The men of Steele Security were the best around. They looked like male models on steroids. Gorgeous does not begin to describe Reaper, Bull, Shadow, or Rebel...their nicknames were also hot as hell. Jack caught me gawking at Bull a few times during the after party, raising an eyebrow at me disapprovingly. I wasn't the only one. They had as many girls fawning over them, as did the rock stars that were mulling around in the room.

The Bayou Stix show was the beginning of several surreal events that occurred for us. Between planning our wedding, the Rolling Stone cover article, and being inundated with countless interviews, before I blinked it was June and I was marrying the man of my dreams.

When we got back from our honeymoon, just as I predicted, I couldn't control the beast. I had an insatiable need for him physically. I was grumpy whenever we had to leave our apartment, which was often due to studio time and basically living our lives. It was also a contradiction to how happy I felt. Actually, happy isn't adequate enough of a description. I was on cloud-fucking-nine-off-the-wall-ecstatic. So when some of our friends mistook my grumpiness as unhappiness, specifically Lori, it pissed me off even further.

When we were dating, Jack once told me he was most looking forward to the mundane, the day-to-day functions that most people take for granted. I now agree whole-heartedly. I love being in our apartment with him, playing house. I love making dinner together, or watching TV, or reading side-by-side in bed. I would be completely content in never leaving. In fact, being home in our apartment has become an acceptable substitute for our cottage in Antigua, minus the ocean, private pool, and private butler.

Our parents did well finding this gem. We decorated it together and the results are a warm, inviting space that our friends love to hang out in. It's perfectly located near the studio. It's our haven, and I adore it.

We were only home from our honeymoon a week when we had to fly out to Springfield, Texas to attend Mike Casiano and Lainey Riley's wedding. Mike owns the security company that our bodyguard Oscar Holden worked for. We met Mike and Lainey last May at a benefit concert that we played in New York City. Lainey is a huge Devil's Lair fan. After a really stressful few months from dealing with a crazy guy who was stalking her, Mike surprised Lainey with a New York getaway.

Oscar escorted them backstage, after the show, to introduce us. Lainey and I became instant friends, and Jack and Mike did as well. I wasn't sure about Mike at first. He has the most unique eyes I've ever seen. They are a really pale shade of blue and at first they seem cold, but when I saw him with Lainey, I saw a different man. He adored her, showed it openly, capable of loving with all of his heart.

It was then I was able to relax around him. He and Lainey had a rough time between his experiences in the Navy and her stalker. I thought about that afterwards. My heart went out to them. Their trauma formed an obvious bond between them that was fierce. I recognized it, because I share the same bond with Jack.

Unbeknownst to Lainey, Mike asked if Jack and I would sing at their wedding. The wedding was on her family ranch. It reminded me of our wedding…simple with closest friends and family.

Jack sang my song, *Reason I Am*, while Lainey walked down the aisle. Her emotions were evident on her face, when she realized what he was singing. I'm so proud of him. My song is beautiful. To have another couple connect to it and want it to be part of their wedding day was such an honor. Jack and I later performed their song, *Love Me Tender* for their first dance. Jack played guitar while I sang. Afterwards, we enjoyed their reception and had a fantastic time. We parted promising to see each other again, once we stopped in Texas on our tour.

The trip to Springfield truly marked the end of our "vacation" period and the beginning of our "get our asses back in gear" period. It was July by the time we got back into the studio to work on our second album. Once there, we all fell into a very comfortable routine. It did nothing, however, to soothe the beast. Jack would just laugh at my predicament and taunt me mercilessly. Every evening when we got home from the studio, he would make it up to me, and in the mornings, and many, many times on the weekends.

It took a few weeks for me to settle back into my old self and to once again become a respectable member of society. It was tough working side by side with the cause of my torment. In the studio, Jack and I kept it professional. His work ethics hadn't changed at all since the last time we were recording. The level of Hunter, Scott, and Trey's sarcasm did, though. They made it their mission to piss him off. Most of the time, their antics were funny. On one of my particularly hornier days, the mama bear/beast in me came out and I lost my shit on them. The looks on their faces were priceless.

If I hadn't been rip-roaring mad, I would have laughed my ass off. Afterwards, they sulked for a few hours, making me feel really bad. A double batch of my brownies the next day was my pathetic attempt at an apology. Since that day I forced myself to behave, especially around the guys.

We did have a lot of work to do, but preparing our second album wasn't as intense of an experience as our first one was. Having just come off a pretty extensive tour, the label appeased me and agreed the next one could be shorter. I explained tour number two should segue into our next tour, which will be coast-to-coast, filling large arenas in several dozen cities and running for six months. My main reason for wanting a short tour was based on having sympathy for the guys. The label doesn't know that, though. It was very hard on Scott and Hunter to be apart from their girls for so many months. Jack and I were extremely fortunate to have each other.

Another reason for my request was because of my former band. We thought, since they had just been signed, it would be an awesome opportunity for them to open for us. By making this a shorter tour, Lori and Jen were successful in pitching the combined Devil's Lair / Cliffhangers dual tour to the label. This tour will be an introduction to the label's newest conquests, Cliffhangers. My guys were signed with L.R.V. Media and will be opening for us this time around. I am so proud of them. They deserve this and more. The fact they will be joining us is the cherry on my sundae.

Once they were signed, their lives began to drastically change. Hoboken was no longer their stomping ground. They were playing in well-known bars throughout the city and recording their album in the studio. The label has been very accommodating to them, and the guys have been proving they made the right choice signing them on. It hasn't been all work and no play. Cliffhangers has been celebrating this achievement for weeks now. My brother moved in with Lizzy. Logan and Alisa are expecting their first child.

Lori and Matt are going strong. I wish I could find Joe that special someone he deserves, that may be my next project. All in all, things are going really well for them.

As promised, Louis had a party for us on his yacht and invited Cliffhangers and their significant others as well. They were uncharacteristically quiet and demure during the entire time we sailed around Manhattan. Jack and I laughed about it afterward. It felt like they were teenagers who were taken to someone's house and was threatened to behave. We later found out they were all in shock from seeing the lavish rewards Louis reaps first hand.

Success has found us…my old band, my new band, and myself. I will be recording an album of my own, which will debut during our third tour. I have decided to continue my solo career, but all touring will only be as a Devil's Lair member. Malcolm wasn't happy with my decision. He said that every solo artist should promote and perform to achieve maximum compensation. I don't care about the money part. In my eyes, I achieved success as a solo artist already. My single made Top Ten and held for months. I don't need the paycheck as validation. Devil's Lair is my first priority. Correction, Jack Lair is my first priority.

After our contracts are up next year, we will be renegotiating for our first worldwide tour in two years. Our past year hasn't been all smiles and rainbows, though. Danny's trial tainted our silver lining. We committed to doing everything in our power to keep that maniac behind bars. Jack's dad pulled in some heavy hitters in the legal council area. Danny was denied bail, and his trial took place at the end of last summer.

It's an experience I would like to forget, but I know I never will. Seeing him arrogantly sitting across the courtroom scared me to death. The man has no remorse. He is pure evil. He was convicted of attempted murder, kidnapping, assault, aggravated murder charges on Jessa's unborn baby, possession of heroin with the intent to distribute, and grand theft auto. Guilty on all counts, he is spending the rest of his life behind bars.

Seeing Jessa wasn't any easier, reminding me of all the crap she pulled. Jack and I don't regret not pressing charges, but there is a part of me that wants her to suffer for what she did to us, more than she already has. Jack did file a restraining order against her, really to just prove a point. If she ever attempted to contact us, he said he would press charges in a heartbeat. She got the message loud and clear. She moved to California shortly after we returned from tour. Except for seeing her at the trial, we haven't heard a peep out of her.

The trial was the hardest thing I ever had to experience in my entire life. Once it was over, the swell of relief flooded me in an emotional release that lasted for days. Jack took me away, just the two of us, sequestering us to a quiet cabin in the woods for an entire weekend. I've never been so exhausted, so mentally drained, and so relieved all at the same time.

Jack isn't taking the fact that Danny is behind bars for granted. He and Evan have been relentless in ensuring Lizzy's and my safety. He had a state-of-the-art alarm system put in our apartment. Oscar would accompany us to any social functions we were obligated to attend. After witnessing how angry Danny still is, I agreed it was better to be safe than sorry, but I also didn't want us to live in constant fear. It's not reality to constantly worry if Danny would reach us from the confines of his jail cell. Jack said he isn't going to make it easy for him, in case he tries.

During most of the past year, I've been in the company of Über-protective Jack. Weirdly enough, his sometimes-Neanderthal ways turn me on, for the most part. The beast in me very much likes caveman Jack. Let's be honest, I love all versions of Jack. Whether it is caveman, sensitive, raunchy, rock star, or husband extraordinaire, there isn't a side of him that I don't adore. We get along very well and rarely fight. One night, he took his protectiveness to a whole new level. We had our worst fight ever…discounting the time I broke up with him. It was the first time I saw a Jack that terrified me.

We were only married a few months. I was out with the girls. We decided to hit a new bar uptown. It was loud and my head was killing me. I decided to call it a night and head home. When I got there, he was sitting in our apartment in the dark. At first, I thought nothing of it, because my alcohol induced daze failed to let me recognize the anger that was rolling off of him in waves. With a flip of the lights, I could then see his fury palpable in the air.

"Where the fuck were you?" he asked. His words accosted me, helping me realize how enraged he really was. He has never spoken to me like that. A flash of fear gripped my heart before being replaced with annoyance. My assumption was he didn't trust me. I couldn't wrap my brain around that possibility. That has never been an issue for either of us, even when his ex-girlfriend tried to break us up. In the few seconds that we stood eyeing each other suspiciously, time suspended for me in an indelible way.

"I was out with the girls. You know that."

"I've been trying to call you for an hour. You didn't leave me with a location. You didn't have Oscar with you. I tried calling each of you. I finally spoke to Liz and Lori. They also tried calling you, after you left. Why would you leave alone? Why the fuck didn't you go home with someone?"

"I have a major headache and I want to get to bed. I also had no idea my cell phone had died in my bag until I got in the cab. We were all the way uptown and it took forever to get home. By then, I figured I'd be seeing you shortly."

“Do you have any idea what you’ve put me through?”

“I do now. I didn’t consciously set out to piss you off.” I threw my bag on a chair and turned back to him.

“For all I knew, you were dead. I called every hospital in the area.” He raked his hands furiously through his hair and then scrubbed them down his face. “I was minutes away from calling the police.” He walked over to the window, and I could see his livid reflection staring back at me.

“Jack, it’s barely been an hour since I left the bar. I feel bad you…”

“I’m so fucking angry with you!” He turned on me, cut me off, and barked, “You have no right making me worry like that!”

“Jack, I didn’t mean to worry you. You need to relax.”

“Jesus Fucking Christ, Leila! Relax? After what you went through, what we went through. How inconsiderate can you be?”

“I understand you were scared. I’m sorry. It was a mistake.”

I did feel bad. I truly did. But that didn’t give him the right to treat me like that. I wanted to both comfort him and tell him to go fuck himself. His next comment made my decision.

“Your irresponsible behavior will not be tolerated,” he said condescendingly, leveling me with both his words and his eyes.

“Tolerated? I am not your teenage daughter who missed curfew. Fuck you, Jack!”

I stormed into our room, slamming and locking the door before he had a chance to get to me.

He cursed, pounded, and commanded me to open the door. I refused and ignored him as best I could. It wasn’t easy. He threatened to break the door down. I threatened to call the police, if he did. The door between us became a proverbial line in the sand. Suddenly he went quiet. My chest constricted painfully from the raw emotions I was feeling, my head still pounded relentlessly.

I've never been scared of him, ever! This Jack terrified me. I sat on my side of the door, dumbfounded from what just happened. A myriad of scenarios ran through my head. The impulsive alarmist in me concluding this damage was irreversible.

I sobbed as quietly as I could. Then he softly called my name through the door.

"Lei, I'm sorry. I was so scared. I didn't know what happened to you, I couldn't imagine what happened to you. I've only been this terrified once, and…" I heard him choke on his words, an agonizing sound followed that broke me. I wasn't able to stifle my sobs any longer. He heard me and knocked again, begging me to open the door.

I had to convince myself that this man loved me and would never, ever hurt me.

When I opened the door, he stood broken and defeated. He immediately pulled me into his arms as sobs convulsed through his body. We held each other for what seemed like hours, each afraid to let go.

There was tension between us for a few days after that awful night. Slowly, we released the hurt and pain we each felt for our own reasons. We discussed it, talked it through, and buried it…neither one of us ever brought it up again. I became more cognizant of the constant worry he has regarding my safety. He became more cognizant of the way he handles situations when he is scared. I came to terms with the fact that he loves me more than anything on this planet. The thought of losing me is what caused him to behave the way he did. I made peace with the realization that he will never relax when it comes to me or to my safety. I accepted the reality, and I need to be more sensitive to his fears.

I did a lot of soul searching after that night. I have been selfish in denying the combination of our exploding popularity coupled with the people in our paths that want to hurt us and have placed a gigantic bulls-eye on our heads. My husband has been carrying a huge amount of anxiety, and I need to be more sensitive regarding that. I tried to put myself in his shoes, tried to imagine what I would have felt if Danny had gotten to Jack instead of me. How would I have felt while sitting in a hospital room, crippled with fear? My husband has been through hell, and I won't put him through that ever again.

So when Jack hired Oscar as our full time security guard, I didn't argue. He is with us almost every day. On days he isn't, Alec, his newly hired assistant, is. When he demanded that I no longer go anywhere unaccompanied by one of them, I didn't argue. I didn't fight him. I conceded that he needed this to feel safe, and I wasn't going to cause him any further strife.

We've both grown a lot in a year and matured in our relationship. Being married to him is better than I could have imagined. Selfishly, I want him all to myself. I know it's a horrible way to think, but I'm not ready to share him. He is a very good husband. I'm a lucky girl. No one could've predicted the hot-man-whore rock star that I met in the studio on my audition day would be a model husband. In hindsight, it's not surprising to me since he is good at everything he does, and I know he's going to be an even better dad. I just hope it's not too soon. We haven't scratched the surface in our careers, yet.

Granted, we've come a very long way. The combination of being a bona fide rock star and being married to the most desired rock star in the nation is both euphoric and difficult. The women chasing Jack have been a bit of a nuisance. They find us everywhere. It's all about them. They have no problem interrupting a dinner, snapping a picture of us anywhere they see fit.

I was once photographed entering a ladies room as Jack waited for me in the hall. The Internet chatter claimed I couldn't wipe my own ass without Jack's help.

Really?

And although we have come so far in just a year, we still have a ton yet to accomplish…and now with a baby?

I look around our bedroom, and at all the little touches that make it so special to me. It's equal parts Jack and me. It's sexy, homey, and warm. I love it here. I'm not ready to leave it yet. I know a baby doesn't take up much room, and we do have a spare bedroom, but it will only be a matter of time before our haven is overrun. I'm not mentally ready to move into the next phase yet. Our newlywed phase went by too quickly.

On the other hand, the thought of Jack as a father warms my heart. I can picture him holding a beautiful baby boy, blessed with his father's grey eyes and dimples. I can see him in a park, tossing a ball to a toddler, laughing adorably. I can even envision him holding a little girl's hand as she dons her pink tutu on the way to ballet class. I just thought it would happen down the proverbial road, and not so soon.

I guess there really is never a good time to start a family, especially if your life takes you on the road so often. I usually put the semantics on how that would work at the back of my mind, reasoning with myself that I had plenty of time to worry about that later. I thought we would try to have kids in a few years, after our worldwide tour ended. The planner in me falsely depended on being able to work in a family when it fit well for Devil's Lair.

Ha, ha, joke's on me.

My nausea takes hold again, sending me back to my new hangout. When Jack returns, he finds me on the bathroom floor, cradling my open laptop.

"What are you doing? I told you to use the pot."

"I'm not using the pot."

"Babe, get up off the floor." He takes the laptop and hoists me up into a standing position. "You need to pee on this," he demands, pulling a pregnancy kit out of the bag.

"Now?"

"No, let's wait nine months and be surprised."

"Smartass," I huff, snatching the test out of his hands. He sits on the edge of the tub, as if he is settling into his front row seat for a show.

"Do I get privacy?"

"Sure," he responds while kicking the door shut.

"I meant from you."

"Oh, no. I'm stayin'."

He ignores my head shaking and watches intently as I take the necessary steps to get the stick to reveal a plus or negative.

As I embarrassingly clean myself up, Jack leans over the thing like it's going to speak to him. I know the results before looking at the test from the smile that spreads across his gorgeous as fuck face.

His arms surround me as he lifts me while spinning slowly. "Baby, we're pregnant!"

My giggles provoke him even more. "Wait, I'm going to throw up."

He stops quickly and puts me back down. "I'm sorry."

Once back on the ground, my stomach settles and my head stops spinning. "Ok, false alarm."

He carries me back to our bed, sitting me on the edge. "Would you like anything? Tea? Crackers?"

"Babe, I can get my own crackers."

"Nope. I got it." He returns a few seconds later with a box of crackers and a glass of milk.

"What's with the milk?"

"Don't pregnant women need milk?"

"What?" I ask, unable to hide my mirth.

"You know, drink it to make it?"

"Oh, my God!"

"What?"

"God, I love you."

He sits next to me, beaming. I palm his face and ask a rhetorical question, "You're happy?"

"Lei, you have no idea. I've been waiting for this day since the day I proposed to you."

I pull him closer for a kiss. He pulls back, concern etched on his face. "You aren't?"

"Baby, I am, but I can't deny I'm really concerned about this. Ultimately, it would have been better to wait a few years." He watches me closely, but the happiness in his eyes is unyielding. I don't want to upset him, but I need him to understand the enormity of our newfound situation. We do have an obligation to fulfill. "I just feel it's not the right time."

"Leila, this is happening now for a reason, and I couldn't be happier. Don't worry about stuff we can't change. Once we know you're due date, we'll call the label and discuss if anything needs to be revised."

"You make it sound so easy."

"It is. The most important thing is you and that baby." Annoyance flashes through his eyes. He's losing his patience with me.

"And you."

"And me. Ok?"

"Yes, ok."

"Who are we telling first?"

“We are supposed to wait until the second trimester. We’ll tell the guys as soon as we leave on tour.”

“That sucks,” he frowns adorably. “That will be more torturous than when we had to keep our relationship a secret.”

“It’s not going to be easy, especially if I feel like this. Let’s see how it goes. For now, we’ll tell our parents, Evan and Lizzy. But that’s it. Besides, these things give false positives all the time. I need to see a doctor to confirm.”

My comment causes his smile to disappear.

“I’m sure I’m pregnant. It all makes sense now. My boobs even hurt.”

“I can help with that.” He skims the backs of his fingers over my t-shirt.

“I must be feeling better. I’m getting turned on.”

“Hold that thought.” He lifts me, gently placing me in the center of our bed. The way he handles me makes me laugh out loud. “What?”

“I’m not going to break.”

“Just humor me,” he huffs while rolling his eyes. He then picks up my cell, scrolling through my contacts again.

“Who are you calling now?”

“*You* are making an appointment as soon as they can squeeze you in, and then I’m making love to the mother of my child.”

“What if I need to throw up during?”

“You’ll use the pot.”

♬ ♬ ♬

My dad and Barb are the first to arrive. We are expecting Jack’s parents, Evan and Lizzy, as well. Once we confirmed that I was indeed pregnant, Jack immediately called them and invited them over for dinner. The Lair's weren't able to make it for a few days, and Jack has been busting at the seams.

I'm still nauseous, and I still have several bouts of morning sickness each day. My doctor said it should end in the second trimester, which did help me feel a tad better. Maybe with luck I won't be sick while on tour.

My doctor did give me tips to help with the nausea and suggested that I identify triggers to avoid. I quickly learned coffee is most definitely a trigger, especially first thing in the morning. I feel awful about that. Jack needs his morning coffee, like an addict needs their daily hit. He said it was no big deal, and that he would give it up for as long as needed. He can get his fill outside of the apartment as I get ready in the morning. More of my amazing husband being amazing.

I've lost some weight. Nothing appeals to me at the moment, except for apple juice, mango sorbet, toast, and potatoes. Mango sorbet? What the fuck? I don't even like mangos. And you would think having potatoes three times a day, prepared in every which way, would make me even queasier. Nope, I can't get enough of them.

The "bible," as we now refer to our pregnancy book that sits on my nightstand, says it's completely normal for strange cravings to appear and for certain foods that were once loved to become triggers. As of right now, besides coffee, I can't take the smell of garlic or look at raw chicken.

The combination of morning sickness and being pregnant has sent my overbearing, overprotective, neurotic husband into a tailspin. He wants me doing absolutely nothing and he's driving me crazy. He called us both in sick for the past few days, claiming we had a stomach flu…a contagious one, in case Hunter considered dropping by to bother us.

I'm going through some crazy changes hormonally. I cry at the drop of a hat. It could be caused from absolutely anything. I've never been the crying type. Jack has only seen me cry a few times during our relationship. Yesterday it was because I burnt my toast. The look he gets on his face when I have one of my episodes is priceless. He gets totally baffled and has no clue how to handle me. After the burnt toast episode, he told me he'd buy me a new burn proof toaster. It was so sweet.

While home, he has doted on me, cleaned the apartment, did the laundry, grocery shopped, and made me potatoes. Anxious for our dinner tonight, he's been up since the crack of dawn, making sure I was taken care of and everything was perfect for our families. Little does he know, while he was out shopping I organized a closet and recleaned the bathroom.

"Leila, you look pale. Are you ok, dear?" Barb asks as Jack's serves them their drinks and my apple juice in a wine glass.

"I'm fine," I can barely utter the words, trying to control my nausea. Today has been a bad day. I take a small sip and reach for a cracker from the cheese platter that Jack put out. Jack instantly knows what I'm dealing with. He grabs a few more for me while rubbing my back and draws attention to my turmoil.

"What's wrong?" my dad asks, watching Jack's every move.

I throw Jack a look, which he chooses to ignore. "Just stomach problems. I'll be fine."

Dad and Barb exchange a look of their own as the door buzzes.

"Finally," Jack mutters and goes to let the rest of our guests in.

"Hey, sorry we're late." Evan says, as he and Lizzy follow Peter and Renatta into the apartment.

"You're killing me, man," Jack mumbles, leaving Evan confused and Lizzy responding defensively, "We aren't that late."

After quick hellos, more drinks for our guests, and small talk regarding what everyone's been up to, everyone is sitting around our living room relaxed and chatting comfortably, when my husband blurts out, "So…we have some news." All eyes focus on him, as he grips my hand in between his.

"Oh, my God!" Renatta exclaims before Jack is able to share.

Jack smiles wide at his mother and announces, "We're having a baby."

The women shriek, the men praise as they each take their turn man-handling us in their own way.

My dad hugs me tight, rocking me back and forth. "I can't believe this. I thought for sure I'd have to wait years for this to happen. I am so happy for you, but more so for me."

I laugh at his candor, "I'm happy for you too, Dad." He strokes my cheek, smiling through tears. "When? When is my grandchild due?"

"First week in January."

"A New Year's baby? That's great. He may be too young for opening day, but he'll be good to go the following year."

"Dad, *he* may be a *she*, and you aren't taking a toddler to Yankee Stadium."

"We'll see."

"Anthony, I have to agree with my wife. His…" Jack shoots me a look and adds, "or her first game should be a Subway Series, Yankees vs. Mets."

When I gape at them, they both simultaneously ask, "What?"

"When did you all find out?" Lizzy asks.

"A few days ago. You are the first and only to know. We don't want to announce until I'm done with my first trimester. So please keep this to yourselves."

They all nod, promising to do so.

"So how are you feeling, dear?" My mother-in-law asks from her new seat next to me. She and Lizzy squeezed Jack out and are now flanking me on the couch.

"It's been rough, but Jack has been great…neurotic, but great." I smile warmly at my husband.

"When I was pregnant with Jack, all I could tolerate for three months were potatoes."

Jack and I burst out laughing at his mom's admission. "Me, too. I eat them every day…and mango sorbet. I saw a commercial for it and had Jack running to the store. It's the only thing that quenches my thirst. Why is that?"

"That's hilarious, I loved orange. Not sure, but I couldn't get enough of those potatoes. Peter became a professional at inventing new ways for me to eat them."

"He'll have to share them with Jack. I'm getting bored with mashed and baked."

"I craved chocolate with Evan. It became a major food group for me."

"Well, that makes sense," I respond to Barb, as Evan nods. He's an absolute chocoholic.

"Lei, will you be canceling the tour?" My dad asks innocently.

"No. Why would we do that?"

"Because, you'll be pregnant and you should be home, not traveling on some bus across the country."

"Don't bother, Anthony. It won't work. She's stubborn. She got her doctor to clear her and she's going," Jack grumbles with a ton of attitude.

"Have you hit your head?" I ask him.

"No," he actually answers me in all seriousness.

"Talk some sense into her. A bus is no place for a pregnant woman." My dad directs his next asinine statement directly to my husband.

"Can you two stop talking about me like I'm not here. I am going on the tour and I'll be fine."

"She's right. Most likely she'll feel great her second trimester. Your mentality is absolutely ridiculous. She's pregnant, for God's sake. Does the world stop when someone is pregnant? Thank God it's not you men procreating," Barb responds impatiently while my dad and my husband throw *me* their dirty looks…jeez.

"So true, Barb." Renatta laughs at Barb's comment. "Men are such BIG babies."

My dad, father-in-law, and Evan scowl at the women who are openly ridiculing them while my husband's eyes remain glued to me. I smile at him warmly through my tears, and he returns one of his own.

As our families celebrate our blessed news around us, the electricity courses between us. The enormity of what we just revealed to our families tonight hits me. We are going to be parents. It doesn't seem possible for our connection to strengthen. It's already ironclad. But as I stare into his gorgeous eyes, I know without a doubt it is now stronger. It's downright bulletproof.

## Chapter 2 – Evan

"Liz…come on, we're very late."

"I'm coming."

She emerges from our bedroom looking like a runway model.

"Holy. Mother. Of. God." I close the distance between us, immediately taking her into my arms. "You look incredible. You always look incredible, but fuck, Liz."

She giggles and leans up to kiss my neck. "So I'm forgiven for making us late?"

"You're most definitely forgiven." I dig my fingers into her hair, bringing her lips to mine to devour her mouth. She moves her hands to the nape of my neck, trying to get even closer. The kiss is nothing but a tease. Normally, I would be carrying her into our bedroom right about now, but instead, I need to calm myself down and get her to the party at Granite.

I pull back to inspect her from head to toe. "You're killing me. I need you again."

"You just reminded me why I'm late. It's actually your fault we had such a late start."

"Oh, yeah." I admit, before kissing the tip of her nose.

"Ok, we really have to move it or Jack is going to kill us both." She pulls away to retrieve her bag. The black dress she is wearing is a second skin over her curves. It's short enough to reveal her gorgeous legs, all toned and tan. Her caramel colored hair hangs long and loose down her back. Deep inside of me there is an alter ego who is completely capable of keeping her captive, tied to my bed, and never letting her leave.

She is by far the best looking woman I have ever seen in my entire life. I'll never forget the day I met her. We were at Granite for her brother's surprise party. She walked across the room and I, literally, felt a jolt coursing through me. At the time I had no idea what it was, but I remember the sensation vividly. Mainly because it still happens every time I see her. She simply knocks the wind out of me…by merely walking into a room, by smiling at me, or by leveling me with her gorgeous grey-blue eyes. It took one date to fall in love with her. None of it made any sense to me, which is why I trusted it.

Her beauty isn't even close to her goodness. She is without question the kindest, most caring person I've ever met.

When she turns toward me, I'm gawking like a loon, as I often do.

"What?"

"I love you."

She throws me her dazzling smile before saying, "I love you, too. Let's go." She takes my hand, leading me out of our apartment. I moved in with her six months ago. We were practically living together anyway.

Once Cliffhangers got signed with the same label that carries Devil's Lair, I packed my things and made the move. Almost overnight my life changed. We quit playing at The Zone, which was tough for all of us. Sal was absolutely fine with it. He said he prepared himself once Leila left that we were right behind her. He has already replaced us, but that place was our second home. It's nerve-wracking to leave something so comfortable and safe behind, only to embark on something so elusive and unknown. Most likely we will achieve success, but there aren't guarantees. Leaving The Zone was the hard part, for all of us. Moving in with Lizzy was a no-brainer.

I was itching to do so a lot sooner than I did. With that fucker Danny and his fixation on her, I was in a constant state of anguish having her so far from me. He's in jail, but I fear he could have someone else executing his deep-rooted need for revenge. Jack feels the same way. Oscar is now employed by Devil's Lair full time. We do benefit from that, when we are in their company, but not on a daily basis. Jack offered to extend Oscar's staff and Lizzy wouldn't have it. She's extremely stubborn. The minute we achieve success, I'm hiring my own personal bodyguard to keep her safe. She promised that she would be careful and never venture out alone. Our building and her office both have security. Regardless, I'm still anxious leaving her.

Granted, it's a short tour. We are headlining for Devil's Lair. We are only playing ten major cities, over a two-month window. I'm looking forward to the experience. It's going to be fantastic traveling with the guys and Leila. Soon, we will all be flying out to Los Angeles. I've never been there and I'm stoked that's our starting point. Our first task will be to meet with the label's main suits and record a new collaboration between DL and Cliffhangers. The label is giving us one week in the studio before opening night. The song will segue into our sets every night. By the time we end our tour, Jen informed us every radio station from coast to coast will be playing it daily.

Shit, that's hard to wrap my brain around. It's easy to watch others you know achieve success from the sidelines. The thought of it happening to us, when only a year ago we were confined to one tiny bar in Hoboken, seems outlandish.

The combination of recording a song with Devil's Lair and touring with them from coast to coast, "will make for a sure shot at success"…Jen's words, not mine. She and Lori have been working together very closely to get us noticed. Leila is peeved they get along so well. Leila and Jen never managed to achieve that. Lori assured her they are most definitely are not

BFFs and she's only "keeping her close to keep an eye on the bitch"…Lori's words, not mine.

After L.A., we will then bus it from stop to stop, crisscrossing our way back to end in New York City. We'll have two back-to-back shows in each city with hotel stays flanking our performance nights. We will also have time to ourselves before and after each show. Leila teased this is a prima-donna tour compared to their last one, more like a vacation. I can't argue with her. She's absolutely right.

Basically, it's going to kick ass and I am beyond excited. The only thing that would make it better would be if Lizzy could come. I'm not the only one who will be missing his significant other. Logan will be leaving behind a very pregnant Alisa, and Nina, our co-lead singer, and her boyfriend will be apart. Matt will be the only one traveling with his girl. Lori, will be joining us as our agent, thus making Matt a very happy man. Joe couldn't give a shit since he is single…again.

Of the Devil's Lair crew, Jack is the only lucky man to have his wife right by his side. Leila is very sympathetic to our situations. She insisted the tour be short. She witnessed the stress and heartache Hunter and Scott went through on their first tour. She wants to spare us the same heartache. That's my sister, always thinking of others. It actually turned out to be a blessing since Jack and Leila are now expecting. Our tour ends a few months before her due date. I've never seen Jack so happy. The man is glowing. He simply cannot wipe the smile off his face.

It was a rough start for them, and I am so happy everything worked out. I'm the first to admit that I didn't feel he was right for Leila. His past reputation was hard to ignore. On several occasions, I wanted to kick his ass. I'm also the first to admit that I was wrong. He and Leila are a perfect fit. They are meant to be, just as Lizzy and I are.

Liz and I agreed that she would join us on tour for a few days, two weeks in and two weeks from the end. She can't come out more than that. Her patients need her and it's not fair for me to expect her to. She's a psychiatrist with a very successful practice that she has poured her sweat and tears into. I'm proud of her. Doesn't mean I'm not selfish in wanting her to be with me twenty-four seven. I am at a loss on how I'm going to handle our separation. She's my missing half. We rarely fight or disagree. Our relationship is easy, and loving, and the best thing to ever happen to me. I can't wait to make her mine.

"What are you thinking about?" she asks as she takes my hand in the cab.

"How much I'm going to miss you."

"I don't want to think about that tonight." She says with a brooding expression on her face.

I take her chin to turn her toward me. "Hey, I'm sorry." I pull her closer to kiss her lips. She responds willingly, her lips teasing me, her hand skimming my thigh. When she dips her tongue in to meet up with mine, I moan into her mouth before pulling away. "Liz. You already worked me up at the apartment. I'll tell this cabbie to turn around, if you keep that up."

She smiles and retreats to her side of the cab. "Ok, I'll be good."

I reach for her hand and pull her closer. "There's no need to be all the way over there."

It's not long before the cab pulls up to Granite. Just as we do, Hunter emerges from the door. It's fairly early for club hours, yet there still is a line of patrons waiting to get in. They take one look at Hunter, and they all start screaming. He turns to them, smiling and waving, and then turns to us like a possessed demon.

“Jesus Christ, what took you so long?” he grumps as we walk toward him. “They are going to be here any minute. He texted me a thousand times.”

“Sorry, my fault,” Lizzy says as she leans in to give him a chaste kiss on the cheek.

“Babe, no it wasn’t,” I correct her.

“Yes, it…”

“Ugh…what…ever,” Hunter cuts her off.

“You need a drink, man,” I mumble, more to myself.

“I need to kill Jack.”

Jack is throwing Leila a surprise party. Her birthday is in a few days. He went all out. The man would do anything for her. I spoke to her earlier today, and she doesn’t have a single clue. She thinks we are all hanging out tonight to celebrate both her and Jack’s birthdays, which are a day apart, as well as our upcoming tour and their first anniversary, which is tomorrow.

There will be over one hundred guests. Most are friends and family, with some rockers, pop-stars, and super models thrown in. Joe is off the wall excited. His main goal is to ‘become attached’ in more ways than one. He’s at the point where he no longer jokes about joining *Match.com*, but is planning his profile page instead.

I’m guessing Hunter has gotten the brunt of Jack and his unreasonable requests. I’ve heard about a few of his demands through Lizzy. He tried to move heaven and hell to get Springsteen here tonight. He wasn’t able to make it, but he did send a note and an autographed CD to Leila as a birthday gift. I know she’s going to freak out over that. Jack sulked for days. He felt that wasn’t good enough.

Hunter says something else, but I can hardly hear him. The noise level outside the club becomes deafening. I motion toward the entrance, and we hurriedly move through the doors to escape the chaos.

Whenever we are in the company of Devil's Lair, anywhere in the city, pandemonium hits. It's insane the attention those guys get, Leila included. We couldn't be happier to be attached to such an awesome rock band. We know we all stepped in shit, and we are thankful that we did.

Hunter briefs us on the quick elevator ride up to the rooftop bar. "They are minutes away. You cut it really close."

Neither of us can argue that, so we take our hand slapping with dignity.

The elevator opens to a room full of guests all turned toward us, waiting patiently. Scott emerges from the crowd and says, "They just pulled up."

Hunter turns on us red-faced and my gorgeous girlfriend kisses his cheek before he can spew a nasty comment. His scowl turns to a smile and he shakes his head, just as the elevator pings.

We barely turn when the room screams, "Surprise!"

We really did cut it close.

Leila stops in her tracks, stunned into silence. She turns to Jack and buries her face in his chest.

He laughs at her embarrassment and pulls her away to whisper something into her ear. She shakes her head while he nods simultaneously.

My sister is not happy with attention. Ironically, she has chosen a career that tests her trepidations on a daily basis, but this is way beyond her comfort zone.

Lizzy and I are the first to approach. "Happy Birthday, Lei." Lizzy pulls her into a hug and passes her to me. She murmurs, "You couldn't warn me about this?"

"Not if I value my life."

"I would have killed him," Jack confirms and adds, "Babe, you have a lot of people to greet."

"I guess I'll be back." She looks around the room, dread mixed with fear passing through her eyes. She takes a deep breath, as if she's about to face a judge.

She is passed around from guest to guest. I watch from a distance, amused with how she wears her feelings on her face so obviously. Joy, when greeted by Dad, Mom, and the Lairs. Awe, when greeted by some of the more famous of her guests such as MACE. Irritation, when greeted by Jen and Malcolm. The look she wears during that five-minute conversation is comical. It's not long after, when she is back with Liz and me while sipping her juice.

"You are hilarious," I admit when she saunters over smiling.

"I'm glad I amuse you by walking across a room."

"No, you worked this room like you were being timed. Plus, the look on your face when you were talking to Jen and Malcolm was priceless."

Leila bites on her bottom lip and mumbles, "Damn it. I need to work on that. Jack has pointed that out to me so many times."

"No one noticed, especially not Mr. and Mrs. Oblivious."

"They are oblivious…and a perfect match."

"How are you feeling?"

"It's getting a little better. As long as I eat every hour or so I don't feel as nauseous, but I'm still tossing my cookies a few times a day."

"Eww."

"You asked."

"Did you decide when you would be telling people?" Lizzy asks.

"I really want to wait, but it's getting harder. It took me an hour to find something to wear."

We both glance down at her belly, and she blushes. "You aren't showing at all," Lizzy comforts her.

"Oh, yes I am!" She subtly lifts her top to reveal a rubber band holding together her waistband. "Lori wanted to go shopping a few days ago. I wanted to so desperately. I really need a few things to wear, but she would know immediately."

"She's going to flip when she finds out."

"She's going to kill me for not telling her."

As if on cue, Lori comes over hand-in-hand with Matt while leading a waitress holding a tray full of Jell-O shots. I watch my sister's face go from smiling to panic-stricken. "Oh crap," she mutters to herself.

"Happy Birthday, Lei!"

"Thanks, Lor."

Jack's radar instantly picks up on the situation, as he saunters over to, no doubt, help his wife. As Lori passes out the shots, Jack and Leila proceed to have an entire conversation with their facial expressions alone.

Jack pulls two shots off the tray and holds them in his hand. "I'll have Lei's. She isn't feeling well."

"What's wrong with you?" Lori stares her down, waiting for a response.

"Um…stomach bug."

"You've had a stomach bug for over a week now."

"It's a slow bug."

"I call bullshit."

Leila moves closer to her best friend and lowers her voice, "Stop talking so loud."

"Oh, my God!" She raises her finger and points at Leila's belly as her other hand covers her gaping mouth.

"Lor, I don't want anyone knowing yet."

"Holy shit." She looks around and announces, "Patio. Pronto."

Lori takes hold of Leila's hand and drags her toward the outdoor patio. Jack follows and so do Matt, Liz, and I. Once we all congregate on the patio, Lori points to me and accuses, "Ev knows?"

"He's my brother. Liz is Jack's sister."

"I'm your sister. Not technically, but really, Lei?"

"I'm sorry. We just told our families. I promise no one else knows."

"I'm not just anyone. I am so hurt," she flips her hair dramatically.

Leila throws me a resigned grimace. "I'll make it up to you."

"Can I name it?"

Leila raises her eyebrows and asks, "It?"

"He…she," she responds, rolling her eyes.

"Um…no."

"What's going on back here?" Hunter and Amanda intrude.

"Ok, I see where this is going. Hunter do me a favor and gather Scott and Trey and bring them back here please." Leila takes control of the situation.

"Are you sure, Babe?" Jack asks.

"I don't think we have a choice."

As Hunter goes to retrieve our friends, Lori shoots questions at Leila and Jack in rapid fire.

"How did this happen?"

"First, I slipped my hand down her pants to get her…"

"Jack!" Leila smacks him to stop his play by play.

"Seriously, dude. That's my sister."

"Sorry," he smirks to keep from laughing.

"I know how, you jackass. I mean *HOW*. Didn't you two want to wait awhile?"

"She did. I never signed up for that plan." Leila throws Jack a look, and he shrugs in apology. "Well, I didn't."

Sighing heavily, Leila shakes her head and says, "Really? Does it matter? It happened."

A commotion causes us all to turn in time to see the rest of DL joining our pregnancy pow-wow.

"So what's with the impromptu meeting?" Hunter asks, looking from face to face.

The tiny outdoor patio cramps us all together in an uncomfortable amount of space. We are practically shoulder-to-shoulder, as we circle Leila and Jack, awaiting their announcement.

They in turn look at each other, clearly stalling. "Um…" Leila raises her eyebrows, in an attempt to get Jack to take control.

"Ok, so we have something to tell you guys. But we really don't want anyone else knowing. It's very early and we wanted to wait until we left, but since…"

"Spill it, dude," Hunter barks.

"Leila is pregnant."

They react with gaping mouths, bulging eyes, and utter silence.

"Well?"

"You're shitting us," Hunter is the first to speak.

"Nope…not shitting you." Jack puts his arm around Leila, pulling her into his side.

No one speaks and Leila looks really uncomfortable.

Hunter finally breaks the tension, "Um…that's fucking…awesome." His words are a complete contradiction to his facial expression.

Jack looks like he's about to hit someone.

"I personally can't wait to be an uncle. That kid is going to be the coolest kid around." I poignantly level each of the three assholes on this patio with my glare. Not sure if it's alcohol or that these idiots are just competently insensitive, but my words work.

"Yeah, guys. That's great. Congrats," Scott adds while nodding.

The reaction that should have occurred after Jack's announcement finally comes. There's hugging, kissing, and congratulations offered.

Jackasses.

Once the noise level lessens, Leila teases, "That was quite a delayed reaction."

"Aw, come on, Lei. Don't be upset. We were just shocked. You can't blame us for that. We are going on tour, and it's hard to imagine our next tour with a baby on board." Hunter pulls her away from Jack and into his own arms. He kisses the top of her head and adds, "Please forgive us. We're idiots."

Trey shakes his head and laughs out loud. "Fuck that. I haven't lost my balls. This is gonna suck." We all turn to stare at him when he adds, "I'm happy for you two, but we're Rock Stars. Rock Stars don't change diapers."

"No one is asking you to change diapers, *Rock Star*," Jack responds through clenched teeth. "This is the best fucking news, and if you guys aren't happy for us because it's going to cramp your style, you can all suck it. I am beyond happy. My wife was worried about how this was going to work. You aren't helping. So either be happy for us, or shut the fuck up."

You can literally see the smoke billowing from his ears. He's pissed, and I can't say I blame him.

"Trey, I get it," Leila reaches for his hand. He takes it and shrugs. "I know it's going to be strange and hard for you, but it is what it is."

"What the fuck?" Jack barks. "Stop consoling him."

Lori moves forward and puts her hands on Jack's shoulders. "Men are mentally incapable of seeing past their own happiness unless it's at the end of their cocks. Give them time." She then hugs Leila and adds, "I'm very happy for you. This kid is one lucky son-of-a-bitch."

Scott and Hunter hang their heads in shame as Trey smiles wickedly at Lori. Matt notices and pulls her back into his chest, circling her possessively with his arms, staking his claim.

Trey tilts his beer up and says directly to Matt, "She's a smart lady."

Matt smiles sardonically and Lori quips, "He knows."

"Don't move, anyone," Hunter calls out as he jogs off the patio, back toward the party.

"When are you due, Lei?" Scott asks remorsefully.

"Early January."

A few minutes later, Jen appears on the patio, arms folded, in her usual confrontational stance. "Ok, so why is my band hiding back here when there are plenty of important people out there they should be schmoozing with?"

Hunter follows behind Jen carrying a tray of shots, looking all kinds of sheepish and shrugs, "Sorry guys. She cornered me."

"What's going on?" she asks directly to Jack.

He looks down at Leila and she nods, giving him permission. "Lei and I have some news."

Jen raises her eyebrows, anticipating what he's going to say and tactlessly asks, "When?"

"January."

You can see the cogs and wheels of her brain in motion. "Ok, so, we need to call the label. This isn't terrible and our third tour shouldn't be affected."

"What the fuck! How about congratulations?" Jack now barks at her, causing her to jump from the volume of his voice.

My sister suddenly looks green and bolts off the patio, leaving us all stunned in silence.

"My wife has been feeling like crap, wracked with nausea and vomiting. She has been a nervous wreck over how this pregnancy is going to affect the tour and is determined to ensure it doesn't. She has had anxiety up to her neck over telling you all and hoping you wouldn't be upset about this. And you just proved her right." He rakes his hand over his face, trying to compose himself. "We are having a baby. It happens every fucking day. I am out-of-this-fucking-world-excited! I don't want to hear how this is going to affect you…" he points to Jen, "or you…" he points to Hunter, "or you!" he ends with Trey.

Jack stalks off the patio without a backwards glance.

"Fuck," Hunter says to no one in particular. "He's right. We need to fix this."

Lori shakes her head condescendingly and pulls Matt back to the party. "This is a Devil's Lair issue, and I feel like I'm intruding."

"We'll leave you guys alone," I offer and follow them out.

The last thing I hear is Hunter asking, "So, Trey, how are you going to fix it?"

# Chapter 3 – Jack

Fucking assholes! I walk into the Ladies Room, not caring who is in there. A supermodel turns toward me smiling, "Well, hello there."

"Can I have some privacy, please?"

"You do realize you are in the Ladies Room?"

"Yes."

She winks and says, "You need help with something?"

I open the door and wave toward it, "Please? I need to speak to my wife."

The smile falls from her face, and she storms out, as I quickly lock the door behind her. "Lei?"

"Yeah?"

"You ok?"

"Yeah."

She opens the door of her stall, and my heart breaks from the look in her eyes. "Baby, please don't let them upset you."

"I'm fine. I just…" she lets out heavy sigh and shakes her head. "I'm more worried about you."

"*Me*?"

"Yes, you. You need to relax."

"I am relaxed."

She throws me a look telling me otherwise. "Jack, I'm sorry, but I can't say I blame them." She regards me as I stand silently stewing and adds, "Stop clenching your jaw." She steps closer and lays her hands on my chest. "Babe, you can't force people to be happy or excited about something. This will affect them. They may be selfish in feeling that, but so what? They are entitled to want what they want. They want a repeat of our last tour, but better. They want to party, and celebrate, and revel in our success. You can't blame them for not being as excited as you are. That doesn't mean they aren't happy for us. Cut them some slack."

I digest her words as she wraps her arms around me. When she looks up into my eyes, she smiles warmly and says, "I love you. I love that you are so ecstatic over our baby…and I am, too. I really am…and I don't want you to think otherwise. Please, don't harp on this."

She steps up on her tiptoes and plants a kiss on my chin, my neck, and finally my lips. I return her kiss, pulling her closer until I can feel her heartbeat against my chest. "I love you, Mrs. Lair."

"I know," she smirks.

I move my hand to cover her belly. "You two are the most important things to me. I'll protect you always."

She covers my hand with hers. "You're turning me on, Mr. Lair. There's nothing sexier than my man protecting me."

"I'd kill for you, Baby."

"I know. I would for you, too. But let's spare our band, at least until we finish the world tour."

"That's years away. I can't promise that."

"Please?"

"Only because you asked."

She giggles and kisses me chastely. "Come, let's celebrate."

"Wait. Seriously, how are you feeling?"

"It passed. I'm good now."

"You haven't eaten. I want you to eat something."

"Ok, let's go get some food. Come."

When we rejoin her party guests, I quickly scan the room searching for the three fucktards. I find them in the corner with their girls, drinking and laughing. Leila watches my face and squeezes my hand, "Smile, Baby."

She pulls me toward them, but then Jen steps into our path. "Hey, I'm sorry you two. This is great news and I apologize for being insensitive. You know I'm always in business mode. Don't take it personally."

"Forgiven. Thanks."

I nod and walk around. When I glance down at Leila, she shakes her head. "Jack."

"What?"

As we approach, Hunter asks, "You gonna hit us man?"

"I'd love to. But my gorgeous wife asked me to spare your lives."

"Thanks, Lei," Hunter has the nerve to look offended.

"So, when again?" Scott asks earnestly.

"Early January."

"If he's born on my birthday, will you name him Hunter?"

"Definitely not," I respond without a doubt.

"Hunter Lair. Has a nice ring to it. Very rock star-like. He'd be a guaranteed rock god, drummer. No doubt. It's in the genes."

"He won't have your genes," I roll my eyes.

"My name genes." He rolls his eyes back at me. "Everyone knows you automatically inherit the person's genes you are named after. I wasn't named after anyone, but the H is after my grandfather. He was also very handsome and very talented. I'm just like him. It's because of the H." We all stare at the jackass for a few seconds, trying to figure out if he is serious or not.

"Ok, let's do a shot so he shuts the fuck up," Scott says while handing us each a shot, bypassing Leila. "Lei, what do you want?"

"Apple juice, please."

Trey looks down at her and smirks, "That's hilarious."

"Shut it," she smiles back at him.

Trini moves forward and abruptly hugs Leila. "Congratulations. I think that's awesome news."

"So much for keeping it to yourselves. Who told you?" I ask, annoyed that they didn't keep their mouths shut.

"I did," Trey says proudly. "Mainly to be sure she doesn't get any ideas."

"You're an ass," Trini accuses before kissing him.

He smacks her butt and responds, "You wouldn't want me any other way."

"Well, I would, but I'd like to keep my job. I'll show you later, though."

"Why wait? Don't you get a break soon?"

Hunter watches their exchange and shakes his head. "Anyway…we did tell the girls, but we swore them to secrecy. Jack, Lei, congratulations. We are very happy for you. Speaking for the three of us, we were thrown off guard and acted like idiots…"

"More like fucking assholes."

He nods at Jack and admits, "Fucking assholes…and we're sorry. I can't wait to meet baby Lair. He'll have a bunch of cool-as-shit uncles to teach him the ropes and one motherfucking awesome godfather to protect him."

"As in you?" Jack asks, amused.

"Yep."

"And if it's a girl?"

"Same deal, only less teaching her the ropes part."

Jack nods, "Appreciate that."

"Yep, don't mention it."

Mandy and Patti each hug Leila and then me. "Congrats, you guys are going to make awesome parents."

"Thanks, Patti," Leila smiles, just as Scott hands her a glass of juice.

"So, what's with the juice?" Trey asks, as if it's the most unusual thing he's ever seen.

"I'm nauseous all the time. It helps."

Trey considers her words and says, "I'm sorry you aren't feeling well."

Wait…Trey Taylor being sensitive?

"Thanks, Trey. That means a lot coming from you."

He frowns and says, "What the hell does that mean?"

"Oh, you know that I love you. You're just usually…" she glances up as if trying to think of the perfect words, "self-absorbed."

He smiles at my wife over the rim of his beer bottle. "I hardly ever have to 'self-absorb'. You must be confusing me with Hunt."

"I did what I had to do. Besides, most of the time it was while I was talking to Mandi." Hunter shrugs as Mandi blushes.

"Shut up, Hunt," she scolds.

"Sweetie, this crew experienced first hand what I went through without you. I missed you and 'self-absorbing' was necessary."

Hunter reminds me of all his grumpiness we had to endure. He was absolutely miserable most of the time…except when on stage. I'm starting to feel bad for jumping down their throats. I'm sure all three had high expectations for this tour. Guilt creeps through me as I realize I was the blame for most of the nonsense that happened last year. They were probably banking on us having an eight-week party on wheels this time around. So, maybe I overreacted a bit.

Trini steps up to Trey and says, "You better learn the art of 'self-absorbing' on this tour, or I'll hunt you down and kick your ass."

Trey purses his lips and nods, "Noted."

My adorable wife giggles at their exchange. Trey points at her and threatens, "Watch yourself, Little Lair."

"This tour is going to be fun," she responds, not at all intimidated by him. "Trini and I may have to exchange cell numbers." Trey points at her again and she sticks out her tongue.

Just as I'm about to kiss her, someone taps my shoulder. I turn to see Jen and Malcolm, hand in hand.

"Hey," I say flatly.

"Stop being a dick."

"I'm being a dick? How's that?"

She rolls her eyes and says, "I apologized. What else do you want?"

"I'll let you know. I'm sure I can come up with something."

Malcolm laughs obnoxiously. "While you two duke it out, I'm going to congratulate my protégé." He pulls Leila into a huge hug. "I'm very happy for you. Let me know when you are ready to record an album of lullabies."

"I can see the dollar signs in your pupils, Malcolm," I grumble before sipping my beer. I then turn to Jen and add, "Don't tell anyone else. We're serious, we don't want people knowing yet."

She shrugs, but doesn't respond otherwise, which means half this room now knows.

"Well, alright then…my wife needs food." Without apology, I tow Leila to the buffet table and away from the mass of annoyance that is my agent and band.

"You ok?"

I stop walking, pull her into my arms, and kiss her like my life depends on it. I could care less we are in the middle of her party with over one hundred guests surrounding us, or that they are all probably focused on our make-out session at the moment.

Whistling and hooting confirm my suspicions, but I keep my ironclad grip on her head, holding her to my lips. After a few seconds, she relaxes and submits, ignoring the catcalls we are soliciting. Once I break the kiss, she sags against me, depending on me to hold her up. Her eyes are still closed when I whisper against her lips, “I am now.”

## Chapter 4 – Leila

Well, at least my old band took it better than my new band did. Obviously, Evan is ecstatic. But I was most surprised by Logan and Joe's reaction. Logan, being a dad-in-waiting himself, is so excited that our kids will be the same age. He worries about his wife, Alisa, and feels that this is a blessing in disguise. I also worry about my friend. She is so pregnant right now and so depressed. She puts on a smile, and tries to hide it from Logan, but I know how she is truly feeling. I can't blame her. This should be a very exciting time for her. She's about to have her first child, but on the same note, her husband's career is about to explode, pulling him away for a few months. Add the fact that both Lori and I are leaving as well, that would make me a bawling mess. We all try to be supportive, but there isn't much we can do or say to make her feel better.

Joe hooted, grabbed me in a bear hug and made quite a scene. I'm sure half the people at this party now know I am pregnant. I can't worry about it. I can't control the gossip mill. There's a part of me that is relieved I won't have to hide it. Then there's the part of me already cringing at the Internet gossip that is hovering in our future. I have become more comfortable with the realization that I can't control what is printed, whether it is lies or truths. I know, Jack knows, and everyone we love know the truth…I finally have come to peace with it. I finally learned to ignore. It's liberating.

Now that our band mates, our friends, and our family know that I'm expecting, I can get excited about the baby. Things will work out. Jack's right, the most important thing is this little human we made together. I can't wait to meet him or her. I tease Jack that it can very well be a girl, but the thought of a mini Jack thrills me.

That man is meant to procreate. I would like nothing more than to populate the Earth with many Jack Lair clones. I watch as my sexy-as-fuck husband chats with Dylan and Krista. How different would my life have been if I ended up with Dylan? I can't even imagine that anymore. There was a time when I would picture myself with Dylan, when I was dead set on denying my feelings for Jack. I felt the worst thing to do would have been to admit to them, and looked to Dylan as the safer choice. I thank the universe for not listening to me. Jack and my fates were on a collision course and I'm not sure anything could have stopped it.

Dylan is meant to be with someone more like him. Krista is a good fit. They've been dating since the tail end of our tour, and they are now engaged to be married. I'm happy for them. He deserves to be happy. He could have easily written us off, from resentment or even jealousy. He didn't. He supported us and helped us. He's a very good man, and I wish him all the best.

The three of them all look over at me at the same time. I can only imagine what Jack's telling them. God, he looks gorgeous in his white button down and dark jeans. He throws me a sexy smile and my insides ignite. The look on his face reminds me of the orgasm-inducing kiss he gifted me with for all our guests to witness. It's the reason I am sitting alone at this table, in fact. I needed to distance myself, and I needed sugar. The birthday cake helped, somewhat, but my mood took a nose-dive.

I'm having a complete déjà vu moment. He did this to me at our wedding reception. He riled me up in front of all our guests. I had to mull around with a nicey-nice smile on my face, mingle with my guests, and eat my cake while watching my sex-god husband lick frosting off his bottom lip while smiling at me knowingly.

The difference is at my reception I was still a respectable member of society. Now, I am a nauseous, emotional, hormonal, pregnant woman with a beast living inside of her. If I weren't pregnant, I would be pounding back the Jell-O shots at this very moment, so sober, horny, frustrated Leila is not a happy camper right now.

Jack strolls over to where I'm sitting and sits across from me. Taking my hands, he asks, "You ok?"

I level him with my glare, and the bastard laughs at me.

"How bad?"

"Bad."

"Do you want to dance?"

"That would make things worse."

"Do you want something to eat?"

"No, I finally feel like I'm not about to hurl."

"Do you want to take a walk?"

I meet his heated gaze, debating his offer. "Where?"

"Downstairs. There's a place."

My heart flips as I realize I can help my situation and then I'll be able to enjoy my party, but then his offer and the insinuation behind it hit me. "How do you know there's a place?"

He shrugs, offering no explanation.

"Great," I mumble as my eyes well with unshed tears.

"Hey, knock it off." He moves closer until my legs are between his opened ones, leaning in so we are face to face. "Just think about what I can be doing to you as we speak." With the intensity of his stare, he wills me to not focus on the one part of him I can't help but hate. He licks my bottom lip, daring me to accept his offer.

"Hurry, before I change my mind."

A smile spreads and he tows me toward his secret "sex" spot. We take the elevator down one flight to a balcony that looks down at the club below. The only light comes from the pulsing strobes. The floor beneath us vibrates from the pounding music. He leads me to the glass banister, and we look down at the mob of writhing bodies on the dance floor.

There are people up here, scattered around the wrap-around deck. None are watching the action below us. They are all participating in their own private parties. I've been to Granite several times and never knew this existed.

"This is so cool," I loudly whisper directly into his ear.

He nods and motions toward a hallway with his head. Wordlessly, we follow it away from the noise as it winds around the space. There are several doors on each side, and one at the end that faces us. He confidently opens the door, locking it behind us.

"This reminds me of the Bellagio." I smile at him in the darkened room. He flips a light and reveals a swanky lounge. It's nicely decorated with a leather couch facing a few club chairs and a small bar in the corner. The one wall is a glass window overlooking the club below. "I was expecting a storage closet. What is this?"

"The owner uses it for private parties."

I smirk at his comment. "Can I assume you've hosted your own private parties in here?"

"No." He pulls me into his hard body, anchoring me with his hands on my ass. "This is my first official private party. The other times were just necessary encounters."

"With Trini?" My question just pops out and it surprises him. He searches my face, concern puckering his brow.

"Does the thought of me and Trini bother you?"

I look away and he moves his head until our eyes align. "Lei?"

"Sometimes. It's easier to deal with all the faceless girls you have been with. The unknown. I love Trini…she's great. Putting a face, a personality to the image is hard for me."

"Why haven't you told me that?"

I shrug, only slightly embarrassed by my confession.

"Baby, I *never* had feelings for Trin, except friendship…*ever*. I've told you this before. Please, don't overthink it. But to answer your question, no, I never had sex with Trini anywhere other than her apartment."

I nod solemnly as my eyes betray me by moistening with emotion. My hormones are all out of whack. I'm normally not this sensitive, or paranoid. I know what I married. I am fully aware of Jack's past. So why am I so insecure suddenly?

He senses my discomfort and kisses me gently before wrapping his arms around me to hold me close.

"I'm sorry. I don't know what's wrong with me. I went from being horny as hell to feeling like my puppy just died."

He chuckles at my analogy. "The 'bible' says your moods are going to be all over the place."

"Screw the 'bible'," I pout.

He laughs again, wiping away a tear that escaped with his thumb.

"I guess we should get back. I'm sorry I ruined our sex-capade." I look around the room before adding, "It would have been fun."

"Ok, but when we get home, I'll remind you how horny you were and we can feed the beast."

Bam…instant desire.

I rub up against him, aligning myself with his arousal, and he smiles wide at my awakening. His dimples further igniting the heat that starts to smolder, slow and powerfully in my core.

"Yeah?"

I nod slowly, planting a kiss on one dimple and then the other. I then drag my tongue across his stubble and down his neck. He moans and his hands find my ass, gripping it firmly.

"I better hurry, before Sybil reappears," he teases.

"Wait, can they see us?" I nod toward the large window.

"No." He sits on the couch, unzips his jeans, freeing himself. My eyes rake over his length, the sight of him practically causing my climax. What the hell is going on with me?

I slide my skirt up, move my panties aside, and ease over him without breaking eye contact. Once he's buried to the hilt, he leans his head back and closes his eyes. His hands on my hips immobilize me and prevent my body from doing what it needs to do. I need to move.

"Jack…" He opens his eyes and nods, knowing what I need. He loosens his grip and lets me take control. I grip his shoulders with my fingernails, practically scoring the cotton fabric that separates them from his skin.

Remembering our kiss upstairs that was to blame for my mood swing earlier, I bend to take his bottom lip in between mine. He moans into my mouth, causing my muscles to clamp around him in a viselike grip.

I reach my climax first, shamelessly using him to pull out every last delicious spasm. Once I slow my movements, he then shamelessly uses me by holding me still as he buries himself within me. I can feel him swell and stiffen, an announcement of his completion. The intensity he always gets in his eyes sparks desires within me, causing a circular loop of need, of want.

He smiles when he feels my core tighten around him again, as if it has a mind of its own. He pulls my lips to his, kissing me in the most erotic of ways, enabling me, encouraging me to ride my second wave. It doesn't take long before my next orgasm takes hold and drains me completely.

As I pant against his mouth with my forehead resting on his and my thighs slick with a film of sweat from my exertion, he smirks and asks, "Feel better?"

"Much. Thank you."

"Anytime," he grins devilishly. "I love you, Mrs. Lair."

"I love you, too."

"We should get back."

I nod wordlessly. I'm good. I can handle the rest of the party. In fact, I can probably even have fun, now that the beast has been fed.

We clean ourselves up and rejoin our guests. Thankfully the party is still in full swing. With luck, no one even knew we were missing in action. Our friends and band mates are all in the center of the dance floor, laughing and drinking. As we approach, Lori shakes her head…so much for wishful thinking.

"What?" I ask with a blush instantly tingeing my cheeks.

"Where were you?"

"Lei wasn't feeling well," Jack responds quickly.

She squints and smirks annoyingly.

I throw her a wicked smile before turning to Jack and announcing, "Come, Baby, I want to dance."

Jack shrugs and says, "We'll be back. I need to satisfy my wife."

"Again," Lori retorts and everyone laughs. I ignore her, because…well, it's true.

He backs me up against him, nuzzling my neck from behind, and starts moving to the music. Our friends follow and surround us on the dance floor, just so they can hurl round after round of sleazy innuendos at us. Jack quips back while I remain silent. Some of them are actually pretty funny.

"Hey, Lei. What's the difference between a pregnant woman and a light bulb?" Trey throws another one-liner at me.

"No clue, Trey," I smirk as he watches me amused.

"You can unscrew a light bulb."

"Bahahahaha!" Hunter cracks up and fist bumps Trey while my husband mutters, "Jackasses."

I'm finally having a good time as we all laugh, dance, and enjoy each other's company.

After a long while, the music changes and slows. Some of them ditch us to hit the bar or grab some food. Even though I am exhausted, I don't want to leave. I'm enjoying the feel of Jack's arms wrapped around my body. My song fills the air and my heart swells. I will never get tired from hearing his words of love. The soulful chords of *Reason I Am* soothe me and fill my heart with the love I feel for this man. He sings directly into my ear, relaxing me in the process. I struggle to stay awake and use him to support my weight.

"You've had a long night. Tired?" He looks down at me, concern filling his eyes.

"I am, but I'm happy. Thank you so much for my wonderful party."

"You're welcome. I wish I could have gotten my surprise here."

I smile warmly, now knowing the backstory of how he tortured Jen, Hunter, and everyone at the label to get Springsteen here tonight. "Babe, this night was perfect as is."

"I wanted you to have the greatest birthday party."

“Mission accomplished. We have a lot more celebrating ahead of us. Can you believe a year ago tomorrow we were on a beach getting married?”

“I know and it went so fast. What do you want to do for our anniversary? I kind of was busy planning this and haven’t made any plans for tomorrow.”

“I would love to spend a nice quiet night with you at home.”

“Sounds good. All partied out?”

“Yes, so no party for your birthday either. Just me and you.” I lean up to kiss him slowly.

“That’s the best kind of party,” he whispers against my lips, and he’s right.

## Chapter 5 – Lori

God, I love this song. I'll never admit that to Jack though, because I get great pleasure from busting his chops. As I watch my best friend swaying to the beautiful ballad her husband wrote for her, recorded for her, bared his heart and soul for her, a seed of jealousy festers in my gut. I am not a jealous person…at all. I'm especially not jealous of Leila. I adore her. She deserves all the happiness in the world. It disgusts me that I feel this way. I watch her dancing with her husband, the obvious adoration he has for her rolling off of him in waves. He simply can't hide how much he loves her, nor can she. Since they got home last year, I've witnessed the most profound love story I've ever seen.

If I hadn't witnessed it with my own eyes, I would scoff at the notion that two people truly need each other to breathe, to exist, and to essentially live. I used to feel it was all bull crap and only found in books. Those two are walking proof it can exist.

Matt squeezes me tighter and nuzzles my neck. I know he cares for me, he's said he loves me and I love him, but something is missing. Our relationship is filled with hot sex and respect, but that all encompassing - I would die without him if he left - obsession is not there. Normally, I wouldn't even notice or care. I finally got this gorgeous man to admit he wants me. It took me a long time. My plan worked perfectly. It was a blessing when Leila came up with the idea that I should be Cliffhangers' agent. It was brilliant. I finally landed the man of my dreams, or so I thought.

Feigning nonchalance and indifference finally woke Matt Rizzo the fuck up. It was like a switch had been flipped and a neon beacon stretched from his eyeballs to my face. He chased, I ignored. Having Trey Taylor in my life at the time was a perfect distraction for me, and a perfect motivator for Matt. Matt Rizzo finally realized he needed me, wanted me, and had to have me. After years of chasing him, I finally got my prize.

Now that I have him, my thoughts of doubt have been fucking with my head. I haven't confided in anyone. I need to soon, or I'm going to do something stupid. We are about to embark on our first tour, and I need a clear head. Normally, I would confide in Lei, but she has been so preoccupied lately. The endless excuses that she gave me on why we couldn't hang out, all make sense now. The egomaniac in me thought that fucker Lair was making her unhappy, when it was just the opposite. She knew I'd call her out and she wasn't prepared to fess up to being pregnant. Truth be told, I am hurt. I thought we told each other everything. I know she loves me dearly, but she has a new partner in crime, a new confidant, and a new best friend. I don't feel like she abandoned me, or our friendship. Without a doubt, if she knew what I was being tormented with, she would be there for me in a heartbeat. She would talk me off this cliff I'm precariously perched on.

A cliff, where behind me is the man of my dreams with his arms wrapped possessively around my waist and his lips whispering into my ear how much he needs me. Below, a gorgeous, turquoise blue Caribbean ocean meeting a serene powder pink beach with a big-ass great white cutting the calm waters as he stalks back and forth.

Who's the shark?

Trey Fucking Taylor.

That man made me feel more than anything in my twenty-seven years ever has. Here's the thing…it's purely physical. Trey Taylor is not capable of love. He's a hot, fucking rocker who can fuck me like no one else ever has. He's exciting, dangerous, dark, and sexy as fuck. He is "fling" material, and not "relationship" material. I've had a fling with him. It was absolutely the best sex I ever had. That was the gist of our relationship. I know nothing about him. Our conversations were usually about what we would do to each other, specifically with our mouths. Besides knowing he's originally from California and he moved here right before Jack and Hunter found him, I haven't a clue who he really is. He's a closed book. He's hard to get to know. He's detached.

So then, why do I keep thinking about him? Why does the image of him and that little tattooed slut – who Leila says is truly a nice person and not to hate on her – make my insides boil?

He acted completely unaffected, when I broke it off with him to finally be with Matt. I get what we had was purely physical, and he probably replaced me hours after my phone call to him, but…

But, what?

Did I expect him to profess his undying love for me? To hop the first plane and show up at the bar, carrying a boom box blasting *In Your Eyes*? At the time, I had no expectations. It was what it was, hot sex and nothing more.

I know if I sent Trey a signal, he would respond without hesitation. I won't go that route. Matt's a cheater…well, he was. He cheated on Leila a few times during their relationship. I threatened his balls if he ever considers that option with me. I am not a hypocrite. So, do I end it with the love of my life for a quick thrill? Do I covet Trey from a distance, ignoring my desire and wish things were different?

Fuck if I know.

The major issue is I've changed. In one year, I went from being the coolest chick I know to being a sappy, mushy, attention seeking mess. I partially blame my one best friend who is living proof love conquers all and is now having a baby. I blame my other best friend who also is living proof that love conquers all and is also having a baby.

And then there's me.

"Where are you at?" Matt asks when I finally make eye contact with him.

"What?"

"You're in a daze. What's wrong?"

"Nothing."

He measures me up, not convinced with my lie. "You're lying."

I wiggle against him, trying to distract his line of thinking. "No, I'm horny as fuck and can't wait to get you flat on your back."

He spontaneously laughs at my comment. "You talk like a guy."

Relieved my tactics worked, I smile devilishly and respond, "I'm no guy."

"That I know, Baby." He presses his hardness against me and adds, "But I am. Ready to blow this party and go home?"

Home is my place, or his. He's asked me to move in with him several times. I can't take that step yet. Some would say that is a big-ass red flag.

Damn it, I'm so confused.

I am ready to forget my whining with hot, steamy sex. I need a distraction and Matt Rizzo is the perfect solution. So what the hell is my problem? I know once we get home, he'll tend to my every need and I will convince myself I am happy. I will forget my inner turmoil…

Until I see Trey…again. Then the lid to my can of worms will pop off and wreak havoc on my brain…again.

"Soon. I just want to hang with the gang a bit more."

He gives me a resigned look, but nods reluctantly. "Fine."

Most of our friends are dancing around us. Alisa sits quietly at a table, by herself. "I'm going to sit with her a bit." I motion toward her.

"Ok. I'll be at the bar."

He gives me a quick kiss, and I watch him walk away toward where Trey is sitting with a few of the rockers who are here tonight. Matt notices him sitting at one end of the bar and heads straight for the other end. Seeing those two on tour together is going to be interesting…and scary. I'll worry about that later.

I smile at my friend, worried about how tired she looks. She smiles warmly in return as I approach. "Hey, Lis. How're you feelin'?"

"Exhausted," she shrugs.

"I know, Babe. Not much longer, though."

Alisa is due in two months, smack during our tour. Logan will be flying home the minute it's necessary. We already have a fill-in for him, provided by the studio. His name is Wade, and he's been rehearsing with us often.

I feel for my friend. We are all leaving her during a time she clearly needs people around. She does have awesome support from her family and her sister, but it must be awful going through the tail end of your pregnancy knowing your husband and best friends will not be there with you.

The sadness in her eyes breaks my heart, which is hard to do since it's made of *Teflon*. "Sweetie, you sure you're ok?"

She nods, emotions clear in her eyes. "Yeah. It is what it is."

"I know. We're only going to be a plane ride away."

"Yeah, I know."

God this is killing me. "Hey, did you have cake?" I ask, trying to improve her mood.

"Yeah."

"Want more?"

"Want more what?" Logan asks as he approaches. He sits next to his wife, kissing her cheek.

"Cake. I'm trying to cheer her up."

"You know my wife well," he teases. She faces him with pouty lips, which he kisses. Again, I witness that consuming love and respect that I covet so much. These two are a bit more reserved than Jack and Leila are with their love, but it's there in spades.

Matt appears with another Cosmo for me and joins us at the table.

He notices the gloom in the air and asks, "What's going on?"

Alisa sighs heavily, "Oh, just feeling sorry for myself. The usual."

I watch as he reaches over and caresses her arm. "Come with us," he suggests. His face lights up like he just thought of the best solution for all involved. See, he is warm and fuzzy and loving, I think to myself, once again defending him and his actions to my demented self.

"She can't, man. She needs to be here, safe at home, where she'll deliver in a hospital with her doctor patiently waiting."

"There are doctors outside of the state of New Jersey, dude."

Alisa and I share an eye roll. "Yes, sweetie. There are," she pats her brother-in-law's hand. "I just feel so uncomfortable. I can't imagine squeezing this fat ass in a small bunk for weeks."

"I'm squeezing my fat ass in a bunk," Leila touts as she drags Jack to our table.

This time Lis and I synchronize our eye rolling. "Shut up."

Jack sits and pulls her onto his lap.

"What? That's why I didn't want to go shopping with you last week, even though I desperately need to get clothes already. My jeans don't fit, and you would harass me as to the reason why."

"Don't bring that up. I'm still mad at you." Leila sighs, and Jack scowls. "Calm down, Lair."

"You're in a mood," he grumbles.

"I didn't get drunk enough tonight." I watch Leila giving me a look over the rim of my Cosmo. I raise my eyebrows in response.

"Is this the old people section?" Hunter asks as he pulls up two chairs for him and Mandi.

"Five, four, three, two…"

"Hey, what's with the private party?" Joe says as he pulls up a chair.

"One." Matt finishes his countdown.

"One, what?" Joe asks.

"Took you five seconds to realize Hunt was over here."

"Fuck off," Joe gripes, causing us all to laugh.

Matt is convinced Joe has a crush on Hunter. It's been an inside joke since we got signed to open for them. Joe says that besides himself, Hunter is the best drummer around. They have a mutual love of the instrument and that's what bonds them…besides their total "awesomeness."

Hunter laughs it off, but he gives Joe a sideways glance and subtly moves his chair to the right.

"What the fuck, man?" Joe throws up his hands. "I'm so hurt."

We all laugh at Joe's drama, even Alisa laughs out loud. I reach over and take her hand, giving it a squeeze. She smiles as well, squeezing back.

As guests file out, all stopping at our table to wish Leila a happy birthday, our party within a party grows to include Evan, Lizzy, Scott, Patti, Nina, and Dylan with his fiancée. Trey is nowhere to be found. I search the few heads left in the darkened club, not seeing him anywhere.

That's good. I wouldn't want him here with us anyway. I wouldn't want Matt to feel uncomfortable.

My brain quips, "Liar…liar."

"So, if any of you haven't noticed, I'm still single," Joe announces. We all laugh and he scowls. "I'm glad that amuses you all."

“Hunter, run,” Jack deadpans.

“Bahahaha. You’re a riot, Lair.”

“Joe, did you honestly think one of these supermodels would take one look at you tonight and beg for your hand in marriage?”

“Yeah, Matt…I did. You people aren’t helping either. I’m very marketable.”

The insults start flying and Joe sits and takes it all. He kids, and jokes, but I know he really wants to meet someone. Here’s Joe looking for any love, hoping for it. Then there’s me, lucky to have it and wishing for more.

Love sucks.

## Chapter 6 – Leila

"Baby."

I nuzzle closer to his warmth, placing my lips on his neck. He is so comfortable. His arms tighten around me and his lips place a sweet kiss on my forehead. I settle back into the very lovely dream I was having.

"Babe."

"Hmmmm."

He places his lips on my ear, the touch of them causes my skin to break out into goose bumps. "Baby, I want to get you home."

I shake my head in my confused state, burrowing further into his hard, warm body. He chuckles, causing his chest to vibrate, bringing me out of my slumber.

"Stop shaking," I grumble.

He laughs again, and so do others. When I open my eyes, confused and disoriented, two pairs of eyes stare back.

"Where are we?"

"Granite." He smiles at my daze and kisses my cheek. "You passed out on me. Everyone left, except us, but we need to go. It's really late and they want to shut down."

I pout like a brat, not wanting to move. The nap that I apparently had making me cranky.

I stare at Evan, and he laughs at me. "What are you looking at, Miller?"

"Good luck, man. She is a gem when she's cranky. I'm sure you know that already."

Jack nods until I scowl at him and then he shakes his head. "Don't know what you are talking about."

"Bye, Lei," Evan says as he kisses my head. Lizzy gives me a hug, which I try to reciprocate as best I can with one arm, my other still wrapped around Jack's warmth.

"Bye, guys. Thank you so much for coming." I settle back against Jack, closing my eyes.

Jack pats my ass and says, "Come on, get up."

"Fine." I stand and stretch, moving closer to give them each a proper goodbye hug.

"We'll talk to you tomorrow…or later, actually.".Evan says as they leave us alone in the dark. The bartenders are cleaning up the bar and a few of the waitresses are still gathering glasses and dishes off the scattered tables.

"What time is it?"

"Two."

"I was out for an hour?"

"You were wiped out. Come, Oscar is waiting downstairs. Let's get out of here." He takes my bag, a larger tote filled with stuff, and my hand.

"What's that?"

"Presents."

"They bought me stuff? That makes me really uncomfortable."

"I clearly said no gifts on the invite. Some didn't listen."

My hubby thought of everything. "After I get in about ten hours of sleep, you are so getting lucky later."

He smiles wide and nods, "Sounds like a plan."

♬ ♬ ♬

This time when I stir, the warm, hard body beside me doesn't move. He lies on his stomach, facing away from me. I slept so hard. If a bomb had gone off last night, I wouldn't have heard it. It's quiet and still. I grab for my phone, pondering what woke me up? It's still early, considering what time we finally crawled into bed. Suddenly my stomach growls loudly, surprising me.

Holy shit, I'm hungry.

I smile to myself, hoping this will be a good day. It is our first wedding anniversary. I throw on Jack's shirt and tiptoe out of our room, closing the door quietly behind me. I'm going to take advantage of my current state. My stomach rumbles again, inspiring me to attempt to make my husband bacon and eggs.

The true test will be coffee. I pull the container out and sniff it tentatively. It's not appealing, but bile doesn't rise, like it usually does. Pushing past the nausea, I'm determined to do this small thing for him. I grab the coffee filters to prep the coffee maker, and a black box sits nestled with the filters. I quickly glance to the door and lift the box. He is so sweet. Not wanting to ruin his surprise, I replace the box and proceed with my task.

While I'm making the eggs my thoughts wander to how thoughtful he is. He threw me an amazing party. I was touched that all those people were there for me. Not that any of them had a choice with Jack, I'm sure. I had no idea he was planning that. I feel bad now. Last year we were away on our honeymoon during our birthdays. This year, with the pregnancy and my ailments, I haven't even thought about it. His birthday is in a few days, and I want to make it very special for him. I'll have to think of something, and I don't have much time.

I'm lost in thought, mechanically finishing up breakfast. When I turn to set the table, I first notice my rock star leaning up against the doorjamb in his black Calvin's.

"How long have you been standing there?"

"A while." He stalks over, smiling wide. "Seeing you in my t-shirt and nothing else does things to me."

He nuzzles my neck, pulling me up against what that particular "thing" is.

"Don't distract me, I'm on a mission."

"What's all this? Does my wife feel better?"

"My rumbling stomach woke me up. Can you believe it?"

"That's awesome news. He knows it's our anniversary and he's trying to make Mommy happy."

"*She* is definitely cooperating today."

He pulls me into his arms, pushing a stray strand of hair out of my eyes. "Happy Anniversary, Baby." Bending, he plants a warm, chaste, single kiss on my lips.

"That's all I get?"

"For now. You made coffee?"

"I did."

He watches me and shrugs, "So, you know."

"No clue what you are talking about."

"Nice try." He reaches into the cabinet to retrieve the filter box. "I thought it was safe in here. What are the odds that today you suddenly can tolerate the smell of coffee?" He smiles sheepishly.

"I didn't look, I promise."

"I believe you." He hands me the box and says, "Happy Anniversary, Babe."

"I thought we agreed no gifts."

"I lied."

Inside the box is a simple silver bracelet with an infinity symbol on the front.

"I love it." I put it on my wrist, becoming very emotional. "Forever."

"Forever." Smiling, he wipes away an errant tear as it falls. "My sweet, emotional, sappy wife." He gathers me in his arms, kissing the top of my head, and I sniffle pathetically. He lets me burrow into his chest for a few minutes, slobbering it up with my tears. When I pull away, he smiles wide. "Done?"

"Yep."

"Good. Ok, this smells too good, so keep cooking, wench. You know I love you, Baby, but there's coffee sitting a foot away from me. Priorities." I swat at his ass as he reaches for the coffee pot and teases, "Hey, old friend. I missed you." He then nuzzles the cup with his nose and intimately kisses it.

"Stop that. I want to eat breakfast before the beast wakes up."

I serve our food, actually excited to take my first bite of a breakfast that is something other than potatoes for the first time in weeks.

"So far, so good," I admit after a few bites.

"Welcome back to the land of the living."

Three loud bangs on our door cause me to jump. "What the hell?"

Jack and I exchange a confused look, when he gets up to answer the door.

"Jack, you aren't dressed."

He looks down at himself and opens the door anyway. Lori flies into the apartment like she's being chased.

"Jesus, Banzini. What the fuck?"

She stops long enough to take in my husband's practically naked torso. "Nice body, Rock Star."

"Jack, go put on pants!" I turn her body to stop her from oogling. "Stop staring at my husband."

"Sorry…and mazel tov by the way," she smirks.

"How did you get in?" I ask, trying to get her to focus.

"Doorman likes me," she states obviously.

"Why are you here?"

"I need to talk to you."

"Did it occur to you to call first?"

She sits at our table, grabbing a piece of bacon. "Spur of the moment decision. I was in the neighborhood." She gets up and helps herself to a cup of coffee and a plate. "Can I have some?"

"Help yourself," I wave at our uneaten breakfasts. I tug on Jack's t-shirt to ensure my parts aren't on display. Lori catches me and smirks.

"This better be important, Banzini, for you to barge in and interrupt our anniversary breakfast and my wife's first attempt at eating real food in weeks."

Lori looks embarrassed for three seconds before shrugging, "I need to talk to her."

He sits at an empty chair and says, "This better be good."

"Alone."

"Are you freaking kidding me?"

"No. Please?" She gives him a pleading look while Jack gives me one.

"Babe, can you give us a few?"

"Unbelievable." He stands and grabs his shoes. "She's just going to tell me anyway, once you leave."

"No, she won't."

"You are exhausting, woman. You got thirty minutes." He gives me a resigned look and asks, "Do you need anything?"

"No, Babe. Just be careful."

"The danger would be if I stayed here." He kisses my cheek and storms out of the apartment.

"Is he not a morning person?"

"Lor…"

"Ok, ok." She takes a deep breath, and then another.

"What's wrong?"

"I had a panic attack this morning."

"Metaphorically?"

"No…actually. A full blown, hyperventilating, chest pains, cold sweat, panic attack."

"Why, are you ok? Are you sick?"

"No. Well, maybe in the head…but no, I'm not sick." She picks at our food, leaving me hanging in suspense.

"What's going on with you?"

"Well, we were lying in bed this morning. He had just given me the most amazing oral sex…"

"No details please."

"Ok, sorry. We were lying together afterwards, and he was being sweet and kind and loving." She stops and fiddles with her hands in her lap.

"And?"

"I'm so messed up."

"Don't you love him?"

Without making eye contact, she nods and responds, "I do. I think. No, I do."

I patiently wait for her to continue, watching as she visibly struggles with her thoughts. When she raises her head, she looks completely lost.

"Something is missing."

"Between you?"

She nods slowly.

"Lor, I watched you pine over Matt for years. You know how I feel about him, but with you, he's different. He's changed. He loves you. You can see it all over his face."

She sits quietly, processing my words. After a few very long minutes, she finally says, "I know he does. This is crazy. I finally have what I always wanted."

"Ok, so what's the problem?"

She releases a sigh and gives me a resigned look. It's almost as if she's embarrassed to say the words. "Well, now that I have it, I'm disappointed."

"In what way?"

"I watch you and Jack, or Lis and Logan, even Evan and Liz, and there's something there. A spark? Something alive that anyone around you can see and witness. I don't have that. I didn't think I wanted it…" she stops, and whispers, "but I do."

"That doesn't always exist, Lori. People have very loving relationships without that spark."

"I had it with Trey."

"Lori…"

"Wait, let me finish. I know Trey is not a relationship kind of guy, but I had that fire with him. Every day was exciting and sexy and hot. With Matt, it's predictable. There's no excitement."

I let out my own heavy sigh, frustrated at her line of thinking. "Lori, I lived with that man on a bus for months, and I can fill a thimble with how much I know about him. Trey is…"

"A self-centered fuck. I know. That's why I'm so confused. I need to work out my shit."

"How are you going to do that?"

She stalls, chewing on her thumbnail while I wait for her to enlighten me. After another prompt from me, she finally says, “I’m going to skip the tour.”

“What? Why?”

She shakes her head and admits, “I shouldn’t be going with you guys. You know I pushed my way onto that tour. Jen is meeting up with you twice during the tour. As the agent to Cliffhangers, I really don’t need to be there more than that as well. Matt Rizzo’s girlfriend and Trey Taylor’s ex-fuck is who was going on that tour.”

“You were so excited about it. You’ll be miserable.”

She doesn’t respond or deny my claim. “I need to figure this out. Besides, Alisa needs me. She’s so depressed. I’ll stay back until Logan gets home. Once he’s with her, I’ll join you guys. Hopefully by then, I’ll have figured out what to do.”

“What will you tell Matt?”

“Just that. Alisa needs me and I decided to stay with her.”

“He’s not going to be happy.”

“He’ll get over it.” The look on her face tells me she isn’t looking forward to that conversation.

“How long have you been feeling like this?”

“Months.”

“Wow, Lori. Why haven’t you said anything?”

She sucks in a heavy breath, not responding for a few minutes. She looks tired. This must have been messing her up big time. For her to have a panic attack, actually recognize it, and be freaked out by it is most definitely unlike her. She is a “fuck-it” kind of girl who doesn’t lose sleep over anything.

I voice my last thought out loud and she confirms.

“Yeah. It’s been a fucking party in my head.”

"I'm so sorry. I wish I could tell you what to do. I do have to give you some advice. I don't want you to walk away from something that meant the world to you and throw it all away for a…"

"A hot fuck," she interrupts me again.

"Ok, a hot fuck."

"Do you think he cared about me at all?" she asks with doubt.

"In a way only Trey can care about something. He was upset when you broke it off. But sweetie, he also got over it very quickly. He copes. He adapts. He survives, any way he can." I watch Lori chew on her lip, contemplating my words.

"Lei, if he was to tell me he loved me, I'd be running. That's what scares me. How can I care about Matt, claim I love him, and have no problem walking out the door if Trey Taylor beckons?" She stands and starts pacing around the room, shaking her head repeatedly. "I'm not even sure I love Trey? I think it's the thought of Trey I love. What the hell is wrong with me? I chased Matt for years. What happens if I do end up leaving Matt for Trey, and once I have him, the same thing happens again? What if I am just not capable of appreciating and loving what I have? What if I'm the type of person who is always looking for better?"

Fuck, she's right. She's been doing this her whole life. She constantly waits for an improvement to show up. When we were in high school, she was asked to the prom in September. No one gets asked that early. She obviously said no and was continuously asked every month until May by various hot jocks in the senior class. She waited until the week before prom to make her decision from all those who asked. Of course once she did, the guy dropped everything to take her.

"Do you think he would ever fall in love?"

"Maybe he just needs someone to openly love him to have an awakening."

She sits heavily, chewing on her nail again. This is so unlike Lori. She seems so insecure. Lori doesn't do insecure. Lori doesn't do emotion. She isn't a cold bitch. She's warm and loving, but she's Lori. She's the female version of Matt and Trey mixed into one. I have to bite my lip to keep from laughing out loud at that realization.

"Stranger things have happened, right? Men can change, right?" she asks earnestly.

"Absolutely. I'm married to one…and Matt has changed tremendously. But sweetie, don't count on it with Trey."

She nods, knowing I speak the truth. "Speaking of, I'm sure your man is pissed as hell at me right now. I'm sorry I ruined your anniversary."

"You didn't ruin it. We'll resume, once you leave."

"Ugh."

I shrug unapologetically.

"Thanks for listening."

"I'm sorry, honey. I wish I could help you with this."

"I know. I've been in denial. Having that attack this morning scared the shit out of me."

"How did you explain it to Matt?"

"I didn't. I ran out."

"Oh, my God, Lori, he's probably frantic."

She holds up her phone to reveal eight missed calls and thirteen missed texts.

"Call him."

"No, he'll flip on me. I'll go home and make things right." She stands and gives me a crushing hug. "I love you, Leila."

"Me, too. Things will work out, you'll see."

As I walk her to the door, she stops and turns, "You can't tell him. Promise me."

"Lori, he wouldn't tell anyone."

"Lei, please?"

"Ugh…you are asking me to lie to my husband?"

She hugs me tighter, using her grip to evoke some sympathy. "Please! You wouldn't be lying, just omitting."

"Fine, I won't tell him. I promise."

"Thank you."

When I open the door, Jack is standing in the hall, waiting patiently, holding a gorgeous bouquet of flowers. "Not tell me what?" he asks, having heard us apparently.

"Aww, Jack. Are those for me?" She ignores his question and reaches for the flowers.

"Get off." He moves them away and swats at her. "Are you done?"

"Babe, you've been out here the whole time?"

"No. I was giving you five more minutes before I barged in, though."

Lori kisses his cheek and quips, "A considerate rock star, who knew?" She saunters down the hall calling out, "Bye, lovebirds. Happy Anniversary."

He watches her walk down the hall and shakes his head. "What was that about?"

"Thanks, Baby. I love them," I take the flowers, returning to the kitchen.

"Hello?" he asks as he follows me. Careful not to look up at him, because that would surely make me crack, I turn my back and fiddle with putting them in a vase.

"Are you going to tell me why that lunatic barged into our home?" He comes to stand behind me, waiting for me to turn.

When I do, I wrap my arms around him and nibble on his chin. “I can’t. But I’ll make it up to you.” Slowly, I drag my lips from his neck to his earlobe, pulling it between my teeth and tugging gently.

“You’re slick.”

“What? I missed you and I want to mark our anniversary properly.”

When I resume nibbling on his stubbled chin, he says, “Hold that thought. We need to leave.”

“Where are we going?”

“Pack a bag. We’re going back to the place we were married.”

“Really?” I squeal from excitement. I’ve wanted to go back there and recreate our wedding night. It was so incredible, the memory still vivid in my mind. “Wait, we have the studio time tomorrow.”

“We’ll drive home in the morning.”

“Really?” I repeat pathetically.

“Yeah, really.” He swats at my ass and says, “Now, let’s go…move it.”

## Chapter 7 – Jack

I may have only thought of this while I was waiting to get back into my apartment, but damn if I admit it is a fantastic idea. It's a gorgeous day. It's a picture-perfect replica of our actual wedding day. I called the bed and breakfast where we were married and was thrilled to see they could accommodate us for the night.

My ire has settled a bit. I couldn't imagine what had that red headed wacko barging in and kicking me out of my own apartment. Once I calmed down and cleared my head, I was able to focus on how I would make our anniversary special. And here we are, driving down the parkway without a care in the world. I love that I can do this for her. I love that we can do this on a whim. This is the benefit of success. This is a bonus to my already full and complete world. My wife and my child is all I need. Anything else is frosting. The money, the fame, is all frosting.

I can't believe less than two years ago I was so far removed from who I am now. It makes me wonder if God said to himself, "Mr. Lair, you are about to be fucked with." Fucked with I was. She not only fucked with my libido, she fucked with my mind, in a way nothing has ever in my entire life…and I wouldn't want it any other way.

She is the most important thing in my life. I simply cannot get enough of her. We are fortunate to be able to spend almost every waking moment together. On the rare occasions we are apart, my mind is on her constantly. I crave her, like I haven't had her in years. I also worry about her and her safety. I will not take her safety for granted, not as long as that motherfucker is still breathing on this earth.

The memory of what I felt, as I saw him throw her in that van and pull away, is something that will forever be ingrained in every cell of my body. The mere thought immediately causes my body to react as it did that day. The way my chest constricted so tightly, I couldn't pull in a single jagged breath without the pain radiating throughout me and settling in my heart. The memory of waiting for her prognosis, of her lying in that hospital bed waiting for her to return to me, all bring me dangerously close to a panic attack.

She accepts my neurotic behavior when it comes to her safety. She allows me to act in my unreasonable ways. The truth is she really has no idea how much it affects me on a daily basis. As crazy and over-bearing as I am, I won't apologize for my behavior. Inside, I'm capable of unspeakable acts if something were ever to happen to her. If that something came at the hands of the prick, so help me God, I'll kill him, if it's the last thing I do. I regret not doing so when I saw him lying lifeless on the ground, after he abducted her. The only thing stopping me was the love of my life lying a few feet away in the same condition.

I steal a glance as she sits with a small smile playing on her beautiful face. Our song *Committed* comes over the radio, and just as she does each and every time, my wife smiles wide and turns it up.

"Will you ever get tired of hearing us on the radio?"

"Never," she shakes her head with a smile. She settles into her seat, closing her eyes and singing along with our voices.

I press down on the gas pedal, forcing Leila's head deeper into the headrest. When she opens her eyes, I can't help the grin that spreads on my face.

"Will you ever get tired of driving this car?" she throws back at me.

"Never," I mimic both her words and her head shaking.

"You love this car, don't you?"

"Not as much as you, but it's a close second."

"Really? I'll remember that when we fight. You can find comfort in her instead of in me." I purse my lips, feigning acceptance, and she swats at me. "Jerk."

Ok, so the *BMW* I'm driving is also a nice perk to success. This was my only real purchase since achieving said success. My sexy-as-fuck, black, two door *BMW 435i Coupe*. Leila wanted us to continue using Betsy, her 2004 Honda Accord. I couldn't do it any more. The thing was a heap of junk. I never had my own car. Never really needed one. I was a married man with a hefty paycheck, driving this piece of shit. Betsy needed to be retired. Leila pouted, argued for her, and then finally succumbed.

We bought my baby when we got home from our honeymoon. I'll never forget that day, or night. We drove out to the beach and found a secluded parking lot facing the ocean, and I fucked her in the driver seat, as well as the passenger seat. She hasn't mentioned Betsy once since that night.

I glance over at my hot wife as she sits in said seat. She has become even more beautiful, if that's possible. She's worried with how quickly her body is changing, self conscious with her new curves. I, personally, am fucking loving them. My wife is thin, but sexy thin. In these past weeks, the changes occurring are fascinating to watch. Her breasts fill my hands, more than they had before. Her belly slopes ever so slightly, when I run my hand down her torso. The biggest change is in her eyes. They glow, almost as if they are now backlit, the gold flecks in them sparkling more than ever.

Her hands cradle her tiny bump. Her crossed tan legs cause her shorts to creep up, and I can't help but run my hand over her smooth skin. She smiles while her eyes remain closed and uncrosses her legs, letting them fall open in the process. My hand has a mind of its own and settles on her heat in between.

"Careful, rock star. I may have you pulling over, if you don't get us there soon." She entwines our fingers, bringing them up to her lips, and plants a firm kiss on my wedding band.

"Enough said," I force my speed further, depending on the built in radar detector to keep us from being pulled over. The parkway is pretty clear since most day beach-goers are already at their destinations. I was never into driving before. It was a menial task that never appealed to me. Since getting this car, I love taking off in different directions. I've lost count how many times I told her to pack a bag and we'd just head out of town. Sometimes north, sometimes south, it didn't matter.

Leila stops singing, and I glance over to see her worrying her bottom lip.

"What are you thinking about?"

"Nothing." She turns to meet my gaze and adds, "Not telling you."

"Fucking Lori."

Leila laughs, but offers no explanation.

"The only thing you are allowed to think about is what I'm going to do to you this weekend. Mr. Raunchy is back." Since we found out she was pregnant, our lovemaking has been sweet, soft, and slow. I'm not complaining, by any means. I love it both ways with her.

As if reading my mind, she teases, "It's been a while since we had kinky fuckery."

The insinuation of her comment goes straight to my cock. It's as if he's napping and she attempts to wake him with her tongue.

"Careful, wife. Words like that will have me pulling over."

"Well, it's been way too long since Mr. Raunchy has been around, and I miss him."

"I know." I grab for her hand, bringing it to my lips. "I love making love to you, but sometimes I need the other stuff, too."

“So do I.” She settles our entwined hands in her lap and says, “You are the one who’s afraid I am going to break.”

“Your point?”

“Just sayin’.”

Her comment reminds me, I haven’t fretted over her since leaving the apartment. “How are you feeling, Babe? Do you want me to stop for anything?”

“No, I’m just going to take a nap to prep for Mr. Raunchy.”

♬ ♬ ♬

“Memories,” she says while surveying the room. “Looks the same, minus the candles and my wedding dress slung over here, or your tux slung over there.”

I embrace her from behind, pulling her into my chest. “One whole year. It went so fast. Before you know it we’ll be married fifty years.”

She spins in my arms to face me, “Can we not jump ahead to fifty? I have a lot to cover between now and then.”

She slowly drags her fingers down my chest, slipping them under my t-shirt to start the climb back up, pulling it off in the process. While pinning me with her eyes, she then slowly unbuttons my jeans and slides her hand in to claim me. Her fingers molding over me, cause me to harden immediately. She drags both my jeans and my briefs off, in the same motion, lowering herself until she is eye level with my throbbing cock.

Seeing her down on her knees, looking up at me innocently, hits a nerve.

“Lei, no,” I lift her, denying her what she wants.

“No what?”

“I don’t want you to.”

"Why?" She gasps, looking like I just punched her in the gut.

"I just don't." She needs *me* to lavish *her* with sensual kisses and erotic touches. In her condition, she should be worshiped slowly with my hands and my lips. What she wants to do to me just feels wrong. Surely I can sacrifice getting sucked off by my wife for a few months?

"What happened to Mr. Raunchy?" she interrupts my inner dialogue.

"He left." I really don't have an explanation to this. It doesn't make sense. I just can't see her in that way right now.

She levels me with her glare. "Don't you dare."

"Dare what?"

"Don't you dare pull this shit!" When I look away, she grabs my chin, forcing me to meet her gaze. "I get the overprotectiveness you have with me, and it is warranted. But this? I am still the same person, Jack. I am not going to break."

"It's not that. It's just..." I release a heavy sigh from my frustrations. We have a silent standoff, her eyes blazing with fury and mine with remorse. "Please, Baby, let me make love to you," I stubbornly try to persuade her. She watches me carefully, her anger replaced with a touch of sadness in her eyes.

"Don't you find me…" She abruptly stops her words, but her eyes continue to plead for answers. The intensity of her scrutiny causes my heart to flip.

"Oh, my God! Don't even finish that thought. Of course I do. You are the sexiest woman I've ever met. It's not you..." I mumble in a pathetic attempt to explain. She is misunderstanding my intentions and I don't want to hurt her.

"Then what is it?"

I shake my head in frustration.

Her response is to push me until I fall on my ass on the edge of the bed. There is a new intensity in her gaze, a determination. With her fiery eyes pinned to mine, she unbuttons her shorts and then lowers the zipper. My cock aches painfully as she removes her shorts and panties. She grabs the hem of her t-shirt and pulls it over her head. Without any preamble, she then unfastens her bra, throwing it into the corner. Her gorgeous body calls to me, beckons me to take it. The tiny bump on her lower belly reminds me of her condition. An image flashes through my mind of Leila nursing our child, her topaz eyes filled with love.

"Lei, please come here. I need to taste you," I offer an alternative.

"No."

I swallow audibly, willing the fucking war that is raging within me to end. We've had sex plenty of times since she became pregnant. It's always been gentle and sweet. I'm now realizing that wasn't by chance.

She licks her fingers and skims her torso until they disappear between her legs. "Are you coming to this party, or am I coming alone?" she challenges.

My head is screaming this is the mother of my child. You can't hurt her. My cock is screaming fuck her hard and fast. It's still Leila. What the fuck is wrong with me?

The motion of her fingers hypnotizes me and clouds my logic. My intense yearning to touch her, to love her, is what propels me to kick off my shoes and jeans. My resolve slips with every movement of her fingers. In an instant, I press her up against the wall, holding both her hands above her head with one of mine.

She leans closer until our lips touch, willing me to take what I want. My turmoil is obvious from my heavy pants and the force of my hold on her. My cock pushes menacingly into her bump. Daring me, she lifts on her toes and parts her legs, so I'm now nestled between her folds. She then bites down on my lower lip, coercing a groan to escape.

"What are you waiting for?" she rasps against my lips. "Fuck me, Jack."

I crush my lips to hers, hitching her leg around my waist. With a single thrust I feel my issues crumbling around me. The familiarity clears my mind and instigates my lust. I plunge deeper and deeper into her, and she gasps against my lips. With every thrust I grunt heavily in return. My tongue invades her mouth brutally as my hands grip her flesh roughly. With every thrust she releases another moan. I can feel her possessing me, taking what she wants without apology. With every thrust I forget what I was conflicted with a few minutes ago.

I break our kiss to stare into her eyes, my engorged cock tightening within the space inside her. The exertion moistens our skin, dampens our hair.

"Jack," she gasps faintly against my lips, "faster."

Her command is so quiet I can barely hear her. Her lips on mine send a jolt of electricity through my body. I can feel the hair raising tingling course through me, traveling down my spine, and settling in the base of my erection. She swallows me whole, enveloping me with her warmth. Using every fiber of my being to slow down my impending release, to prolong this mind-blowing sensation, to relish in her voracious greed, I fail miserably. My attempt to control the situation is in vain as the strain causes my muscles to shudder and my cock to betray me.

"Come now," I demand, my words sounding ridiculous to my own ears. With them she constricts around me, bringing me to a ferocious climax…one that comes too fast…one that is hard and necessary.

"Fuuuuck," I cry out as I empty myself into her. It seems to go on forever, draining me completely. I release her hands and she brings them down to my shoulders to hold onto for support. While our tremors hold us prisoners to the position we are in, we rely on the wall to keep us upright. I bury my face in her neck, breathing in her scent and needing it more than air. Once we successfully control our breathing, she pierces me with her angry glare.

"Don't ever do that again."

I loosen my grip to hold her gently. Repentance fills me as I cup her face to kiss her softly. "I'm sorry," I mutter when I pull away. She holds me captive with her eyes, and I feel the need to repeat my apology before I slowly release her to turn away to sit on the bed.

"What was that?" she asks quietly.

"I don't know. Seeing you like that..."

She sits next to me, silently watching as I drag my hands through my hair. I turn toward her and take both her hands in between my own.

I pull her onto my lap and hide my face in her neck. When I lift my head to stare into her eyes, I attempt an explanation. "You misunderstood."

Her lips, still swollen from my forcefulness beckon to be kissed, which I do softly.

"You scared me," she admits. "Jack, I need that from you and I need to do that for you, as much as I need the sweet and gentle. Please don't take that from me."

"I won't. I promise. I love you and I didn't mean to hurt you. Ironically, I was trying to protect you and my head was fucking with me and…" The silence stretches between us. I don't know what else to say to justify my actions. She skims her hand across my cheek, studying me closely.

"I know," she says, excusing my sudden loss for words. "Hey, that was awesome."

"Yeah, that was pretty awesome."

"Want to do it again?" Just as she asks, her stomach rumbles loudly. "After you feed me?" she adds with a smile.

I squeeze her to my chest, openly laughing at her.

"What?"

"Seems your appetite for both raunch and food decided to come back? Is my baby hungry?" I ask as I caress her bare belly. "Do you think he can hear me?"

"Not sure. It wouldn't hurt to talk to her." When I place my lips on her belly, repeatedly murmuring *I love you*, her stomach growls viciously for the second time. I can't help but laugh out loud once again.

"Holy shit. Is that you or him?" I ask incredulously. "Was that his first rock scream?"

"That was me."

"Ready to eat?"

"Apparently."

"I'll hurry, in case it's a fluke."

"I hope not. This would be a terrible tease if I were to go back to constant nausea and vomiting."

"That *would* suck. Plus, I didn't bring the pot."

## Chapter 8 – Lori

Their departure date is a week away. All my friends claim that time is flying by. For me, it's slinking by at a snail's pace. I've been stalling, avoiding, and lying to Matt every minute of every day since the day I spilled my torment to Leila six days ago. I was all prepared to tell Matt of my plans to skip the tour. I wasn't going to tell him the real reason why, only a semi-truthful version that had me staying behind because of Alisa. It didn't matter what version I prepped in my head over and over on the walk back to his apartment, because when I got there, I chickened out.

He was waiting for me and he was pissed. Like a coward, I texted him to let him know I was on my way back. Once home, my explanation of the panic attack was lame. I lied and said I forgot to fill my birth control pills. I had to run to the pharmacy at that moment, in a life or death situation. He made it very clear, he didn't believe me. After prodding relentlessly for a few days, he finally dropped it. I can be pretty stubborn.

My new game plan was to act normal, and once he didn't see me on the bus, he would figure it out. I thought it was a good plan, but I wasn't executing the act normal part very well. Regardless, I probably would've still been holding it all in if Leila hadn't threatened me.

When I did finally tell him the abridged version of why I was skipping the tour, he flipped out. I wasn't sure what I expected. Maybe indifference? His reaction only made me more confused. He truly cares for me. I feel like such a bitch. When I'm with him, I spend most of the time pointing out all his finer points. It's almost as if I'm making a mental pro and con list. It needs to be said that his pro list is beating Trey's by a mile.

Trey has one pro…he's Trey.

In an attempt to soothe his crossness, I've been very sweet and loving. I'm not a complete insensitive bitch. I don't want him leaving upset. It's not fair to do that to him. He deserves to leave with a clear head and satisfied libido. I've been busy ensuring he has everything he needs. Apparently, my atypical behavior has made him more suspicious.

My band's opinion on the subject of me staying home has been split. Joe was quick to point out that it'll be *my* fault for Matt's constant bad mood. I can sympathize with him. Matt can brood more than I can, and that's saying a lot.

Logan is thrilled I'm staying behind. The poor guy has been so distraught over leaving his very pregnant wife. He sent me a huge bouquet of flowers as a thank you.

Alisa is still crying a lot, but not from sadness like she used to. The day I told her, she insisted I should go. She would feel guilty if I stayed home to be with her. I argued that she didn't have a choice, that my mind was made up, and to get over it. She hugged me for a solid twelve minutes. I may be staying behind for other reasons, but I'm so happy to be doing this for her, as well. It's the only bright spot in this mess.

Evan understands my "motives," but is sad I won't be there to keep Leila company. He knows how excited she was to finally have a confidant on tour. Sure Nina will be there, but they don't have anything in common or have a relationship to speak of, besides being acquaintances.

As for me, I am no closer to clarity than I was three weeks ago. I keep rationalizing that once everyone is gone, especially the two reasons I'm in this predicament to begin with, I'll have an "aha" moment. Let's hope that moment comes sooner than later.

In another attempt at making nice-nice, I picked up breakfast and am standing at Matt's apartment door. After a quick knock, I hear him faintly calling that he's coming. I'm starting to get peeved when a few minutes go by and he still doesn't answer the door. He knows it's me and is probably moving slower than necessary to punish me.

He opens the door with a grim look on his face.

"Hey, Babe, I got breakfast."

Without a word he moves aside to let me in.

"How long are you going to hate me?"

"Still debating that."

I put the coffee and muffins down and encircle him in my arms. "It's Saturday. We have no plans, and I plan on reminding you of all the reasons that you love me." (*And reminding myself*) my inner monologue adds its two cents.

He looks down into my eyes, and a tiny smile tugs on one corner of his lips. "I'm waiting."

It's his normal arrogant - I'm gorgeous and I know it - smile. Thankfully, I feel the familiar twinge in the pit of my stomach and the tingle on my girly parts. I wrap my fingers in his hair and slowly pull him down until our lips touch. His remain still, firm, unmoving. I take the lead and begin to coax him to reciprocate. When I slip my tongue into his mouth, he comes to life.

He presses his fingers into the small of my back, pulling me into his hard body. I can feel his excitement firmly pressing into my belly. He invades my mouth, pushing his way in and holding my own tongue hostage in the process. By the time he breaks our kiss, I'm a panting mess.

He quirks one eyebrow up and asks, "What else you got?"

Without any further explanation, as if one is needed, he drags me down the hall to his room. Normally, I'm the dominant one in our sex life. I'm not a riding crop yielding dominant, but I do like to control how I reach orgasms. He hasn't complained, because part of my turn-on is turning him on.

Watching his eyes cloud over, or his jaw tightening, or his cock growing to a thick painful hardness are all triggers for me. Knowing I've gotten this man to a point of no return is a power trip like no other. That may be part of the problem. I never had that power over Trey. I was never close to being able to dominate him, but I was ok with that. Maybe if I saw Matt in the same erotic way things could be different.

As my mind drifts to that mental pro/con list, I'm reminded of whom I'm with now by his gruff voice commanding, "Get naked."

Without argument I remove one article of clothing at a time until I stand before him in my bra and panties. He comes closer and skims his hand from my hip to my breast, holding it firmly while running his thumb over my nipple. He dips his other hand into my panties and slides a single finger back and forth. He pins me with his gaze, almost daring me to react. Except for my attempt at controlling my breathing, I keep my facial expression bored and unaffected.

When he slips his finger inside of me, my façade starts to crumble. That sexy smirk appears and he slips in another. Without breaking eye contact he drags his tongue across my bottom lip.

Fuck control.

I lunge, pulling him into me. The hand that held my breast now moves to my ass. He grips it tightly to hold me close. His fingers continue to plunge in and out, in and out. He's bringing me to the edge, and I'm not ready to jump yet.

I push him away, trying to gain some sort of control. His amused grin widens. He takes it upon himself to remove my bra and panties and leaves me open and vulnerable to his penetrating stare as he removes his clothes. Once he is gloriously naked, he begins to stroke himself slowly and deliberately.

My heart races and I forget to breathe for a second. I feel dizzy from the flow of blood that's desperately trying to make its way to my brain and the lack of oxygen in my lungs. My audible gulp of air clues him in to how close I am to cracking. Without warning he turns me and firmly pushes my back until I am bent in half.

And then, nothing.

The tip of his cock sits at my entrance. The heat emanating off of it makes it feel like he dipped it in hot wax. The hands that are holding my hips shift. One slides to the middle of my back, almost as if he's daring me to move. His other slides around to my clit and slowly starts circling, over and over, with the slightest bit of pressure. It's just enough to instigate me to respond. I clutch the fabric of the comforter tightly between my fingers. He can't see my eyes cinched shut, but his rough chuckle tells me he knows he got to me.

Without invitation he plunges into me in one fast thrust. The tempo of his fingers quicken to the same pace of his hips. All too soon, I lose complete control. He broke me, and I can't fight my muscles any longer. With a mind of their own they surround him, they clench, they tighten, and they bring me a crushing orgasm.

Once they soften and return to their normal state, he wraps both arms around me and holds me tight, forcing me to accept every inch of him. His savage grunt in my ear is such a delicious sound.

We collapse together, both spent and drained.

I shift to face him and run my fingers through his hair. "Wow!"

"Yeah," he agrees, but he looks so sad when he meets my gaze. It tugs on my conscience. I'm robbing him of the excitement he should be feeling right now.

"Matt, it's only a few weeks."

He nods quietly, lost in thought. When he finally says something, it crushes me. "It's actually fifty-eight long, unbearable days."

This gorgeous, sexy man loves me.

My eyes swell with emotion, and I bury my face in his chest embarrassingly.

He holds me close and tries to soothe me with his caresses. He thinks I'm upset because of our separation. My guilt rushes through me with such force it causes a sob to escape. I'm evil. I'm a coward. I'm so selfish. I've been so consumed with my own problem that I not once stopped to consider what he is feeling over all of this.

I am so messed up in the head that I forgot what my heart has always wanted.

"We need to talk," his voice breaks my reverie.

I nod into his chest, taking the cowardly way out. He doesn't allow me that out and pulls away, so I am exposed to him and his coming interrogation. "I know this isn't about you being a great friend and choosing to hang out with Alisa. Something else is up." My silence confirms his suspicion. "What's going on with you?"

"I don't know."

"Oh, come on, Lori. Do you think I'm an idiot? Give me more credit than that."

"Are you happy?" I ask, throwing the ball in his court.

He looks surprised for a second before shrugging, "Yeah."

"That's it? I get a shrug and a yeah?"

"What are you looking for? A signed contract?" he responds arrogantly.

"Don't be a dick. I'm not in the mood."

"You're not in the mood? Well, I'm tired of your moods."

He hits a nerve like it's a bull's eye. I leave the bed and throw on his t-shirt. I can't have this discussion while naked. He pulls on his jeans before following me out to his kitchen.

Busying myself with reheating our coffee and pulling out the muffins, he leans against the counter watching me silently. After trying to ignore him, he finally breaks me without ever saying a word.

"I feel like we're missing something."

"Missing something?" Sadness passes through his eyes, but it's fleeting and quickly replaced with annoyance. He waits for further explanation.

When I continue to ignore him, he finally speaks in an icy tone. "I'll stand here all day until you tell me what the fuck is going on."

Damn him. Actually, damn me. Did I think I could avoid him and his concerns? Did I honestly think he would drive off into the sunset without calling me out on my shit?

Time to pay the piper.

"Matt, I'm not a mushy, lovey-dovey type. You know that. I'm a no games, no gimmicks kind of girl. I'm not a hopeless romantic. I think you love that part of me. What I'm struggling with is I'm no longer feeling like that Lori."

"What the hell are you talking about?"

I release a heavy sigh. I'm already exhausted with this conversation. "I want more. I want more than hot sex, and I want more than a comfortable, expected relationship. I want my world rocked."

He shakes his head mockingly. "Ok, I see where this is going."

"No, you don't."

"The fuck I don't. You are still hung up on that fucking rocker?"

His statement makes me cringe from guilt. I silently chastise myself for using the fucking word "rocked." I can tell by his expression that he is stuck on the word and not the meaning behind it. Because of this, I truly don't know how to respond to him. My unexpected silence further fuels his fire. He grabs his coffee off the counter and stalks over to the couch. Now, I'll never get through to him.

I sit across from him to purposefully keep my distance. The way he waits expectantly for me to explain myself ticks me off. I have no right being angry with him, but I am. I'm pissed he guessed my issue and that he can't miraculously read my mind and give me what I want. Forget the fact I don't know what I want…and I'm fully aware I sound like a psychopath, even to my own ears.

"You want to end this?"

"No."

"No? Then what do you want, Lori?"

"I want you to want me more than life itself." There, I said it. Not only did I finally let out what's bothering me, I said it with attitude. He sits gawking at me, as if I've lost my mind.

"So, loving you the way I do, the amount I do, isn't enough for you? You need some sort of validation written in my blood?"

This conversation is killing me. I've never had to analyze my feelings or actions before, or explain them to someone. "No, I need to know if I walked out that door, you would be wrecked."

"I just admitted I'm going to be lost without you. Let me ask you a few questions. Do you want me more than life itself? If I were to walk out that door, would you be wrecked?"

"That's my point," I mumble more to myself, but he heard me. He got my message, and the look on his face is one of complete defeat. He now understands that we aren't the be-all and end-all to each other.

I move to sit next to him and wait for him to meet my gaze. When he refuses to, I turn his head for him. His gorgeous eyes look lost. It kills me to see him look so pained. "I didn't want to do this. This is what I was hoping to avoid, by avoiding the whole subject. I was hoping, once you got back, I would have worked it all out and never had to explain my stupid issues."

"They aren't stupid, especially if they have you questioning your feelings for me."

"Matt, I love you. I'm just confused…but it's my problem. I need time to work this through on my own. I wanted to figure myself out before we even had this conversation. Since we're having it now, I need to know you love me, and you'll wait for me to figure it all out."

"And if you don't? If you decide I'm not what you want or need? Then what?"

I can't answer that question. I'm not ready to voice the outcome I foresee, if I decide this isn't enough.

"Lori, I love you, too. Am I ready to propose marriage or promise to be your forever? No, I'm not. But that doesn't make what I feel for you any less valid. Nor does it make our relationship any less real. I may not have fireworks exploding in my goddamn head every time we kiss, but I know there are times when you look at me from across the room and I feel my heart is being squeezed from the inside. Or if you text me one of your quirky little comments, I can't wait to see you again to kiss your smartass mouth." He takes my hands in between his and says, "I guess none of that is enough for you."

I shake my head through my tears. "You're wrong. It is enough for me. I just never knew it. You've never told me any of that."

"I didn't know I had to." He releases my hands and adds, "I assumed by saying I love you, you understand how I feel for you. Fuck, I'm not good at this. Clearly you know my history with relationships fucking sucks. Communication is new to me. But you aren't exactly a walking *Hallmark* card yourself."

"You're right. I suck at this, too." He leans back into the couch and stares at the ceiling. I lean against him, my head on his shoulder. The fact he doesn't move away or push me away makes me feel slightly better.

"So now what?" he asks hesitantly.

"Now I wish I could rewind the past twenty minutes so it never happened. Because I don't want you to think, while you are away from me, that I don't love you or want to be with you. Now that we have had this talk, we both have a lot of thinking to do. I need to make sure that at this point in my life what we have together, whether it be good or bad, is what I want." I sit up so I can look into his eyes. "You need to decide that as well. If you can't see me in your future, you need to admit that. This separation will be good for both of us."

He pulls me into the crook of his arm and kisses the top of my head. "You drive me nuts, you know that?"

"I know, but you do love me."

"It's the only reason I haven't kicked you to the curb yet."

"I'd kick you back."

He laughs and kisses me. "I know you would."

# Chapter 9 - Leila

I look ridiculous.

"I can't wear this!" I announce when she walks in. I've been standing at the mirror, mortified while also on the verge of tears. This is the fifth thing I've tried on. I summoned for our wardrobe stylist, and now the poor woman looks lost as I animatedly flail my arms in frustration.

"Mrs. Lair, this is what I was told to give to you."

"Angel, I apologize, this isn't your fault," I turn to the mirror, motioning at the mounds of flesh popping out of the top of the camisole, "but I can't wear this. I'm not sure anyone at the label, or if my always-efficient agent, has mentioned that I'm pregnant. This rack of *Frederick's of Hollywood* clothing they sent is not going to work today, or for the tour."

She shakes her head and rolls her eyes, mumbling under her breath. "I'm sorry, no one has mentioned that. Let me see what else I can find," she adds with sympathy. "I'll be back." Obviously she agrees with my gripes.

Except for yoga pants, t-shirts, and pajamas, none of my current wardrobe fits. I've bought a few things, like jeans and an industrial sports bra to hold my newly acquired C-cups. I've postponed a shopping trip until I saw what the label was supplying. Staring at the scraps of fabric hanging before me, they apparently confuse me for a porn star.

We are back at Pierre's studio to shoot some publicity shots for the tour. The last time I was here, I wore a sexy red leather bustier and very tight jeans. I was embarrassed at the time. I felt the choices the MALE stylist made for me screamed of sex and I was less than thrilled with that marketing strategy. In comparison, that was nothing compared to what I look like now. This time, they want me in a black lace camisole and black leather pants. The lacy cups barely cover my nipples. In fact, double-sided sticky tape will be needed to ensure they do.

Are they fucking kidding me?

I'm thankful to the label for covering my clothing costs…but seriously?

With tears still threatening I resume rummaging through the rack, searching for something to wear to this damn shoot.

I went from not being able to hold anything down to wanting to eat an elephant if you served it up with some ketchup. I've gained back the pounds I lost, plus five more, and I think most of it appeared in my boobs. At this rate, I'll be a house by the time I deliver this child.

Jack enters just as I throw a red cut-off top across the room. "What did that thing do to you to deserve such a fate?"

When I turn toward him, his eyes practically bulge out of his head. "Um." He grips the back of his neck and stumbles with his words.

"Yeah, exactly…UM!"

"You can't wear that."

"No shit?"

He comes up behind me as I scrutinize myself in the mirror. "Don't get me wrong, Baby, I love them. I hope they stay for a while, but there's no fucking way I want the world seeing them."

"No worries, rock star. We're on the same page." I yank the scrap of lace off my body and throw it to join the red one on the floor.

Jack picks it up tenderly and says, "Don't be mean to it. I want you to take this one home."

I throw him a murderous look and pounce over to the rack, trying for a third time to see what my choices are. A pink halter-top that's loose and flowing catches my eye. This may work. I can probably even use the leather pants. The top is long enough to hide the fact the top button will be undone. I quickly change into my new option and model it for Jack. The fabric clings to the girls, but if I stand sideways, my exposed back distracts from them.

"How's this?"

He circles me, like he's checking his *BMW* for dings. "Walk to me."

I take a few steps as his eyes zone in on the twins.

"Better, but they are still very obvious. Can you wear a sports bra or something?"

I throw him an exasperated look. "It's backless!"

"Then just hide behind me."

"For six more months?"

"I wouldn't mind."

"You're not helping," I whine and pathetically stomp my foot. "Do I look like a circus tent?" I turn first right, then left. "Ugh, I do look like a tent."

He steps up to me and digs his fingers into my hair, holding my gaze. "Babe, you look hot."

"You have to say that, you're my husband. I wish Lor were here. She would tell me the truth."

Jack pulls out his phone, takes a picture and texts it. "Next best thing."

As we wait for Lori to talk me off the ledge, I focus on my image in the mirror. The changes to my body aren't the only transformations I am going through. I look different. My face looks older, more mature. It's filled out a touch, but it's something else. Something I can't pinpoint, but is there nonetheless.

"All good. She approves," Jack shows me his phone displaying the huge thumbs up icon in the center.

"You're so smart."

"I know. What would you do without me?"

"Well, for one thing, I wouldn't be knocked up as I'm about to tour."

"Ha ha."

"Kidding. I love being knocked up. I just hope the haters take mercy on me when I'm out to here." I form a circle with my outstretched arms.

"Fuck the haters." Jack spits out. He is the only one who gets irate when reading their posts. I can laugh about it now, we all can. I've grown so much in this fishbowl we live in. It no longer upsets me in the least. I am confident in my talent, I have the support of my friends and family, and I sleep beside the hottest, sexiest, sweetest man on earth every night. He's right, fuck the haters.

I say that now…ask me again, once they start their lies.

News broke of my pregnancy days after my birthday party. I wasn't at all surprised. It spread at the party like a wildfire. Someone was bound to leak the news. Of course my haters absolutely hate that I'm having Jack's baby. I'm trapping him. It's the only way he'll stay with me. I'm pathetic. I'm a gold-digger. Some of their pet names for me are hilarious. Trey has taken to calling me a gold-digging skank.

One last inspection of my face and hair, and I'm ready to get this over with. "Ok, I'm ready, let's go." I drag him by the hand into the hall when we run into Angel.

"I found a few things, but what you chose looks great."

"Thank you. I'm going to need that whole rack replaced. I'll take whatever you can find."

"Ok, I'll keep working on it. I'll also get multiple sizes of each item, so you can grow into them. I'm annoyed I wasn't told you were expecting. I'm on it now."

"I appreciate it. Angel, you are truly an angel. Thank you. I'm sorry I lost it on you."

“No worries. Mother of three here, I can relate.” She pats my shoulder and walks away, leaving me shaking my damn head.

What the fuck? Goddamn Jen. I find it hard to believe she forgot I was pregnant. There is no way it slipped her mind to tell wardrobe. That woman consistently pisses me off. Since the wedding, she’s been lying low. Jack had a pretty big blow-up with her right before. She wanted Jack and the guys to do a publicity event, alone. Jack said if I couldn’t be involved, then he wanted no part of it. She explained that it was during Greek Week at a college where a few of the sorority houses were major Devil’s Lair fans. They were throwing a charity event and wanted to auction off date nights with each of them. After trying to patiently explain he wasn’t interested and rather just donate to their charity, she threw a fit. She claimed that me being there would “upset the female fans and hamper the event.”

Her tantrum was nothing compared to Jack’s. He’d had it with her and the fact that she totally would disrespect me at every turn. She claimed she was the reason that Devil’s Lair was so successful. He claimed she was a jealous bitch who benefited from our success and that she’s the one who needs us. On and on it went. It took days to get them to swallow their pride and meet face to face.

Jack came dangerously close to firing her ass, but I wouldn’t allow it. With all her faults and all the things I despise about her, she is still a top-notch agent. The boys have benefited from her hard-ass, don’t-fuck-with me attitude. I wouldn’t be the reason to derail their train, and from getting it to where it was bound. The boys and I sat Jack down and calmly convinced him to work things out with her. He finally agreed and was sure to tell her that it was me who she should be thanking for not becoming unemployed. Since then, she’s been pathetically kissing *his* ass.

She married Malcolm, and for a while I felt she was trying to change her methods and be more supportive of me, until now. I haven't felt like wanting to stab her for a long time. I can only attribute the old Jen resurfacing because of my pregnancy.

Bitch.

"What was that about?" Jack asks as Angel walks away.

"The poor woman got the brunt of my tantrum. Can you believe Jen didn't mention I was pregnant to wardrobe?"

"And that surprises you how?"

"You're right. It shouldn't." I haul ass down the hall toward the studio. "Hurry, the quicker we are done, the quicker you can buy me a cheeseburger."

♫ ♫ ♫

"So, our bus now includes Oscar. Cliffhangers will have their own bus with the roadies. The third bus is Dylan, the drivers, and Will?" Hunter recaps as we all scoff down our lunch.

We bolted to Leo's Diner the minute the shoot ended. I've been craving their apple pie, which I've had as an appetizer. I nod at Hunter with my face full of a cheeseburger since he directed his question to me.

"Lei, will there be room in that tiny bedroom for you, Jack, and your traveling companions?" Trey asks with a serious expression.

"What traveling companions?"

He zones in on my boobs, and I can feel the blush creep up, starting from my toes. I pick up a fry and throw it at his head. He lets out a belly laugh and fist bumps a laughing Hunter.

"Screw you all," I mumble more to myself.

"Are you hoping for a death wish?" Jack asks Trey.

"Chill out, man. It's a compliment. You're a lucky dude." He turns toward Hunter and asks, "Weren't we just sayin' how lucky he is?"

"Seriously. Stop talking about my wife's boobs, or I'm going to hurt you."

"Baby, I can fight my own battles. As soon as I'm done with my burger, I'll kick his ass."

"Bring it, Little Lair," Trey says with a wink.

Trey has been in a great mood lately. It happened to have surfaced once news broke that Lori would not be traveling with us. Not that I feel Trey ever stresses over anything, but I do feel he wasn't looking forward to having a front row seat to the Lori/Matt love affair, which confirms my suspicions that Trey isn't over Lori. I haven't shared that with Lori. I don't want to fuel her irrational confliction. I love Trey, but he isn't someone to throw a stable, loving relationship out the window for. A tiny part of me feels he is capable of changing, but it's improbable.

"It's funny that the girls are meeting up with us in Chicago again," Scott says, trying to change the subject. "And Miami. It's like a repeat of our last tour."

"Let's hope not too much of a repeat," I mumble out loud. Jack looks down at me with unmasked trepidation. I immediately regret my comment. I work hard at shielding him from my fears. I don't want to live in constant fear. Truth is, I do get nervous whenever we are performing in a public forum. He'd quit and have me shacked up in a secluded location for the rest of our lives, if he actually knew I struggle with that.

The upside is we aren't performing at the same festival we did when Danny tried to kill me. I don't think I would be able to revisit that venue ever again. Terror engulfs me when I visualize the parking lot or Jack's face as he was trying desperately to reach me. A shiver takes hold of my body as I sit and stare into space reliving that horror.

"You ok?" Jack looks down at me with concern.

"Yeah, I'm fine." I lie from necessity. The entire subject enrages him, understandably so. Feeling the weight of his penetrating gaze, I check my cell phone for the time. "Guys, we gotta go."

We are heading to the larger studio this afternoon to have our first rehearsal with Cliffhangers. We are recording a song together when we arrive in Los Angeles next week and need to squeeze in as many rehearsals as we can until we leave. It's exciting that we will be tied together for all of eternity in this piece of music that represents so much. Their lives are about to change, and it's an absolute honor to be part of that.

After my husband settles the bill, because he refuses to let anyone else pay for lunch, we pile into the waiting SUV. The reality that we aren't walking three blocks to our destination is comical. The guys love to tease me that it's because of the flocks of females that seem to have their own personal *LoJack* device on my husband's ass. In all honesty, it's a nice diversion from the truth, so I let them tease me all they want. I would gladly accept the hoards of touchy, feely females over having Danny Sorenson walking this earth.

When we get to the studio, my former band mates are waiting for us with excitement written all over their faces.

"You guys ready for this?" Jack asks while smiling widely.

"Yeah, we've gone over the sheet music and Nina memorized the lyrics…" Evan recaps until Jack cuts him off.

"I mean what's about to happen to you."

They look to each other smiling before Matt says, "Fuck yeah. I'm ready."

"Where's Lori?" I ask with my eyes focused on Matt's and avoiding Trey's. I'm really not a good actress. The fact that I now know how she feels and that they are going to be in the same room is worrying me.

As if on cue, Lori and Jen walk into the foyer while chatting quietly. Lori sees me and winks. The irony that she's calm and collected while I'm not isn't lost on me.

"How was the shoot?" Jen asks Jack when she sees us.

"I need to talk to you."

"Jack, not now."

He ignores me and pulls me past Jen. "Hallway," he commands as we walk by her.

She follows us down the hall and asks, "What happened?"

"Shoot was fine, once Lei figured out what to wear. Did it slip your mind that she's pregnant?"

Jen drifts her gaze down to my belly. "She's showing already?"

What a *bitch.*

"Yes, Jen. I'm showing. I worked it out and Angel from wardrobe is revisiting my options."

"Oh, good. Problem solved," she says with a plastered smile.

"No thanks to you. Where were you anyway?" he asks, folding his arms expectantly.

"I had a meeting."

"How convenient."

"Jack, let it go," I huff in frustration.

When will my husband learn it won't work? She simply will not change. She has had a problem with me since the first day I walked into the studio. Nothing has changed, nor do I expect it to. I don't understand her issues. I thought I knew what they were. I used to feel that she felt I was a threat, specifically to her. My female presence would distract from her authority. Then as things progressed and our popularity increased exponentially, I felt that she felt I was a distraction from the four rock gods she's devoted her life to. Once we achieved fame, and Jack's popularity still increased with single females from coast to coast, in spite of our relationship, I thought she would back off.

Apparently, it's personal.

Well, I'm not going anywhere. It gives me a bit of leverage, power, and even satisfaction to know she isn't able to do a thing about that.

"Everything ok?" Lori asks, interrupting our private chat without apology.

"Peachy," I wink, and she gets the message.

"Ready to start this?"

"More than you know."

Our agents take the lead and run the show. They had already discussed what the run down should be and proceed to throw out orders as we all sit and listen.

The song is called *In The Cards*. Jack wrote the lyrics and Hunter and Evan wrote the music. I've heard Jack's rough draft, only with his guitar and I love it. It's perfect. Jack was able to capture what we are all feeling, thinking, and hoping for in one perfect rock song. I can only imagine what it will sound like with all of us performing it.

The introduction to the song will start with Trey and Evan dueling in a haunting bass riff. When they settle, the rest of the guys will bridge them to the first verse. Jack and Matt will both sing the first verse. I come in with Nina shortly after. The next three verses will be sung by all four of us. Jack and I will then share the second chorus, and Matt and Nina the last. It's brilliant.

As expected, it takes a few run-throughs before we are all in sync. Jen was hoping we could record a demo today, but was quickly put in her place by Jack. After he is satisfied with how we sound, he ends rehearsal to her dismay.

"I feel you should crack out one recording today," she voices while in her, *arms-folded-because-I'm-always-right* stance.

Jack purposefully waits a few minutes before responding, causing steam to billow out of her ears. "We'll record tomorrow. We have three more days to get a demo recorded and I'm not rushing it." He turns his back on her, as the tension in the room becomes stifling.

"Um…ok, so tomorrow morning?" Lori asks hesitantly.

"Sure. We'll meet here around eleven," Jack doesn't give Jen a chance to respond.

"Apparently, I'm not needed here." Jen gripes and waits for Jack to disagree. When she's met with silence, she adds, "Text me when you've recorded, I'll be back then."

"Looking forward to it," Jack responds curtly. Jen flips her hair and walks out.

"Dude, you need to back off," Hunter offers his opinion to Jack, even though it wasn't solicited.

"Really? When she behaves herself, I'll back off. I'm sick and tired of her nonsense and her attitude."

"We get attitude from Lori all the time, and it actually turns me on." Joseph deadpans. Lori crumples a piece of paper and throws it at his head.

"Dickhead."

While everyone else laughs I can see the tension rolling off Jack's shoulders in waves. As we all gather our things to head home, Lori comes over and mumbles, "I talked to him."

"Wait, what?"

"I'll call you later," she says, leaving me hanging.

With that Evan comes up beside me and whispers, "I need to talk to you."

"Why are you whispering?" I whisper back.

"Tonight's the night."

My mouth drops at his announcement. I've been waiting for him to give me a hint as to when he was going to finally ask her. "Really? I'm so happy. Where?"

"She's meeting me at our favorite place. Then we'll head to the apartment. Do you mind going over for me and setting up?"

"Not at all. Are you ready to tell him? He can use some good news." We both shift our gaze to Jack, just as he looks up.

"Yeah, I'm ready. I'll walk out with you guys."

"What's going on?" He asks as he comes over, guitar slung over one shoulder and our bag over the other.

"You ready to leave?"

"Yeah. The guys are heading out for a drink, but I'm exhausted. Do you mind skipping?" he asks, quietly.

"No. Actually, I have to make a stop on the way home. Come, Evan and I will fill you in."

Evan appears nervous as we walk out of the studio. Tables are turned. Jack had told me how nervous he was when he called my dad and Evan right before he proposed. They weren't big Jack fans then and gave him a hard time. Their relationship is great now, and they've grown very close. Jack confided that Evan is like a brother, and Evan is proud of the man that married his sister.

I find it funny Evan is nervous. I guess in his mind, it's his turn to now ask Jack for his sister's hand, and his turn to grovel.

## Chapter 10 - Evan

There's a ton of shit that needs to happen before you go on tour. Besides all the personal crap you need to get done, there are photo shoots and paperwork to be signed, wardrobes to be approved, and rehearsing and recording in the studio. Through it all, I made a life-altering decision. So among the stress of packing and preparing to leave, I also decided I want to propose to Lizzy.

I already knew I was going to propose down the road, but I decided now is as good a time as any. I want her to be mine in every sense of the word, and there's no reason to wait.

I also put tremendous amount of pressure on myself to create the perfect evening. I made a reservation at her favorite restaurant. I arranged for Leila to romanticize our apartment while we were out.

Leila was the only other person, other than myself, to know of my plan. I mainly confided in her to be sure I did everything right. I trust her opinion and I know she would want the best for Lizzy. Originally, I was going to propose at the restaurant. Leila said that was a big mistake. Public displays like that are cheesy. Who knew?

The plan is to head back to our place afterwards, where candles, flowers, and romantic music will be waiting for us when we get there. Lei helped me pick the perfect ring. I've called her dad and asked for permission. I told Jack after rehearsal. He wasn't surprised and gave me his complete blessing. He actually went pretty easy on me, considering how hard I was on him when he called asking for Leila's hand. He could have given me a good dose of my own medicine, but he didn't.

So now, I'm all set.

I've been walking around all day with the ring in my pocket. During rehearsal Joe picked up on my nerves. He antagonized me with his practical jokes and snide comments. He assumed I was in a pissy mood because I was leaving Lizzy and bet me a hundred bucks that I won't be able to go an hour without calling her. No way I'm taking that sucker bet.

Liz and I decided to meet at the restaurant to save time. She usually works late and promised to leave on time tonight. She isn't here yet, but she's always late…always. She doesn't mean to be. Since I've come into her life, she claims her tardiness has gotten much worse. I may be the blame some of the time, but mostly it's all on her.

She was an hour late on our first date. I was convinced she stood me up. I was minutes away from walking when I got a text from Leila who heard from Jack that her phone died, her cab had a fender bender, and she didn't know my number by heart. I was so impressed she went through all that to get in touch with me. They were on tour at the time, and she did all she could to get in touch with me.

I've gotten used to her running late. It's part of who she is. Doesn't lessen the anxiety I'm feeling right now, or the sweat from drenching my pits.

I feel her before I see her as I watch her walk toward me frowning.

"I'm so sorry, Hon."

When I pretend to be annoyed, she gifts me with a delicious kiss. "Ok, you're forgiven."

"Yay."

She takes her seat and smiles warmly. "Tough day. I really need a romantic date night with my man."

"Lucky for you I have a romantic date night planned."

She chats animatedly as we order our dinners and sip our drinks. She tells me about her day and some details of her patients. I remain quiet, nodding and smiling robotically. I shouldn't have listened to my sister, as I'm having a hard time getting through this dinner. My plan would already have me on my knee and her wearing the ring.

My nerves are so obvious during our meal that she looks up concerned and asks, "What's wrong, Hon?"

"Nothing."

"Evan? You're sweating. Do you feel ok?"

"Yeah, I'm fine. It's hot in here." I pathetically admit and subtly wipe my brow. I can feel my heart pounding through my chest. What the fuck am I freaking out over? The possibility she'll say no?

Just as I try to rationalize what is causing my panic, she reaches over and takes my hand, and all is right in my world.

"You ready to go?" I ask, gripping her hand tightly.

She nods, smiling warmly. "I'm ready to get you home to take care of you."

When I wiggle my eyebrows, she laughs and says, "You can't be all that sick with that one track mind."

I nervously tap my foot as I wait to settle the bill. The minute the waiter hands me my receipt, I pull her out of the restaurant and to a waiting cab.

"Jeez, what's going on with you?"

"I just can't wait to be alone with you. I missed you today. The closer I get to leaving, the more desperate I am to be with you."

She smiles at my words and caresses my face. "Me, too. I'm going to miss you so much. Did you set up your *Skype* account?" she reminds me.

"Yes, it's all ready to go." My nervous foot tapping starts again, but she doesn't seem to notice this time. She settles against me in the cab, content in being within my embrace. Our commute back to our apartment doesn't take long at all. Hand in hand, we enter our building and then the elevator. She's quiet on the way up. I study her as she stares ahead. Her eyes are moist with emotion. My guess is the realization that I'm leaving in a few days is hitting her.

"Hey, Baby. Please don't cry. You'll kill me." I encircle her in a tight hold. My hug that's meant to soothe backfires, as she quietly starts to sob in my arms. The elevator opens to our floor, and she swipes away her tears as I wait for her to exit. She follows me to our apartment, sniffling quietly.

My hand shakes as I attempt to unlock the door. Once I finally unhitch the lock, I push open to reveal the room glowing from the dozens of tiny votive candles flickering romantically. Over the speakers, our song, *Only Place I Call Home* by *Every Avenue*, plays softly in the background.

Lizzy stands stunned.

She looks up at me with new tears in her eyes, but a breathtaking smile on her face. "What's all this?"

I quietly shut and lock the door, moving to stand before her. When I take her hands, they tremble in my hold.

"Baby, meeting you was the best thing that ever happened to me. You are the most beautiful person I've ever met. Your beauty goes way beyond your stunning looks. It's deep, deep inside. Your kindness, your love, your compassion for all things takes my breath away. The fact you actually fell in love with me doesn't seem logical. Why me? Why was I so lucky to have you fall in love with me?"

The tears freely stream down her face as she blesses me with her stunning gaze. I bring her hands up to my lips, kissing each softly. My next move causes her to gasp. I slowly bend on one knee, reaching in my pocket for her ring.

"Elizabeth Ann Lair, I love you more than anything in this entire world. It breaks my heart I'm leaving you for these next eight weeks. My heart will be firmly anchored to you as you wait for me to return. The only thing that helps me get through the torment of our separation is knowing you'll be here when I get back. Please tell me you'll be here, waiting to marry me."

I slip the ring on her finger, kissing her hand before standing. She looks up into my eyes and smiles wide through her tears.

"Evan, I love you so much. I would be *honored* to be your wife."

Her tears continue to flow, and I smile at her when I gently wipe them away.

"Can I confess I was a nervous wreck over this?" Still holding her face, I brush my lips against hers softly, then again, and again.

"Is this what you were so tense about? You were nervous I would say no? Evan, I would rather die than be without you."

How the hell was I nervous over this? This incredible woman has owned my heart since I first met her. How could I have doubted this? She pulls me to the couch and settles against me. Her upturned face is begging to be kissed. When I sink my fingers into her silky hair, she closes the gap between us. Tasting her is like heaven. I attach my mouth to hers in an attempt to inhale her, consume her whole. She wraps her fingers around the nape of my neck to ensure I continue doing so.

The music plays softly, the candles flicker shadows across the room, and time stands still. Every emotion within me pours into her with this kiss. I love this woman with every fiber of my being.

She's the first to pull away. I would have gone on for days if she let me. Her soft pants and smile bring me back to pick up exactly where we left off. I can't get enough of her. The second time that she breaks our kiss gives me the chance to take in a much-needed breath. In a fog, I watch as she stands and tugs on my hand to follow. I'd follow her to hell and back, if she wanted me to. She leads me to our bedroom, closing the door behind us.

Wasting no time, she resumes our kiss while pressing her body flush into mine. I skim my hands up her back slowly until I sink into her gorgeous hair to firmly cradle her head. She slips her hands beneath my shirt, dragging them up the center of my back. Her touch sends tiny jolts through me, causing a moan to escape from my mouth into hers.

"I need you," I rasp against her lips. She nods as my lips travel along the smooth skin on her neck to her ear. "Now," I voice directly into her ear.

A shiver runs through her, spurring me on further. I lift her effortlessly and carry her to our bed. She watches as I remove my clothes, her eyes heavy with desire. A desire that she has for me, and that I know of first hand, as well. It's a craving like no other I've ever experienced. It's a need that courses through me. I've never felt this way before in my entire life.

I then take it upon myself to remove her clothes, one piece at a time. It takes every effort I have to go slow and not rush into what I desperately want, that connection we have when I enter her. I'd like nothing more than to reach that end result, but I also want to savor every second with her. In a few days, I'll crave this while being thousands of miles away. The recreation of our lovemaking will be the only thing I can take with me to satisfy this hunger I'll have deep inside. It's an inadequate solution, but necessary for me to survive without her.

There isn't an inch of skin I won't taste tonight. Our naked bodies are pressed against each other when I start with her lips. She lets me move my lips over her body at my unhurried pace. The unspoken words of what we are each desperately trying to achieve tonight hangs over us like a thick black cloud. Besides committing to memory every moment of this evening to replay over and over in our minds…besides trying to brand our love into the other's heart as evidence of our connection…most importantly we are becoming one, both physically and symbolically.

I watch as she pulls her bottom lip between her teeth when I drag my tongue across her hardened nipple. I mold her breast with my hands, chasing after her with each rise and fall of her chest. Her moan, when I move to the other breast, causes my cock to jerk. Her fingers tangle in my hair, holding me to her with just the slightest of pressure. When I skim one hand down the center of her body, right to her parted legs, she releases my hair and grips the bedding beneath her. The instant my fingertips touch her, she sucks in a ragged breath through clenched teeth.

Her body heaves as I fondle her slowly. She utters my name when I skim my tongue down the path my hand made earlier. I replace my touch with my lips. Her legs fall open, granting me full access. I slip my hands under and lift to angle her so I'm able to access every fold, every crevice, and every sensitive nerve with my mouth. When I devour her, she trembles. I alternate long, slow strokes with short, quick sucks. My eyes are pinned to her beautiful face as she climbs closer to her climax beneath me. I lace my fingers with hers and her grip tightens during the peak of her orgasm. After several long seconds, she loosens her hold on my hand, her eyes still closed, her body softening slowly.

She meets my gaze and smiles when I align myself to her entrance. She reaches up and takes hold of my neck, bringing my face down to hers. She strokes my tongue with hers as I enter her inch by inch. There aren't words to adequately explain what she feels like. With our faces inches apart, I move myself in and out of her warmth and she meets me each time. Her legs wrap around me to keep me close. Our breathing becomes labored, our bodies slick from the heat between us, and we come together in an explosion of sensations.

I collapse beside her, exhausted from the exertion of my release. She plays with my hair lovingly. When I open my eyes, I can see clear into her soul. “I love you, Liz. So very much.”

“I know. I feel the same. I can’t wait to be your wife.”

She settles into my side, her head resting on my chest. I watch as she admires her ring, tilting her hand to look at it from all sides.

“Do you like it?”

“I love it. It’s perfect.”

“No, it’s a ring. You’re perfect.”

“Evan, you’ve made me so happy. I don’t deserve you.”

I shake my head in disbelief. “Baby, you have it all wrong. It’s the other way around.” I tighten my hold, memorizing the feel of her body against mine, wishing beyond reason that I could close my eyes and wake up eight weeks from now.

## Chapter 11 – Jack

I don't impress easily. My apartment was sparsely decorated. I'm a *Levi* and t-shirt kind of guy. I didn't own my first car until this past year. I've never been very materialistic, but fuck if I can't appreciate a private jet.

We are flying to LA in L.R.V.'s corporate plane. This thing is amazing. More like a living room on wings. Totally equipped with a large flat screen TV, the softest leather couches, lots of mahogany tables in between big, plush captain chairs.

Un-fucking-real.

The gaping mouths around me must feel the same. No one is speaking, just gawking. My wife included. She sits in awe, taking in every detail. She was a nervous wreck this morning. She doesn't like to fly and her nerves got the best of her. She also couldn't get past the fact that practically everyone she loves in this entire world would be on one plane. I tried to distract her and it worked for a few minutes, but she then went back to being a Nervous Nelly.

Apparently, she's now forgotten her strife, as she opens cubbies and shakes her head at the opulence around us. She lifts an armrest that separates us to find a small cooler filled with beverages.

"Holy shit, look," she says as she plucks out an ice cold water. "Isn't this amazing?"

"Yep, it's pretty amazing," I smile wide at her enthusiasm.

The flight attendants are making their rounds, asking for drink orders, and reminding us to fasten our seatbelts in preparation for takeoff. We are scattered throughout the plane. Joe is grilling Hunter over his drumming skills as Nina watches amused. She and her boyfriend just broke up. She actually is the one who ended it. There are trust issues there, and she didn't want her suspicions to hamper her experience. I have to give her credit. It was a brave thing to do.

Scott is giving Matt details of how he survived being separated from Patti during the last tour. Evan is on the phone, no doubt with my sister. Logan is on the phone, no doubt with Alisa. Oscar and Alec are discussing schedules.

Leila and I are sitting across from Trey. He watches her with amusement as she continues to snoop and touch things.

She throws him a sideways glance and touts, "Whatcha lookin' at, Taylor?"

"It's just a plane, Little Lair."

"You aren't impressed at all?" she asks disbelievingly.

"Nope."

"You're full of crap," she challenges.

"No, I'm not…its just stuff. I rather check out that piece of ass," he motions with his head at the leggy blonde serving drinks.

Leila flips her head back to Trey with a scowl on her face. "Really? We are still on the tarmac and you're already acting like a man whore?" She shakes her head and adds, "What about Trini?"

"What about Trini?"

"Don't be an ass, Trey."

He looks insulted for a split second and then controls his features in an arrogant smirk. "I ended it with Trini."

"You did not, man," I challenge.

"Uh, yeah…I did."

Leila looks devastated. "Why?"

"It's for the best."

"For who?"

"For both of us." He gives Leila another arrogant smirk, just as the blonde makes her way over to us.

"What can I get you, sir?" She flashes me a brilliant smile. I can see Leila stiffen beside me. I subtly take her hand and the blonde quirks an eyebrow.

"I'll have a beer." I turn to Leila and ask, "Babe, what do you want?"

"I'm fine, thanks."

The blonde then turns toward Trey, and he flips up his shades. He only flips his shades when he's putting on a move.

"I'll also have a beer and a private tour," he leans his head until it's inches away from her ample boobs and reads her tag, "Chrissy."

Leila and I exchange a look.

Hers is asking - *Is he for real*? Mine is responding - *Yep*.

Chrissy smiles wide and offers, "Once we are safely cruising at the Captain's intended altitude, I'd be happy to."

She turns and strolls through the plane to the galley.

"You're a fucking dog," I accuse.

Shrugging he says, "It's a long flight." He replaces his shades and leans back in his seat. My wife levels him with her glare. "I see you looking at me. Can I help you?"

"What's your deal?"

"My deal?"

"Yeah, your deal."

"You see what you get. I'm an open book."

She laughs out loud at his analogy. "An open book? That's hilarious. I've known you now for two years, and your book is definitely closed tight. Tell me about yourself, I'm curious."

"Babe, it won't work." Trey looks over at me and now it's my turn to shrug. "What? Man, I've known you for almost ten years, and *I* know nothing about you. Hunt is convinced you were an axe-murderer in your previous life."

Hunter walks over at the mention of his name.

"Sir, please remain seated."

"Yeah, yeah. I'm sitting." He takes the seat next to Trey and looks around. "What are we talking about?"

"I just asked Trey to tell me about himself. Apparently, he says there's nothing to tell."

Hunter shakes his head at Leila and says, "It's not gonna happen. He's an asshole, who apparently was spawned by some immaculate conception."

Now it's Trey's turn to laugh out loud at Hunter's comment. "Definitely not immaculate."

"Didn't you guys do a background check on him when you hired him?" She directs her question to me, but Hunter responds.

"Of course not. He could play a wicked bass, that's all we needed to know."

"Well, that explains Danny," she mumbles, but I heard her.

"Not funny."

She looks up and pouts, "Sorry." Unable to resist, I plant a kiss on her pouting lips. "Trey, were you born in California?"

"No clue."

"You don't know where you were born?" she asks incredulously.

"Infants don't retain that kind of info."

She folds her arms and raises her eyebrows.

He mimics her posture.

"Hunt, it looks like my wife is getting a lesson in Trey Taylor 101."

Hunter nods and adds, "Yeah, I could use some popcorn right about now."

"Trey!"

"What do you want, woman? There's nothing to tell."

We have tried to get to know Trey over these years, and we have all given up. It's pointless. He wants no part of his past and made it very clear that he will not talk about it. We've speculated, and some of our scenarios have been pretty creative, but the truth is we haven't a clue.

I couldn't imagine being completely alone in this world. Over the years, he's never indicated he has friends, to speak of, besides us. He's never mentioned family. He never had a girlfriend for more than a few months at a time. He rented a fully furnished apartment. All his possessions include enough clothes to fill one suitcase, his trademark shades, and his beloved guitar.

Before Leila came along, Trey barely interacted with us. He would obviously give one hundred and ten percent while performing. He'd hang out with us whenever we asked him to. Most of the time, he'd disappear with a random chick he picked up and would see us all the next day. No explanation as to where he disappeared to or with whom.

The strangest part of his elusive behavior is his dodging of all and any family related functions. My wedding was the first time Trey attended such an event. Over the years, he has avoided each and every one. My parents would invite him to parties, Hunter's sister invited us all to her wedding, even Scott's family attempted to get him to join them at their yearly summer barbeques. He refused their invites with a polite no, without any explanation.

The man knows we would do anything for him and he would do the same for us. It's an unspoken assumption. He's never said those words per se, but we know he's got our backs. We've tried to scale the wall he intentionally hides behind and have gotten shot down each time. In fact, Leila is the first person to cause a tiny fissure in his stone façade. He has a very comfortable and easy relationship with her. He doesn't apologize for who he is, but he humors her at every turn. I love him for that.

When Leila was in the hospital, he practically sat vigil in the waiting room. He would chastise the press that hung out in the parking lot. He would play tricks on them and punk them. It was hilarious and showed me a bit of the real Trey. The dude has a good heart. Beneath the arrogance, there is a good man. I wish he would meet someone who.would rock his world. He needs his own version of a Leila to come in, fuck him up, and walk away with his balls…like she did to me.

I was hopeful it would have been Lori. He seemed different with her, happier. No such luck. I was surprised by his relationship with Trini. A few weeks in, I knew it wouldn't last long. He wasn't invested in her. He didn't see her every night, only once or twice a week. I haven't a clue if he was even faithful to her. I haven't really talked to her, like we used to. It was always more than just sex with her. She truly was a good friend. But, after Leila and I became a couple, I felt it was no longer appropriate to continue our friendship along those lines. I do care for her and only want the best. She's been desperate to find her other half and she deserves happiness. If he broke her heart, I'll kill him.

I watch as he and Leila spar back and forth. For every one of her questions, he has a smart-ass response. I can see her becoming increasingly frustrated, and all he does is laugh.

"Taylor, knock it off or I'll hurt you," I warn him after his last comment has her growling audibly.

"Big Bad Papa Lair is protecting Little Lair…I'm shaking in my boots."

"Prick."

While she sits and scowls at him for not cooperating, he says, "Hey, Little Lair. Wanna hear a joke?"

"No."

Ignoring her, he asks, "What should I do if my girl starts smoking?"

"I know I'm going to regret this," she responds as she rolls her eyes. "What?"

"I should slow down and possibly use a lubricant."

Hunter cracks up and fist bumps a laughing Trey. Leila fights desperately to keep a straight face and loses the battle when she sees mine.

"That was stupid," she rebuts, but her words contradict her smile.

"No lubricant needed for you two, huh? Congrats." Trey nods at me, smiling wide.

"You get great pleasure in embarrassing me, don't you?" The tint on her cheeks confirms her statement.

"Come on, that one was tame. Here's another. Why did God give men penises?" Her response is to sigh. "Men needed one way to shut women up."

"Are you insinuating I need to shut up?"

"Well, Babe, I'm flattered. But your hubby may not go for that." She squints and scowls and he laughs again.

"I'm seriously going to hurt you," I threaten, again.

"You know I heavily like your Little Lair, Papa."

She gives him a lop-sided grin and asks, "You love me?"

"Heavily like," he clarifies, and then adds, "like a brother and his annoying, irritating, whiny baby sister." She throws her uneaten apple at his head, and he catches it one handed. "So annoying," he confirms, pretending to be annoyed.

The leggy blonde appears asking if we are ready for our meals. She serves us each, saving Trey for last. When she hands him his lunch, he shakes his head. "Not hungry…yet. Can you direct me to the restroom?"

"Sure, sir. Follow me."

"I'll be back," he calls over his shoulder as he follows her to the back of the plane.

Hunter watches Trey follow the blonde and rolls his eyes. "One day his dick is gonna fall off."

"Isn't she concerned she'll get fired?" Leila asks as she watches them walk away.

"Maybe it's part of her job description."

"Shut. Up." She analyzes my facial expression to see if I'm kidding.

"I'm serious. I'm sure this plane has transported some heavy-duty rock stars. It wouldn't be smart for the label to employ the faint at heart."

"He's right. I'm sure Trey is being serviced as we speak," Hunter says with pure conviction.

"Ugh," she responds in disgust.

"I'm not saying they require her to do that. I'm saying they probably hire women who would," I clarify, but it doesn't take the scowl off her face. She sizes me up, as if I am the one being *serviced.*

"Why are you giving me a dirty look?" I pretend innocence.

"Men are pigs," she says, and I pretend to look hurt.

Ironically, before she arrived I probably would have been. I was most definitely a pig…but a respectful one. I can only wonder how I would have acted if I also had money and fame at the time. Combine that with my immaturity, irresponsibility, promiscuousness and cockiness, and the notion makes me cringe uncomfortably. I give her a sideways glance. She's watching me speculatively, as if she can read my thoughts.

“Not all men. I’m a catch,” Hunter nods arrogantly.

She shifts to get comfortable and settles against my shoulder. “Wake me when we get there.”

“Baby, eat something.”

“I lost my appetite.”

♬ ♬ ♬

The ride from the airport to the hotel feels like a class trip. When did I become the chaperone to this crew? The label has supplied us with another one of their lavish forms of transportation. We all got comfortable in the stretch *Hummer* that is fully stocked with top shelf alcohol. They have all been taking full advantage. Shots are flowing, and the decibels are increasing. It’s only a thirty-minute drive to the hotel from *LAX*, and from the look of things, they are pretty toasted. They did get a head start on the flight over.

We aren’t due in the studio until Monday, and we are taking full advantage of L.R.V. Media. We flew out a few days early for some R&R before our grueling schedule begins. I plan on spending most of the time showing Leila the sights and enjoying our cushy room at *The Four Seasons*.

Hunter’s audience all start laughing as he pulls a box of *Fruit Loops* out of his carry-on and concocts a God-awful new way of eating them using *Patron*.

“That’s disgusting,” I call out when he slurps them down noisily.

“Don’t knock it unless you try it.” He toasts me with his cup and shoots them down his throat. The girls giggle as he continues to down more of the crap he loves so much.

Showing disgust all over my face, I challenge, "I bet fifty that you'll be puking in Technicolor by the time we hit the hotel."

"I'll take that bet," Trey quickly jumps in.

"Me, too," Scott agrees.

As Trey and Scott encourage the jackass to keep drinking, I turn to my wife and ask, "Ready to see LA with me?"

"Really? You hate sight-seeing."

"As I recall, I promised to bring you back the last time we were here. You and I are in tourist mode this weekend."

She leans in closer, putting her lips directly on my ear, and asks, "Just the two of us?"

I nod slowly, watching her lips as I do.

She smiles and says, "Thank God. I need to be alone with you."

Unable to resist them any longer, I bend to kiss her first softly, and then more forcibly. The noise level in the limo plunges when Hunter annoyingly slurs, "Oh, here we go. We haven't even been here ten minutes, and you're already making ush nau…sheous."

Leila pulls away from me embarrassed and shakes her head.

"I'm pretty sure it's your dumbass drink choice making you nauseous."

He stares into his cup, turning a shade of green and mumbles, "Maybe."

"Looks like Hunter is about to cough up some dough, among other things," Trey touts with a big smile.

"Just as long as he doesn't do it in here," Scott adds.

"I never shooook on it," he grumps before mumbling, "I think I'm getting car sick."

Trey and Scott bolt down to my end of the limo, squeezing themselves into what little space there is beside Leila and me.

"Yep, definitely just the two of us." She giggles at my confirmation.

When we pull into the hotel parking lot, everyone starts yapping at the same time. Most of our crew announces they are heading out to see the sights. I announce that Leila and I are spending the day *alone*. Hunter announces he'll be in his room for a while.

We all scatter to our respective rooms. Once in ours, I tip the bellhop, lock the door, and pull my wife into my arms. "I need you."

"Can I unpack first?" she asks as I nibble on her neck.

"Later."

She gives in very easily, becoming boneless in my arms. My lips find the soft spot under her ear. Her fingers flex on my arms with each stroke of my tongue. There aren't any words exchanged. There isn't a need to. We are both completely in tune to the other, knowing exactly what the other wants, craves, and needs.

We undress, and kiss, and pet our way to the bed. Her naked body, stretched out beside me, stirs me in predictable ways. Our eyes lock in an impenetrable connection, a steel tether that binds us. My lips need to taste her. I slant my mouth over hers in a heated kiss, luring her tongue to follow my own. She clings to me as I pull away. Selfishly, I want all of her. She's mine, and every time we make love, I need to stake my claim. It's as important to me as the act itself. It's validation that this gorgeous woman belongs to me.

I slowly drag my hand down her cheek, over her chin, down the center of her neck to her perfect breast. Never breaking eye contact, I circle her nipple until it lengthens beneath my touch. My lips follow the path, taking a perfect peak into my mouth. The more I taste, the more I want. Her smooth skin is like an open canvas to an anxious artist. I grip her thighs as I kiss her tattoo before moving the fraction of space lower to claim her. When I reach her clit, she whimpers softly. I pull her between my lips, and she digs her fingers into my hair. My cock throbs from hearing the tiny moans she's gifting me with.

I look up to see her eyes tightly closed, her lip caught between her teeth. Never breaking stride, I stroke her clit with the tip of my tongue and slip my middle finger into her as deep as I can go.

I cradle her ass with my other hand, tilting her for better access. I then suck on her forcibly. She gasps and bucks against my mouth, opening her eyes in surprise, only to see me holding her prisoner with my gaze. Her eyes are unable to hide the heat and lust that swirl in their topaz depths. Seconds later, she tightens around me and trembles. I remove my finger from deep inside and bring it to my mouth to taste her essence.

She watches in a daze as I lay beside her. I slant my mouth across hers, needing to feel the silk of her tongue. I lure her tongue into my mouth, and once there, I suck on it and refuse to let it go. My hand possessively cradles her belly, and she imprisons it with both of hers. She lays limp beside me, but I need more of her.

"Can I have you?"

She nods wordlessly, her brow puckered from attempting to control her breathing.

I kneel between her legs, holding myself and dragging my hardness across her folds. She bucks and mewls, trying to get me to quicken my pace. With a small smile I place myself inside of her warmth. She takes hold and pulls me in deeper by clenching around me. I grip her thigh, pushing against it to open her wider. With my other hand I caress her where we are joined.

My movements become jerky and awkward as my brain forgets to control my dexterity.

"Jack, faster," she pleads.

I accommodate willingly, plunging deeper and deeper with each push of my hips. I can feel every part of her surrounding every inch of me. I anchor myself to the mattress with both hands firmly planted on either side of her waist and increase my tempo. She nods over and over as I bring us both to release at the exact same time. Since this is my first, it rolls on much longer than hers. She pulls me down by my neck and kisses me, dragging its duration out even further.

"Holy fuck, I needed that," I admit when I collapse on top of her, trapping her with my exhausted body.

"Me, too." She draws lazy circles on my back.

"You are going to kill me."

"No, I need you around. This baby needs you around." I move to lie beside her, and she turns, backs up against me, and pulls my arms around her to get comfortable. After a few minutes she stills, making me think she fell asleep.

We have dinner reservations, but I want her to rest for as long as possible. She stubbornly refuses to admit when she's tired. I can see the signs, and I probably know her body better than she does. I also have been reading the "bible" every day, combing it page by page. I know that at this point in her pregnancy, her body is working the hardest, building the placenta.

Huh…there's a word I've never used in a sentence before.

I chuckle softly at my thoughts, and she whispers, "What's so funny?"

"Why aren't you asleep?" I ask, surprised that she is awake. I thought for sure she was out cold.

"Just thinking."

"What about?"

"Have you thought about baby names yet?"

I shift her to face me, intrigued by her question. "Not really. Have you?"

"A little, but only if it's a girl."

"What did you come up with?" When she looks up, there is sadness in her eyes. "Babe, what's wrong?"

She shakes her head as she comforts, "Nothing's wrong. I've just been thinking about this for a few days and it would mean a lot to me if…" She stops for a beat and then continues, "if it's a girl, can we name her after my mom?"

"Of course! Marie…did she have a middle name?"

"No. Marie Siarra Marino was her full name. I'd like to reverse it though, maybe Siarra Marie?"

"I love it. Siarra Marie. Done."

"Are you sure?" She asks with uncertainty. "It is your daughter, too. I'll understand if you rather combine our mom's names."

"We'll name our next daughter after my mom."

"One baby at a time, please?"

"Fine. Mom will understand. I really do love it. Siarra Marie Lair. It's gorgeous, just like her mom." I skim a fingertip across her cheek. She smiles warmly and gives me a chaste kiss. "Why were you afraid to ask me that?"

"I wasn't afraid. I was just emotional about it. Every time I call her name, I'll have a constant reminder of my mother. It's a huge burden to put on a little baby. I needed to be sure it was something I wanted before I asked you to agree."

"What about if it's a boy?"

She shrugs, "I have no freaking clue. You?"

"I got nothin'," I admit as well.

"Well, now that we've named Little Jack, Jack Junior, we really can't use Jackson."

"Never little," I quip confidently, "and nor would I want to."

"Then I would like him to have Jackson as a middle name."

"Ugh. Why?"

"I love it. Please?" She sidles up against me and pulls my earlobe in between her lips.

"You don't play fair, my wife." I catch her by the chin and turn her face level with mine. "It depends on what his first name would be."

She rests her chin on my chest, looking up expectantly. I haven't even thought about names yet. A touch of superstition stopped me from thinking too hard on the subject. "I do know he has to have a rock star worthy name," I say what I'm thinking.

"Does he, rock star? So George or Fred wouldn't do?"

"Fuck no." I scan my brain for some legendary rock stars that would also be acceptable boy names "Jagger?"

"No. What about Jersey?" she asks straight-faced.

"As in the state?"

"Yeah."

"You can't be serious," I scowl as she laughs. "Jersey. You've lost your mind."

She stares back at me deep in thought. Her lips pursing before saying, "Presley?"

"As in Elvis?"

"Yeah."

"Um…no." She frowns when I roll my eyes and sigh. "Two strikes. You get one more."

"I don't see you coming up with any."

"Hendrix?"

"No."

"Blaze?"

"As in fire, as in Devil's Lair logo, as in no."

I exaggerate a groan from frustration. "Rocco?"

She bursts out laughing. "Rocco?"

"Yeah, rock star…Rocco."

"That was your fourth strike."

"Ok, hot shot, what do you have?"

"River?"

"Um, no."

"Michael?"

"Michael…Jackson…Lair?"

"Yeah. I love Michael." The look on her face tells me she doesn't realize her choice.

"Michael…Jackson?"

Her eyes widen when it sinks in. "Oh, I guess not."

"We have plenty of time to think of something. Right now I want you to get dressed so I can take you out to a nice dinner and a night out. We have a reservation at the hottest spot in LA, and we can't be late. It was a bitch to get."

"How did you manage that?"

"I had to promise our first born."

"Not funny." She leans up, plants a kiss on my lips, and scoots off the bed. I sit up, watching her as she moves around the room, unpacking things from our suitcases. She's very comfortable around me now. Of course she should be, we're married. But there was a time when she would immediately cover herself with one of my t-shirts.

She is so goddamn beautiful. She has cut her hair some since I met her. It falls past her shoulders in rich, silky waves, and no longer to the middle of her back. Her body is fucking amazing, even more so now. It seems to be changing right before my very eyes. Her breasts are fuller and perfectly positioned. I hate to admit, I really hope they stay, as I would miss them. Her legs are toned and sexy as hell, but the sexiest part of her is her baby bump. I didn't think it was possible, and if you had said to me a year ago I would love her even more now, I'd say you were fucking nuts. It's true. I love her more.

"Hey, Mr. Lazy. Help me," she says while pulling things out of her bag. She turns to see me watching her, my cock at full mast. "*Really*?" she motions to Junior.

"What do you expect parading around like that?" I cross the distance between us, and put my hands on her ass, pulling her into my now hard cock. "You turn me the fuck on, and I can't help that."

"I'm so sorry. I'll stop parading around you naked."

"Fuck no!" I kiss her passionately, egging her on in the process. I lift her and sit her ass on the edge of the dresser. Our bodies immediately align like a magnet to metal. She closes her eyes, losing herself to the physicality between us. As always, I can feel her body submitting willingly. Her breath hitches, her eyes close, her hips move forward. I'm a second away from closing the gap when she shakes her head.

"Jack, we don't have time."

"You're still a kill joy," I accuse against her lips.

"You're the one that made the iron-clad reservation."

"True. Ok, I have an idea. We both have to shower. Let's multitask." I hoist her over my shoulder. She squeals and giggles as I carry her into the bathroom.

## Chapter 12 – Leila

Last night Jack and I enjoyed a lovely dinner on Rodeo Drive. While sitting at the restaurant's street side patio we counted dozens of celebrities walking by. Each and every time I saw one, my eyes would bulge, my mouth would gape open, and my husband would laugh. As we strolled down the street afterwards hand in hand, with Oscar on our heals, a few giddy fans spotted Jack and asked for pictures and autographs. I've become accustomed to being asked to take the picture rather than be in it. He was charming and flirty, winking at me playfully. I've also become accustomed to the attention he gets. It is what it is, the downside of being married to a hot as hell rock star who is becoming more and more famous every single day.

I was exhausted from traveling. We retired early so I could be well rested for the busy day he planned. He still hasn't told me where we are going, and it's driving me nuts. We also have tomorrow to ourselves before reporting to the studio bright and early on Monday morning.

He watches me watch him in the bathroom mirror. "What?"

"Where are we going today?" I ask for the fiftieth time.

"You just can't help yourself, can you?" he turns back to shaving, dismissing me once again.

"Please? I'd like to know what to wear," I throw out the fiftieth excuse for wanting to know. "You know how limited my wardrobe is, and I don't want to waste an outfit if it's not appropriate for where we are going."

He continues to watch me impassively, as if I'm speaking a foreign language. After a few minutes, I smile wide and bat my eyelashes. "You are a pain in the ass when you want to know something. You know that right?"

"Yep."

He sighs and shakes his head. "First, I have a stop to make. You'll know when we get there what it is. Then I booked a cheesy tourist tour on one of those double decker buses. We'll be seeing it all, from the *Walk of Fame* to *Grauman's* to *Hollywood Boulevard*."

"Really?" I ask, giddy with excitement. "I've always wanted to do one of those tours. Will we be driving by any celebrity homes?"

"Some."

"Yay." I wrap my arms around him, and he laughs at my enthusiasm.

"Do I know my wife, or what?"

"Yep, you know me well."

"Hurry up and get done. I have the first appointment, and I can't be late."

"Where?"

He quirks an eyebrow, "Na uh…I've told you enough. Move it," he commands before smacking my ass.

True to his word, he wouldn't tell me any other details. When Oscar pulls up to a tattoo parlor, Jack announces, "We're here."

"I've already branded myself to you. You want me to do it again?"

"Only if you want to…but no, this time is for me."

"You're getting a tattoo? Of what?"

"My mistress's name." He sidesteps away from my swat and opens the door, allowing me access.

"Jack Lair?" the bald headed dude, with barely any skin showing, asks when we walk up to the front counter.

"That's me. Thanks for opening up early for me. I appreciate it."

"No worries, man. I'm usually here anyways. Ready?"

"Yep."

"Are you both getting inked today?" he looks over at me expectantly.

Jack looks down and smiles. "I think just me."

"Cool. I'm Dix. Follow me, I'll get you prepped and you can tell me what you want."

We follow Dix to the back of the shop. This is swankier than your normal tattoo parlor. The décor is actually more on the lines of a high-end spa. As we walk down the hall, there are dozens of celebrity photos lining the walls, displaying their new ink. I jerk to a stop to admire picture after picture when Jack tugs on my arm. "We have a double decker bus to catch, stop stalling."

"So, what are we doing today?" Dix asks as he pulls out supplies, inkbottles, and rubber gloves.

Jack looks at me while responding to Dix, "I want the infinity symbol with both our names as part of the loops. In the center, I want the lyrics *Baby you are the reason I am* connecting the loops."

"Sounds good. What's the pretty lady's name?"

He throws me a small smile and responds, "Leila."

"I love that. When did you think of this?"

"I've been wanting to get your name tattooed, but I wanted something special. This just came to me when I bought your bracelet."

"Where do you want it, man?"

"Over my heart."

After Jack spells my name out for him, Dix mocks up a few paper versions for Jack to choose from.

"This one."

"Is this big enough?" Dix asks. It measures about two inches long and one inch wide.

"Yeah, that's perfect."

As Dix preps Jack I'm stunned into silence. I love what Dix came up with. He added a tiny heart next to my name that perfectly matches the heart on my own tat. He added a tiny guitar next to Jack's name. Running diagonally in the center are his lyrics. It's unique to us. I love that he is doing this for me. I now know how he felt after I got my tattoo. It's sexy as hell to know he will forever have my name over his heart.

I hold his hand as Dix goes to work. The whole thing takes fifteen minutes from start to finish. "All done, man."

He holds up a mirror and Jack inspects it closely. "Looks great. Thanks."

"Sure thing." Dix bandages Jack up and hands him a sheet of paper. "Here are your care instructions."

Jack pays Dix and we head out to catch our tour. "You're very quiet," he says as we climb into our car.

"Jack, what you just did for me, left me speechless."

"In a good way?" he asks, uncertainty written all over his face.

"Of course in a good way. You have no idea what this means to me." I gently caress his face, my eyes moist with all the emotion I feel for him, for this act of love that he showed me today.

"It shouldn't surprise you. I love you more than anything or anyone in this entire world…forever."

A tear escapes as I nod and repeat, "Forever."

♬ ♬ ♬

"Aren't you hot?" Hunter asks Trey as we get settled. It is hot, not stifling, but the black t-shirt and black denim Trey is wearing does look uncomfortable…that's Trey. I've never seen him wear anything other than a variation of what he is sporting now. "You stand out like a hard cock."

"Really, Hunt?" I scold.

"Sorry, Lei."

"No, man, I'm not hot. Stop fucking annoying me."

"Hee hee. You said that you're not hot," Hunter antagonizes him further.

"I'm going to pummel you," Trey threatens.

These guys are exhausting. We are trying to squeeze in our last bit of relaxation before tomorrow's whirlwind begins. We decided to go to Santa Monica for the day. When the guys found out, they invited themselves in spite of Jack's claim he wanted to be alone. I was fine with it. I was also surprised Trey was accompanying us to the beach. Seems so un-Trey-like. Cliffhangers are doing their own thing, leaving the five of us to enjoy this gorgeous day in the sun.

Jack is looking all sorts of gorgeous in his trunks and t-shirt. I watch conspicuously from behind my sunglasses as he positions our chairs under the shade of the umbrella. They hang low on his waist and it's hard not to look. Hunter and Scott are also in bathing suits. Trey is the only one who stands out like a sore thumb.

"Trey, do you own a bathing suit?" I ask. The look on his face tells me he knows what I'm up to. I've been nonchalantly throwing questions out at him every opportunity I have to get to know him better…it's now an obsession. Unfortunately, I haven't had any luck. His retaliation is to throw egregious, tasteless jokes at me.

"Nope," is all he says in return. "Do you own a bathing suit?" He motions to my t-shirt and shorts.

"Yep," I give him a dose of his own medicine.

He smirks and asks, "Don't want us seeing the girls today?"

I kick sand at him, just as my husband turns with his hands on his hips in a threatening stance.

"Calm down, Papa Lair." Trey holds up his hands and openly laughs at him.

Once Jack has my chair set up next to his, I take a seat and continue to oogle him. His shirt hikes up as he bends and twists. He tugs off his t-shirt, allowing me a lovely view of his washboard abs. I see him naked all the time, but having him out here in public like this is stirring the beast.

He notices me smiling like a Cheshire cat and sits next to me. "You like?" he asks directly into my ear and sucks on my earlobe while he's there.

"Very much."

"Whoa, whoa, whoa! What the fuck is that?" Hunter points at Jack's new tattoo, now prominently displayed on his left pec.

"What's it look like?"

"It looks like you're even more whipped today than you were yesterday," Hunter touts back.

"Babe, make sure you keep it out of the sun. Dix said you can't get it sunburned while it's healing," I say, making the mistake of voicing it out loud.

"Yep, even more whipped," Hunter confirms.

Just as Jack is about to respond, a semi-hysterical girl comes right up to our circle. "OH. MY. GOD. You're Jack Lair!" The girl then scans the rest of us and announces rather loudly, "You're Devil's Lair!"

Jack hushes her quickly while I hide behind my hat. The rest of our band has varying responses from Trey's eye rolling to Scott's blushing to Hunter's ear-to-ear grin.

The beach is packed, but there are so many celebrities around, we thought we could be inconspicuous among the throngs of gorgeous California natives.

Apparently not.

"Um…if you quiet down, we'll give you a picture…how's that?" Jack murmurs to the girl as she motions for her friends. Five other bikini-clad girls come barreling over, causing even more of a commotion.

They all start yapping at once. "We've got tickets to your show next week. I can't believe you are here. This is amazing!"

They all start throwing out their names to get as personal with their objects of desire as possible - Trish. Kim. Steph. Cheryl. Jessica.

A cute brunette sidles up beside Hunter and offers, "I'm Rachel, and I adore you and would follow you anywhere."

"Why thank you, Rachel. I am attached, but if I weren't…" Hunter leaves the prospect dangling and Rachel giggles on cue.

"Can we get backstage passes?" The hot blonde asks Trey.

"That can be arranged," he responds with a smirk. I want to smack the two of them upside their heads to stop them from encouraging the crazy.

"I'm texting Drew. He's not going to believe this."

"Is it true you're going to be a daddy?"

"Ssh, girls. Please keep it down," Jack pleads as his eyes scan the hordes of teenagers all turning their attention to our corner. Oscar moves in quick, lowering his voice so only they can hear. They all nod, gawking at us like we are attractions at the zoo. He hands them a card, which they accept while giggling.

Oscar takes charge, arranging them in between us and snaps a few pictures. "Ok, girls. Time to go." He ushers them away and is back in a flash.

"Stupid idea," Jack grumps to no one in particular.

"We need to change locations or this will go on all day," Oscar suggests, causing the rest of us to start grabbing our things to make a getaway. We've become professionals at traveling light and getting the fuck out of a place before anyone realizes we are gone. When we were planning our day, Oscar thought it would be best to stay on protected properties, such as the beach club the label has a membership at.

Jack wanted me to experience California to the fullest. He wanted me to see Santa Monica and all its attractions. We purposefully found a quiet, secluded area of beach that was close to the pier. He meant well, and he can't quite come to grips with this new lifestyle we are forced to live. Our fame and popularity is spreading slowly, but from week-to-week, we can see a difference in how it's affecting our lives. We've avoided public places where college kids frequent in New York City. We are local celebrities there and understand what to avoid.

But we're in California, and on the fame-o-meter we're like a two. So I can't blame my husband for desperately wanting to have a normal day at the beach and thinking we would be able to.

Once in the safety of our van, we start plotting where we should go next. It's mid-afternoon and we decide on lunch in Malibu and hopefully that beach will have less screaming, giddy girl fans.

Oscar finds us a quaint beachside bistro. We are able to have a wonderful lunch before heading out to relax on the quiet, pristine beach below. It's a dramatic change from Santa Monica's beach. I guess those who frequent Malibu couldn't be bothered lying out on a gorgeous day to do nothing…too many Botox appointments to keep.

The guys are quiet, all lost in their own thoughts. This tour is going to be so different than our last one. The stress of not knowing what the hell we were doing is gone. Where I was so nervous and scared to perform as part of Devil's Lair, I now am comfortable and at ease with that whole part of that process. I don't feel anxious or insecure. I don't have a psycho ex-girlfriend who is threatening the love of my life with her unborn baby. Danny is still a concern, but not nearly as much as he had been. Overall, I'm blessed to be doing this and appreciate it so much more this time around.

"Whatcha' thinking about, Babe?" Jack asks quietly.

"Just how different things are from our last tour."

"Yeah, this time we're legit rock stars," Hunter nods like it's now the law.

"Yes, there's that, but also, it's so much less stressful this time." Jack watches me closely and frowns. "What? Don't you agree?"

"It's a different stress," he admits.

"You're feeling stressed?" His admission surprises me. "What about?"

He glances down and raises his brow. "Really? You're carrying my child on a bus as we cross the country. I'm freaking out over this."

It never occurred to me he was worried about this. Sure, he's super protective and I know he's been a tad neurotic, but to be stressing over this is silly. "Jack, I'm fine. I'll be fine. I want you to enjoy this tour. We are very lucky, and I don't want you to miss out on this awesome experience because you're worried."

"I can't promise that. It's more important you relax and enjoy this tour. I want that for you more than anything. I caused you such heartache on the last one."

"It wasn't you, man," Scott corrects immediately.

"Yes, it was."

"Jack..." I try to derail his line of thinking, and he shakes his head and cuts me off.

"It was because of me...all of it. What I put you through. What I put them through," he points to his band, "completely my fault. So this time around, I want you all to sit back, relax, and have the fucking time of your lives. I need you to have it."

"And we will. What's with all this negative crap? We are fucking DEVIL'S LAIR and we have arrived!" Hunter raises his arms, as if we are his private cult following.

I laugh at his normal, self-appreciating antics. Hunter is Hunter's biggest fan.

"Hey, Lei," Trey calls over to me.

"What?"

"How do you pick out the blind man at a nudist beach?"

"I can't wait to find out."

"It's not hard."

"Bahahahaha!" Hunter goes hysterical, slapping his knee like an idiot.

"It wasn't that funny."

"No? Your husband thought it was," Trey points out. I glance at Jack and he's failing miserably at keeping a straight face.

"I'll just have to keep trying." Trey shrugs, not deterred by my indifference.

"Can't wait."

"Here's another. Why are hurricanes normally named after women?"

I sigh and know if I don't go along, this can go on all day. "Why?"

"When they come they're wet and wild, but when they go, they take your house and car with them."

He throws me a rare Trey Taylor, panty-melting grin as the guys laugh at his stupid joke. He's very handsome. When I joined the band, he constantly wore his shoulder length hair in a ponytail. He now wears it longer on top and shaved on the sides. He's been a blonde, he's been a brunette, and he's even been blue. Currently he's sporting black.

He catches me staring at his tattoo sleeve and raises an eyebrow. The design is so intricate that you really can't make any of it out. He waits patiently for the question he knows is coming. When I open my mouth to speak, he smirks.

"How long did it take to get that done?"

"Years."

"Why only the one arm?"

"It hurt." I falter with my next question. I wasn't expecting an honest response from him. "Cat got your tongue?"

"You can feel?"

"Bahahahaha," Hunter blurts out again. "Good comeback, Lei."

Trey nods while smiling. "I'm impressed, Little Lair."

"Thanks." Little by little, I'm chipping away at his stone wall. I'll breach it…trust me. I'll wear him down.

"Have you always had long hair?"

"No."

"What's your favorite food?"

"Pie."

Hunter guffaws again and I pretend to throw up a bit in my mouth. I can feel my cheeks blazing from embarrassment, and a few long seconds pass where I'm rendered speechless. He absolutely knows how to shut me up.

"You done?"

"For now." I purse my lips, and add, "And they don't hurt that much."

"How would you know?" Three pairs of eyes assess. I turn to Jack for help, not realizing I was opening this can of worms. He folds his arms, leaning back and leaving me to navigate this one on my own.

"Jack told me."

"He's got two rinky-dink tats. He isn't the authority on them," Hunter quips.

“Nah, she’s lying. You have one, don’t you?” Trey calls me out. My deepening blush tells of my truth. “Yeah, you do.” He points a finger at me. “Where is it?”

“None of your business,” Jack finally decides to chime in.

Hunter and Trey exchange glances while nodding.

“Scott, why don’t you have any?” I try to deflect pathetically.

“I bruise like a peach,” he shrugs, and we lose ourselves in hysterics.

## Chapter 13 – Evan

"I'm taking off. I'll see you guys in the morning." I take a few steps from the table and add, "Hey, Joe. Take your time getting back."

"Sure thing, bud," he winks. "Make sure you use moisturizer, you don't want to chafe."

"Shut up. I just want to be alone with her for a bit."

"Exactly, make sure you tell her where you want her mouth."

"Dude, that's my sister you're talking about," Jack says to Joe, and he shrugs.

Their laughter is the last thing I hear as I walk away. We all congregated, sort of by accident, in the hotel bar. Jack, Leila, and the guys saw us on their way back from the beach, and an impromptu party began.

It's great how we all get along so well. There's a touch of animosity between Matt and Trey, but that is to be expected. I chatted about it with Leila yesterday, and we both agree it is a blessing Lori decided not to come. The dynamics of all three together would have put a completely different vibe on this tour.

For the most part, we all like each other. Joe has us all in stitches most of the time, and it's hard to leave when I'm having so much fun hanging with everyone. But I haven't had a chance to really speak to Liz since we arrived. Joe's rooming with me, and it's difficult to get some alone time. Logan and Matt are also sharing. Nina is the only one of us with her own room, and we're all jealous.

It's understandable the label has Cliffhangers sharing rooms. We're lucky they put us up at the *Four Seasons* at all. They could have easily shipped us off to a *Motel 6*.

Privacy is not a luxury that I'm going to have on this tour. I need to take every opportunity as it comes. I figure I have at least fifteen or twenty minutes until Joe shows up. I'm so anxious to talk to her, I start dialing while walking down the hall to my room. It's late there, but I just need to hear her voice, if only for a few minutes. She answers the phone, her voice raspy and thick with sleep.

"Hey, Babe. How are you?"

I should hang up. She needs to work in the morning. Selfishly, I can't. I miss her terribly, and it's only been two days. Hearing her voice is both satisfying a deep need and instigating a painful longing. Both are combating viciously inside of me, and my head and heart are the victims.

"I'm miserable," I admit while unlocking my door. "I'm sorry, I know it's late. I just needed to hear your voice."

"You call me anytime you want. I know it's difficult to get a few minutes alone while rooming with Joe and with your busy schedule."

"Are you being careful?" I ask the first thing that's been bothering me since leaving her. I am so worried about her being there alone. I've spoken to all our friends and her family and made them swear to me they would watch over her.

"Yes, I am. I promise," she responds before releasing a yawn.

"Liz, you're tired."

"No! Don't hang up, please?"

"Ok, I won't." And I feel like a heel saying that. I'm so goddamn selfish.

"So, how's California?"

"California is ok. I don't know what all the fuss is about. Everything seems so fake."

"Have you seen any sights?"

"Some. I'm ready to hit the studio tomorrow. I think all this downtime isn't good for me. I need to keep busy."

"I feel the same way. This weekend dragged by. I did spend some time with my parents. My mom is already in full-blown wedding mode. When I got to the house, she had twelve bridal magazines waiting for me."

I chuckle into the phone. "You are her only daughter. You had to have expected that."

"I guess. I just would love to do what Jack and Leila did. Would you be opposed to that? Having a simple, quiet ceremony with our closest friends and family? I would even entertain eloping, but that would break her heart."

"We can't do that do her."

"I know. When do you want to, though? Have you thought about it?"

"Tomorrow." She giggles adorably, and my hunger for her becomes unbearable. "God, I love that sound."

"I thought you love when I moan," she teases in a breathy whisper.

"Oh, God. Don't say things like that to me, Liz."

"No? You don't want me to tell you that I wish you were here right now, your lips on my neck, your fingers stroking me?"

Instantly, my cock swells painfully. I throw my head back in frustration, slamming it against the headboard, repeatedly.

"What's that noise?"

"I'm banging my head." She giggles again, and I can't take it anymore. "Keep talking to me," I pant as I slip my hand into my jeans. "I don't care what you say, sing the fucking alphabet. I need to hear you."

She stops, her silence is an indicator that she understands what I want, what I need. "Ev, my voice is a poor substitute of what I would be doing to you right now, if I were in that room, lying in your bed."

"What would that be?" I ask, my own voice sounding foreign to my ears.

"You know that little spot under your jaw? That spot that I love sucking on? I would start there."

I close my eyes, imagining exactly what she describes. Her soft warm lips parting slightly to take my skin into her mouth as she sucks with just the slightest bit of pressure, but enough to project my cock into a throbbing hard-on. My hand works over my length, dragging over it slowly from base to tip. I haven't jerked off in over a year, but I guess it's like riding a bike. Joe's advice flashes through my thoughts, and I literally shake my head to focus on Lizzy and her voice.

"Did I lose you?"

"No," is all I can manage to say.

"Good. Do you know where I would go next?" She doesn't wait for me to respond. She sucks in an audible breath and says, "I'd go down your chest, and I'd swirl my tongue around your flat, warm nipple. Can you feel it? Now picture me opening my mouth and sucking until your hips buck to find a release."

"Holy shit."

"My hand has a mind of its own, you know that. As I'm licking and sucking my hand grips you firmly, pumping you slowly. Not enough to get you there, just enough to drive you insane."

My heavy breathing sounds pathetic over the phone. It sounds desperate and eager, and I couldn't give a shit. You couldn't stop me now if you tried…nothing could.

"Ev?"

She laughs at my guttural groan.

"I need to taste you. God, you're so warm and so hard. Can you feel my mouth on you?"

"Fuck."

"Ev, I can feel you…at the back of my throat, filling my mouth completely. I can taste you, too. I want more of you. I'm sucking you hard and fast. I'm dragging my lips over your head, down your length, and back up. I'm repeating it over and over, slower and slower."

"Fuck, Liz. I'm close."

"Baby, I'm working my hand over your base, my mouth is sucking harder now. I won't stop until you get there."

The image plays like a movie in my mind. It's so vivid and so real. I swear I could smell her perfume. My exertion is obvious with each sound that escapes from my parted lips.

"Ev, I need you to come for me. Can you do that?"

"Ahhh, fuck. God, Liz, oh God." A groan erupts as I shoot my load into my own hand. "Fuck. Fuck." She waits as I moan repeatedly. It feels like it takes hours before I can speak. I can only continue my pathetic pants. God, I love that she did this for me. Only Lizzy can turn phone sex into a complete act of giving, selflessness, and love.

"Babe?" I finally say after several long minutes.

"Yeah?"

"I wish you were here."

"Me, too."

"Thank you. I needed this. I needed your voice tonight."

Silence fills the space between us again. I can tell she's close to crying. I can hear it in her shaky breaths. She helped me through tonight and I'm not able to be there to help her. My arms ache to hold her right now. "Baby?"

"Yeah?" she whispers.

"I love you so much. I am wrapping my arms around you right now. I'm holding you close, your face is on my chest, listening to my pounding heart."

"Ok," she says so quietly, I can barely hear her.

"Are you ok?"

"Yeah, I'm just missing you."

"I know, Babe." She remains quiet on the phone. I don't want to let her go. Part of me would love to just listen to her breathing until it's time for her to go to work. But I've kept her long enough, and it's not fair to her. "Liz, it's late. I'll talk to you tomorrow?"

"Of course. I love you."

"I love you more."

"Not possible. Sweet dreams, Ev."

When the line goes dead, so does a piece of me. I get so completely lost in my thoughts that I'm pathetically still holding my dick when I hear someone at the door. Not wanting to be caught with my spunk all over me, I dart into the bathroom to clean myself up. I'm sporting a semi, and a cold shower is the only thing that can remedy my situation. The last thing I need is a sleepless night, with a raging hard-on, and Joe snoring beside me.

"Bud?" he calls out as I climb into the shower.

"Yeah. I'll be out in a minute."

"Take your time. I'm ordering porn."

Oh, fuck. Goddamn Joe. "Ugh, hurry up!"

♬ ♬ ♬

Our time in the studio was both exhilarating and exhausting. The song we recorded sounds amazing. It perfectly showcases each and every one of our strengths. My brother-in-law impressed me more than ever. He is truly a talented man and a phenomenal musician. Even with all the ball busting and the fooling around, DL is a very focused bunch that bring their "A" game when the pressure is on. They are comfortable and confident in their skills, and it shows in everything they do.

Behind the scenes, their agent is even more impressive. I understand now why my sister has turned the other cheek when it comes to Jen. She is incomparable in her efforts of making Devil's Lair a household name, and her achievements speak for themselves. Her methods may be maddening, but her results are proven. She has taken Lori under her wing, and it will only benefit us, as well.

Goddamn we stepped in shit, and we know it. Who knows if we ever would have been discovered, if it weren't for Leila joining DL and for her agent giving us this chance to shine? She said she believes in us and believes we have the necessary ingredients to be a successful rock band.

The minute the demo was approved, Jen practically ran out of the studio with it. She, Malcolm, and Lori will be working their asses off promoting it to every radio station from coast to coast, ensuring they debut it to coincide with opening night.

The downside of successfully recording our single so quickly had me facing forty-eight hours of downtime. It stretched before me like a never-ending walk in the desert. With the help of my sister and brother-in-law I miraculously survived. Leila kept me busy to a fault, ensuring I didn't have any time to brood. I appreciated it and shamelessly spent every waking moment with them. If I hadn't, I knew my only sign of relief would have been my fleeting phone calls from Liz and more embarrassing intimate moments in the shower with my fist.

I also knew once opening night arrived, my brain would be working overtime to contain my nervous energy. We had an early rehearsal to accommodate the Pre-show Meet and Greet the studio arranged. Just as predicted, I've barely had time to miss Liz today, in between the scared as fuck moments and the holy shit episodes plaguing me. Devil's Lair has been giving us pointers and tips on how to handle the fans.

From what Leila described, their previous Meet and Greets were more of an open forum of sorts. The fans could mingle with the band and interact with them on a more personal level.

Jack said those days were over. He wanted an organized event with security monitoring everyone attending. There was an incident on their last tour when a male fan got a little too frisky with Leila. Jack came dangerously close to beating the crap out of the guy, and that was when there weren't nearly as well known as they are now. This time around, having a room full of Devil's Lair groupies without any form of organization or policing could cause a riot. Tonight's session will run differently.

Since there are so many of us, they will be ushered in a line around the room, getting a brief opportunity for a picture or autograph. I can't help but feel we, (as in Cliffhangers), will all be left standing around holding our dicks while watching the fans drooling over DL and essentially walking right past us, ignoring us completely. Why would they even give us the time of day? Leila said I'm being ridiculous…and I said we'd see.

So here we are, waiting for the first of the groupies to file in, and the adrenaline we all feel is coursing around the room, like an indoor electrical storm. Jen, Malcolm, and Dylan rush into the room as we all stand and wait. "You all ready?" she asks.

"Yes, let's do this already," Jack responds to her first, his apprehension clear in the tone of his voice.

He has confided in me about how stressed out he feels going into this tour. He hasn't shared every detail with Leila, as he doesn't want to upset her. But, she knows he is having a hard time keeping his paranoia in check. I watch as my sister tries to loosen him up, whispering in his ear. He quirks a lop-sided smile at her and kisses her chastely before plastering his game face back on.

The line of us stretches around the room with Leila and Jack at the very end. Oscar and Alec are both positioned in opposite corners. *The Staples Center* has provided a security guard, as well, and he is manning the door.

"Shit, my balls are sweating," Joe leans in close and whispers, although not too quietly. He successfully breaks the tension in the room, sending Leila and Nina into a fit of giggles.

We can instantly tell once they have arrived based on the influx of activity that resonates through the hall and into the holding room. A cluster of wide-eyed females are the first fans that rush through the door. Surprisingly, they make their way around the room, knowing each of our names and wanting pictures and autographs. These are our very first fans. The surrealism of the moment is not lost on me. I may remember what each of these girls are wearing, because I know without a doubt I'll never forget this.

When one of the girls gets to me, she starts squealing, "Oh, my God! Evan, I adore you! Can you sign my boobs?"

"Um…" I pathetically shrug, not at all prepared for her to immediately lift her shirt and thrust her perky breasts into my face.

"Holy shit," Joe lets slip as he gawks at the girl and her exposed chest.

"Ok, this wasn't in the manual," I mumble to no one in particular. When I look around the room for some guidance, most of the guys are nodding encouragingly, Leila is catching flies and Jack is leveling me with his ice-cold stare.

"Sign them, man. Make sure you write it nice and big across both of them," Joe steps closer, taking it upon himself to coach me. "Center it, and don't write your normal chicken scratch. Be neat."

“Can you shut the fuck up?”

I quickly scribble my name across her pale skin, and she turns to her friends to show off her new acquisition.

“Wow, I would have guessed Matt would have been the first to sign boobs. I think you’re my new hero, Ev.” Joe pretends to unbutton his pants and adds, “Can you sign my ass?”

“How about I kick it, you ass.”

My autograph request is tame compared to some of the requests made of DL. Phone numbers are slipped into pockets. Female hands grope, just as the shot is taken. Lips meet necks, captured for all of eternity in that one perfect shot that they will use as bragging rights to everyone they know. I can tell, from where I’m standing, that my sister’s patience is wearing thin. Jack is pawed at, groped, and kissed more than any of us, but each of the other DL members all get their fair share of crazy.

All things considered, Cliffhangers hold our own throughout the process. There are only a few times when a crazed fan moves right past us to her intended target. Most of the time it is one person she is interested in, and nothing could stop her from getting to him. The male fans all play it cool until they get to Nina or my sister. Jack quickly moves them along, if they linger longer than their allotted forty-five seconds.

As we robotically smile, pose, and sign for every fan that walks past us, the time flies by, and Jen is already announcing the Meet and Greet is over. Once the last fan is ushered out of the holding room, everyone takes a collective sigh of relief.

“Shit, that was…weird,” Joe voices.

Jen starts barking commands, like a drill sergeant, reminding us that we have fifteen minutes until we are on. Suddenly I feel sick to my stomach.

Fuck, this is our first opening night, on our first tour, and we are playing the *Staples Center*. I guess it's sink or swim time for Cliffhangers.

I lock gazes with Leila, and she watches me closely from where she is standing. She walks over with an all-knowing smile on her face. "Relax, Ev. You guys will be great."

"Lei, it's the fucking *Staples Center*. I don't think we're ready for this." Based on the fact none of my band are objecting, I'd have to think they all agree.

"You *are* ready. Here's a tip. You won't see a thing. It'll be dark and the lights are blinding. The first time I performed, I imagined we were playing The Zone. It worked for me."

The next fifteen minutes are spent getting all sorts of pointers from Scott, Jack, and Leila, one-liners from Trey, and asinine comments from Hunter.

"Ok, Cliffhangers. You're up," Dylan announces with a smile and a clap. The five of us stand rooted, not moving. This is stage fright at its finest.

"We'll be right there, side stage, watching you guys," Leila comforts and gives me a quick hug.

Logan takes control and commands us all to get our asses on stage. I have never, ever, been this nervous in my entire life. When we quietly congregate at the foot of the stage steps, I offer up a quick prayer for this not to be a disaster. When I glance at the rest of my band, they are all stone still, eyes closed, murmuring to themselves. I can only guess they are all praying as well.

## Chapter 14 – Jack

“Hey, Los Angeles. How are ya’ tonight?” Matt smoothly calls out into the microphone, and the arena erupts for him.

Even in the dark, I can clearly see the pride emanating off of my wife’s face from her ear-to-ear, beaming smile. Like a proud mama, she stands with her hands clasped together over her mouth. Her eyes wide, she repeatedly bounces on her toes. This is huge for her boys. Even bigger than what we experienced. Before she joined us our first tour was opening for MACE. The experience was phenomenal, but not nearly to this scale. The arenas weren’t as big as what we are playing this stretch. Most importantly, we really weren’t comfortable in our own skin yet.

Even during our own tour last year, the audience size we played for were a few thousand at best. We only experienced huge arenas when we opened for Bayou Stix, played the charity concert, and our closing nights in New York City. To take the stage for the very first time ever, before almost twenty thousand people, is something to be proud of. Cliffhangers should be very proud.

Matt strolls along the stage, engaging them with his banter, and they are responding to him enthusiastically. He reminds me a bit of me, when performing that is. He’s a completely different person up there than he is in everyday life. The real Matt is cocky, has an attitude, and has a chip on his shoulder. Put Matt up on stage and suddenly he’s charming, engaging, and likable. Combined with his movie star looks, the dude has what it takes.

I’ve gotten to know him better these past few days. I usually avoid him. After our first introduction where he was a complete dick, I wanted nothing to do with him. It didn’t help that he screwed my wife and cheated on her. I can't get past that and I can't stop visualizing it. There is nothing between them now. Even friendship would be considered a stretch. They also avoid each other as much as possible. The other guys handle him much like they would a petulant child. His brother Logan can put him in his place quicker than anyone. I take that back, Lori can put him in his place quicker than anyone. With one look, he visibly shrinks before your eyes.

So watching him on stage now, almost a carbon copy of me, is fucking strange. I never saw him perform, except for that fateful night at The Zone. I'm feeling a newfound respect for the dude, professionally speaking ONLY.

He's good.

It doesn't take long for the rest of the band to lose the deer in headlights expressions and adapt to their environment. They sound fantastic. They're edgier than we are, a touch more metal. Leila said they added that after she joined DL. She took with her a significant part of their sound. They needed to tweak and change their repertoire, so they didn't sound like carbon copies of Devil's Lair. I respect that. They recognized what a huge influence Leila's voice was to them. Instead of fighting it, they changed it. The results produced the new and improved Cliffhangers, who are unique in their own way.

They have this place rocking. I know exactly what they all must be feeling at the moment. It's that euphoria combined with pure adrenaline, which makes you feel high as a kite. I never did drugs, besides the night Leila dumped me, and smoking the occasional joint…but I can't imagine a recreational drug giving you the same results.

Leila sings along with most of their songs, occasionally turning to show me her beaming smile. Time goes by quickly since their set is shorter than ours. In no time at all, Matt introduces the rest of the band and takes them into their last song in the set.

Our shared single is the bridge between our sets. Our instruments are all positioned, ensuring the transition is seamless. This was intentional. When an intermission is taken, it causes a break in the flow in the atmosphere of a concert. I hate them when I attend a concert. I purposefully avoid them in our shows. Why would any band want to work so hard to work the crowd up, only to leave them hanging while you take a break?

It's not my style. So to keep with the integrity of a Devil's Lair concert, the bridge will bring Cliffhangers' set directly into ours.

Matt thanks the crowd for coming. I'm not even sure the crowd hears his words, the screaming, applause, and hooting is deafening.

Just before we take our places on stage, I pull Leila into my arms. It is so loud that I have to shout my words into her ear for her to hear me.

"They did it, Babe! They were fucking awesome!" She nods, smiling wide, kissing me quickly before we take our positions in the dark. Matt continues to talk to the crowd, hinting and teasing of what's to come next. He asks the crowd was there someone else they wanted to see.

The entire arena screams out as one, "Devil's Lair!"

He chuckles, "Who?"

"DEVIL'S LAIR!"

While still in the dark Matt responds to the crowd, "I don't think I know them. Are you sure you're in the right place?"

Chaos ensues and he laughs into the mic, "Ok, ok. I guess now wouldn't be a good time to tell you that they all left?"

With that, the stage lights come on, and the arena vibrates beneath our feet from the intensity of their cheers and feet stomping.

"He's a funny man. Hello, Los Angeles!" I take over the banter, openly laughing at their response. "Thank you! Thank you for being here! Thank you for joining us on our *In The Cards* tour. We have an awesome surprise for you tonight. This is the first time we are performing this beauty live. We hope you like it."

Immediately following my words, Trey and Evan begin their dueling bass riff. They face off, center stage and frantically work their fingers over the strings, creating the tone for the rest of the song.

The song becomes a party for us, a celebration of what we are privileged to be experiencing. It's raw and honest. My lyrics hit the nail on the head. Once we come into the ending, all ten of us sing and play as one. Any doubts I had that this tour was going to be anything less than spectacular leaves me, as we relish in the audience's response to our performance. We're off to a great start and tonight we set the bar pretty high.

♬ ♬ ♬

We're drenched, we're exhausted, and we are beyond delirious. Tonight was epic. It was beyond epic. We've opened our tour spectacularly. Leila clutches my hand, a delirious grin plastered on her face. The minute our feet hit the holding room, she bolts to Evan and right into his arms.

"You guys were unbelievable. How did it feel?"

He laughs at her hold on him. "Lei, let go."

"Oh, sorry." She steps away, waiting for him to respond.

"It was unreal. I've never felt that before in my entire life. It was both scary and exhilarating."

"Quite a rush, right?" I ask, joining their circle.

"A rush is an understatement. I can see how this becomes addicting."

"Best drug ever."

"Where's my hug?" Joe asks, giving her a wounded puppy face.

She gives Joe a hug, then Logan, Nina, and pats Matt on his back.

"We need to celebrate. Where are we going?" Hunter asks out loud. I quickly look to my wife, gauging her carefully. She needs to go right to bed. But I don't want to ruin her fun.

As they all start throwing options around I step closer and ask, "Are you tired?"

She looks up, schooling her annoyance, but I can see it. When I raise my brows, she quips, "Nope. I'm fresh as a daisy."

"And you would tell me otherwise?"

"Probably not." In one of her classic forms of distraction, she wraps her arms around me and murmurs against my neck, "One drink. Please? I just want to be part of their celebration. It means a lot to me." She pulls the skin her lips are touching into her mouth, sucking gently. She leans up on her tippy toes so her lips can travel from my neck to my ear. "Please?"

"Christ, woman."

She giggles and adds, "Yay, three drinks."

"Don't push it."

"I promise I'll sleep in tomorrow." She looks up innocently, pursing her lips in a pleading manner. Not being able to resist her lips that are perfectly puckered and waiting to be tasted, I do just that. I slant my mouth over hers, stealing a much needed kiss. Even after a year of dating and another of marriage, she still dulls all my senses with just a kiss.

"So, you two coming? To the bar, that is," Hunter asks, interrupting our intimate moment.

"Go away." I bend back down to resume, when she smiles against my lips.

"God, man. Can you just leave her alone? I should put a wager on you two. She'll be knocked up days after this one pops out." He pulls her out of my hold, wrapping an arm around her shoulders and ushers her out the door.

"Um, hello?"

"Just follow your wife's ass."

"Ok, that's easy."

We pile in our van and head to our destination.

Our clan is hard to ignore. We elicit some unwanted attention, but this is expected no matter where we go. Oscar added another security guard to his team. He, Alec, and the new guy Ryan, have secured our corner. Except for the gawkers, we are pretty much left alone to our celebrations.

Hunter holds up his beer, smiling as he glances at each of our faces. "Speaking for the rest of us," he looks at me for confirmation and I nod in agreement, "we couldn't have picked a better band to open for us. You guys fucking rocked it tonight. It was an unbelievable start to what's sure to be a fucking awesome tour. I thank **fate** every day for bringing you all into our lives. To FATE."

"To FATE," we all repeat in agreement.

Tonight marks the beginning of our journey. I know it's about to be a fantastic one.

## Chapter 15 – Leila

While in L.A. I received a very emotional text from Lainey Casiano regarding her cousin's daughter, Keeley Stanton. She has been diagnosed with leukemia. We had met Keeley's parents, Aubrey and Trevor when we attended Mike and Lainey's wedding. Trevor was on crutches at the time, recovering from a war injury.

The video Lainey sent had Keeley's dad, Trevor, catching her singing and dancing along with our song *In The Cards*. As our song played in the background Keeley squealed with excitement, her adorable face beaming with joy.

"Daddy, dance!!" she called to Trevor, when the instrumental part came on. Trevor handed Aubrey his phone and obeyed his daughter's command. The line to the port for her chemo treatment did nothing to deter her from swaying to the music in her daddy's arms. When the song ended, she shouted, "Again!"

"You need to rest, Baby," Aubrey said while still recording.

"Nope. I gots ta practice," Keeley replied.

"Practice for what, ladybug?" Trevor asked, looking down at his daughter's determined face.

"For when I get to sing with Jack!"

Trevor laughed, "You think you're gonna sing with Jack Lair?"

Keeley nodded, "Uh huh."

"What song would you sing with him?"

She rolled her eyes, losing her patience with him. "Daddy! In The Cawds."

Trevor laughed at his daughter's response. "But Mrs. Leila sings with Jack," Aubrey reminded her.

"She can sing, too. But I sing with Jack."

Trevor met Aubrey's gaze as she continued to point the phone in their direction. "God help me, my daughter's in love with a rock star," he groaned.

Later that night, he forwarded the video to Lainey, who then sent it to me.

"Babe, it looks like I have major competition," I admitted when sharing it with Jack. My husband sat riveted to the tiny phone screen. Once done, he replayed it twice more.

"We need to go see her," he stated, without doubt.

I nodded in agreement. "We'll fly out after our show tomorrow. We'll meet up with the tour in Vegas."

Jack simply nodded, not being able to speak in return.

I made all the arrangements, and we arrived in Springfield the next day. When Jack and I walked into Keeley's room, the tears that threatened were hard to contain. I had to muster all my energy to smile warmly, when Keeley looked up and noticed Jack. A flash of surprise on her pale face was immediately replaced with a beaming smile. Her body couldn't cooperate with the elation she felt. Our only indication of her joy was on her beautiful face.

Jack and I each sat on the side of her bed, talking quietly with her, holding her small hands in ours.

"Would you like to hear some songs?" Jack asked her after a few minutes. She looked so tired, and we didn't want to exhaust her further. She nodded eagerly, and we sang her a few songs as she watched in awe, her eyes never leaving his face, or his hands as he strummed his guitar.

He then sang *Reason I Am* as she slowly drifted off to sleep.

Aubrey approached, her tears falling freely. "Thank you, both, so much. You don't know how much that meant to her."

"She is adorable," I responded, unable to look away from her beautiful face. "I'm glad we could help."

Jack, who has yet to speak after he sang, shook Trevor's hand silently. I could see the emotion all over his face.

On our way out Jack said to each of them, "We'd like to do something to help. We're going to be playing at the *AT&T Stadium* in Dallas in a few weeks. If she's feeling better, we'd love to have Keeley be there, join us on stage. We want to donate the proceeds of that show to children's cancer research."

"That would be awesome, man, thanks," Trevor responded, moved by our suggestion.

Aubrey continued to cry, hugging me tightly and thanking me repeatedly.

Dallas was a few stops away, but Keeley remained on my mind the entire time.

I kept in contact with Aubrey, wanting to know how Keeley was feeling each day that went by. Aubrey said the video Trevor uploaded on YouTube went viral. Within a week Keeley's video had over a million views. News programs began coming out of the woodwork, asking if they could interview Keeley. Unfortunately, the effects of the chemo had Keeley too weak to participate in any interviews. Aubrey also shared some heart-wrenching news with me. Trevor is a Navy SEAL and was on assignment when Aubrey discovered she was pregnant. Keeley was a result of their brief encounter. When Keeley was just two-years of age, she was diagnosed with leukemia. Trevor had no idea he had a daughter, or that she was fighting for her life. Aubrey had no intentions of telling Trevor that he was Keeley's father.

He was injured and only learned of Keeley and her illness after returning home for treatment. By then, Aubrey knew Keeley needed a bone marrow transplant, and both she and her mother weren't a match. Fate stepped in and made it necessary to tell Trevor of Keeley's existence. They are now battling her illness together while also trying to work out their relationship.

This family deserves happiness. While Trevor selflessly served our country Aubrey was battling Keeley's horrific prognosis alone. Their story tore at my heart. Giving Keeley this experience became an obsession for me. I silently said a prayer every day, in hopes she would be strong enough to meet us in Dallas and join us on stage. Thankfully, a few days before our show, Aubrey confirmed Keeley was feeling better and they would like to surprise her with our offer.

Aubrey and Trevor came along with Mike and Lainey Casiano. They joined us backstage before the show started. Jack carried Keeley in his arms the entire time as we gave them a mini tour of the backstage area. She barely saw any of it, as she gazed up at Jack, smiling shyly.

Mike, Lainey, Trevor, and Aubrey stood side stage when we joined Cliffhangers for our bridge. My new band and my former band were all as excited as we were to get to this part of our show.

After Matt introduced us, Jack wasted no time. "As you know, I adore my wife." The band behind him groaned at his admission. "Zip it. Anyway, I love my wife very much," he turned toward me and added, "but, Baby, I gotta admit…there's another girl in my life."

He smiled and ran a hand through his hair when I put my hands on my hips, pretending to be outraged.

He shrugged, smiled wide, and said, "Sorry, Baby, but she stole my heart. And I think she stole every one of our hearts, including Trey's. I didn't know he had a heart to be stolen."

Trey nodded, and the audience laughed.

"That's ok, Baby. I'll overlook it. This one time," I conceded.

"Yea? Well, that's good, because I told her she could sing your part in our next song. You ok with that?"

"Completely."

"Ladies and gentlemen, please show some love to the beautiful, Miss Keeley Stanton!" He smiled over at Keeley, sitting in her daddy's arms, clapping excitedly to what Jack was saying to the crowd. Trevor set her down, and she ran right into Jack's arms. She had the crowd eating from the palm of her hand. She had my husband head over heels in love. After her debut, she stayed for a few more songs before Aubrey and Trevor left to take her home.

That night was one of the best nights of my life. This little person, this beautiful little girl successfully stole our hearts and ran away with them. She has become very important to us, and we will be there for her and her parents, every step of the way. We were destined to meet Mike and Lainey Casiano, and even more so Aubrey, Trevor, and Keeley. We have become great friends, and they will forever be in our lives.

## PART TWO – LOVE

# Chapter 16 – Jack

I watch as she sleeps soundly beside me. Her hair fans around her pillow. Her lips part with every breath she takes. The sheet clings to her form, revealing her now obvious pregnant belly. My hand twitches with the desire to touch her. I don't want to wake her. She stubbornly claims she's not tired. She constantly fights me on getting more rest. I want her to sleep as much as possible on our final drive back to New York City. I threatened the guys that I would pounce if I heard one sound from the front of the bus. They must have known I meant business, because I haven't heard a peep from them yet, and it's practically noon.

This tiny room may provide us some privacy, but the walls are very thin. We learned of that reality the hard way on our last tour. My wife has become a professional at keeping her voice down during sex. It seems like yesterday when we were spending a lot of our free time locked in a similar room while getting to know each other. It's hard to believe how fast time has gone by. Now here we are married a year, completing our second tour, and about to start a family.

This tour has been a much different experience for all of us. Their stress levels have been nonexistent this time around. I've been stressing the entire time. The two monthly appointments she had while on the road did little to relieve my anxiety. I requested her OB-GYN to give us the best doctor recommendations in each city, leaving nothing to chance. Especially since her first sonogram was due early in our tour.

I sat nervously in the exam room while Leila lay on the examination table. Unable to remain seated, I started to pace back and forth, allowing my nerves to get the best of me.

"Please sit down," she pleaded. "You're making me nervous."

I did as she asked, but began to tap my foot, like a man strung out on crack. By the time the doctor entered the room, I was two seconds away from going out there and dragging him in by his collar.

The doctor introduced himself and explained what he was about to do. He coated her belly with gel and started to move a hand held device over it. Every time he moved it, the picture on the monitor would shift.

I moved to Leila's side to get a better view of the chaos on the monitor.

"Are there twins in your families?"

Huh?

Neither of us spoke. He looked up from the screen and asked again.

"Um, no. Not in mine," Leila responded while watching me.

"Uh…my grandfather was a twin."

Shock appeared all over her face. "Were you planning on telling me this?"

"I forgot."

"Well, it seems you are having twins." He turned the screen so we could get a better look. We both leaned closer, trying to decipher what we were looking at. All I saw was greyness and static. He chuckled at our dumbstruck expressions and pointed to two tiny alien looking things on the screen. "That there is one...and there is the second."

Twins?

While he clicked away on the keyboard we sat completely frozen. Neither of us moved.

Twins?

He printed a few images of the grainy blips that were supposedly our babies and handed them to me.

"Everything looks great. From the size of the fetuses, you are about twelve or thirteen weeks. You'll follow up with your normal monthly visit. You'll be receiving a sonogram at every visit since you are carrying twins. We want to be sure everything is ok." He pulled a gadget from his pocket, plugged in some numbers, and added, "Your due date is the seventh of January, but you most likely will deliver two to three weeks earlier."

Neither of us muttered a word.

"You two ok?" We nodded robotically and he chuckled some more. "Very normal reaction. You aren't the only ones. You've been doubly blessed, congratulations."

When he left us alone, my voice finally retuned. "Baby, I can't believe it, twins."

"Two…two babies at once? I can't do this."

"Yes, you can."

"No…I can't," she repeated stubbornly, crossing her arms.

I laughed out loud at the expression of determination on her face. "You don't have a choice. I'll be there with you."

"I'm about to slug you."

She wasn't amused when I laughed again. My heart went through a gamut of emotions that day. I understood her panic. I've been much more receptive to our pregnancy than she's been. Now add a second baby to the mix and her freak-out tendencies were in over-drive.

We both decided to keep the news of twins to ourselves. We wanted to tell our parents and siblings first, once we got home.

My overprotectiveness skyrocketed. I constantly worried whether she was resting enough, eating enough, often annoying her to the point where she actually did slug me a few times.

The guys would moan and groan over my nagging. I didn't give a flying fuck and made no apology for my behavior. Trey has been relentless in fucking with me, calling me every variation of wuss, pussy, and pansy-ass that he could think of. I have to give him credit, as some were pretty creative, even making it hard for Leila or me to keep a straight face. My favorites were Cock Star, Queen Kong, and Baron Von Pussy-whipped.

In spite of my neurosis, overall, this time on the road has been a great experience. Not having a lunatic ex-girlfriend or ex-band mate stalking us surprisingly made a world of difference. For the most part, we have enjoyed ourselves and relished in our good fortune. Having Cliffhangers with us has been a blast. I feel they are an extension of us. It's amazing how well we all mesh and how much we all have in common.

During our tour, Trey smartly stayed clear of Matt. There were times it was awkward between them, but not having Lori around definitely lessened how thwarting things could have been. The only time she joined us was in Chicago, where Trey smartly stayed clear of our group outings. She was also supposed to join the rest of the girls on our Miami stop, but Alisa was late and Lori decided to stay with her until her scheduled C-Section. Leila misses her very much. She also said she's worried about her. She didn't elaborate, and I suspect it had to do with Lori's surprise visit on our anniversary.

She'll be reunited with her friend shortly. Tomorrow nights show in New York City marks the end of our tour. I've already warned Leila her reality will be total rest and relaxation for the next few weeks and no stress...especially by getting involved with that wacko redhead's issues. Leila is over-due for her monthly sonogram. She tried to convince me it was ok to postpone it, and then had her doctor do the same. He assured us she could have it done as soon as we got home. Twins are monitored differently than single births, but she isn't high risk.

I've been wondering what she's carrying, boy, girl, or both? I am dying to meet them. My gut tells me one of them is definitely a boy. I'm not sure why. It has nothing to do with wanting a son over a daughter. I would love a mini version of Leila and will probably keep trying until I get one. But this time around, I feel at least one of them in there is a boy just waiting to arrive.

We felt them kick for the first time a few days ago. It was after our show in Charlotte. As we do after every show, Leila and I were just about to have sex when I felt a nudge against my abs. It didn't register until her eyes flew open in shock.

"Did you feel that?" she asked incredulously.

"Yea, what was that?"

"The babies!"

I immediately moved to lie beside her, and she placed my hand on the spot she felt the kick. A few seconds later, one of them kicked again. It was the most surreal moment of my entire life, a confirmation that they were real. Up until then, her pregnancy wasn't a tangible thing to me. It was more of an idea, a mystery that was yet to present itself. After that kick, it hit me that there was indeed two perfect little people in there waiting to come out. The enormity of this monumental event hit me like a freight train. The only other time I felt so much emotion was when I realized I loved their mother.

Leila smiled through her tears, instigating my own emotions to swell within me.

So basically, my theory that one of them is a boy comes from the fact that he chose to introduce himself just before his mother and I were about to…well, let's say that I feel he's a chip off the old block. Leila said I was ridiculous and balked at my reasoning. Since that day my hands have been glued to her belly, constantly waiting for another kick. Hunter has brazenly taken up the habit of touching her belly as well, until I told him to knock up Mandi and get his own pregnant woman to manhandle.

They've been very active in there. Now that we've felt the first kick, they are coming frequently. Every one of my band members has had the pleasure of feeling my babies kick.

In fact, as she lies beside me now, she subconsciously moves her hand to her belly. A habit she has developed, even in her sleep. She blinks her eyes open, and focuses on my face. "Hey."

"Hey."

"What are you doing?"

"I'm watching you sleep."

She shoves at my chest. "You're a creeper."

"Yep," I respond, not bothering to deny it.

Her hand flexes on her belly again, reminding her of what woke her up. Recognizing the signs, I immediately lay my hands beside hers. The minute my hands mold over her belly there's a kick, and then again.

"They're playing soccer with my bladder. I need to pee." She flies out of bed and toward the bathroom. I literally stop myself from following, selfishly wanting to keep touching her and feeling them. I can't imagine what that feels like for her. Every movement felt first hand. They come so frequently that she probably takes them for granted. I, on the other hand, want to feel as many kicks as possible, always afraid of missing one if I'm not touching her belly.

A few minutes later she returns, closing the door behind her. "The guys are up. Are you ready to have breakfast?"

"Not yet."

She folds her arms and smirks, as if she knows what I want.

Ignoring her stance, I place my hands on her, waiting for more signs of life.

"Wow. My boobs were usually what you went for. They're starting to get jealous."

"No worries. Tell them I'll be coming for them soon." Sure enough, the twins make it known they are wide awake and ready to play, based on the movements I feel under my palms. I shift my hands every few seconds, covering the entire area to ensure I don't miss any. When I lean my ear against her, she laughs.

"What?"

"The only thing you are going to hear is my stomach rumbling. I'm starving."

"Humor me." I continue to listen intently, as if they are going to speak to me from her womb.

"So, I thought of another name. How about Arsen?"

"No," she immediately responds.

"Why? What's wrong with Arsen?"

"Besides it being a crime?"

"It's cool."

She shakes her head, "No, it's stupid."

I pull her onto my lap. "Ok, I got one more. Madden."

"Madden?" She purses her lips in thought. "Madden Jackson?" I nibble on her neck while waiting for her to mull it around. This is the first time she hasn't instantly vetoed my suggestion. "Madden Jackson Lair and Siarra Marie Lair. I think I like it."

Lifting my head, I ask, "Really?"

"Really. It's cool, it's definitely rock star worthy, and it's unique."

"Well, fucking yay."

"Now we just need another boy and another girl name. It only took us weeks to find the one, we should be good by January."

"Or, we could revisit some of your vetoes." I frame her belly with my hands before leaning down to murmur, "Hey, are you a Madden and a Siarra? Daddy can't wait to meet you guys."

"Right now Siarra is rolling her eyes at you."

"Maybe, but most likely Madden is fist bumping me as we speak."

No sooner do I finish my statement, when a tiny nudge pushes against my hand. "Aha, see. Fist bump."

"Wow, that was strange. Maybe you're right."

"I know I'm right. There's definitely a boy in there. Maybe two."

"Two more male Lairs? Great. The female population is not ready for that."

"Well, they better get ready. I plan on having several."

"*You* plan on having?"

"Me, us…whatever. If these two are boys, then our next one will be Siarra Marie, and if not then, the one after that or the one after that."

"A litter?"

"A Lair litter. Let's practice." I kiss her passionately until a loud knock on our door interrupts our moment.

"Ignore it, they'll go away."

"I heard that," Hunter responds through the thin wood panel.

"We're sleeping."

"Nice try. Get out here, Jen is on the phone."

Leila shrugs, "Sorry, Babe." She stands quickly, leaving me to adjust myself.

"I should go out there just as I am. It would serve them right." I point down to my tenting briefs.

"I'm sure Trey would love that." She grabs my jeans and throws them at me. "Hurry up. I'm curious as to what she wants."

"I'm surrounded by cock-blockers," I mumble as she walks out. I follow, scanning their expectant faces as I do.

"So, what's so important?" I ask into the phone that's sitting on the table.

"I have some news." Jen responds through the speaker. "*Rolling Stone* wants to follow up their article with a series of feature articles detailing your lives. They will have a mini biography on each of you, as well as a recap article of the band."

"You're shittin' us," Hunter accuses.

"No, Hunter. It's true."

"Holy fuck!" he yells back. "This is fucking awesome."

"The rest of you agree?" she asks unnecessarily.

"Of course we agree." Hunter is right. Holy fuck. I grin at Leila and she returns one of her own. I've collected those special edition *RS* magazines over the years, and now I'm going to be featured in one?

We basically all ignore Jen as we start yapping over each other, voicing our individual responses simultaneously.

Jen interrupts our chaos, calling out, "Jack?"

"What?"

"Do you and Leila want a combined feature or solos? The writer wants to know."

I glance at my wife and she immediately agrees to Jen's first suggestion. Of course she doesn't want the spotlight solely on her. I could give a damn, as well. We are a unit, a team. What I have to say, most likely has something to do with her. They could cover my pre-Leila existence within one paragraph for all I care.

"Combined is fine," I confirm to Jen and Leila smiles.

"Good. I'll let them know. They want a meeting next week. Stay tuned to the day and time after I confirm with them." She clears her throat and then asks, "So, DC was good?"

A few seconds of silence follows her question. DC was a good show, but there was an incident afterwards. Obviously our agent is aware of it and is fishing for a confirmation. My cowardly band mates, specifically Trey, all sit silently and wait for me to do the talking.

Feigning innocence, I respond, "Yep, DC was great."

"Uh huh. That's how you want to play it?"

"Not sure what you are talking about. Bye, Jen. We'll see you tomorrow after the show." I disconnect the call and Trey starts laughing uncontrollably.

"Fuck you," Hunter responds to his annoying reaction.

"What?" he deadpans.

"You should have come clean. It was your mess."

"Literally," Scott adds.

"Fucking jackass," Hunter grumbles at Trey.

He responds, "I'm innocent."

Leila tries to hide her giggles, failing miserably. Not wanting to give Schmuck One and Schmuck Two the satisfaction, I turn my back to get myself a cup of coffee, hiding my own grin.

The memory of the DC fiasco comes flooding to my mind. Damn Trey and his whoring ways. After our show, we hung out back stage for a bit, relaxing before we headed back to our hotel. It was just Cliffhangers and us until Trey dragged in one of his groupies. The girl was hot as hell, but dumb as dirt – which suited Trey just fine. She drank like a fish, pawing him the entire time. He dragged her out of the room to get down to the reason she was there.

Apparently, on their way out, they stumbled upon Hunter's drum set sitting on stage waiting to be packed by the roadies. Trey's conquest bolted toward it and started playing them erratically. Hunter's sense of hearing is impeccable when it comes to his drums. He made it out to his beloved set just as she barfed all over them.

Long story short, there was crying, chasing, and a lot of disinfectant. It cost the roadies hours of extra work. Hunter needs to resort to his practice set while his good set is being professionally cleaned. He may not have them back in time for our closing show. He is not a happy camper. Trey didn't apologize and Hunt is holding a grudge. Trey is now taunting him relentlessly.

"Hey, Hunt?"

Hunter doesn't bother responding and just levels him with his icy glare.

"What do you do if you accidentally run over a drummer?" Trey waits for a response that doesn't come. "You back up." Hunter continues to glare and Trey tries again. "No? How about this one? What do you call a drummer with half a brain?"

"I'm going to pummel you," Hunter fuels his fire.

"Errrr…wrong answer. A drummer with half a brain is *gifted*."

Scott hides his snicker with a cough. Trey lets out a belly laugh and all hell breaks loose. Fruit Loops are used as Hunter's weapon of choice. Leila hides behind me, trying to evade the adolescent food fight.

When Hunter uses up all his ammunition, he quips, "Yeah? Just for that I'm going to go jerk off in your bunk." He makes a dash for it and Trey chases after him.

"Really?" I ask no one in particular.

“The natives are getting restless,” Leila says while shaking her head. “Good thing we are almost home.”

“Hey, Tom?” Our driver meets my eyes in the rearview mirror. “Can we dump them somewhere on the side of the road?”

“Just say where, boss.”

Apparently they are getting on everyone’s nerves. Tom is the most easy-going man I know. Scott joins Leila and me in the booth while their arguing gets louder and louder. “You guys didn’t hear them going at it most of the night?”

“No, thank God. We both passed out from exhaustion. I may have killed them.”

“I almost did,” Scott admits. “We may need a second bus next tour. I can’t be held responsible for their demise.”

Correction, Scott is the most easy-going man I know.

Trey strolls back toward us like he doesn’t have a care in the world.

“What did you do to him?”

“Nothing. I just kept throwing one liners at him,” Trey brags. “He’ll hide for the rest of the trip.” He plops himself on the couch and smiles. “You’re welcome.”

“Hey, man, I’m all for busting Hunt’s chops, but don’t you think you’re laying it on thick?”

Trey faces me, slowly folding his arms. “No.”

“Those drums are his pride and joy. Your chick barfed all over them.” It’s impossible to know what he’s thinking since I can’t see his eyes. His silence tells me he knows I’m right.

After a short pause, he shrugs and says, “She’s not my chick, and I’m not her keeper.”

I shake my head in frustration. “Whatever.”

“Trey, I know you aren’t that cold and insensitive,” Leila now tries to get through to him. One side of his mouth quirks up in a semi-smirk, otherwise he holds his defensive stance.

“You, too, Little Lair?”

“Cut him some slack. For me?”

His smirk turns into a sly smile. Still, it’s impossible to know what he’s thinking. Sometimes I feel I don’t know this man at all. All the years we’ve spent together, and I have no true understanding of how his brain works. How can someone go through life so detached? There was a time I was insulted by his indifference. I felt if he really were a true friend, he would trust us with his past, with his secrets. I’d then feel guilty for feeling that way, because I knew viscerally he was a true friend, and he would defend us with his life. It’s almost as if there are two Treys, both conflicting each other, both warring against each other.

My wife waits patiently as he refuses to let down his guard. Scott doesn’t say a word, he knows better. We all know better. She’s wasting her time, but there’s a part of me that would like to see if Leila is able to make any progress with him. Actually, she has made more progress these past two years than we have these past ten. To our defense, we’re guys. We push things under the rug and ignore them. He could also tell us to fuck off and leave him alone. He wouldn’t do that to Leila, I know he wouldn’t.

Trey breaks out into a smile and slowly shakes his head back and forth.

“What?” she asks innocently.

“You’re a pain in my ass, Little Lair.”

“Trey, you’re about to be an uncle. I want my baby to look up to you guys, to idolize you. I know you want that, too. Even the Grinch had a heart. I know yours is in there somewhere.”

“Nope, I’m heartless.”

"No, I think it's been broken. I think you're afraid it will be again. Isn't there a tiny part of you that's tired of acting like you don't give a shit?"

"I don't."

"Yes, you do." She nails him with her mega-watt smile and adds, "You give a shit about me."

The more he stares at her the more she smiles. "Fine, I'll apologize to drum-head, once he comes out. Happy?"

Leila breaks out into an even bigger grin. "Very. Thank you."

"Hey, Little Lair…"

"Stop," she holds up a hand, interrupting him. "Do not ruin our moment."

"Ok, I'll save it for later."

"I can't wait." She responds while basking in her victory.

Brick by brick, she's breaking down his wall. They banter as Scott and I exchange incredulous looks.

How the fuck did she do that?

Hunter appears from his bunk and scowls while pulling out a new box of *Fruit Loops*. He wordlessly pours himself a bowl and heads back to the bunks.

"Amatto," Trey calls out at his retreating back. Hunt stops for a second without turning around.

"What?"

"I'm sorry, man."

"For what?" Now Hunt is being a ball buster.

Trey sighs. I know he's going to tell him to fuck off at any moment. He watches Leila as she encourages him silently. Trey grits his teeth at her, yet says, "For the drums, for busting on you, for being a prick."

Hunter slowly turns around, meeting Trey's gaze. "You're forgiven." He walks to Trey and adds, "Now kiss my feet," raising one toward him.

"Fuck off." Trey swats him away and looks at me. "Can I kill him now?"

"Yeah, go for it."

Hunter looks panicked for a second and darts back to his bunk, leaving a trail of *Fruit Loops* in his path. Leila giggles and Trey laughs along with her.

"You're still a pain in my ass."

"But you love me," she responds confidently.

"I don't love. I heavily like you," he responds.

"Whatever."

"Ok, you're going to be the disciplinarian. I'm impressed." I bend to kiss her chastely. "I'm also turned on," I add directly into her ear.

"I'm not surprised."

"We have at least another hour to go. Let's take a nap."

"Nap my ass. Go screw your brains out. Scott, you can go be with your boyfriend. I'd like some peace and quiet," Trey suggests. "You all gave me a headache."

"I need off this bus and away from you all, no offense, Leila. You're all driving me fucking crazy." Scott voices out loud. "I can't wait to get away from you, no offense, Leila, and fuck Patti's brains out. I'm this close to hitchhiking. You're all getting on my fucking nerves. Jack, you aren't the only man on Earth whose wife is having a baby. Jesus Christ, enough with the fucking nagging already. Hunter and his goddamn jerking off two feet above my head, not to mention Mr. Joke-man and his humongous ego." He stands and opens the fridge, searching for something while continuing to mumble incoherently. Every few seconds his head pops out to utter an insult at us, and his face is red as a tomato.

Hunter has become a crybaby.

Trey has become partly human.

Scott has become a bit unstable.

Damn, I wish I got all of this on video. This shit would have gone viral.

## Chapter 17 - Lori

My nerves are getting the best of me. I wanted to be sure I was here on time, waiting for them as they pulled in. I haven't seen Matt in weeks.

The first time I joined him on tour was two weeks after they left. He was standoffish and detached. I knew he would be. He was quick to tell me how upset he was that I wasn't there to experience their opening night. He was hoping I would surprise him and just show up. The way he described the show to me over the phone had my heart aching with guilt. It was the best experience of his life, and he said he would never forget the disappointment he felt afterwards that effectively killed his buzz.

So it was to no surprise that the tension was thick between us, when I joined him a few weeks later. I was nervous as fuck sitting on my flight to Chicago. I flew out with Liz, Mandi, and Patti. I put on a brave face, but inside I was a mess. I'm ashamed to say that seeing Matt was only part of my anxiety. Seeing Trey played just as equal a part, if not slightly more.

Leila said to focus on Matt, so I planned on taking her advice. The day we arrived was a free day for the bands. The guys made no plans, wanting nothing more than to spend their reunions in complete privacy. The girls were more than ok with their decision. I, however, was dreading it.

The guys met us at the airport. The other girls got panty-soaking receptions from their men. I got a peck on the cheek and a half-hearted hug. He held my hand on our ride back to the hotel, but barely said a word.

Unlike the others, who couldn't wait to get behind closed doors, Matt suggested we grab dinner instead. After receiving a few snide comments, we headed out, each lost in our own thoughts. When I got him alone in the cab, I pounced.

"Are you going to give me the silent treatment for the next three days? Because I'll take my sorry ass back to New York on the next flight." He cut his eyes toward me, watching me silently. "I'm here. I wouldn't be here if I didn't want to be. The question is, do you want me here? I should have asked that and not assumed you did. But goddamn it, Matt…you have to cut me some slack."

"You got it all wrong, Lor. You have to cut me some."

Ok, so he had a point.

I softened my features and tried a different approach. I'll never forget the irritated look he gave me as I closed the distance between us. It wasn't exactly the kind of look that could set my insides on fire, but I went in anyway.

That kiss set the tone for the rest of our time together. He remained distant, annoyed, and curt. I continued to initiate, engage, and beg. Our lovemaking was forced. Our alone time was awkward. Our reunion sucked.

The best part was watching them perform. I was so proud of the band they became. I was even more proud of him. He didn't use our situation as an excuse to underperform, just the opposite. He was the Matt I used to lust after. He was the sexy, cocky fuck that I haven't seen in a while. By the end of their show, I was a horny mess. I skipped DL's segment, instead dragging Matt into an empty holding room and fucked him senseless.

So maybe it was just a temporary fix to our surmounting issues…but it was just what I needed to firmly put his sexy ass back into my mind. Mind you, Trey's ass was still in a far corner of my mind, as well. Thankfully, he avoided us and made himself very scarce during my visit. The only time I really saw him was during their shows. By then, Matt had successfully infiltrated my mind. He firmly planted himself back into my thoughts.

It sent me back home with a longing that I haven't felt in a long time. Once my feet hit the New York pavement, I missed Matt Rizzo…a lot.

I started texting him daily with the things I wanted to do to him and the things I wanted him to do to me. The first few days, my texts went unanswered. When we spoke on the phone, he acknowledged he received them. Instead of getting angry, I gave him phone sex.

After a few days of my newfound lust, he slowly started coming around. First I got a smiley face, and then a one-word response. The day I got an actual sext from him, I felt like we were back in high school. It made me giddy, anticipating what our next reunion would be like.

I kept a journal. I needed a reminder of all the times he stirred my insides. This was my issue, my missing spark. The fact that I was feeling it again, it needed to be validated and documented. There were days I thought, what the fuck am I doing? I felt like a lawyer busy preparing her case. This wasn't normal. It shouldn't be this forced, this calculated. Then I would receive a sweet text from him, or he would call me baby over the phone, and I knew my methods were necessary. I was working on our relationship and, although unconventional, it was necessary.

We were finding our way back to each other, even with the miles that separated us. Leila said he wasn't brooding any longer. He was happier. I had to admit, I was also. I kept busy with promoting them from afar. I met with Jen several times to discuss publicity, and I spent a lot of time with Alisa during her last stretch of pregnancy.

The next scheduled trip to see him was supposed to be in Miami. Based on her size, we all thought that Alisa would have delivered by then. Logan would have been home with his wife and baby, and I could then join Matt for the last leg of the tour.

Alisa was late.

Her doctor scheduled to induce her, two weeks after her due date. Logan made preparations to be home the morning of. Alisa went from desperately wanting this child to be born to claiming she wasn't uncomfortable at all. She actually had the nerve to claim she could make it another two weeks. Of course she was lying. It was the dead of summer and a thousand degrees out. She sat in her air-conditioned apartment day after day, refusing to move or go anywhere. She desperately wanted her husband to be with her. I couldn't blame her for that. I silently said a prayer hoping for the same thing.

Alisa being late is the best-case scenario for Logan. He then would only be missing one stop, as the last one was NYC. The powers that be felt for the Rizzo's and Alisa delivered a beautiful baby girl with her husband by her side. Michelle Lynn Rizzo has her mom's coloring and her dad's eyes. She already has her dad wrapped around her little finger.

I've been spending even more time with them, helping Alisa as much as possible. The birth of Michelle further instigated my sappy thoughts. I want one. I want one of my own and I want to be happy. I want a loving family. I want a strong, solid marriage. I want to be a wife. I want all this with Matt Rizzo.

He hasn't a clue I've made this revelation. He still thinks I'm sitting with my stupid-ass thoughts. I had a brain-fart these past few months. I can't blame it on a mid-life crisis. Whatever it was, it's over. Trey was an awesome time, and hot fling, that was fun while it lasted. Trey is not my soul mate. Matt is.

So now I'm waiting at the curb in front of *The Garden*, where Matt's bus should be pulling in at any moment. The crowd lining the sidewalk is quiet now, but soon all chaos will break loose. There are barricades set up to contain the fans. A few policemen are already positioned, waiting for the rock stars to appear.

Leila, being the only person who knows of my revelation, texted me announcing their arrival will be in minutes. He'll see me before I see him, and when he does, he'll know what I've decided. I simply can't wipe the smile off my face.

Wait, what if he doesn't want the same? A flash of panic suddenly courses through me. What if during my soul searching, he realized I'm not it for him? It hadn't occurred to me. There was a time he wanted nothing to do with me, he could easily have decided I'm so not worth it.

In an instant, my euphoria morphs into paranoia. By the time the buses pull up, I'm a mess. I don't have a back up plan. It's too late to run.

Two of the three buses park nose to ass along the curb. Seconds later a flux of activity starts to pour off the buses. Roadies congregate on the sidewalk and immediately start unpacking equipment, wheeling it all into the loading dock of *The Garden*. The mob starts to get loud, waiting for Devil's Lair to appear. Ignoring it all, I stand rooted, waiting patiently for the Cliffhanger bus to arrive.

Dylan and their security guards move into action keeping the fans at bay. Trey bounds off his bus, like he's on fire, smiling arrogantly at the screaming fans. He stops in his tracks when he sees me. The tiniest flutter takes hold of my heart. It's fleeting and gone before I realize what it is. Surprisingly, he strolls toward me instead of ignoring, which has been his usual response to me lately. My eyes dart to see if Matt's bus is approaching. It wouldn't serve my reunion well if it arrived as I was speaking to Trey. But I'm too curious to know why Trey is giving me the time of day at the moment.

"Hey."

"Hey. How are you?"

He nods slowly, "I'm great. Tour was awesome."

"Yes, I know. You all should be proud."

An uncomfortable silence falls between us, each waiting for the other to speak. He turns his head, waving at the fans that are screaming his name. Finally, I decide to be the one to walk away. “Um, well…I need to go.”

I barely take a few steps when Trey says, “Wait.” I turn expectantly, dying of curiosity.

He comes closer and says, “You, me, it was great, but it’s done.”

I instantly blanch from the choice of his words. Why would he be telling me this? Why now?

“I know that,” I respond defensively.

He shakes his head, “I’m not sure you do,” he disagrees.

“Trey, I have to go. Just get to the point.”

“I overheard Leila on the phone with you.”

Fuck. Fuck. Fuck!

“Leila is always on the phone with me. Can you specify?”

“I’m not it for you. Move on.”

What an arrogant prick.

I keep my face as stoic as possible, considering my insides are quaking and my legs are having a hard time holding me up. “Well, no worries. I have moved on. It was great and I had a blast, but I know Matt is it for me.”

“Good. I want you to be happy.” He strokes my cheek gently and stalks off without a backwards glance.

Well, fuck me. If that isn’t a sign I’ve made the right decision, I don’t know what is.

“What was that about?” Leila practically has to shout above the screams as she approaches with Jack. I violently gnaw on my bottom lip, debating whether I should tell her now or wait until we are alone. I want to move on and put all this behind me, so I decide to come clean.

“Um…he told me to move on.”

"Why would he tell you that?" she asks, confused.

"He heard one of our conversations."

Leila pales and looks like she's about to cry. "I'm so sorry, Lor. I didn't…"

"Ssh…don't worry about it. It's for the best. No more secrets. I want to move on. I decided that without Trey Fucking Taylor's help."

Jack watches our exchange silently and wraps an arm around her. She looks up at him, reminded he's standing next to her.

"Wait…I can finally know why you barged in on our anniversary morning?"

"Sure, Lair. Your wife will fill you in." Changing the subject, I touch her belly in awe. "Fuck, Lei, you're huge."

"She is not." Jack immediately comes to her defense.

"Oh, relax." I pull Leila into a huge hug and add, "When can I come over for dinner?"

"Anytime."

"Only if you bring dinner." Jack adds. "She needs to take it easy."

I roll my eyes, ignoring him, hugging her again. "I missed you so much. I'm glad you're home."

"Me, too. How are Lis and the baby? I can't wait to see them."

"She's great, and Michelle is absolutely adorable." I pull away and even offer a hug to Jack. "I missed you, too, Lair. Just don't mess with our 'girl' time. I will level you. We have a lot to make up for."

"Oh, God. I think it's time to move."

"You must be kidding, I'd find you." The third bus finally pulls up, evoking a huge grin to spread across my face. Leila and Jack follow my gaze. "Ok, I have to go find my rock star now. Bye, lovebirds." With purpose I walk to Matt's bus, impatient to see him and speak to him.

I position myself right in front of the door. When it opens, Matt stands before me, looking more beautiful than I remember. A small smile plays on his lips, his eyes are heated, and his hands are shoved into his pockets. Time suspends, and the noise behind us ceases as we each take in every detail of the other. His hair is a bit longer and he's tan, but otherwise, he's still my gorgeous Matt.

"Hey. What are you doing here? I thought we were meeting at your place tonight."

"I couldn't wait to see you. Do you have to stay or can we leave now?"

"Let me tell the guys that I'm going."

After a few minutes, he joins me again, taking my hand. "Where to?"

"My place."

♫ ♫ ♫

I put all my eggs into my "Matt will want to be with me" basket. Thank God above, it's playing out just as I need it to. I prepared his favorite meal, had his favorite beer, we had a nice dinner. He filled me in on all I missed without an attitude. He's been attentive and sweet, and now I'm quickly cleaning up as he relaxes on my couch. He even offered to help. Things were looking up.

When I move to sit next to him, he raises his arm around my shoulders and pulls me close to his body. He doesn't speak. I know that he knows I'm stalling. He wanted to have a conversation when we got here, but I held him off. I am stalling. I wanted his undivided attention. I wanted him fed and relaxed. I don't play fair.

After many long minutes of staring at some car race he's watching, I pick up the clicker and turn off the TV.

"It sure took you long enough."

"Ha ha." I twist on the couch to face him fully. He follows my lead and waits. "Ok, hear me out. Let me get it all out, ok?"

"I'm listening."

I pull in a huge breath and dive right in.

"Matt. What I went through these past few months, what I put us through, had nothing to do with Trey. Well, it did, but not in the way you think. I have no feelings for Trey. I swear. I don't want you to think it was the reason for my stupid behavior. Trey was just more of what I've always had my entire adult life. It was physical and hot and that's it. I've realized that, in itself, was my problem. I've only ever had physical relationships. All my past relationships have only been about sex. And that was fine. I *was* only about sex. I couldn't give a shit about the hearts and flowers. That's not who I was. I've never been in love…until you.

"I love you. I have loved you for years. I think I loved you even when you were a douche in high school." He tries to interrupt, but I barrel through.

"Everything was perfect in my life. I had my dream job. I had a hot as hell boyfriend who loved me. I had the best friends a girl could ask for. The only thing I was missing was the romance. When you aren't looking for something, you don't miss it. It's not something I searched for. I don't know why I suddenly woke up at the age of twenty-seven and decided that I want that. Maybe it's because I never had it. Maybe it's because I'm surrounded by it. My two best friends live it daily. So now, I want the same thing. I believe I deserve it.

"I'm high maintenance. You already know that. I need to be made to feel like I'm your entire universe. I need you to constantly make the effort to blow my mind. When we got together, my only focus was that I had to have you. I needed you. Once that happened, we settled in, we got comfortable, and we got boring.

"Do you know what did it for me? What made me realize you're it for me?" He shakes his head wordlessly. "This may sound shallow, but it was seeing you on stage flirting with those girls in the front row. That's what I need from you every day. I know it's in there. I know you can be very sweet and very loving…mostly, I know you can be cocky and a sexy tease. Knowing it's in there and knowing you only pull it out when you perform, kills me. I'm a selfish person. I want that from you all the time.

"I know what you're thinking. What about me? I didn't really make any efforts either. You pointed that out and I thought about that a lot. You're right, I didn't and I will. I will remember to bring the spark. It's the least I can do when I'm complaining we don't have any sparks between us. I failed on my end, and I'm sorry."

I stop for a second as he processes my words. "Are you done?"

"No, one more thing." I pull in a huge breath, steeling myself for possible rejection. This is it. This is the million-dollar question. This is where he can walk out and never come back, because this is a deal breaker for me. If he doesn't feel the same, I cannot be in this relationship. I want it all, the golden ticket, the brass ring, and the forever after.

"Matt, I want to spend the rest of my life with you. I want the wedding, I want the babies, I want the dog, the white picket fence, the Kitchen Aid mixer, the Volvo, the fairy tale…all of it."

His hazel eyes bore holes right through me to my soul. Except for his breathing, he doesn't move otherwise…and neither do I.

"What the fuck is a Kitchen Aid mixer?"

I laugh out loud and he joins me before taking my hands in his. "Lori, you are a royal pain in my ass. You are definitely high maintenance. You are pushy, and selfish, and a bitch when you don't get your way. You're also sexy as fuck, and smart as a whip, and beautiful, and stunning, and gorgeous, and the love of my life. If it's romance you want, fine. I'll do whatever you want, but I'm not driving a Volvo."

"Suburu?"

"Fuck no." He pulls me into his arms, kissing my head as I cling to him for life. "I'm not going anywhere."

"Really?"

"Really." When I look into his eyes, he nods with pure conviction. "I'm not ever going anywhere." Never breaking eye contact, he sinks his hands into my hair, holding my head hostage to his beautiful gaze and adds, "Unless you pull this shit again. I will not go through this again. You tortured me these past few months. It's not fair to me, and I'll walk the next time it happens. Ok?"

"Yes." We are face to face, and my lips desperately want to touch his. I pull forward, trying to reach him, but his hold is unyielding.

He waits a few seconds, and then says, "I love you."

Only then does he bring my lips to his. The first touch is soft, barely a kiss. He moves his lips over mine in an excruciatingly slow tempo. With each contact our kiss becomes more passionate, more heated, until we both completely loose ourselves.

He stands, wordlessly pulls me into my bedroom, and spends the next several hours blowing my mind.

# Chapter 18 – Leila

I'm proud of Trey. I'm proud for two reasons. He must have heard my conversation with Lori weeks ago. He never mentioned it. He probably knows how upset I would be. He's seen my emotions first hand. The fact he kept it to himself is commendable. I understand men are different than women and we would be singing like canaries. I still feel it was a sensitive gesture on his part, even if unintentional.

I'm also proud of him for telling Lori to move on. I could tell her until I'm blue in the face, but hearing it from him probably did the trick. She had worked it out with herself and came to the conclusion on her own. I know my friend well, she'll forever wonder if she made the right choice. Trey's poignant advice will give her the closure she needs. Once she closes a book, she'll never revisit it. Trey just firmly closed her book.

After we pulled up to *The Garden*, we quickly convened in the arena, had a quick pow-wow about tomorrow night's show, and then all took off for different reasons. The guys practically sprinted to their girls, and Jack practically dragged me to our apartment. The quick ride was spent recapping Lori's issues. Now that Jack is up to speed, he wholeheartedly agrees she made the right decision, and she most definitely should be with Matt.

"Home sweet home," I say the minute my feet hit our apartment. We are finally home and I'm wiped out. Our closing show isn't until tomorrow night. I plan on passing out until the morning. It's only seven p.m., but I'm exhausted. Jack follows behind me with our bags.

"Hungry?"

"Not really, more so sleepy."

He wraps his arms around me and I burrow my nose in his t-shirt.

He smells so good. He feels so good.

Maybe sleep after sex.

My belly makes it difficult to mold my body into his, so I resort to driving him crazy with my lips. I lift up on my toes to kiss his neck, then his chin, and then the corner of his mouth.

"What are you doing?"

"Nothing." Another kiss below his ear, and my jig is up.

"Babe."

"What?"

"Tomorrow. You're tired and we have a show tomorrow night. You need sleep."

Continuing on my mission, I move my lips across his stubbled chin to the opposite corner of his mouth and back up to his ear.

"Lei."

"Please?" I pull his lobe in between my lips, and he moans. "I'll make it quick." I whisper directly into his ear.

In lightening speed he scoops me up and carries me to our bedroom. When he sees me smiling wide, he says, "You're in big trouble."

"Ooh, punish me?"

He crashes his lips against mine as he lowers us both onto the bed. I love our bed. It's big, soft, and squishy, and having Jack in my bed is a female wet dream. I dig my fingers into his hair, more so to prevent him from stopping his assault on my tongue. He sucks forcibly, driving me insane in the process. I pull away first to take a quick breath. It confounds me how he never has to do so. He can go forever without taking a breath. As I pant pathetically, he moves on.

Piece by piece he removes my clothes until I am completely naked and squirming with desire. I wanted a quickie. I should know by now that there isn't such a thing with Mr. Jack Lair. Well, that is unless we are in a storage closet or a private room in a crowded club.

He uses two hands to hold my breast while he lavishes it with his tongue. I can't contain myself any longer, desperately tugging on his hands to get his attention. He looks up amused. "Yes?"

"Please. I'm very close and I can't guarantee I won't pass out once I'm done."

He contemplates my admission. Before granting my request he gently kisses my pregnant belly twice, once for each baby. Quickly, he removes his clothes and positions himself between my legs. "Ready, Baby?" He skims his fingers through my folds.

I nod and press my fingers into his flesh to get him to move faster. He gives me a crotch-clenching smile and sinks in slowly. I am so worked up at this point, that it's only a few seconds later when I tighten around him. He controls his movement the way he knows I need it, deep and fast and hard…my method of choice when I'm at the point of no return. He knows me so well. Our eyes connect and through my release he strokes my hair, runs the pad of his thumb over my bottom lip, and watches in awe as I come undone.

A small smile plays on his lips when I relax beneath him. It's now my turn to watch his stormy grey eyes darken further and feel his fingers tightening in my hair. He uses one hand to hold his weight, careful not to press on my belly. I do miss feeling the length of him when making love. Most of the time, he now has me on top to avoid hurting me.

"Baby," he breathes out in a rush. He takes his time, prolonging his pinnacle by kissing me deeply.

"Mmm. Thank you."

“You’re welcome,” he responds before giving me a chaste kiss. When he withdraws, I immediately feel the loss and crave him again. He wraps me in his arms, running patterns up and down my back. “It’s really good to be home. I missed this place.”

“Me, too. I love our place.” I sit up suddenly when a thought occurs to me. “Jack, we’re going to have to move.”

“Why?”

“We’re having two.”

“So, we have a spare room. They can share for a few years.”

I hadn’t thought about that yet. Have two babies in this apartment? Granted it is more spacious than most NYC apartments, but it isn’t roomy by any means. We can definitely fit two cribs in the spare room, but it’ll be tight.

“Babe, we don’t have to worry about this now. We knew we needed to move sooner or later. So it may be sooner.”

“But, I love this place.”

“So do I, but it’s just a place, and I love my family more.”

“Aww, that is one of the sweetest things you’ve ever said.”

“It’s true. Now go to sleep. You’re exhausted and I can see your brain working overtime right now.”

He kisses me softly before I nestle against his side to get comfortable. Once I’m relaxed, the twins decide it’s playtime. Jack’s hand takes up shop on my stomach, and he chuckles every time he feels a nudge. I’m so exhausted I drift into a deep sleep, in spite of the play date they are having in my womb.

♬ ♬ ♬

Closing night, tour two at *The Garden*. I'll never get used to this…ever. Our faces on the marquee out front, our posters lining the walls in the main concourse…I just can't process any of it in my head. I sometimes feel I'm hovering above, watching our success from a far. I'm still me. I'm still the ambitious, back-up singer from Hoboken, N.J. I'll never get used to the fame, the recognition, or the success. Jack agrees with my assessment. Even when our faces land on the cover of a magazine, or a quick blurb is featured on the evening news, it seems like they are talking about someone else.

Our last tour gave us a taste of Internet gossip, but that's just what it was, for the most part contained on the Internet. This time around, it's exploded outside the confines of someone's laptop. The relentless paparazzi, especially when we are back in New York, have memorized the places we frequent. The entertainment shows, that have an obvious obsession with my husband, will announce everything we do, short of taking a crap.

My dad tracks it all, every single thing. His Google alerts are set to hourly. He unwinds at the end of each day by catching up on all the news about his daughter. I've lectured him repeatedly, warning him that most of it wasn't true. He doesn't care and refuses to stop reading them.

I am impressed how he has managed my fame. The only times I know a story has gotten to him is when he sends me a text with the link. Thankfully, they are few and far between, but I usually have to do some damage control and heavy convincing when they do come. As good as he is at weeding out the trash, there are always those stories that just seem too real to ignore. I now understand the importance of ignoring them. It consumes way too much of my time stewing over an article that is blatantly filled with lies.

I had a brief memory lapse after we got married. I made the mistake of setting a Google alert on Jack, not because I didn't trust him…that was never an issue. I wanted to know what was being said. I would complain to Jen whenever something hurtful or insulting was thrown out in gossip-land. She would explain, as if I was a child, that unless it's slanderous information, all gossip was good gossip. Easy for her to say, it wasn't her frowning face on a cover, caught for all of eternity in the most unflattering of ways, claiming my husband was cheating on me, once again. I could have been frowning because I stubbed my toe, but according to the gossip world, I'd had my heart ripped from my chest by my philandering husband.

Jack sat me down and reminded me of the chat we had when the Jessa nonsense was constantly hitting me in the face. After that, I pulled back, ignoring all that was printed, and I've been much happier.

My former bandmates are still fairly safe from evils of success. They are able to live their lives with little to no disruption. The only times they are witnesses to the chaos is when they are with Devil's Lair. I wish I had mentors when we were starting out. They are learning through us. Mind you, they didn't have to deal with major scandals while at the same time trying to make a name for themselves. They play their music and let the powers that be, within the music industry, carry them. It's happening slowly and naturally, the way it should. It's not the onslaught of scary hyperbole crap that we were enduring. We would have reached the same levels without the crap, but perhaps not as quickly as we did. That reality causes a contradiction within me. The worst moment of my life is forever linked to the best.

I quickly glance at the clock and hurry to finish getting ready. I want to be out front from the minute Cliffhangers touch the stage. I've seen them perform tons of times, but this is closing night of their debut tour on their home turf. I don't want to miss one thing. I sent Jack out to secure a spot with the best view. One quick glance in the mirror, and I rush back to the stage.

The arena is buzzing with noise. The house lights are all on. I can see the glow, even from where I'm walking down the darkened halls of the backstage area. As soon as I approach Jack turns, his smile instantly lighting up his face. He is so in tune to me and me to him.

"Hey, Babe. Is this good?"

"Yes, this is perfect. Thank you." I turn to peek out at the masses. The memories of our first closing night flood my mind. I was so nervous, more than I had ever been. I know they are all very nervous, even though they try to play it cool. I haven't seen them since rehearsal. I don't want to add to their anxiety.

Jack takes my hand and squeezes. "You excited for your boys?"

"So much. They deserve this."

Hunter, Trey, and Scott join us in our viewing area. The girls are all in the first two rows, wanting to see the show from the seats.

"The minute this is over, we are partying!" Hunter announces. He looks over at me and adds, "Not you."

I stick out my tongue at him. "I have a neurotic babysitter, I don't need another." His response is to kiss my cheek. He's in a much happier mood. His precious drum set has been cleaned and delivered, and he will be reuniting with them tonight. This gave Trey the green light to commence the ball busting.

Hunter plans on proposing to Mandi in the next few weeks. He has only confided that info to Jack and me, and I am so happy for him. Except for Trey, we will all be happily married by our next tour. I wonder how that will change the dynamics of our relationships. Will marriage alter Hunter's personality? He's a different person when he's around Mandi. Jack told me Hunter is typically shy out in the real world. He feels his connection to Mandi is for that exact reason. They are two peas in a pod. I told him he's delusional. Hunter is the opposite of shy, but I wasn't around when he was single. Jack says being with Mandi has made him much more confident, more comfortable in his own skin. This also doesn't make sense to me. Hunter is a very attractive man. I've seen girls fawning over him repeatedly. I find it hard to believe he's insecure.

I sometimes wish I met this crew sooner, when they were young and unattached, just to see what they were all like. Things do happen for a reason, and I may have been completely turned off and wanted nothing to do with them.

Ha ha, that's hilarious. Who am I kidding?

The house lights dim and *The Garden* explodes in applause. I watch as the guys trot up the stairs, one by one, onto the stage. I can see their grins, even in the dark. They are ecstatic, and I want them to enjoy every single minute of this night.

Matt's voice announces their arrival, even before the stage lights turn on. He does this at every show. He likes to rile up the crowd before they have the chance to see them. By the time the lights do come on, Matt has worked them up into a frenzy with his flirting and charming self.

Their set flows flawlessly. They move from song to song without a hitch. Their repertoire is filled with hot, compelling songs that immediately pull you in. I've sang most of these songs with them for years, but that doesn't stop me from completely fan-girling over them, like one of our Devil's Lair groupies. The rest of my band is now familiar with their songs as well, mouthing the words along with Matt.

Evan has a solo during the show, and the response he gets is off the charts. Their fans have dubbed Evan their poster boy, Matt is their bad boy, Logan is the serious one, and Joe is their teddy bear. He isn't happy with that persona and grumps about being sabotaged.

I recognize their second to last song, which is my cue to go pee. "I'll be back." I shout into Jack's ear. He nods and follows.

Once we get further down the hall, I tout, "Jack, I'm fine."

"Maybe I have to pee, too," he responds defensively, which I know damn well is a lie. Using the music as my time clock, I'm back in position with Jack at my side minutes later in preparation of our introduction.

Cliffhangers take their final bow and the stage goes dark. Our single with them is the last song of their set, and the first of ours. Matt addresses the crowd while the lights are still out. Once my husband's voice rings through the mic, pandemonium hits *The Garden.*

"NEW YORK CITY, we missed you!" he shouts out, trying to compete with the noise levels. "How awesome were Cliffhangers?" The crowd enthusiastically agrees. Matt and Jack tag team them with flirty comments and sexual innuendos. They have mastered their teasing and the fans love this part of our shows. It's about ten minutes later before we actually sing our single together. Matt, Nina, Jack, and I are all performing front and center while the guys are behind us dueling and meshing their portions flawlessly. It's the perfect ending to a perfect tour.

Once our song is over, Cliffhangers swap places with us, assuming their spots side stage to now watch our show. We switched up our playlist, making it a best of Devil's Lair, including Jack's song *Reason I Am*, and my single *Constant Torment.* We also throw in *Dream On*, as it's very sentimental to Jack and me. That song changed my life, and it will forever be tied to my success. I remember our opening show when he had me perform that song and how green I was to this entire lifestyle. How nervous I was with both starting my career and starting my relationship. It seems like I've been doing this for years now, when that night was a mere two years ago. That's not a long time at all, and yet, so much has happened during it. Song by song we get closer to closing this chapter and closer to beginning our next one.

Jack calls Cliffhangers back up on stage to share in our encore. We chose a brand new song of theirs and a brand new one of ours to end the tour with. We're giving the fans a sneak peak of what's to come, and from the reaction of the crowd, they love them.

"New York City, we are so proud to call you our home. Thank you so much for coming out tonight. We'll be back soon, we promise! Next time you see me, I'll be someone's dad. That's a fucking scary thought!"

He rubs my belly for all to see. My cheeks heat with embarrassment, but at the same time I find it so sexy. More than half this arena probably wants this beautiful man standing beside me…and he's all mine.

Jack takes my hand as we give our final bow. We haven't even left the stage when he asks, "How are you feeling?"

"Fantastic!"

"Are you tired? We can go home."

I roll my eyes in a very exaggerating manner. "I. Am. Not. Going. Home."

"Ok, we'll stay for a little while. First thing you are going to do is eat something and sit down. You've been standing for hours."

"Yes, Daddy." I've learned that it's so much easier to just agree and distract him later.

He swats at my ass as we all make our way to the party room. Hunter bitched he wanted our bash to be in a cool place, and not in the dull backstage area of *The Garden*. But Jack insisted we stay here to avoid the chaos. I knew his real motive. He didn't want me shuffling around the city after an exhausting night. He denied it of course, but I called bullshit.

He sets me up on one of the couches with food and water before he works the room. Our parents were at the show, but chose not to join us at the after party, claiming it was no place for old geezers like them. I decide to mingle a bit, but end up right back on the couch soon after with an aching back and throbbing feet. I don't mind, as I have a great vantage point of the room and am able to watch all the activity. It's better than watching TV.

Everyone that we know is here. Matt and Lori attached at the hip all night. They look like they did when they started dating. Trey has a blonde on his arm. I've been watching Lori. Not once has she looked over at him. That is definitely a great sign. Logan took off right after the show to be with his wife and baby. Jen and Malcolm are also here, but haven't been their annoying selves. Jen's been uncharacteristically quiet and Malcolm's been drinking like a fish at the bar.

One by one my friends feel the need to check on me, I'm sure either from guilt or Jack's insistence. Evan takes a seat next to me and smiles.

"It's your turn?"

"What's my turn?"

"To babysit the preggo." He laughs, but doesn't confirm nor deny my accusation. "I am so proud of you guys. You're naturals out there."

"I don't know if I'd go that far, but it has been quite a blast." He glances down at my belly before asking, "How ya' feelin'?"

I haven't yet told Evan we are having twins. We plan on telling our families, once we get home. I avoid his gaze, feeling guilty I'm hiding such huge news.

"I feel good. I'm tired, but if you tell my over-bearing husband, I'll deny it."

He laughs at my comment. "He's pretty overprotective. Lei, I never told you this, but he's a good man. I'm so glad you found each other. He obviously adores you, and I pegged him totally wrong in the beginning."

"Thanks, Ev. Circumstances did paint him in a pretty ugly picture, but he has such a good heart. I knew. I saw it."

"Well, Sis, you were right. It's the stock he comes from. His sister is an angel. I can't believe I've gotten so lucky." He stares at her from across the room. Evan always gets this glaze over his eyes whenever he speaks of, or thinks of, Lizzy. We both watch as she chats and laughs with Jack, the similarities between them leave no doubt they are related.

"I'd say we both got lucky. So hurry up and marry that woman so you can give me a niece or nephew. It's the least you can do."

"I'll keep that in mind."

We watch as Joe leaves the room. Less than a minute later, Nina leaves as well. Evan and I exchange a look. "Was that as obvious as I think it was?" I ask out loud.

"Um…yeah, it was."

Jack and Lizzy join us on the couches. Evan moves to the one adjacent to sit with his girl. "What are you guys up to? You look guilty," she asks suspiciously.

"It's Leila. She's speculating."

"Nah, not my wife. She doesn't speculate." I pinch his side, and he openly laughs at me.

"So, when is the big day, Liz?"

"Well…funny you should mention that. We want it to be one month from now."

"One month?" I gauge my brother's face and he smiles. "Why so quick? Are you hiding something?"

"See, no speculation at all," Jack quips, and he gets an elbow this time.

"No, we aren't hiding something. We just want to be married. It's a very small wedding. Neither of us wants a big to do." She looks up at Evan and adds, "We'd like you two to be our Best Man and Matron of Honor."

"Ugh…Matron?"

"Well, you're married," Liz laughs at my aversion to the word.

"The Matron who is going to be waddling down the aisle?"

She shrugs and smiles. "Sorry."

"No worries. I'd waddle for you two any day."

"You can wear anything you want."

"A muumuu?" She laughs, even though I'm dead serious. "Do Dad and Barb know?"

Evan nods, "Yes, they do. They're very happy for us."

"The only reason we aren't eloping is because Mom threw a fit," Lizzy admits. "We suspected she would. So the compromise was small and quick. She's been handling everything. We will get married at the house. There are a total of fifty guests. Just the way we want it."

"Did you get your dress yet?"

Liz smiles, "Yes. I love it. It's so me. We're all set. Really, we were just waiting for you all to return. We figured we'd give everyone a month to settle in. Ev isn't due in the studio until October. It will give us just enough time to get married and have our honeymoon."

"I'm thrilled for you guys. I was just telling my brother to hurry up so you can give this little one a cousin."

Liz and Evan exchange a loving glance, and he bends to kiss her sweetly.

Joe sneaks back into the party. "Ev," I motion with my head. He turns to see Joe heading for the bar, looking very disheveled. Sure enough, a minute later Nina returns looking even worse.

"What?" Jack asks.

"They left at the same time, and now they come back at the same time?" I whisper loud enough for just the four of us to hear. "Something is up."

"You're speculating again," he teases.

"I'm right about this. Mark my words."

While Jack chats with Evan about the tour my eyes follow Joe and Nina. They do look adorable together. She's tiny, blonde, and has the female version of Joe's sense of humor. She had a boyfriend when she signed on with the band. She ended it right before leaving on tour. If these two have been hooking up, they sure did a great job keeping it discreet.

"Ev, did you notice anything between them on the bus?"

"Nope," he turns back to Jack and continues their conversation.

"Ev."

"What?"

"Leila," Jack interrupts. "Let them be."

"I am," I pout. "I just think it's a perfect match, and I'd be really happy for Joe if this was happening."

"If it is, we'll find out when they are ready to tell us."

"Fine." I lean into his side and a huge yawn escapes from my betraying mouth. I wish I could crawl onto his lap and pass out.

"Ok, time to go," Jack says annoyingly. "We have to be at the studio very early tomorrow." I choose not to argue this one and save it for the next time. I predict many more battles to fight over the next four and a half months.

## Chapter 19 – Jack

Jen was serious when she said we would be meeting with the writer from *Rolling Stone* immediately upon our return. She wants us all in the studio today, nine a.m., no excuses. When I was filling the guys in last night on this new development, they grumbled a little, but, for the most part, they kept their gripes to themselves. Trey was the only one to voice his opinion and said it would be easier to stay up all night than to have to try to get up at such an ungodly hour. Whatever, as long as his ass is there I couldn't give a shit.

This is huge. Bigger than the article they ran on us last year. If these mini-biographies are well received, it could lead to a book deal with a traditional publisher. Jen pointed out, in these exact words, "Do *not* fuck this up."

Jen has been working around the clock on her cash cow. She delegated her other accounts to her assistant and is exclusively handling Devil's Lair practically twenty-four seven. Malcolm, her sleazy agent husband, is still handling Leila's career and is still pushy as ever. My wife has made it very clear to him that her career is exactly where she wants it to be. Her solo success will be treated as a secondary goal. Last year her single exploded, climbed the charts, and caught up with ours. Malcolm keeps insisting she needs to record an album and tour to properly promote it. She is simply not interested and it's killing him. Another agent would have moved on by now, but he knows the gem he has with Leila as his client. He also thinks he can charm her into doing what he wants. He apparently doesn't know my wife very well.

Leila has never been a huge Malcolm fan. She was almost forced to deal with him. I've told her she can choose a new agent and be done with him.

She knows another agent wouldn't stand for her fickleness, and she enjoys tormenting him.

God, I love her.

Malcolm reached out to me to try to persuade her. I made it very clear I want whatever she wants, and I will not push her into something she isn't comfortable with, just to appease him. That being said, I did have many conversations with her regarding her career. I've tried to encourage her to follow his advice, only because I don't want her to ever have any regrets. I assured her that nothing would change with us, because I simply wouldn't allow it. If I needed to put DL on a short hiatus to accommodate her, I would in a heart beat. She will not have it and says she isn't interested at this moment. If it is to occur, it will be on her terms when she is ready. Now that she is pregnant, there is absolutely no way she would change her mind. If anything, it just delayed Malcolm and his ambitions even more.

Surprisingly, Jen hasn't gotten involved with Leila and Malcolm's relationship. She never brings it up, and she never tries to persuade Leila in her husband's favor. I suspect something is up with them and voiced my suspicion to Leila.

Leila comes into the bathroom, sleepy and grumpy, just as I begin shaving. "Hey, Babe. Tired?"

"No."

I chuckle at her frowning, angry face. She slips her arms around me and lays her cheek against my bare back. After a few minutes, I feel her weight against me, almost as if she fell asleep standing up.

"Babe?"

"Mmm?"

"Wake up."

"I am awake," she stubbornly admits, but makes no attempt to move. I allow her to continue her nap against me until I finish with my shave. Once done, I turn to face her and wrap her in my arms. Her heavy breathing continues, undisrupted.

She is stunning, even standing here with nothing but my t-shirt and panties on. I skim my hands down her back, slipping them under the t-shirt and into her panties. I can feel her grin against my chest, but she doesn't move otherwise. A squeeze of her ass elicits a sexy moan.

"Don't start something you can't finish," she says into my chest. When she raises her head, she's smiling, but her eyes remain closed. I can't resist tasting her lips. Once my lips touch hers, she pulls away. "Ugh. I haven't brushed my teeth, yet."

"Don't care," I ignore and continue nibbling on her while still gripping her ass. "Get in the shower or things are gonna get ugly." A quick pat and I leave her standing in the bathroom. If I stay, we will never get out of here. I need to be the responsible one, as stupid as that sounds, and get us to the studio on time. I let her sleep later than she should have and we are dangerously close to being late.

With great effort on my part, Oscar has us at the studio five minutes early. I deserve a freaking medal. Leaving nothing to chance, I had Alec and Ryan picking up the rest of my band to ensure they were on time. When Leila and I walk into the conference room, their scowls tell me they aren't happy they beat us there.

"How is everyone today?"

"Fuck off," Hunter responds, and I blatantly laugh as he glares at me.

Jen walks in followed by a stunning blonde. They could actually be sisters with similar straight blonde hair. The difference lies in the way this woman smiles warmly, emitting a very approachable aura about her. In comparison, she makes Jen look angry, even though that's Jen's normal face.

"Well, you are all on time. I'm proud of you boys," Jen attempts a compliment.

"It's practically the middle of the night. It's a good thing you had coffee and donuts waiting," Hunter responds, not caring there is a stranger among us.

The blonde giggles at Hunter and says, "I'm sorry. It's kinda my fault you are all here so early today. I'm leaving town for a few weeks, and I needed to schedule our sessions before my flight. I know you guys had a really late night. I was at the show and it was phenomenal. I'm Tara Rodston, and I'll be writing your biography pieces."

She offers her hand to Hunter, and he shakes it slowly. One by one she shakes each of our hands, calling us by name. She congratulates Leila and me, asking when she is due. She also compliments Leila on her single and admits she can't wait to hear more from her. She congratulates Scott on his engagement. How the hell does she know that? He proposed yesterday the minute he reunited with Patti. Maybe Jen told her? Patti was flaunting that ring at the after party like it was the Hope Diamond.

Her last introduction is with Trey. Trey removes, not lifts, but removes his shades. He then gives her one of his rare smiles while assessing her from head to toe.

"Mr. Trey Taylor. It's an honor to meet you, I'm a huge fan."

"That's a coincidence, so am I."

She smiles in return, her big brown eyes never leaving his pale blue ones.

We all sit and watch this unfold, stunned into silence. Trey and Tara's hands remain clasped in the longest handshake I have ever seen. Jen clears her throat in a pathetic attempt to move on.

Trey stands and pulls a chair out for Tara, leaving Jen standing awkwardly. "Thank you very much," she says, still smiling.

"My pleasure." He lays his shades on the table, watching Tara instead of Jen.

Hunter and I lock amused gazes, trying desperately not to laugh. This is classic. Has Trey been abducted by aliens since last night? This man is not Trey Taylor.

Leila sits beside me, smiling wide. I can see the wheels in motion in her head. I take her hand below the table and she gives me a sideways glance. A subtle squeeze tells her to not get involved. Their relationship is very comfortable now, and Leila desperately wants Trey to find love. I personally don't think it will ever happen. She scoffs at my opinion, claiming he is looking and hasn't found it yet. My wife is ever the hopeless romantic.

"So, Tara will be setting up appointments with each of you. Each feature biography will span an issue, ending with a recap and the history of Devil's Lair as the last feature. Jack and Leila will be the first interviewed, and then the rest of you following. Tara, you can fill them in on how the sessions will run."

Tara smiles at Jen, then turns to us. "Using Jack and Leila as an example, I will meet with them initially, just to have an open chat session, more so to get to know them. The second meeting will be to create an outline of what we all want covered in the feature and a list of questions I will be asking. The third will be the actual interview. The final will be a review of the written feature for approval. I'd like to span the four sessions over a two week period, leaving me two weeks for editing and publication." She makes eye contact with each of us during her run-down and ends with her eyes pinned on Trey.

"Sounds great. When do we start?" I ask, and a few seconds pass before she actually makes eye contact with me.

"I'd like to start as soon as I return."

"Where are you going?" Trey asks, and all eyes focus on his face. He ignores us all and instead focuses on Tara.

"I'm going to London for two weeks for an exclusive interview."

"Who?"

"If I tell you, I'd have to kill you," she smiles.

"Sounds intriguing," he responds without smiling, "I love a challenge."

Holy shit, what's happening here?

"Um, ok, anyone have any other questions for Tara?" Jen asks.

We all shake our heads, except for Trey.

"Ok, then we'll touch base when Tara returns." Jen gathers her things and walks to the door. "Tara?"

"Yes?"

"Do you need a lift back to the office?"

"No, I'm fine. I have a cab picking me up. I'm heading directly to the airport."

Jen nods and walks out without a goodbye.

"Ready, Babe?"

Leila nods with a small smile playing on her face. Hunter and Scott are watching Trey, dumbstruck. I'm the first to stand. "Tara, it was really nice meeting you. We look forward to working with you."

"Thank you, same here."

Leila offers her hand and adds, "Have a safe trip."

"Thank you."

Hunter and Scott also say their goodbyes. Trey remains seated, and so does Tara.

♫ ♫ ♫

"Did you see the way they were looking at each other?" Leila brings it up, yet again. Oscar is taking us to her sonogram appointment. I've been nervous all morning, yet my wife has been distracted. I'm actually thankful for the distraction, because I want her calm for this appointment.

For the past few days all she's been talking about is Trey. When we left the studio, she relentlessly yapped and yapped about the look in his eyes. I reminded her that what Trey saw was a hot, conservative woman, who was also a challenge or conquest. She disagreed, claiming I had no idea what I was talking about.

She asked Trey the very next day. He smiled and said she was losing her mind. With every question Leila asked, Trey threw her a one-liner, and my wife became more and more agitated. He finally gave her a hug and said even though she was a loon he still "heavily liked" her.

"But he couldn't stop looking at her."

"Yes, Leila, I know…but please don't get your hopes up. When Trey sets his sights on a hot chick, he is relentless until he gets her." She looks out her window, basically ignoring what I said.

"You also think she's hot?"

Um…

"Not as hot as you."

She quirks her mouth at my response, "Good answer."

"Seriously, Babe, I don't want you to get disappointed. I can predict that Trey will chase her and then he'll be done."

She meets my gaze and nods, "Ok. I won't get my hopes up."

"Good. Are you ready to see our babies?" I squeeze her hand and she smiles.

"Very."

The ride to her OB-GYN is short. When we are situated in the exam room, my nerves once again kick in. I'm much more comfortable with the environment, having been to several appointments with her already. But the anxiety of wanting to be sure that my children are ok is causing a queasiness to settle in the pit of my stomach.

Dr. Rand enters the room and smiles warmly at Leila. "Welcome back. How are we feeling?"

"Good, really good."

"Glad to hear. Your guest doctors have all kept me very informed. Your pressure is a bit elevated, but nothing to be concerned about, yet. We'll keep an eye on it." He reads her chart over and adds, "Congratulations are in order."

"Thank you," she responds while looking up at me. "It was a bit of a shock."

"It usually is. Let's take a look at the munchkins, shall we?" He starts prepping Leila's belly with the gel. "Tired?"

"Not very," she responds, blatantly avoiding my gaze.

Dr. Rand looks at my lying wife and nods. "That's great. Second trimester is usually when women feel at their best."

She smirks at me as if to say, "I told you so," and I roll my eyes in return.

Dr. Rand moves the hand-held device across Leila's swollen belly, and instantly there are two grainy images of two tiny babies on the screen.

Leila gasps when her eyes land on the monitor. One is facing us while the other is turned facing its twin. I'm completely mesmerized. She looks back at me, tears threatening. "Babe."

I can barely speak. I wasn't prepared to see actual babies. I assumed we would see more unrecognizable shapes. I also wasn't prepared for the onslaught of emotion I'm currently feeling. I expected anxiety and fear, but the swell of love that engulfs me is instantaneous.

"Everything looks great. They're breech, but there's plenty of time for them to turn," he says as he continues to move over her bump and type simultaneously. I squeeze my wife's hand because I simply can't form words at the moment.

Those are my babies, my kids. I have fucking kids.

There are four hands, four feet, one of them is a tiny bit bigger than the other, and they look perfect.

"Do you see this one sucking a thumb?" Dr. Rand points to the monitor and sure enough, a tiny hand is shoved into a tiny mouth.

"Look, Jack," she says in awe.

I am looking. I can't believe this. That little baby is in there right now doing something as normal as sucking a thumb? This is fucking insane.

"Do we want to know their sex?"

"You can tell?"

He nods slowly. "Yes, I can tell one of them very obviously. The other is hiding, but sometimes if we turn the mother on her side, they will also move and cooperate."

Leila and I exchange confused looks. "Do you, Babe?"

"Do you?" she repeats.

"I'll give you guys a minute to discuss." Dr. Rand leaves us, closing the door on his way out.

"I think I want to know," she says quietly. "I feel like they want us to get to know them."

"Ok, whatever you want." I pull in a deep breath, "Let's meet our kids."

When Dr. Rand returns, he finds us in a mini make-out session. "Do you need more time?" he asks, very amused.

"No, we're good," I respond as my wife turns beet red. "We'd like to know."

"Ok, here we go." He resumes his task, and the suspense is fucking killing me. It must be killing Leila also, as her grip becomes death-like on my hand. "Well," he points to the bigger baby and says, "this one here is a boy."

"Jack," Leila breathes out in a whisper.

"I knew it." I look down at her for a split second, not wanting to miss one thing on the screen. "I told you so."

"Yes, you did, Babe."

"The little one is a bit shy. Let's see if we can get him or her to cooperate." He removes the hand-held and says, "Leila, move to your right side." Leila rolls to her right, taking my hand with her, bringing me even closer to the monitor. "Ok, let's see what we got here."

He moves the device and types, and moves it again and types. Minutes pass and he finally says, "Well, well. It looks like you are also having a girl."

Leila bursts into tears. I do my damnedest to hold back mine. "Babe, Madden and Siarra."

She nods, unable to speak.

"Congratulations." He pushes a few buttons and a few images release from the printer. He then inserts a CD and pushes some more. After a few minutes, he hands me the pictures and Leila the CD. "Your first home movie."

"Is everything ok?"

“Yes, all looks great.”

I reach out, offering my hand. “Thank you so much, Dr. Rand.”

“You’re very welcome.” He pats Leila on her leg and says, “See you next month.”

I bend to kiss her gently, and then again. Skimming her tears away with my thumbs. She clings to me, her arms circling my chest, her fingers gripping the shirt on my back.

“Jack.” She utters into my chest, still struggling with her words.

“I know, Baby. I know.”

## Chapter 20 – Leila

The waterworks haven't stopped since my sonogram appointment. I'm completely out of control. I am so emotional, I spend more time crying than not. Jack has no idea what to do for me. He struggles with comforting me. He now understands that they are happy tears. I am so happy. I feel as if we met our children. We've been officially introduced and they are just as anxious to meet us in person as we are to meet them. The sonogram photos, their first official portraits, sit proudly in a frame in our room, as well as on our fridge. It's a constant reminder of the precious cargo I am carrying.

We have a lot to do. Parenthood is looming in our future and I feel like we suddenly need to cram for a final exam. We don't have much time. I have so much to prepare for and so much to learn. Alisa, Barb, and even Renatta, assure me most of it comes naturally. How can it? How can you suddenly come home from the hospital with a tiny person, dependent on you for everything, and just know what to do?

I slipped up and voiced my concern to Jack.

Big mistake…huge.

His neurosis is now on steroids. Besides the constant worrying about my safety, he's now constantly reading the bible regarding my pregnancy. Not in the same way he used to either. He would read along with the month I was in to be sure I was doing what I was supposed to. He has now taken to reading ahead to the chapters that detail after the baby arrives. He suggested purchasing a doll. After I calmed down from my laughing fit, he explained the pregnancy book suggested it to practice changing diapers. I felt bad for laughing. I think I fell in love with him even more that day.

Yesterday, I walked into our bedroom and caught my hot as fuck husband, naked in bed, researching the best strollers, car seats, and baby carriers one can buy.

Holy hell...it was the sexiest thing I've ever seen.

The visual pulled the beast out of hiding. My emotional state has curtailed my raging libido for the past few days. He didn't know what hit him when the laptop went sailing across the bed and I straddled him without an invitation. Afterwards, I cried because I'm a mother-to-be and I shouldn't be acting like that. Jack looked at me dumbstruck, like I've just announced a sex change. I love being pregnant, but I can't wait to be myself again. I feel like a mental patient.

Today we are having our families over to share our news. I almost slipped a few times referring to the "babies" I was carrying and not the "baby." It will be a relief to finally have them all know.

Evan said Dad mentioned having some news of his own. Of course, we've been speculating on what it is. He and Barb still live in separate houses, but spend all their free time together. I predict they may be getting married. Evan says they'll just be moving in together. He's convinced his mom would never marry again.

I have to disagree with him. I've had several conversations with my dad. I think he worries how I will feel if they were to commit to each other. This is unchartered territory for him, for us. I don't ever remember him dating as I was growing up. When I got older, I'd encourage him to date, but he'd claim he was happy and wasn't interested. Little did I know all the platonic dates he had with Barb to diners, movies, and baseball games weren't so platonic. Dad finally came clean and said he and Barb have been seeing each other in the romantic sense for years, which is a contradiction to what he admitted to Evan. So my theory is dead on. Evan has no clue what he's talking about.

I'm so convinced they're getting married that I picked up a bottle of champagne for our dinner tonight. I'm actually making dinner for everyone. I've been feeling so useless and wanted to do something nice, instead of just ordering food in. Jack was about to object, but decided not to for fear of sending me into hysterics, again. Asking how he could help, I sent him out for some last minute ingredients to make him feel needed and to get him out of my way.

The door buzzer makes me jump, practically causing me to drop the brownie pan. Assuming it's Evan and Lizzy, I'm surprised to hear from the front desk that it's Lori and Matt. I unlock the door for them, surprised to see them.

"Hey, what's up?"

"Just saying hi. Busy?"

"Come in."

"Ooh, what smells so good?" Lori asks, pulling me into a hug. She pats my belly, yelling, "Hi, baby, Auntie Lori is here!"

"You don't have to shout."

"There's a lot of muck in there. I want to be sure she hears me."

"Hey, Matt, how are you?" I ask over her head.

He smiles at me and moves Lori aside to give me a hug. We sure have come a long way since the days of me hating him and him avoiding me. This Matt is not the same guy who cheated on me repeatedly and broke my heart twice. There was a time being in the same room with him was difficult. I no longer have any ill feelings toward him.

"How ya' feeling?" he asks while looking at my belly.

"Fat."

"I'm glad you brought it up, Lei. Damn, you're huge," Lori puts in her five cents before stealing a tomato from my salad.

"I can't wait 'til you're pregnant. I'm keeping notes."

"I'm going to be supermodel pregnant."

"What exactly is supermodel pregnant?"

She throws me a look and explains slowly, "When you only look pregnant from the side." She smiles wide and helps herself to a glass of wine and grabs a beer for Matt.

"So who's all this for?"

"Our parents, Evan and Liz. Do you want to stay? I have plenty."

"No, we have plans. We can hang out for a little bit, if that's ok."

"Of course."

Matt settles on the couch and Lori sits at the island watching me finish preparing the lasagna I'm making. Every few seconds, she steals an ingredient and pops it into her mouth.

"Hey, so I met with Jen yesterday. She wasn't wearing her wedding rings."

I look up in shock. "She wasn't?"

Lori shakes her head slowly. "Nope. I thought it was strange. She normally uses that rock as a flashing beacon."

It's true. It's huge and I've never seen it off her finger since the day Malcolm put it there. "Jack suspected something was up with them. I agreed she's been acting weird, or weirder for Jen. I haven't paid attention and try not to waste brain cells on either of them."

"If she isn't wearing it again the next time I meet with her, I'm asking." Lori announces determinedly.

Jack returns from his errands with his Mets hat pulled low over his eyes and his *Ray Bans* on. He takes one look at Lori and asks, "What do you want, Banzini?"

"Jeez, I'm starting to get paranoid that you don't like me."

"I don't," he responds with a mega-watt Lair smile.

"Oh, no. How will I sleep tonight knowing Jack Lair doesn't like me?"

"Smartass." He plants a peck on her cheek and notices Matt on the couch. "Hey, Matt."

They exchange handshakes and Jack carries the grocery bag into the kitchen. "Did you purposefully send me on a wild goose chase?"

"What are you talking about?" I feign innocence, removing his hat and glasses for him.

He pulls out the specific brand of chocolate that I absolutely had to have for my brownies from the bag and announces, "Three stores. I went to three stores before I found it." I turn my back to hide my face. "Yeah, I thought so," he calls me out. "You owe Ryan an apology." He sniffs the air and opens the oven door. "Wait…you already *made* the brownies?"

"I found some of the chocolate in the cabinet."

He shuts the door, half smirk half grimace on his face. "You are a very bad liar."

I wrap my arms around him, getting as close as I can. "Thank you, Babe. I truly appreciate you."

"Uh huh," he kisses the top of my head and adds, "you wanted me out of here so I couldn't see what you did and how hard you worked. I'm so on to you now."

Lori claps and says, "I'm impressed."

We fall into a fit of giggles as my sulking hubby grabs a beer and joins Matt on the couch. "You both suck," he mumbles.

"I'll pass, but she'll oblige later," Lori shoots back. She smiles wide at Matt and Jack and winks at me. She and Trey have the same exact sense of humor. It's scary.

Lori and Matt hang around long enough to see our parents and siblings. I try to convince them to have dinner with us, but they both decline. Since they are here, I'd like them to hear our news. It's the least I could do to make up for the fact Lori was kept in the dark regarding my pregnancy.

Jack and I are in the kitchen, finishing up preparing dinner when my father-in-law joins us.

"Hey, you two. I have some interesting news for you."

We both look up, curious as to what he needs to tell us. The look on Jack's face prompts him to add, "I..I think you'll be happy about it."

"What is it?"

"I received a phone call today from the prosecutor in Danny's trial. It seems…" he clears his throat and starts again, "apparently, he made a lot of enemies in prison. Someone killed him last night."

A shocking gasp escapes as Jack puts an arm around my shoulders, pulling me closer into his body.

"Are you serious?"

Peter nods, "Completely, Son. They found him stabbed to death in his cell."

I bury my face into Jack's chest, trying to hide my sobs. The relief that washes through me is the most forceful thing I've ever felt. Jack consoles me, shushing me and telling me it's over.

He got what he deserved. I'll never have to worry about Danny Sorenson hurting us ever again.

The rest of our guests notice my episode and all turn to Peter for an explanation. As he explains what he just said to us Jack holds me in his arms, rocking me back and forth, kissing my head, and rubbing my back.

Lori and Matt interrupt to tell us they are leaving. "Is it sick that I want to congratulate you on his death? I'm sorry, that sick fuck deserved everything he got." She says with no sympathy.

"I'm just glad it's over," Jack admits.

Once I calm down, I run my hands over my belly and release a breath through my pursed lips. "Ok, this is the last time I spend one iota of time thinking about him. It's time for happy thoughts." I wipe my tears, kiss my husband, and remove the sonogram picture out of the draw where I hid it earlier today. "Who wants to see Baby Lair?" I call out for all to hear.

The eight of them focus on the photo that I'm holding. "Bring that here right now!" Renatta commands.

Jack and I walk over to his mom and she snatches it before anyone else can. Her mouth drops open as she stares at the twins in awe. "Really?"

She passes the photo around the room, and one by one they mimic Renatta's reaction of a few minutes ago. When it lands with my dad, his eyes swell with tears.

"Sweetheart, twins?"

"Yes, apparently they run in Jack's family."

"This is the best day of my life," my dad proclaims. That's when I completely lose my ever-loving shit. I smile as my own tears stream down my face. Jack wraps an arm around my shoulders, kissing the top of my head.

"Do we know their sex?" Peter asks hesitantly, almost as if he's afraid to ask or know.

"We'd like you to meet Madden Jackson and Siarra Marie."

"I love them, so unique! How did you come up with them?" Lizzy asks while wiping her own tears.

"Jack came up with Madden. Jackson was a definite that I wouldn't bend on." I look over at my dad and add, "My mom's name was Marie Siarra Marino. I reversed her names."

"So beautiful. Which one is Siarra?"

"The smaller one. Her brother is already protecting her in the womb."

Lori tugs me away from Jack's arm and into her own. "This is so amazing. I'm so happy for you guys."

"Thanks, Lor. I'm glad you were here today to hear our news."

"Nah ah, you still owe me big," she quips, pretending to be angry, "and I'm glad I was too. This explains why you're so big."

I shake my head, "You are exhausting."

The emotion in our apartment after our announcement is incredible. These two babies are coming into a very loving, very supportive family. I will make sure they are aware of how fortunate they are, every day of their lives.

Lori and Matt leave right before I serve dinner. Once we all sit to eat, my dad clears his throat. He raises his wine glass and smiles warmly. "Seems like it's a day for happy news." Evan and I exchange a glance as my dad smiles at Barb sitting beside him. "Barb and I are getting married."

I throw my brother a very cocky "I told you so" look and clap at my dad's announcement. I am so happy for him and Barb. She's had a rough time these past two years while battling her breast cancer and rebuilding her relationship with Evan. My dad has also had his fair share of heartache and I've never seen him happier than he's been recently. He and Evan are back on solid footing, and their relationship is even better than it was before.

The rest of our night is spent laughing and sharing plans. Jack opens the champagne for everyone with dessert. We have much to celebrate. The next several months will have us all very busy with Evan and Lizzy's wedding, followed by Dad and Barbs', the holidays directly after and the arrival of the twins in January. I know before I can blink my due date will be here. I think back five or so months and realize how fast that went.

Later, as Jack and I lay in bed recapping our day, he lifts my chin until my eyes focus on his. The raw emotion he is feeling is obvious in his stormy grey eyes. "Thank you," he says in a raspy whisper.

"What for?"

"For everything…for walking into that studio, for loving me, for my babies. Thank you." He bends to kiss me passionately before kissing my belly sweetly.

He has it all wrong. I should be thanking him. He has made every single dream of mine come true. Everything I ever hoped for, or wished for since I was a little girl, has come to fruition because Jack Lair fell in love with me.

I try to speak and my voice hitches, getting caught in my throat. He looks up and smiles, knowingly. "I know, Babe," he gives me an out, yet once again. It's become a common occurrence between us, our knack to communicate without words.

He holds me as I fall asleep with visions of Jack holding our babies, gifting me with his beautiful smile.

♬ ♬ ♬

Lori and I are on our way to Hoboken to visit Alisa and the baby. Jack needed to meet with his dad on the island and didn't want me sitting home alone. He also was sick of hearing me whining that I should visit Lis. So he called Oscar and Lori and arranged for it to happen today. I've become a master procrastinator among everything else.

"Oh, my God, I forgot to tell you," Lori interrupts my thoughts. "Guess what?"

"What?"

"I caught them."

"Who?" I feel like I'm playing a game of twenty questions.

"Joe and Nina."

"No way!" I yell while turning sideways, as much as I physically can in my seatbelt. Oscar smiles in the rear view mirror and I shrug.

"Yes, way. We went out for dinner last night. Afterwards, we decided to visit The Zone. Sal says hello and is mad at you by the way."

"Why?"

"Because you aren't naming a twin after him," she scolds and shakes her head, "Anyway, the lovebirds were there. They were in a corner booth, sitting on the same side, whispering."

"We need to ask him."

"Pfft. I went right up to their table. They looked up and went pale."

"I wish I was there to see it."

Lori smiles deviously. "It was priceless. They fumbled with their words. Matt and I stood, waiting for them to form one coherent sentence between them. It took like three minutes."

"What did they say?"

"They claimed they were meeting on a new song idea. Yeah, ok, drummer and singer collaborating on a song? Do they think we're fucking idiots?"

"Apparently." I smile wide, finally having a pseudo-confirmation.

"Well, they got busted. Matt and I sat and I fired away with all my questions. They first got together in Vegas."

"That was only our second week on tour."

"Yep. Joe was trying to figure out how to make his move."

"He's liked her all along?"

"He's had a crush on her since she replaced you. He said the day he found out she broke it off with her boyfriend, he spent hours planning his approach."

"Are you supposed to be telling me this?"

"Of course. I told them I would be telling you. Stop interrupting me. So, Nina also had a crush on Joe. She had no idea if he felt the same. She said he would flirt with her and tease her. She felt like she was in grade school again. Finally the night you were all in Vegas, once you all got back to your rooms, she knocked on his door."

"She went to him?"

"Yep. She was tired of waiting. She wanted to know what his deal was and thought maybe he was gay!"

I belly laugh at the prospect. I could just imagine Joe's face when Nina confronted him with that suspicion.

"So Joe pulled her into his arms and kissed the thought right out of her head, and they've been together since."

"So are they out?"

"Yep. They said that they'd come clean the next time we are all together."

"I can't wait to get home and call him."

One by one my friends are finding love. I have been hoping for Joe to find his for years. He is one of the nicest guys I know and his heart is pure gold. I am so happy for him. Last one left is Trey. He better get his act together, or I'm taking matters into my own hands. I don't care what Jack says.

“They are happy. So, it seems like we are all paired off now.” She looks at me and smirks, “Except him.”

“How have you been with your decision? Please don’t tell me you are still thinking about Trey.”

She shakes her head before I even finish my statement. “Nope, not at all. I’m happy.”

I take her hand and confirm, “You look happy.”

When we get to Alisa’s house, she opens the door smiling wide, holding Michelle. “Hey, I can’t believe we are all here, together, in one state.”

“I can’t believe how big she got,” I gently touch her soft blonde hair. It’s the exact shade as her mom’s. In fact, she looks just like Alisa, except for her daddy’s eyes. Alisa ushers us in and we pick up right where we all left off. The three musketeers reunited again. The bond we hold will forever be there, I don’t have a doubt in my mind.

## Chapter 21– Jack

I hate lying to her, but I truly want to surprise her. The excuse I gave sounded pathetic, even to my own ears. I couldn't believe she bought it. I claimed I had to meet with my dad, because he had some papers for me to sign regarding his practice. I called my dad to fill him in on the lie, just in case.

As I coast down the Garden State Parkway I increase my speed, pushing the limit. I can't wait to see this place. The pictures looked amazing. My realtor said I had to get my ass down there pronto because this kind of gem wouldn't be on the market for long. She gave me a tip, advising the property isn't listed yet. I had to spin my wheels moving an appointment at the studio and getting Leila occupied for the day. By some stroke of luck, it all worked out.

I've been tossing the idea of surprising Leila for a few weeks now. Once we found out we were having twins, my decision was made. I want a place to get away from the city, yet close enough. I want a place to raise our children and accommodate any more we will be having. Somewhere we can entertain for Christmas or Birthday parties.

I want a home.

Once I made the decision, this place popped up. I feel getting this house is meant to be. This house fits my tall order perfectly. It's a waterfront property on the Jersey Shore. It's less than an hour from the city by water ferry, about ninety minutes by car. Another option could have been searching in Long Island, but I know my Jersey girl wouldn't be happy on any beach other than the Jersey Shore.

The closer I get, the more I know I'll love it. It's in a gated community and the views are spectacular. It's pricey, but we can afford it. I'd pay double if necessary. This is our future and you can't put a price tag on that.

When I pull through the private entrance, I can barely contain myself. Once out of the car, I snap pictures of the front, the view, and the grounds. Ellen the realtor is waiting at the door when I approach.

"So? Beautiful, right?"

"Very. This place is incredible."

"Wait until you see the inside." She ushers me in, taking me from room to room, explaining all the finer points of the house. Truth be told, she had me at the front door. I snap some more pictures of both the inside and the spectacular deck with stairs leading down to the private beach. By the time I head home, I'm a bundle of nervous, anxious energy.

I hope she likes it. I put in a bid, just to position myself if anyone else came in and did the same. I want Leila to see it, though. I would never make such a huge decision without her input. As much as I know she'll love it, I won't tell her I submitted a bid. Knowing my wife, if she knew I had put in an offer, she would feel obligated to like it…just to avoid hurting my feelings.

I visualize her in every room, moving around with our babies teetering after her. I can actually picture her laughing and playing with them. Consumed by my daydreams, the ride home feels much faster than the one going. I was on autopilot the entire time, not once remembering the road or the journey. It's not until I see the New York skyline in my vision that I realize I'm almost there. The blue-tooth on my dash lights up with Leila's name.

"Hey, Babe. I'm approaching the city. How's your visit with Alisa going?"

"Jack…"

Just the tone of her voice sends a chill running up my spine, settling in the base of my neck. "What's wrong?"

I can hear her crying, and I fight myself internally not to panic. "LEILA!"

"I'm at the hospital. I'm bleeding."

I don't understand how my grip doesn't crack the steering wheel beneath my fingers. My heart immediately starts pounding, making it very difficult to breath. "I'm on my way. Baby, I'm coming. I'm very close. Do not worry. Everything will be fine."

Her sobs over the speaker crack me in half. The pain in my chest becomes unbearable. In a shaky voice she adds, "Lori is here with me. Please drive careful, don't make me worry."

"Baby, put her on."

"Hey."

"How bad is she bleeding?"

Lori pulls in a deep breath. I hear shuffling and assume she is walking away from Leila. "She went to the bathroom at Lis's house. She became hysterical. I finally got her to calm down. I didn't want to scare her, but…" Lori stops abruptly.

"But what?"

"Jack, she's bleeding enough to have to wear a pad."

I can feel the blood drain from my face. What the fuck is this? This can't be normal. I can't lose these babies. I can't lose my wife.

"When did this start?"

"Just as we were leaving Alisa's. We just got here. I tried calling you, but…"

"I didn't get any calls!" I bark back, interrupting her.

"I meant to call you. Jack, she was beyond hysterical. I had my hands full on the drive over. I forgot to leave your number with Lis. My first priority was to get her here."

"Ok, I'm sorry. Where's Oscar?"

"He's here. She begged him to let her call you herself. Just hurry. Her blood pressure is very high. They are concerned with that, as well. She's making herself crazy."

I can just picture her, and the realization that I'm not there holding her hand is crushing me. I've let her down. When she needs me the most, I'm not there.

"Jack, she keeps saying this is her fault, that she did something to cause this."

"Put her on, please."

After a few very long seconds, Lori passes the phone back to her. She doesn't speak, but I know she's listening. I need to put all my own angst aside and concentrate on calming her down.

"Baby, listen to me. You are at the right place, and they are going to take good care of you and our babies. You need to do something for me, ok? You have one job right now, and that's to stay calm. You need to…ok?"

"Yes," she sobs through the phone.

"I'm just about heading into the tunnel. I'm on my way."

It's a miracle in itself I get to the hospital in one piece. I slam into a parking spot closest to the door, not giving a fuck if it gets towed or stolen. My feet can't carry me fast enough to the information desk. "Maternity."

"Seventh floor."

When I come barreling around the corner toward the central desk, I run into Dr. Rand. He's writing on a clipboard and suddenly looks up alarmed until he sees it's me. He quickly schools his features, so there isn't any way I can tell what he's thinking.

"She's hooked up to fetal monitoring. From what we can tell, the babies are showing no signs of distress," he starts off, no doubt to calm me down. "Our main concern is her pressure. If it continues to spike, it will affect them."

"Does she know this?"

"She knows they are stable, but it's doing little to settle her at the moment."

"What about the bleeding?"

"We don't know yet. Once her pressure stabilizes a little, we'll do an internal ultrasound. It could be a placenta abruption, or the weight on her cervix, or a polyp. All these scenarios are manageable. The most important concern at the moment is her pressure."

"Can you give her something to bring it down?"

"No. Unfortunately, ACE inhibitors and angiotensin receptor blockers can harm the babies during pregnancy."

"English, please," I show my frustrations for the first time in my tone.

He smiles and adds, "Blood pressure medicine can be very harmful to the babies."

"So, how can she get it down?"

"For now, bed rest."

"For the rest of her pregnancy?"

"Yes. If we can't control it that way, and she develops severe preeclampsia, we'll have to induce."

"What can be causing her high blood pressure?" I worry it's stress that I transferred to her by being so neurotic myself.

"It could be anything. Possibly the pressure of the babies on her cervix can be causing both her to bleed and her spike in pressure. It's not unusual when carrying twins, especially if the woman is of thin build."

I nod robotically, feeling slightly better, but not happy with the frown that remains on his face. He watches me process his explanation. "I was just about to go in and speak to her. I'm sure your presence alone will calm her down."

He leads me to her room. When she looks up and sees me, she bursts into tears.

"Baby, stop. You can't keep crying like this." I wrap her in my arms, smoothing her hair as she sobs hysterically. Lori sits in the corner, looking completely lost and out of her element. I feel bad she was the one subjected to this. I can barely handle Leila myself when she gets herself worked up.

"Dr. Rand said the babies are ok."

She looks up, her red-rimmed eyes swollen beyond recognition.

Dr. Rand repeats everything he said to me in the hall, and she listens intently. Her body still trembles in my arms, and her sobs still cause her to pull in ragged breaths during his explanation.

"Leila, you need to calm down. High blood pressure during pregnancy can also cause less blood flow through the placenta, thus less oxygen and nutrients to the babies. Hypertension can cause placenta abruption. That may be the reason you are bleeding. It's treatable and nothing to worry about, but if your pressure continues to elevate, it can cause preterm birth. They are too tiny for that scenario. They aren't ready to arrive yet. Do you understand?"

She nods. "Did I do something wrong?" she asks in a quivering voice.

"No, dear. This sometimes happens when carrying twins. As long as it's managed early, there's no need for concern. Ok?"

She nods again.

"Ok. I'm going to do an internal ultrasound to be sure you don't have a cervical polyp that is causing the bleeding. Then we'll discuss how to get your pressure down. You hear those two tiny heartbeats?"

"Yes."

"You listen to that. That's what you need to focus on. Right now, your babies are fine. We will make sure they stay that way. Your job is to remain calm. Can you do that?"

"I don't know."

"Sing to your wife to relax her. I'll be back." He leaves the room quietly.

Lori stands and says, "I'll give you two some privacy. Is there anyone you want me to call?"

"Evan. Tell him to fill in my dad and Liz," Leila responds in a shaky but more forceful tone.

"You got it."

"Lor?" She turns and smiles at me. "Thank you."

"No thanks needed."

Leila looks up at me, completely defeated, "I'm sorry."

"Stop it, Lei. I mean it. It's no ones fault. It happens and we'll manage it." She remains silent. "Leila? Do you hear me? You need to stop. Do you want me to sing to you?" I ask with a smile.

She gives me a weak smile in return. "Maybe later. Just hold me."

"Scoot over." I lay besides her, wrapping her completely in my embrace. The monitor alerts us to her rapid heart rate, as well as the twins'.

"How did your appointment with Dad go?"

"Good," I lie again. This isn't the time to share my news with her. My cell buzzes in my pocket. My initial reaction is to ignore it. I quickly take the call from her dad. "Hey, Anthony."

"Where's Leila?"

"She's here. The babies are fine. Her blood pressure is high and she needs to calm down. Can we call you back?" Anthony agrees, after a pregnant pause. "Can you tell Evan that we'll call him later?"

"Do you want us to come?" Anthony asks, desperately.

"No, we'll call you after we know some more. Most important thing is the babies are fine and they are taking good care of them and Lei."

"Ok," he hangs up and she continues to tremble in my arms.

"Ready for my song?" I distract her from her thoughts.

She nods and I sing her song directly into her ear. I can feel her softening against me, no longer rigid and stiff with tension. The monitor doesn't slow its rapid beat, but I feel her calming down little by little.

Dr. Rand comes back to give her an internal. He doesn't see any polyps or other reason for the bleeding. He concludes it's from the spike in her pressure and the weight of the babies.

"Leila, we need to get you to at least thirty-five weeks. We need to lower your pressure to ensure you get there."

"Is there something I can take to lower it?"

He shakes his head and says, "No, there isn't.

"So how do I lower it?"

"The weight of the babies has caused the placenta abruption that caused the bleeding. Your high blood pressure has thinned your blood and aggravated the amount of the bleeding. It's a vicious cycle." After his explanation, he drops the bomb. "The only way to attempt to lower your pressure is complete bed rest."

Her mouth drops open in shock. "Complete?" He nods and waits for her to process his diagnosis. This is not going to help calm her down. How fucking ironic that her direct orders to de-stress is going to cause her more stress?

"Leila…"

"What?" She cuts me off. "Jack, complete bed rest? For the next eleven weeks?"

I use her spark of anger to fuel my own. "Yes, complete bed rest. You don't have a choice. There is absolutely nothing that needs to be done for the next eleven weeks but to get those babies matured and ready to arrive. Nothing!"

"Jack's right, Leila. That is your main focus. Enjoy the time. Let Jack pamper you, read, relax."

She pouts like a child who has just been scolded. Dr. Rand makes some more suggestions. I listen intently, because my stubborn wife probably isn't paying attention while trying to figure out how she's going to manage this.

The minute he leaves her room, I grasp her chin, holding her hostage to my gaze.

"Stop."

"Jack, we have two weddings, the holidays…not to mention shopping for all we need…"

"Listen up. I'm going to say this once, and you are going to listen to me. Before you know it we will be back here in for the birth of our babies. From now until then, you are to worry and focus on that one event."

"But…"

"That. One. Event."

She moves her head to look away, and I let her. She needs to find a way to accept her fate for the next three months. That's all on her. I can't help her with that. But I'll be reminding her constantly and making damn sure she does just as Dr. Rand ordered.

♬ ♬ ♬

Leila remains in the hospital for a few days before they finally release her. On the drive back to our apartment, she throws question after question at me in rapid fire, and I have a response and solution ready for each and every one.

"What about Evan and Lizzy's wedding?" – "They'll postpone."

"My dad and Barb's?" - "They waited this long, a few more months won't matter."

"This is going to delay the album." – "We'll extend our dates."

"You can't stay home with me for eleven weeks." – "I'll hire an aide."

"The holidays will suck." – "Next year we'll make up for it with our twins."

"You can't handle buying everything we need." – "I'll take Mom and Barb with me."

When she finally quiets down, I know I won this battle, but I'm sure there will be many more coming.

The next few days are spent setting parameters.

It's bed or couch.

No showering without me.

No cooking or cleaning.

I loaded a huge gift card on her *Amazon* account for any reading material she needs or wants on her *Kindle*. I arrange for a manicure and a pedicure with Lori weekly at the apartment (this was Lori's suggestion). If I have to leave for extended periods of time, her new aide, Dotty, is a phone call away. I purchased a home blood pressure device to monitor her daily. I stocked the fridge and the pantry with all her favorites.

I loaded up our social calendar with visits from our friends and family. Tonight I have some of her friends coming over for drinks. In a few days I'll have my guys coming as well. I'll keep planning things to keep her mind occupied. I'll make her dinner and watch a movie with her. I'm going to make sure her sequestered time is as pleasant as possible.

This morning I told her about the house, in hopes to better her mood. I showed her the pictures, watching her closely as she flipped through each one.

"Jack, this is beautiful."

"I was going to drive you down to see it. Leila, it's perfect. But we can wait and find something together."

"No…I don't want to lose this. I trust you and if you love it, I'll love it. Can we afford it?"

"Yes, Babe. Don't you worry about that. Are you sure you don't want to wait to shop around?"

"I'm positive. I can't wait to see it. When will we know?"

"Not sure. Just keep your fingers crossed." I planted a kiss on her cheek and said, "Wait until you see the kitchen in person. You will love entertaining in there." The size of our kitchen is her only complaint with our apartment.

"I can't wait," she said pensively with a faraway look on her face. I ached for her to smile and laugh. I ached for her to be happy. It's killing me that such a happy time in her life is anything but right now.

She's been very cranky since getting home, and I've been teasing her mercilessly, trying to cheer her up. Dr. Rand said because of her bleeding that we should hold off from intercourse for a few days, but any other sexual activity could continue as normal. I have no shame in admitting that I'm about to use it to my advantage.

I watch as she stares into space on the couch while I prepare some snacks for our guests. She feels my gaze on her and looks up at me.

"Like what you see, Mrs. Lair?"

The scowl disappears as she fights to hide her grin. "No."

"I'm done here. I thought I could be of service to you before our friends arrive." I wash my hands before stalking toward her as she sits on the couch. "Would you like to be serviced?"

"No," she smirks.

I sit next to her, never breaking eye contact. "I think you're lying." Slowly sweeping her hair off her neck, I bend to kiss a trail from her neck to her ear. When I pull her earlobe in between my lips, a small puff of air hits my cheek.

"Feel good?"

"No," she lies again.

I chuckle at her response. "That's too bad. We have some time. There is so much I can do," I say directly into her ear. Goosebumps appear down her arms, betraying her completely. "But if this doesn't feel good for you…"

She grips my neck and pulls my mouth to hers. My smile against her lips provokes her more. "Here's my girl."

"I'm sorry," she says remorsefully. "You're doing everything to make me happy and comfortable and I'm being a complete bitch. I just feel so useless."

"You aren't useless." She laughs at my obvious exclusion of the word bitch. "Babe, you've got a very important job to do."

"I feel like a human incubator."

"You are." She swats at me and I laugh. "A sexy as fuck one, though. I need to devour you."

"That's another thing I'm feeling guilty over. This can't be easy for you not having sex."

"Lei, when are you going to get that I love watching you come almost as much as I love coming myself?"

"Now who's the liar?" she asks before kissing me. "I love you."

"I know. Can I eat your pussy now?"

"Can you wait until later? I'm afraid once the beast arrives it won't leave."

"Sure, Babe. I guess I can wait, if you can," I trail a fingertip along the seam of her pants. Her response is to kiss me, hard. She moves her lips over mine, slowly stirring me up. She dips her tongue in and then swipes it along my bottom lip before inviting mine to chase it. When I follow, she pulls my tongue into her mouth and sucks with just enough pressure to send a jolt right to my cock.

"Are you sure you want to wait?" I ask after breaking our very erotic kiss. "I think your pussy is telling me she disagrees," I tease as I cup her obvious wetness.

"You're evil. If they arrive, and you leave me like this, I'll get you back."

I place her flat on her back and gently spread her legs until I am sitting between them. "No worries. This won't take long. I'm that good," I inform her as I slide her pants and panties off her legs, throwing them to the side.

She watches me quietly. I skim my hands over her very pregnant belly that sits above her like a basketball. I move my palms over her tight skin, beneath her shirt. When I move the fabric up to expose her, I can't resist planting kiss after kiss on her bump. The lower I go, the harder she breathes.

I kiss her tattoo and then I take one long, slow swipe with my tongue. I feel her fingers tangle in my hair. She arches her back immediately. I know just what she craves from me. I know her body very well. Predictably, a moan escapes when I slip two fingers into her. Only after I find and rub her g-spot, do I start to lick her clit. Tiny flicks of my tongue cause the muscles on her thighs to flex. I know she isn't ready yet, but she's climbing. By the time I suck on her clit, she is writhing against me, desperate for more of my mouth. I don't stop until the tremors coursing through her calm and cease, and the muscles of her pussy relax around my fingers.

She opens her eyes and smiles lovingly. "You always know just what I need."

"Feel better?"

"Yes." She sits up and kisses me passionately. "Thank you."

"You're welcome."

The door buzzes and her eyes fly open in surprise. "Jack, they're here!"

I laugh at her panic. "Fuck, I really am that good. That was perfect timing."

## Chapter 22 – Evan

"Evan, I'm so sorry," she says for the millionth time.

"Will you *stop*?" I respond for the millionth and one. "Lei, how many times do I have to tell you that we are fine? It's a piece of paper. We'll have the wedding next year after the twins are born."

"I still feel bad."

"I didn't tell you this to make you feel bad."

I thought I would distract her a bit and fill her in on the wedding plans. Since we will now be getting married in the dead of winter, the wedding will no longer be in the Lairs' back yard. We will instead have it at a country club nearby. The reception room overlooks the golf course. It's beautiful and Lizzy and I fell in love with it when we saw it. Besides the location and the actual date, nothing else has changed.

Neither Lizzy nor I are the least bit disappointed the wedding has been delayed. Sure we are anxious to get married, but our niece and nephew's arrival is more important. Unfortunately, my thick skulled sister can't get that through her thick skull.

"Who cares what you say?"

"You are sincerely getting on my nerves."

"Join the club," she responds snippily. "I'm getting on my own nerves."

"I'm sure you are." Her grunt through the phone makes me laugh out loud. "Hey, look at the bright side…you won't be waddling down the aisle now. That would be sure to ruin the video. With every step the ground would move beneath you and the camera would shake, causing the frame to become unfocused."

"Jerk."

I laugh again and switch gears. "So tell me about this fabulous house."

"It's so gorgeous. I have pictures that I can show you. It's right on the beach." A small amount of excitement is evident in the sound of her voice, but as quickly as it comes, it goes. She falls silent on her end, and I try again.

"Whatcha' been up to?"

"This is absolute torture. Evan, I love my apartment. I now can't stand the sight of it. Why did I paint it this putrid grey color? Can you answer that?"

"You loved that color. It was the perfect shade of grey."

"Who asked you?"

I laugh at her again, "Wow, you are really cranky."

"Ya' think?"

"How is Jack living with you? I would have duct taped your mouth by now."

"Believe me, he tried." She sighs into the phone, "Let's change the subject. How are the lovebirds?"

"Which ones?" I ask amused. "We are surrounded by them."

"Joe and Nina. They are the only two who haven't visited. Even Trey came by with a bag full of joke books, that bastard."

"That's hilarious."

"Yeah, ha ha. Anyway, Joe calls me every day and apologizes for not coming to see me. Lori thinks it's because he's afraid to get yelled at. Apparently, every one is afraid of prisoner, Leila."

"I don't blame them," I mumble very quietly.

"I heard that."

"Joe and Nina are great. They are attached at the hip. Rehearsals are very interesting. Now that they are out, they are out of control. Matt wants to push Joe's head through his snare drum."

She laughs over the phone. It's the first time I've heard a genuine laugh from her in days.

"Hey, is that Leila?" Lizzy asks when she comes into the living room. "I need to ask her something."

I nod and pass her the phone. Lizzy sits on my lap. As long as she does, I take it upon myself to nibble on her neck. She smiles at my assault and says, "Hey, Lei. Are you going to be home tonight?" Lizzy laughs at Leila's response. "Just kidding. I'm coming by. I want your opinion of flowers."

I know for a fact Lizzy could give a crap about the flowers. She has allowed her mother to handle most of the wedding minutia. My fiancé is trying to keep my sister's mind occupied. "Sure, Ev will come, too. We'll bring dinner…Sounds good…Love ya'…Here's Ev."

She smiles as she walks away. Distracted by watching her gorgeous ass, I don't hear my sister until she repeats my name.

"Huh?"

"What are you doing?"

"Nothing."

"Did you hear what I said?"

"Uh huh."

"Liar. I'll see you later," she pouts and hangs up.

Liz comes back in to see me shaking my head. "What's wrong?"

"She sure is a cranky-ass."

"Can you blame her? I feel bad. She was feeling so great and so excited. The poor thing."

"I feel bad, too."

"Come on, I want to pick up some stuff to cheer her up."

"Wait, we aren't…"

She put's her hands on her hips. "No, sweetie, we aren't. Your sister needs us."

♫ ♫ ♫

The look on Jack's face is priceless when he opens the door. "Thank God you're here," he whispers and rolls his eyes.

We come loaded with dinner, dessert, flowers, bridal magazines, baby magazines, two teddy bears, and a bottle of tequila for Jack.

"Moving in?" he asks in all seriousness.

"It's to help cheer her up."

I hand Jack the bottle and add, "And this is for your sanity."

Jack takes the bottle and nods, "I just may open it tonight. Ev, I love your sister, but I'm really struggling with her. She's just…" He scrubs his hand down his face. He looks exhausted.

"Where is she?"

"In our room. Liz, she's crying again."

"Ev, stay with Jack. I'm going in." She walks down the hall, deliberately taking her time.

Jack grabs us each a beer and joins me in the living room. "I called her doctor today. I was that worried. This can't be good for her blood pressure."

"What did he say?"

"He said hormones are often very erratic during pregnancy, add to it twins and bed rest, and it could send Mother Teresa into hysterics."

"She's almost there, just a few more weeks. How big are they now?"

"They're still tiny, but they can gain most of their weight in the next three weeks. This stretch is crucial. He hopes to induce by the end of the month."

"That's great news. So we just have to keep her preoccupied with Thanksgiving."

"Yeah, piece of cake," he responds sarcastically. "She called Dr. Rand begging to be let out for Thanksgiving. She even volunteered to use a wheel chair. She's that desperate."

"Can't blame her, man. This has to be rough on her."

"I'm not doubting that it is. I'm doing all I can for her, and she appreciates it. That's what causes her periods of utter guilt, thus, causing her crying. The fact I'm sentenced to this along with her is consuming her. But I don't care. I just want her and the babies to be ok." He stands and grabs us two more beers.

"Did he give her permission?"

"Surprisingly, yes. My parents were planning on hosting it for all of us here, but Leila's little shenanigans have my mom overjoyed."

"How are your *Rolling Stone* sessions going?"

"Good. We are pretty much done, just waiting on the final to approve. Leila and Tara get along really well."

"That's awesome. I can't imagine how that must feel, seeing your face on a magazine, your story on the pages."

"You'll get there. It's surreal, strange, but mostly it blows my mind."

Lizzy and Leila join us. Leila is actually laughing at something Lizzy said. My girl always amazes me.

"Hey, Babe. Feel better?" Jack asks as he moves over to give her space to sit.

"Very," she rubs her belly as she smiles wide. "Liz was just telling me about one of her patients. I feel sane in comparison."

Jack and I exchange confused expressions. "Good." He says, kissing her cheek. "Are you hungry?"

"I'm starving."

"It's probably cold now," Lizzy shrugs.

"I love cold pizza," Leila says with a smile. Jack smiles down at her and she leans up to give him a chaste kiss.

"Cold pizza it is."

The door buzzer sounds and we all sit and stare at each other. "Expecting someone?" Leila asks.

Jack shakes his head and goes to answer. "It's us. Let us in." Hunter shouts into the intercom.

"There's no need to yell, jackass," Jack ok's their visit and waits for them by the door.

A few minutes later, Hunter bounds through, Mandi, Scott, and Patti following behind.

"What's going on?" Leila asks, as the four stand grinning like fools.

Hunter lifts Mandi's hand and thrusts it out toward us.

The girls start screaming as if on cue. "Mandi, it's absolutely gorgeous. I'm so happy for you. Come closer, I need a better look."

Mandi blushes and comes to sit beside my sister.

"You finally did it. It sure took you long enough, man," Jack shakes Hunter's hand.

"What are you griping about? I'm the one he kept practicing on," Scott admits.

"Do not tell Trey that, he will never let you live it down," Jack says as he grabs them each a beer.

"When's the wedding?" Leila asks.

"We just freakin' got engaged!" Hunter blurts out.

Mandi shakes her head and says, "I'd like next summer."

“We are going to be a busy bunch of rock stars next year,” Leila says. “Let’s see, we have Evan and Liz in February, then Scott and Patti in April, now you guys in the summer. If we can convince Matt, and Trey to get engaged, we can squeeze you all into the same year. It would help me remember anniversaries.”

“I’m sure Trey would get hitched just to help you out there, Little Lair,” Hunter says, and she sticks her tongue out at him. “Speaking of, he’s been out with Tara four times now.”

Jack looks at Hunter. “Dude, you gossip like a girl.”

“Fuck you,” he responds, but it doesn’t deter him to give a play-by-play on Trey’s love life.

Leila laughs, looking more like her self as we all sit and listen to Hunter’s stories. My brother-in-law looks like a different person than when we first got here a few hours ago. It’s amazing how much he is wrapped up in my sister’s happiness. It seems to fuel him, to give him sustenance to thrive. I know exactly how he feels.

## Chapter 23 – Leila

It's the day after Thanksgiving and our babies are coming.

The time during bed rest torturously dragged on. Besides being bored out of my mind, I was more emotional than ever. When my blood pressure showed little signs of improving, Jack called in his sister to help. I had no idea at the time, but he was so desperate to make me feel better, he begged her to have a talk with me. She helped with the guilt I was feeling. She counseled me on how to focus. She suggested meditating and visualizing our family once the twins arrived. She requested I keep a journal to help me understand what caused my bouts of depression. I did all she asked and soon began to feel better.

Since I wasn't able to leave our apartment, Jack arranged a mid-wife to give us our personal *Lamaze* session. She spent an entire afternoon with us, teaching us breathing techniques, methods that Jack can use to keep me calm, and relaxation tactics, such as using pictures for visualization and calming music. Everything was going well until she showed us a video of an actual birth. Jack's pallor turned a cartoonish shade of green, and he swallowed audibly at least a dozen times. Each time he would glance my way, a fake smile would spread across his face.

At my next appointment, my blood pressure improved. A sonogram confirmed the twins were both substantial in size and Dr. Rand took pity. He scheduled for me to be induced on the first day of my thirty-sixth week. Well, the day after, because yesterday was a holiday and I didn't want to ruin it for everyone.

We arrived at my in-laws the day before Thanksgiving. Jack spent most of the day installing the car seats, checking them and re-checking them, running to the store over and over for things he kept forgetting, and assembling the stroller with his dad's help.

My mother-in-law made a delicious dinner and we all had a lovely holiday. My husband then excused us right after dessert, so I would have a full night's sleep. I reminded him I would be having one, if we could leave for the hospital the next morning at a reasonable hour. Once again, he pretended he didn't hear me.

Oscar offered to pick us up, but Jack declined. He told him to enjoy his holiday and meet us at the hospital. Now that Danny is no longer a threat to us, we won't need his constant watch. Jack feels as long as we utilize him during public appearances and or public places where our fans can get out of control, we should be fine otherwise.

"Ok, so that wasn't so bad," Jack says as we drive to the city. He's been randomly babbling all morning.

"What wasn't so bad?"

He looks at me confused for a second, and then remembers what he was referring to. "Oh, traffic."

"That's because everyone is still sleeping." He doubled the amount of time it usually takes to get back to the city to cover any traffic we might hit. When I mentioned it was probably going to be smooth sailing, since most are still off for the holiday, he pretended he didn't hear a word I said.

"I think I need more diapers."

"Have you been drinking?"

"No," he answers, offended at my question.

I bite down on my bottom lip to stop from laughing. He's absolutely losing it. He's a nervous wreck and doesn't know how to channel his anxiety.

"Babe, are you going to be ok in the delivery room?" I ask, truly curious and concerned.

"Of course," he responds, not too convincingly. "Did you remember to pack underwear?"

"Are you serious?"

He gives me a sideways glance, "I'm completely serious."

"Yes, Baby. I remembered to pack underwear."

He nods, frowning as he concentrates on the road.

"Babe?" He looks at me again. "I love you."

My words erase the scowl he's been sporting. "I love you, too."

"Please relax. I know you are trying to play it cool, but I also know you are freaking out right now."

"Am not," he responds defensively, but his smile says I'm dead on.

"Have you noticed that whenever I freak out, you're calm…and whenever you freak out, I'm calm? Why is that?"

"Because we're perfect together," he states the obvious.

"You're so smart."

He clasps our hands and places them on his thigh. "I can't believe we are about to be parents. Baby, I'm about to be a dad."

"You're about to be a great dad."

"I hope so. I'll have you to make sure I am." He lifts our hands and places a kiss on my knuckles. "Are you ok? Are you feeling calm?"

"Surprising enough, I am. Ask me again once we get there, though."

I settle against my seat, closing my eyes. I've been measuring my breathing and purposefully visualizing us holding our babies, soft music playing in the background. I've worked very hard to keep myself calm, and I'm not about to have it all go to pot now.

Jack's nerves are actually distracting me from my own, giving me something else to focus on. Dr. Rand walked me through what would happen today. Once there, they will attach the fetal monitors. I'll be administered a drug called Pitocin to induce contractions. Once I am fully dilated, I'll begin delivery.

Piece of cake.

I have no idea what to expect. Alisa said it felt like your worst menstrual cramps on crack. I never really suffered from cramps, so that analogy was lost on me. I'm usually good with pain, but I am a bit freaked out about that part, especially since it's times two. I'm hoping by then Jack will be calm, so I can freak out.

As I predicted, the ride to the city was traffic free. We arrived with plenty of time.

"Babe, did you forget anything? We have time to actually go to the apartment if you want." He smirks without looking at me. "No? An extra pair of underwear maybe?"

Still nothing.

"We actually have time to run to Hoboken to get some fresh cannoli. You game?" He draws his bottom lip up to cover his top. "Ooh, I can really go for some cannoli."

He finally throws me a smile, and says, "Smart ass."

"*You were right, Baby* - would be all I need to hear from you, for me to stop."

"You were right, Baby," he repeats.

"I know."

He pulls up to the hospital, hopping out to help me. Once he does, he grabs my bag from the back. Oscar comes through the main doors, joining us on the sidewalk. "I got the car. Go."

He takes Jack's keys and pulls away. "Remind me to give him a raise," Jack says and I agree. That man has been a Godsend…always available for us, always reliable.

Jack helps me to the desk, I check in, and shortly after we are on our way to Maternity. It's still very early and very quiet. My dad wanted to meet us here, and I told him there was no need. I could be here for hours. I didn't want to have to worry about him sitting and waiting for me to deliver.

It's not long before I am all hooked up and prepped, and now we're just waiting for Dr. Rand to arrive.

"Jack?"

"Yeah, Babe?"

"I apologize for anything I may say to you later."

He laughs at me and nods. "Apology accepted."

♬ ♬ ♬

*GODDAMN!*

*Holy fucking cocksucker, motherfucker!*

I feel like a car fell across my midsection, and I'm still only at four centimeters dilated. I'm obsessed with watching the needle on the seismometer that is monitoring the earthquake wreaking havoc on my pelvic area. That fucking machine keeps telling me another one is coming. Who invented this sick contraption? Most likely, it was a goddamn man who hates women.

I can't stop watching. I've tried closing my eyes, focusing on something else, specifically my sexy husband, but every few minutes my eyes fly back to that evil box sitting next to me.

Dr. Rand has already been in once to check on me. He said that one twin is in proper position, but unfortunately, one is not. Once I deliver Baby A, they will attempt to turn Baby B. If they aren't successful, I will have to have a C-Section. I'm not worrying about that, yet. I need to take one minute at a time. My blood pressure has been cooperating so far, but with each contraction it's starting to creep up.

I tried to keep it cool at first. Muffled, unrecognizable sounds the only thing I would allow to escape my lips. I smiled at my dad and Jack's parents, who were all in the room with us. I desperately tried to shield them from what I was feeling inside my body. I especially didn't want to further upset Jack, or instigate his angst. Unfortunately, the martyr in me is slowly dying a long and painful death. The last contraction was the nail in its coffin.

I ask Jack to ask them to leave. The more contractions that come, the stronger they are. I'm slowly losing my cool and I don't want any of them to witness it. I apologize profusely on their way out, feeling bad for kicking them out.

Once they all leave, Jack commences his relaxation technique by slowly stroking my hair. My heart sinks because that means another is coming. I'm so exhausted. I have no idea how I'm going to have the energy to deliver these kids. I've been at it all day, and I'm done. I'm ready to go home.

Fuck, this one is worse than the last one was.

"Goddamn it, if you come near me again with that fucking mother-fucking cock of yours, I'll bite it off, spit it out, and throw it out of our twelfth story window, directly into the stream of oncoming TRAFFIC!" The stream of curses that come flying out of my mouth next would make Trey Taylor blush.

Jack watches wide-eyed as I score his skin with my nails. He methodically caresses my hair and encourages me to breathe. It's not until I relax into the mattress and pant forcefully, then he asks, "Over?"

"Yes. I'm sorry, Baby. I didn't mean that."

"I know, or I hope." He bends and places a sweet kiss on my forehead. He offers me some ice chips and wipes my forehead with a cool compress.

He's been an excellent coach. I told him so in between contractions. He said not to compliment him so quickly, as he hasn't witnessed anything horrific yet.

"Ready for drugs?" he asks again. I shake my head, not bothering to open my eyes. I am so tired. "Leila, you need drugs. They'll be happier if their mommy is happier. Please, Baby, you're suffering unnecessarily. I'm worried about you."

"I really didn't want to go that route. I've stressed our kids out so much, I wanted to spare them anything unnatural, but Jack I don't know if I can finish this."

Dr. Rand enters my birthing room, smiling pleasantly. I would love to wipe that smile right off his face. "How are we doing?"

"She's being stubborn. She's wiped out."

"Do you really want to piss me off right now?" I ask through clenched teeth, all sugar and spice gone as another contraction starts again.

Dr. Rand checks the monitor and the printout. "Your contractions are coming a few minutes apart. Let's see how dilated you are."

He shoves two fingers inside and Jack flinches. I wonder if it's the fact that another man has his fingers shoved into my vagina that's upsetting him, or that I've now latched onto the hair on his arm.

"Am I at ten?" I ask, still gritting my teeth from the pain that's ripping me in half.

"Not yet."

"Can she have an epidural now?" Jack asks.

Dr. Rand moves over to the monitor and studies it closely. "Afraid not," he responds distractedly.

"Leila," Jack scolds, like I'm a child. Fuck me and my stubborn ass tendencies.

"Only because I feel I should perform a C-section," He quickly adds. Jack and I lock gazes.

"Your blood pressure is starting to elevate. I'm a bit concerned about that. You also haven't progressed much in the past hour. I feel these circumstances, combined with Baby B in a breach position, requires a C-Section." Dr. Rand further explains as he watches the monitor. He waits until another contraction starts and concentrates on the screen as I ride it out. Once it's over he says, "Let's get you prepped."

I was hoping for better news, something along the lines of, "*You're at ten centimeters and your babies will pop out without any pain in the next few seconds*."

I've never felt this way in my entire life. I feel defeated, beaten. I can't move. I am utterly spent.

"Will she be ok? The babies?" Jack asks, unable to hide his fear.

"I'll take good care of them," he replies as he smiles and leaves the room.

Tears blur my vision, and I try to blink them away. "Hey, stop. We're almost there. You've done your job, Baby."

I nod and he wraps his arms around me.

Suddenly nurses appear, Jack is pushed aside and asked to put scrubs on over his clothes, wires are removed, monitors unplugged, and we're moving down the hall. Panic starts to swell inside, all the complications I've read on multiple births and C-sections coming to the forefront of my mind. Jack catches up and reaches for my hand.

"Babe, you'll be fine," he says as he quickens his pace to keep up with my hospital bed being pushed rapidly by two nurses, also in scrubs. His face is etched with concern, but he's smiling for my benefit. Once inside the OR, a curtain is stretched across my midsection, blocking the view of my lower half. Jack can see over it if he stands. Instead, he bends so he is closer to me, making his obvious choice.

"Mr. Lair, you can sit if you prefer." The nurse drags a chair over, thankfully reading his mind.

Another nurse attaches a new IV bag to the stand. Jack continues to watch my face instead of the plastic port she fiddles with that's protruding from my hand.

There are like a dozen people in the room. "Jack, there's so many people here."

"Just a precaution, dear. They are NICU nurses standing by, in case the babies have lung issues. At thirty-six weeks, they could be just fine."

Her words do nothing to soothe me and only cause me more panic. Jack immediately knows what I'm thinking. "They are going to be just fine. We got this. You got this…ok?" he voices, for both of us. I ignore all the activity that's happening on the other side of the curtain and focus on his gorgeous eyes. He keeps assuring me with his words, his kisses, and his touch. His eyes never leaving mine. Whatever they administer works very quickly, as I feel no pain, just pressure and tugging. After a few minutes, a cry resonates through the room.

"Madden is here," Dr. Rand says, and Madden cries on cue. The nurse carries him off to the side, and above his screams, we hear suction sounds.

"They'll just clean him up and administer his APGAR test before you see him. That's a good cry. It means his lungs are working." A few minutes later, the nurse returns, carrying a squirming baby wrapped in a blue blanket. He has on a tiny cap with a sticky note that says "A."

"He's five pounds, three ounces," she says smiling.

"He's so small."

"Completely normal for twins at this stage," Dr. Rand responds. She places him near my face so I can give him a quick kiss. He's so warm and soft. Jack stands mesmerized, staring at Madden in awe. He bends and plants a tender kiss on his forehead.

"Jack."

"I know, Baby. He's perfect."

She moves him away just as Dr. Rand announces Siarra's arrival.

The same process occurs with Siarra. Where her brother is screaming bloody murder, she gives out one short, loud cry and then settles down. Siarra is only four pounds, seven ounces.

"She's not crying much," Leila voices my thoughts.

"It's ok. They've got her. She may just need some more suctioning," Dr. Rand explains.

All too soon, both babies are put into the same bassinet and taken to the nursery. My emotions flood, tears blur my vision and stream down my face.

"Jack, go, they need you," I plead through my tears.

He looks torn, conflicted as he stands rooted to the ground.

"Go ahead, Jack. It'll be a while before Leila is stitched up and cleared from the anesthesiologist. You can meet her in recovery with your children."

Jack wipes his eyes and places a kiss on my forehead and then my lips. "Thank you. You have given me the best gifts imaginable…first your love, and now my family. I love you so much."

"I love you, too."

He kisses me again and follows a nurse and our babies.

## Chapter 24 – Jack

I've never felt so torn in all of my life. I hate leaving her, but my kids are alone, and who knows, maybe even scared. I follow their bassinet to the nursery. I barely got to see them. Their faces are only a quick flash in my memory. Siarra looks so tiny, so fragile. She's almost a whole pound smaller than her brother. Madden cried, where Siarra was quiet.

The look on Leila's face broke my heart. It was a mixture of awe and want. I could see how desperately she wanted to hold them, to touch them. I am struggling with the same emotions.

When we arrive at the nursery, I quickly punch out a text to my mom announcing their arrival and that Leila had a C-section. Her response is immediate and I add that they are waiting to meet Leila and I'll text her soon. When I hesitantly enter the nursery, the twins are separated and tended to. I stand uselessly, completely lost in my element.

"Dad, you can video them if you want, so Mommy can see what she missed."

Wow, that's a great idea. I pull out my phone again and hit record, getting it all on video, snapping random pictures as well.

"Do we have names picked out?"

"Yes. Madden Jackson and Siarra Marie."

She smiles while filling out two cards, one blue and one pink. "Nice names."

The two nurses mechanically attach bracelets, check vitals, suction their noses and mouths, and bathe them rather roughly. During the entire process, both twins voice exactly how they feel about being manhandled. I don't blame them. It's irritating me that they aren't gentler with them.

After fifteen or so minutes, one of the nurses finally addresses me. "You can wash up there. It's time to hold your babies."

"I can hold them?"

"Of course."

I obediently wash my hands and sit in the rocking chair she points to. "Here's your son first," she says as she places him in my arms.

"He's so light."

"He's a pretty good size for a preemie twin," she informs me. "Where's your phone? I'll take a few shots."

I hand her my phone and watch Madden as she snaps shot after shot of my son and me. He still isn't happy and is scrunching his eyes shut as he cries. I have no idea what his eyes look like, but his little button nose and mouth are perfect. I gently stroke a finger along his smooth cheek. He's so warm and so soft.

"Hey, Bud. It's Daddy. I've been waiting to meet you for so long. I want to thank you for taking care of your sister in there. There may be times where she's a pain in your ass…um, I mean butt, but she'll always depend on you to protect her. I'm counting on you, Buddy."

The nurse stands near by, holding Siarra while I give Madden a gentle kiss on his forehead. He smells incredible. I'll never forget the way his skin feels against my lips.

"Ready to swap?"

I hesitantly hand her Madden, "Careful, don't drop him."

She laughs at my comment, "Darlin' I can juggle three at one time."

Without putting Madden down she hands me Siarra. I sit with my daughter, studying her features, cataloging them in my mind. She stares straight into my eyes, hers a very deep grey/blue in color. She has since calmed down and watches me quietly while measuring me up, as well.

"Hey, Princess. I can't wait until you meet Mommy. She's so beautiful." I look up at the nurse and ask, "Does she have hair? Can I take off her cap?"

"Of course."

I gently remove her tiny pink cap, revealing a small patch of chestnut brown hair. It's almost exact in color to Leila's. My gorgeous daughter is already a little mini-me to my gorgeous wife. The texture is so soft. I place a small kiss on her head, also inhaling her intoxicating scent.

"Smile, Daddy," she says as she takes a few more pictures. "Ok, now hold both of them." The look of shock I give her causes her to laugh. "You can do it."

She settles my son back in my left arm. He has settled down and is now wide-eyed, taking in his surroundings. I stiffen from fear, my muscles locked into place. I keep a cautious eye on each of them to anticipate any sudden movements or wiggling that may cause me to drop either or both. No movement comes as they lay contently in my arms, completely at ease with the fact that I have no experience in holding two babies at once. Come to think of it, I don't even remember ever holding one baby before. My children are the first babies I've held. The notion, although ridiculous, is also monumental in meaning.

"Ok, Mommy should just about be done. Let's get you all to recovery for a proper welcome."

As she settles them in their bassinets she instructs, "You can take those scrubs off now."

I actually had forgotten I was wearing them. I remove them, my eyes on my kids the entire time. As she wheels them down the hall Madden starts crying and Siarra follows his lead. "Why are they crying now? What's wrong?"

"They're probably hungry. They've had quite a day and want their dinner. Is your wife planning on breast-feeding?"

"Yes, she is."

"Ok, they'll have to wait."

"But they're crying."

She laughs at me again and says, "Yes, and they will…a lot. Get used to it, Daddy."

I don't like hearing them cry. It's heartbreaking. I don't think I'll ever get used to that sound. When we get into the recovery room, I drag a chair up to their bassinets and softly sing to them, but they aren't interested. The nurse opens a drawer, pulls out two pacifiers, and shoves them into their mouths.

They immediately stop crying, the only sounds now coming from their synchronized sucking. They look so cute, side-by-side. I can't tear my eyes away. I'm completely enthralled in everything they do.

"That's a good photo opp, Dad."

I quickly take a few shots as my cell buzzes in my hand. "Hey, Mom."

"Jack, we're dying here."

"I'm sorry, I'm kind of distracted."

"Please tell me everything is ok."

I only then realize how worried our families probably are. Sitting out in the waiting room, not having heard more than a few words via text. "I'm sorry. Leila is fine, and they are just perfect."

"Oh, Jack. I can't wait to see them."

"I know. We're waiting for Leila to come to recovery. She should be here any minute. Once she meets them and we move to her room, I'll text you."

"Ok, dear. I can't wait. Anthony and Barb are here, as well as Lizzy. Evan is on his way with Lori."

"Ok."

The door opens wide, and my wife gets wheeled into the room. Her eyes dart around, looking for her babies. When she sees them side by side, the tears are instant. They position her bed and one of the nurses stays behind to help us, no doubt. We both couldn't look more clueless if we tried. She raises Leila's bed, attaches her IV bag to the stationary pole that's bedside, and wheels the babies closer. This woman is amazing. Her calm demeanor is most definitely helping me.

"I'm Jean. I'll be with you until tomorrow morning. Leila, I'll be your best friend, dear. Anything you need, you call me. Ok, before these two loose it because they're hungry, let's get some more photos, Dad," she reminds me again.

God, I can't even remember to take a picture.

She hands Madden over to Leila, and I'm lucky enough to capture the gamut of emotions she experiences. She touches his nose, his eyebrow, all while her own mouth gapes open. She tugs on his pacifier and an audible popping sound makes her laugh. The minute his face crumples up, she replaces it without delay.

"Ssh, don't cry. I don't want you to ever cry," she voices my own sentiments. "Hi, Madden. I'm so happy to meet you. I'm sorry Mommy gave you a hard time, I really didn't mean to."

My eyes prick from her words, and I clear my throat. She looks up, remembering I'm standing a few feet away. "He's so beautiful."

"He is."

She brings him up to her face, inhaling deeply. "He smells amazing." She whispers terms of endearment to him, sings softly to him, and kisses him repeatedly on his forehead. She lifts his cap, stroking his baldhead before replacing it.

"Can I meet my daughter now?"

The nurse swaps babies with her, holding Madden while I film Leila's introduction to our daughter.

"She's so tiny," she says, her voice thick with emotion.

"She's perfectly fine. Twins are always smaller than single births," her nurse explained to her as she did to me earlier.

"Siarra, I'm Mommy. I'm sorry I gave you a hard time, too. Thank you for being patient with me." She repeats the words she just uttered to Madden, kissing her repeatedly. She then lifts her cap and smiles at the difference in the amount of hair she has compared to her brother.

"She looks like you, Babe."

Leila looks up smiling, "She does?"

"She does. She's beautiful."

Our nurse replaces my phone with Madden, "Time for your first family portrait." She snaps away, as I stand beside Leila first holding Madden. Then we switch, and I hold Siarra for several shots.

"What a beautiful family," she says as she hands me the phone.

My family…I have a family.

We went from two to four. The three of them need me…and I, more so, need them.

♬ ♬ ♬

After our family time the day they were born, our parents and siblings came to meet Madden and Siarra. My job was to remind everyone to wash his or her hands. Jean gave me that task, and I've been taking it very seriously. Jean also suggested we keep the visits short and sweet. Between Leila needing her rest, and her breastfeeding every hour, there was no need for long visits. I'm glad Jean said something, because if I had, I know my wife would have fought me.

Besides the physical exhaustion, she must be completely spent emotionally. Her crying hasn't improved much, but her reasons are different. She's very happy and promises these are tears of pure joy. I understand what she's feeling. It's very overwhelming seeing your parents holding their grandchildren for the first time.

Anthony cried, my dad cried, I cried.

Our friends didn't come until day three. Seeing them interacting with my kids was both hilarious and touching. The first ten minutes were very awkward. None of them offered to hold them on their own volition. Instead, they stood and watched me handle them expertly. Yes, I can now hold each of them alone, or together, just like a pro. Hunter took Madden, Scott took Siarra, and Trey hovered in the corner.

Leila laughed at his obvious inexperience with babies. We are all inexperienced, but Trey takes it to another level. He has absolutely no clue how they work.

"They don't have cooties, man," Hunter shook his head in his typical - Trey is an idiot – fashion.

"I just don't want one…or two," Trey responded, never taking his eyes off my kids.

"I'm pretty sure you know it doesn't work that way," Leila threw back. "Unless, you haven't been careful and there are a dozen or so Trey Juniors running around telling dirty jokes to their teachers."

"Fuck no…I double wrap."

"Dude, the language," I scolded

By the end of their visit, he pulled up a chair to their bassinets and watched them sleep. "They are very cute," he admitted and Leila almost died of shock. When he looked up to see her surprised expression, he added, "What? Of course you would have cute babies."

"Well, what do you know? Trey Taylor is a sweetheart."

"Shut it, Little Lair, or I'll tell them their first inappropriate joke."

When it was time to feed the twins, I kicked my band out. There's no way they are witnessing that.

"Damn it. The only reason I stuck around was to finally get a glimpse of Leila's other twins," Trey smirked.

"Get the fuck out," I responded. "Fuck, you made me curse in front of my kids."

On their way out, Trey quipped, "I predict Madden's first words will be Fucking Hunter."

"Babe, we really need to stop cursing," I said to Leila, once they left.

"We?"

"Fine, me."

I always felt like the most responsible of our group until Leila came along. She definitely keeps us in line. I will now have to step it up and keep those jackasses in line.

Not to pat myself on the back, but I've become pretty responsible, literally overnight. I've changed their diapers. I've held one while Leila fed the other, bonding with them in my own way. I can't wait to feed them. Once we get home today, Leila will be "pumping" and I'll be able to give them bottles for the first time.

Leila's blood pressure returned to normal shortly after their birth. She was discharged four days later, but the twins needed to stay due to their jaundice. Dr. Rand assured us it was normal, and there was absolutely no need for concern. It's been six days since their birth. Leila and I would leave the hospital very late at night and head back first thing in the morning. Both nights, she'd cry having to leave them. Once I got her home, she'd pass out until the alarm went off at the crack of dawn.

I'm so tired. I can only imagine how exhausted she must be. Of course, I have no clue since she still stubbornly refuses to admit she's tired. My only indication is the dark circles under her eyes. Otherwise, she's still beautiful. Even while sporting the messy ponytail and wrinkled clothes she laughed about. She's insane. She has no clue how stunning she is. As I watch her now, feeding Madden, I am captivated by her beauty. It confounds me how unassuming she is with her looks. She turns heads wherever we go. When I point that out to her, she claims they're probably gay and looking at me.

There's something very sensual and erotic about the woman you love becoming a mother. I can't explain it and probably never will be able to. Seeing her in this new role has not only made me fall in love with her harder, it's made me want her more than ever.

Of course with the combination of her C-section recovery, and having newborn twins to deal with, I predict our sex life is going to take a hit. It doesn't matter, because I know the build will create for one memorable night.

When I pull out my phone to take a picture of her, she scowls and says, "Ugh, I look gross."

"Shut up," I respond, rolling my eyes at her comment.

"I feel like a milk machine," she gripes while smiling.

"You're a very sexy milk machine."

Leila is handling breastfeeding like a pro. She immediately took to it and both babies "latched on" without an issue. That surprised her. She read up on the subject, learning that it's normal for some women to have issues. Either their milk doesn't come in or the babies don't latch on. I have gotten quite a lesson on the subject and love watching her pull her boob out to feed our children.

We are waiting for the twins to be discharged, and she's giving them a snack to hold them over until we get home. Once Siarra's done, I take her from Leila and place her next to her brother.

I stare down at my children, both content and quiet. They've changed a bit. Their features are more recognizable. I've studied them intently. Siarra has Leila's lips where Madden has her nose. Siarra is impulsive, letting out one short, loud wail one minute, and falling asleep fitfully once fed, where Madden builds to the point of no return until he is fed and is more alert afterwards.

My wife lets out a very loud yawn, drawing my attention away from the babies.

"Tired?"

"No," she gives her standard response while smiling.

"Liar. Once we get home, I'll take care of them so you can take a nice long bath."

"Yeah?"

"Why do you look so surprised?" I ask offended.

She laughs at my expression. "I'm sorry. I'm not surprised. You've been fantastic with them, Jack. I'm so proud of you."

"You don't have faith in me?"

"I do, I just…I'm in awe of you."

"I'm the one who is in awe." I bend and place a tender kiss on her lips.

Dr. Rand pokes his head in and asks, "Am I interrupting…again?" He must think we do nothing but make-out. "Ready to take the munchkins home?"

"We're ready."

"You're all set. They're cleared to go. I'll see you in a week in my office. Good luck to you guys and enjoy every minute. You may feel it's overwhelming and the crying and dirty diapers will never end, but believe me, this phase will go by so quickly. You'll look back and realize that it flew by. So be sure to enjoy it and take it all with a touch of humor. You two are rock solid, and you'll all be just fine."

"Thank you so much, for everything. Thank you for taking such wonderful care of my wife and my babies."

"You are most welcome." He shakes our hands and leaves just as Jean comes in.

"Ok, this is the part when most parents freak out. No freaking out, ok?"

We both nod, but not too convincingly.

Jean helps us dress them, bundle them, and watches as we strap them into their car seats.

I hired a private nurse to help Leila the first few days she's home, as she's also still healing from her C-section and shouldn't be exerting herself. My mom offered to help, but I prefer to have a professional nurse be with them. When I told her so, she laughed, but chose not to argue. So now, there isn't anything left to do but take my family home.

As I secure them all into the car, I say a tiny prayer. I'm not a religious man, and the only other time he heard from me was when Leila was in the hospital, but I'm hoping he's forgiving.

*Please, please protect them always. Keep them safe, healthy, and happy. I* ***love*** *these three people more than anything on this planet.*

*Please...*

## Chapter 25 – Leila

Two weeks after the twins' birth, I was finally starting to feel like myself. We fell into a routine. We had hoards of help and shamelessly took all of it. The OCD in me had a schedule taped to the fridge, detailing feedings and diaper changes. At the end of each night, Jack and I would crash into bed, beyond exhausted.

As we played house, our careers were put on a short hiatus. The guys took the opportunity to spend every waking moment with their girls. Jack pointed out it was almost as if they were squirrels, burrowing nuts to find later when our next tour came up. Scott and Patti were neck deep in wedding planning. Scott was involved in every aspect. Hunter and Mandi were as well, but the difference was Hunter just wanted to be told when and where to show up. Both weddings are scheduled this summer and fall before we leave on tour. Both brides-to-be will be staying behind due to their jobs.

This is the nature of the beast we all chose as a profession. Jack and I do not have the same heartache as leaving our loves behind. We've been lucky to have each other the entire time. Our conundrum is now due to the fact that we are parents. It will be difficult touring with two little ones. The subject of our next tour is constantly hovering above. Every time I try to bring it up, Jack says he doesn't want to talk about it.

We are scheduled to tour just as the twins are a year old. Jack has been working with the label, feverishly trying to postpone it. I knew this would be an issue, but I wasn't going to remind him of that and add to his frustrations.

He used our success as a constant bargaining chip. We have surpassed all their goals. Our feature articles are being published in *Rolling Stone,* as we speak. We also recently received news that we were nominated for four Grammys. I remember the moment perfectly. Jack and I were in the apartment, having a rare moment of peace. Jen called and ordered us to put on the entertainment news channel.

Jack obeyed, flipping through the stations until he found the right one. After the commercial break, they went into their lead story. I heard our names and the categories we were nominated for, but it didn't sink in.

"What did they just say?" I asked him. He was sitting beside me with the same dumbstruck look on his face. Seconds later, our phone started ringing off the hook.

Jen called us all into the studio for a band meeting the very next evening. Jack's initial reaction was to say no. After being cooped up for months, I ripped him a new one. My doctor cleared me, and there was absolutely no reason I couldn't go to the studio. We had baby-sitters practically banging down our door. Once I secured my mother-in-law to watch the twins, I showered, primped, and dressed as if I were actually going to the Grammy's.

When we arrived, Jen waited with Krista and Dylan. They are now married, and Dylan couldn't look happier. We missed the wedding since I was sentenced to bed rest. Charles and Louis from our label were there, as well as Malcolm, since my single was up for its own Grammy. There was a very impressive spread and several bottles of champagne. Louis had gifts for the twins and new contracts for us to sign. The most obvious changes were accommodations during our next tour, as well as our world tour in two years.

At the end of the night, Jack arrogantly informed Louis that our next tour would be postponed in exchange for a new album. We would postpone it by nine months and extend it by one. This would put the twins at almost two years of age. We would travel with a nanny and have our own bus. Our world tour would be scheduled over an extended period of time, having us in the best hotels in each country. Our stay at each tour stop would be no less than a week. His demands seemed too extravagant to me, and I feared Louis would tell him to take a hike. Surprisingly, Louis didn't argue. The pride I felt for Jack that night swelled to mega proportions.

I consciously thought to myself, this is all too much good. Too many great things were happening, and a flash of fear coursed through me.

Later that night, while lying in bed, I shared my thoughts with him.

I'm not a superstitious person by nature. I've always felt things happen for a reason. I believe in fate. I believe in destiny. But the Leila of late, the rock star-wife-mother Leila, is finding it hard to accept all the good fortune I've found. I've become a praying, knocking-on-wood, version of myself.

Sure, we've had our share of bad luck…if you consider a pregnant ex-girlfriend and a furious ex-band member wanting to take you down as misfortune. Afterwards, clarity helped me understand all that happened wasn't the end of the world. We were still healthy and we still had each other…so in reality, we were very fortunate. Through the black clouds, our silver lining prevailed.

Now here we are, happily married with two gorgeous babies. Our careers are on fire. Our families are happy and healthy. Our friends are all securing their own happily ever afters. Every day I worry the bottom will drop out. Can someone go through life blessed beyond reason? I pray to God that we can. I pray daily for my husband and my kids to only have happiness, good health, and more good fortune.

I struggled with trying to understand why some seem to have so much, while others so little. I've decided, for my own peace of mind, to pay it forward. I need to, in order to maintain a level of humility and appreciation. I don't want to ever forget how lucky I am.

I pitched my suggestion to the guys, offering several charities we should donate to. They were all for it and agreed they all felt the same. I then contacted Krista, asking for her help. After our experience with Keeley, we decided on the children's cancer research charity and one for the arts. That girl stole our hearts. Keeley has completed her chemo, and we are all waiting anxiously to hear the news that she is in remission. She has remained in my prayers every single day since meeting her. Jack has continuously sent text messages, notes, and gifts to her since that night in Dallas. We plan on having the Casianos and Keeley, Aubrey, and Trevor out to visit with us this summer.

Krista set up our charity choices on our website and worked with Dylan on a percentage of profits that would be donated to each from Devil's Lair.

I love being home with Jack and the babies. We are both very laid back, easygoing parents. Possibly it's because we have each other twenty-four seven? I'm not sure why it is, but we're enjoying our children, and it's been a wonderful experience so far. Even when it's complete and utter chaos, when both are screaming bloody murder, and we are running on fumes, it's been wonderful.

We've taken the opportunity to visit his parents for a few days, or my dad for a few days. We've become professionals at packing up the car with everything we need. Our apartment is the hub of activity for our friends, and a revolving door for all their therapy sessions. Apparently, becoming parents has qualified us to be their therapists, as well.

The most surprising visit came from Trey. He still isn't very comfortable around the babies, so I was shocked to see him at our door one night out of the blue.

Jack let him in, and I could immediately tell something was wrong. He wasn't his normal cocky self and was very quiet during his visit. When I asked him if he was ok, he nodded quickly, but his eyes said otherwise. Afterwards, when I was putting the twins to bed, he hinted to Jack that Tara was messing with his mind. The minute Jack started firing questions at him Trey clammed up. Soon after, he made a very hasty exit.

So basically, their conversation consisted of two sentences. Regardless, I went off on a tangent, speculating all sorts of scenarios. This had to be good news. There was no way Trey would show up at our apartment unless he was desperate. I knew they had seen each other a few times, but this must mean they are in a relationship. If they are in a relationship, that must mean he's ready to settle down. If all went well, Trey and Tara could be married in a year. Jack finally grabbed me by my shoulders and kissed me passionately, just to shut me up.

When the twins were three weeks old, Jack took me away to our new house. I had yet to see it and was busting at the seams. His parents came to stay with the twins. He didn't tell me we were staying overnight until we got there. He was afraid I would refuse to go. I haven't spent one night away from them, and he was absolutely right, I would have.

My emotions have been almost back to normal. Since coming home, I only cried a few times. One of them being when I found Jack in the nursery, rocking both babies and singing softly to them. I stood in the doorway, silently bawling my eyes out.

When he pulled up to our new home, I lost it. It was incredible. He made the perfect choice. I had seen many pictures, but they didn't do the house justice. He had it decorated for the holidays, and it looked so pretty that I wished we could keep the lights up all year. The inside was even more spectacular. There were two fully decorated Christmas trees, the banister was decorated, and each room had a touch of the holidays.

It's sparsely furnished. He ordered just the necessities to get us through when we would visit. He wants me to furnish it the way I want to and each purchase that he did make was approved by me. The kitchen has all the modern conveniences and then some. We have a beautiful mahogany master bedroom set. He duplicated the same nursery as we have at the apartment. He didn't want the twins to get confused when we would visit. He also ordered some comfy couches, a huge flat screen, guest beds, a dining table and chairs, and a grill and deck furniture.

He ushered me through each room, obviously repeating verbatim what the realtor had told him on his tour. I began to sound like a recording, repeating over and over how much I loved it. When he showed me the deck, I was stunned. I imagined us having many family dinners as the kids ran around on the beach below.

The last thing he revealed was the garage. I was confused why he chose to save this room for last. When he flicked on the lights, a brand new black *BMW X3 SUV* sat waiting with a giant bow.

"Baby, I don't know what to say."

"Do you like it?"

"I love it. It's perfect."

He gathered me in his arms, kissing me passionately. By the time we parted, my breath was coming in short pants and my insides were about to detonate. I wanted nothing more than to christen our new bedroom that night, as well as the couches, and deck lounge under a few blankets for warmth. I still wasn't allowed to have sex and admitted that being alone in that house with him platonically was pure torture. He said he had other plans, and then preceded to show me all the creative methods he could bring me to an orgasm without actually having sex. Loopholes, he called them.

We had Christmas at the house with our parents, Evan, and Liz. Oscar, who doesn't have any family to speak of, is now part of ours and joined us. Of all our friends, Trey was our only guest. The rest were all with their families. Trey initially refused the invite. Jack said not to take it personally, that he always refused invites to family functions. He was surprised he actually came to our wedding. I wouldn't accept that as an option. I wore him down with constant phone calls and texts. I went as far as claiming I would cancel our plans, and Jack and I would show up at his apartment with Christmas dinner.

"You're a pain in my ass, Little Lair," he grumped into the phone.

Victory.

Not only did Trey come, but also stayed over and had a very nice Christmas with all of us. It made me so happy to have him and to see him socializing on a normal level.

Jack and I spent New Year's at home with our children. "Wow, have things changed," he said as we watched the festivities that were in full swing uptown.

"Do you regret it?" I asked, worrying the domestic life had finally gotten to him. He's a rock star, a hot talented one. Others like him are living it up, whoring about, and squandering their money.

"You did not just ask me that," he leveled me with his grey eyes.

I shrugged, focusing back on the *Times Square* coverage.

He gripped my chin, turning my head until I met his gaze. "Right here, is the only place I want to be. Got it?"

We rang in the New Year in our home, wrapped in each other's arms, just where we both wanted to be.

When the twins were six weeks old, Dr. Rand finally gave us the clearance to commence sex. To my dismay, Jack still refrained. Kissing was pretty much all I got from him, and I never knew if that was the kiss that would release Mr. Raunchy. I teased him with my body mercilessly. The beast within me was hard to contain. I gave him a note-worthy blowjob in the shower. I paraded around naked as much as possible. It wasn't until I sang my song while naked, pretending I wasn't aware he was watching me, when he finally caved.

We knew we didn't have much time. It was rushed, hurried, hard, and perfect. Mr. Raunchy gave me one hundred percent, and I took it all. We aren't back to having sex daily like we were, but it's now several times a week.

Progress.

The Grammy Awards were surreal, emotional, and scary as hell. It was the first time we had to leave the twins more than a night. The rest of our friends flew out to LA a few days before, to prolong the celebrations. Jack and I flew out the day before the event, and came back on the red-eye. Sitting in the same arena where we opened our tour last year was a very humbling experience. Seeing all the guys dressed so handsomely, made me teary-eyed. Jack held my hand during the announcement of our categories, squeezing tightly as they opened the envelopes. When the sound of our band name resonated through the Staples Center, the delayed reaction from the five of us was comical. We won two out of the four we were nominated for, Best Rock Song, Best Rock Album. I didn't win for Best Rock Song, but I still couldn't be happier. Once we all returned from LA, we celebrated properly at our favorite place, Granite.

Now that the holidays and the Grammy's are over, all wedding planning has resumed. My dad and Barb are the first ones up. They had decided on

Valentine's Day, which is a few days away. My dad claims it's not as much as the significance of the day, as it would be easy to remember his anniversary each year.

I am so happy for them. Barb has put her house up for sale and has already moved into my dad's. So for all intents and purposes, it is only a piece of paper, but one that they both deserve.

Jack and I offered our house for the wedding, and he and Barb accepted. I want them to have a lovely wedding. It's the least I can do. I still carry some guilt for ruining their original plans. I can't get past the notion that they would all be married for months by now. We're expecting a few dozen guests. Since most of our house is empty, we arranged the ceremony to be in the dining room. The dinner will be in the living room, and the foyer is reserved for dancing.

We've hired a DJ, bartenders, wait staff, and a catering company. I've arranged the house to be decorated with tons of flowers. There is snow on the ground, and the pictures that they will take out on the deck, with the beach as a background, will be stunning.

Evan is the Best Man, and I'm the Matron of Honor. Evan and Lizzy are up next and will be getting married two weeks later at a country club on Long Island.

"Hey, Babe?"

"I'm in here," I call out from our room. Jack was out with the guys tonight. They all went to The Zone to give my dad a mock bachelor party. Sal arranged the whole thing. He's been my dad's best friend forever. Their relationship gets stronger as time goes by. I'm so proud of all the guys. Even Hunter, Scott, and Trey went. My dad's always been a father figure to the guys in Cliffhangers, but my newer band mates have also adopted him as Papa Marino.

Jack walks in to see me breastfeeding Madden. His eyes immediately zone in on his son, who continues to suck enthusiastically. "Why do I find this so damn sexy? Is that sick?"

"Yeah, it kinda is. How was it?"

"It was great. Your dad really enjoyed himself. Sal had food set up. It was fun. That new band he hired is really good. You need to hear them."

"I need to get my ass over there. Sal's mad at me. I predict a lashing when I see him at the wedding."

"Well, you have been kind of busy." Jack lies beside me, gently caressing Madden's head as he continues his meal. Madden isn't phased in the least and never breaks stride. "Siarra's done?"

"Yes, but she was very fussy tonight. I predict a long night."

"I'm going to jump in the shower."

He starts to strip, distracting me from Madden. The all too familiar yearning for him ignites, and the beast rears its horny head. He notices me drooling and smirks and asks, "Missed me?"

"What do you think?"

"I think I need to hurry so we can get Bud to bed and boink before Princess is up."

"Boink? I thought I told you only old people use that word."

"Keeping it clean, Babe." With that he drops his briefs to the floor and saunters into the bathroom completely naked.

"You're evil," I call after him, and he chuckles at my expense.

♫ ♫ ♫

Lizzy and I put the finishing touches on Barb's face. "You look so beautiful," I voice as I meet her gaze in the mirror. She chose a cream tailored dress and my dad is wearing a charcoal grey suit.

She takes my hand, as well as Lizzy's. "I just wanted to thank you two. I am gaining two incredible daughters. My son is a lucky man having such a wonderful sister and a spectacular fiancée. I love you both very much."

"Barb, I can honestly say, I'm the one who should be thanking you. Your strength, your resolve, and your love for my father have given me the security I need to know that he is going to be just fine."

She accepts hugs from us and says, "Ok, let's do this."

Barb's older brother, John, is giving her away today. He is Evan's only blood relative on Barb's side, and they are as close as can be, considering he lives across the country. His wife, children, and their families are also here for the wedding. They will all be staying until Evan and Lizzy's wedding in two weeks. The few aunts, uncles, and cousins I have are here. I haven't seen them since my wedding and look forward to catching up.

Lizzy and I are both wearing champagne colored cocktail dresses, and Evan and Jack are in black suits. I hand Barb her bouquet and wait for our cue. In the distance, we can hear the music change. John approaches as we wait in the hall.

"Ready, Sis?" he asks.

She nods while smiling with a look of contentment settling on her features. She's a fighter and her battles are won. It's time for her to relish in some happiness for once in her life.

We parade down the stairs, and then toward my dad and the minister. The guys stand to his left, watching expectantly as we approach. My babies are in their double stroller, so far cooperating and keeping quiet. Renatta is prepared with pacifiers and bottles if they decide to get vocal.

My dad watches Barb, smiling warmly. My thoughts drift to my mother. I know he misses her terribly, and I wonder what he is feeling right now. It took him a very long time to finally replace her. She will always hold a very huge part of his heart, but I know he has given the rest of it to Barb.

The ceremony is traditional and short. Jack and I exchange glances on more than one occasion. He returns my smile and gives me a wink. Evan's eyes are glued to Liz while sporting his own Cheshire cat smile as well.

The minister announces them man and wife, and my dad embraces Barb, giving her a sweet chaste kiss.

"That's all you got, Anthony?" Sal chimes from the front row.

"She knows what I got," Dad quips back, and Jack laughs at my spontaneous grimace.

Barb moves to hug Evan, Dad comes over to hug me. "I'm so happy for you, Dad."

"Thanks, sweetheart. I am happy." He strokes my cheek softly, his eyes full of emotion. "I'll always love your mom, you know that."

I nod, fighting back the tears that threaten. "I know, and she knows. Barb's a good woman."

He glances over his shoulder at his new bride then turns back to me and says, "She is a rock. She is one of the strongest people I know, and her heart goes on forever." He wraps his arms around me, kissing the top of my head. "I want to say something to my son."

"Ok, go."

Jack congratulates him as he walks to Evan.

"He looks really happy, Babe."

"He is…and he should be." I lean up to give him a peck on his cheek. "You look so damn handsome in a black suit."

He presses his lips against my ear and says, "We may have to sneak away during the party."

"You are an enabler."

"My favorite thing is to enable you." I shake my head at him. I'm still amazed he can make my lower half ignite with need, just from a few simple, very mundane words.

"What?" he asks, amused by my pouting lips.

"You're mean." The twins start fussing, cutting his next thought to the quick. "Well, duty calls," I shrug while pressing my engorged breasts into his hard body.

"I'm the mean one?"

Renatta insists on feeding them their bottles, so I can enjoy the party. I make a quick exit to pump and relieve some of the pressure, returning to find Jack dancing with Barb.

During the course of the night, the party takes on a very laid back, casual vibe. It feels like we are all hanging out, enjoying each other's company. The traditional wedding moments that occur remind us all why we are here, as portraits are taken, first dances are danced, and a modest tiered cake is cut.

Jack dances a slow dance with his daughter tucked into his arms, the photographer capturing the moment for us. I can't wait to frame that beauty.

Once Barb throws her bouquet, she and Dad take off, leaving us all behind to continue with the celebration. They are heading to a secluded cabin in the country for a week and promise they will "try" to keep in touch.

"Hey, Little Lair?"

I meet Trey's eyes, bracing myself for what's coming. He gives himself away every time he starts with, "Hey, Little Lair?"

He came alone, again surprising Jack that he even came at all. Jack admitted he must really care for my dad and me. Tara is traveling at the moment, which gives me an opportunity to ask him some very pressing questions.

"How weird is it knowing your dad is on his way to having mad animal sex?"

"You. Are. Disgusting."

He holds out his hand and asks, "Are you so repulsed, you wouldn't dance with me?"

Payback…

I accept his hand and drag him out to the foyer quickly before he changes his mind. Now is my chance to pick his brain.

"So how are you?" I ask after a few seconds.

"Fine."

"How's Tara?"

He looks down at me, trying to keep an indifferent look on his face. "Fine, I guess. You need to ask her."

I squint at his poker face. "Funny you should mention that, I did." He smirks, but otherwise doesn't respond. "You're spending a lot of time together, that's great."

Still nothing, not even a nod. So I go in for the kill. "She actually said…wait, what were the exact words she used?" I pretend to search my brain for the exact quote. "Oh, yeah. She said 'I've never felt this way before.' What could she mean?"

"No clue."

"Hmm…I wonder. I guess it could go one of two ways. Either, you have successfully damaged her in every way a man can damage a woman, or she's falling for you."

"You been hitting the bottle again?"

"No, the downside of breastfeeding. I'm completely sober."

He pointedly stares at my chest. "Still sporting the giant hooters, I see."

I desperately try to keep a straight face, but fail miserably. "You suck."

"I'm pretty sure that would be Madden and Siarra's job…and most likely Jack's. If I know my horn-bag friend, he's having a field day on those…"

"Ok, that's enough. I call uncle."

"I was wondering how far I'd have to go."

"Trey, all kidding aside, I just want you to be happy."

"Who says I'm not happy? More importantly, who says I need someone to be happy?"

"True. I just think you deserve someone to make you happy."

He contemplates my words as we continue to sway to the music. "Hey, why do men find it difficult to make eye contact?"

"You are impossible," I breathe out from frustration.

"Because breasts don't have eyes." He throws me his panty-soaking smile. "Thanks for the dance."

"Thanks for being an ass," I respond with my own smile.

"I try."

Jack cuts in, "Get your hands off my wife and stop staring at her boobs."

"I'm done with her, she's all yours." He plants a sweet kiss on my cheek and adds, "I'm outta here."

"Trey?" He looks at me over his shoulder and I ask, "Please be careful on that stupid bike?"

A quick nod is all I get before he takes off.

Jack pulls me into his arms to continue the dance. "What was that all about?" he asks while searching my eyes.

"I think our friend is falling for Tara."

"He said that?" Jack asks incredulously.

"No."

He gives me a heavy sigh and says, "Leila, you need to…"

"Jack, a woman knows. Trust me."

His response is to pull me closer, moving his body against mine in an erotic dance. He knows better than to argue with me. Knowing my husband, he's sitting back anxiously waiting for me to either prove myself right, or Trey to prove me wrong. After a few minutes of rubbing Jack Junior against me, he asks, "Can we kick everyone out yet? I'm ready to rock your world."

"Soon, Babe." I promise. "Are the walls soundproof?"

He understands my question and nods, "Completely. I tested them already."

"Good. Seeing you in your suit has riled me up. Tonight is going to be a loud one."

Jack's parents are spending the night. They want to take care of the twins so Jack and I can sleep in tomorrow. Evan and Lizzy are also staying. The few guests that are still mulling around all bid their goodbyes as they file out. Once the last one is gone, I drag my husband straight to our room. I plan on making good on my promise. I also plan on rocking his world.

We stop to check on the twins. They both are sleeping fitfully, at the moment. I tug him out of their room, quietly closing the door behind us. "Hurry."

He throws me over his shoulder and trots down the hall to our room.

In one motion, he closes the door and pushes me up against it. I moan when he captures my earlobe in between his teeth. "God, I love that sound." He presses his open mouth to mine and drags his tongue across the roof of mine. His hands find my zipper at the back of my dress. My hands unbutton his shirt, quickly tugging it from his slacks.

We break long enough to remove our clothes, and then resume with more fervor than before. He captures my lace-covered nipple in between his teeth and tugs while his hands expertly work at unfastening my bra in the back. It drops to the floor, and he slips a hand into my panties and takes my now bare, pebbled nipple back into his mouth. He sucks shamelessly…my husband is a fan of breast milk.

He strokes me slowly, deliberately, right before sinking two fingers into me. I throw my head back, banging it into the wood door, causing a loud knock. "Ssh. You're going to wake them up," he scolds.

"Then stop driving me crazy."

"I have a better idea." He lifts me and carries me to our bed, placing me with my head at the foot. While standing at my head he skims his hands down my torso, snagging my panties in the process and sliding them down my legs…and in the process, Jack Junior rests on my forehead.

"Good idea," I murmur with my lips against him. He looks down at me between our bodies, just as I take him into my mouth and palm his heavy sack.

"Ah fuck, Babe."

I grip his thighs to hold his position above me. The motion of my mouth spurs his groans. He rests his head against my thigh, panting against it. Suddenly his mouth is on me, covering me completely. The more he sucks, the more I do. It gets to a point where I no longer can concentrate on him, because of what he is doing to me. The angle of his head, the position of his mouth, and the voraciousness of his sucks, all bring me to a severe orgasm. As it rolls on, he increases his tempo, bringing me right into my second one. Jack Junior abandoned, laying in wait against my face.

When I stop shuddering beneath him, he places one chaste kiss against my still very sensitive pussy. Now that I can concentrate again, I reclaim him.

He pushes up to a standing position, groaning erotically before saying, "Babe, I need to bury myself in you."

He pulls out of my mouth, turns around, and does just what he claimed he would do. While buried completely inside of me he kisses me erotically and I lose it for the third time. As I clench around him he seizes above me, muttering my name against my ear.

"Fuck, Babe. That was…"

"Perfect."

## Chapter 26 – Evan

Today is the day I've been waiting for since our fifth date. It was on that night while we had sex for the first time that I decided I would marry this woman. I kept my revelation to myself. We barely knew each other, most would think I lost my mind…but I knew. I knew, without a shadow of a doubt, she would be Mrs. Evan Miller.

Here we are, two years later, proving my premonition true. My nerves have moved beyond nervousness and into anxiousness. This day has dragged on torturously slow. I feel like someone keeps moving the clock back, just to fuck with me.

It's finally here.

The music changes as my sister walks down the aisle. She smiles shyly, locking gazes with her husband standing to my left. My niece and nephew sit adorably beside him, facing our guests. At three months of age, they are probably the youngest ring bearer and flower girl ever assigned. Every so often, Jack rocks the stroller to settle their fussiness. Madden is wearing the tiniest tux I've ever seen. Siarra is in a tiny version of Leila's dress. It was Liz's idea. The only accessories that are not wedding approved are the pink and blue binkies they are currently sporting.

Liz and Peter appear in the aisle, and I feel the oxygen leaving my lungs. She is spectacular. She looks more like a runway model than a bride. Her form-fitted dress is very plain. Except for it being off white, it doesn't resemble a wedding dress at all. Her hair is long and loose, just the way I love it. She smiles warmly, her smoky eyes piercing me from across the room. It takes all my efforts to not move to her, and instead stay rooted at the altar.

I'm vaguely aware of her dad placing her hand in mine and patting me on my shoulder. She steps closer, never taking her eyes off of me.

"You are stunning."

She squeezes my hand and smiles wider. The ceremony is fairly quick, my only suggestion during the wedding planning. I predicted I wouldn't be able to calmly stand at her side for a long duration, and I was right. Only ten minutes in, and I'm ready to kiss my bride.

Just as we exchange our vows, Madden voices his opinion. Everyone laughs when Jack shrugs apologetically. Leila fights a grin as she watches Jack remove his son to bounce him in his arms. The minister tries to project his voice above Madden's cry and fails. He rushes through his words and pronounces us man and wife, probably cutting our ceremony shorter even further. After I kiss my bride in a very inappropriate manner, I turn to fist bump my nephew. "Thanks, Bud."

Everyone laughs, except Madden, who serenades us as we walk down the aisle hand in hand. Jack follows with a screaming Madden and Leila pushes the stroller.

"Congrats you two, I'm so sorry."

"Don't be. That was awesome," I admit.

"Well, I better calm him down or Siarra will join in," Leila apologizes and kisses us each before rushing off with a screaming Madden, with Jack and Siarra in tow.

Lizzy giggles adorably. "God, I love those babies," she says.

"Yeah? I'm pretty sure we can take one without them noticing."

She wraps her arms around my back, tilting her face up toward mine. "I want one of our own."

"Ok, I'm all up for getting started now if you'd like. I love a challenge. You've just given me a mission."

She lifts up on her toes until her lips are against my ear, "Mission accomplished."

I hear her words, but I'm having trouble processing them. Our guests rush down the aisle, anxious to congratulate the happy couple. Liz smiles casually while she accepts well wishes, kisses, and hugs. Every few seconds she meets my still stunned gaze and winks.

I'm going to be a dad? Did I misunderstand her?

She can't drop a bomb like that and leave me hanging!

I patiently wait, for what seems like an eternity, until our first dance is announced. Liz and I chose Jack's song *Reason I Am.* We both fell in love with the lyrics. He sings it live for us as a wedding present while I wrap her in my arms and sway to the melody.

"Babe, you can't do that to me. Are you serious?"

For a split second she looks unsure and nervous. "Are you freaking out?"

"No…no, definitely not. I would be thrilled. Is it true?"

She smiles and nods, "Yes, sweetie. I found out yesterday. I've been so busy, I missed my last shot. I was scared you would think it was too soon."

"Babe, I couldn't be happier."

"Oh, thank God," she says, clearly relieved.

"Holy shit, I'm going to be a dad?"

"A great one. Let's keep it to ourselves until we get back. I want to enjoy the peace and quiet for a bit. Once my mom finds out, we're done."

I laugh at her admission. "Good point."

During our conversation, I didn't even notice others joined us on the dance floor until Joe bumps me with his ass, from behind.

"Congrats, you two."

We stop dancing to allow Joe and Nina to embrace each of us. "Who would have thought a year ago all this would be happening? Leila is a freakin' mother! Logan is a dad. You're married, and even Matt is attached. Damn Ev, it's all surreal."

"I know." I focus on the hand he has clasped with Nina's. "I wonder who's next?"

Joe chuckles and looks down at his very petite girlfriend, choosing not to respond. During the course of the night, most of my band mates all voice the same observations that Joe had. We're all changing, for the better…but changing, nonetheless.

I'm a married man with a baby on the way. It scares me to know I'm about to cross over a very major threshold in my life. I watch Liz from across the room, mingling and laughing. She's such a light in my life, a positive influence. I don't have many, but the ones I have are gems…my mom being one of them. It took me a long time to forgive what she and Anthony did. Leila helped me understand the circumstances better. I now get why she did what she did. She'd do anything to protect me, even if it was keeping me from my biological father for years and years. Would I do something so extreme to protect my child?

What if I suck as a dad? I haven't a doubt that my wife would ensure that would never happen, but it scares me anyway. The thought that I will be molding a person, contributing to their make-up is very scary. I'm sure most of it has to do with your genes and your DNA. I'd worry more if Doug were my biological father. The man was an asshole, but he's not my father and Anthony is. Anthony is one of the best dads on Earth. He patiently waited for me to work out my shit. He was always there, always ready to support and love me, once I did. I can only hope to be half as good of a dad as he is.

Maybe it does take a village. Maybe it's all the other influences in a baby's life that also help mold who they become. If that's the case, between my parents, my sister, my wife, and my in-laws, our baby will be the luckiest baby on Earth.

"You're lost in thought. Are you ok?" Leila asks as she takes a chair beside me.

"I'm more than ok. I'm kind of sitting here, counting my blessings, and praying I'll always have them."

She smiles and takes my hand. "We are so alike. I feel the same. It's sometimes scary as hell to accept all the good and not worry. Ev, you deserve this happiness and more."

"Thanks, Lei." I nod toward Jack, who is holding Siarra while chatting with his band mates. "Who would have thought, huh? He's a great dad."

"He is the best." She looks around the room, smiling warmly. "Things are changing, but for the better. I had this exact vision at my own wedding. I didn't share it with anyone, but I pictured this exact scene. I also visualized us years from now, getting together to celebrate a birthday or a milestone in our careers. Our kids running around, loving life." She stops to contemplate a thought before adding, "Such is life, I guess. Every one of us was destined for this. Every path leading right to this moment."

The look on her face causes me to laugh. "You've become very philosophical in your old age."

"Shut it, you dork," she shoves me lovingly.

"And there's my annoying sister."

Liz strolls over, smiling wide. "What are you two up to?"

I pull her onto my lap, kissing her before answering her question. "My sister was just reminding me of how lucky I am."

"You are one lucky son of a bitch," she deadpans. She kisses me and adds, "Ready to live happily ever after?"

"I couldn't be more ready."

## Chapter 27 – Lori

I hang up the call, grinning from ear to ear. Jen may be a bitch, but she's a brilliant one. She, for whatever reason, has taken me under her wing. The woman likes me. My loyalty will always be with Leila, but I do exploit Jen's kindness without shame. My goal was to get Cliffhangers noticed, and it's finally happened.

The label was very impressed with my boys and how they handled touring with Devil's Lair. They were more impressed with their music and their fan following. It's been growing in leaps and bounds, and L.R.V. Media aren't idiots. They have a new cash cow on their hands, and they aren't going to let it go. My appreciation for Jen is valid, because none of this would have happened, if it weren't for her.

My band has yet to know what we've been plotting. Evan has been away on his honeymoon, and I wasn't going to make the announcement without him. The more time that passes, the more anxious I get to share our news. Wasting no time, I scheduled a band meeting the night after Evan gets home. I want to break the news to them alone before we have to meet with the suits from the label. I've asked them to join me at The Zone, feeling it was apropos to go back to where it all began.

I'm very proud of myself. I haven't told a soul, not even Matt. I'm usually not good at keeping secrets. Usually, my thoughts get the best of me and I somehow crack under pressure. I haven't let on, or hinted at what's coming for the guys. Honestly, I haven't really had time to anyway. With all these weddings and life events taking over our lives, I've been quite busy.

Matt moved in with me a few weeks ago. We rarely spent a night apart anyway. It was silly to both be paying rent. The obvious choice was my place since it's a hell of a lot nicer than his. It was an adjustment for me, a big one. I can be a tad selfish and sharing my space proved to be a challenge. At first, I set aside a few drawers and a tiny corner of my closet. When he saw how "generous" I was being, he scoffed and made due. He knew better, but he also knew how to handle me. Over the next few weeks, he has successfully invaded my home, in more ways than one. I never saw it happening, until one day I looked around and he was everywhere.

We've been getting along so well. Sure we fight, and when we do, we are both stubborn as hell. He usually is the one to cave first and offer an apology. That serves me well, since I hold a grudge better than the rest of them.

He also knows how to give me my space. He understands I need it at times more than air. Today he informed me he was helping his brother, Logan, with some house stuff. He left early this morning and said he'd see me later this afternoon. I'm sure whatever Logan needs help with will not take up an entire day, but my boyfriend has fallen in love with his little niece, Michelle, and finds it difficult to leave once he gets there.

I'll never admit to him that I no longer need as much space as I used to. That would mean I'd have to admit I miss him…but I do. I'm not the dependent - *I can't stand being away from him* - type. I am finding I miss him more often than not and can't wait for his return.

Part of the problem is all my friends ditched me. Alisa is busy with Michelle. Leila has her hands full with the twins and her annoying husband. I don't have many friends, for some reason women don't like me. I'm lucky to have the two best friends that I do. I've gotten a little closer to Nina, but it's not the same. Besides, she's always with Joe anyway. So, I'm bored…a lot…just as I am right now.

I look around my apartment trying to come up with a task. I hate shopping alone and I hate cleaning. Matt's dirty jeans sitting in the corner call out and guilt me into thinking that I most definitely should be doing laundry.

Crap, when has my life become so normal?

I start throwing articles of clothing into the laundry basket, including Matt's clothes. I'm feeling generous today. I mechanically start rummaging through pockets to be sure nothing of importance is left in them, the memory of washing his cell phone coming to my mind. That was a disaster, and I learned my lesson.

In the back pocket of his jeans is a crumpled up piece of paper.

*Lily 201-555-9090.*

What the fuck? I grip the paper in between my clenched fingers, the steam rising within me. Would he be that stupid? This is his handwriting. He wrote out this chick's name and number.

I search my mind back to the time when he cheated on Leila. The things she shared with me back then sticking in my subconscious. She had no idea he was cheating on her. He was always attentive, romantic, sweet. There were no red flags. She once called him a serial cheater, who was very good at it. As if uncorked, all these memories come flooding back. All the conversations I had with her, convincing her he was a prick and it wasn't her fault. All the tears she shed over him. All of it comes rushing back, as if it were yesterday.

I call the number hastily as a private caller. I have no idea why. A breathy hello comes over the line. She repeats it and hangs up. I don't know what to do. I have no idea how I should handle this.

I need Leila.

"Hello?"

"Can I come over?"

"What's wrong?"

"I don't want to get into it over the phone," I respond in a throaty whisper.

"Lor, you're scaring me."

"Please?"

"Yes, absolutely."

I'm at her apartment building in record time. She immediately approves my arrival and stands waiting at her apartment door. "Lor, what happened?"

"I'm scared."

The short trek it takes to get to her apartment is long enough to have me ready to dump his ass, as soon as possible. She ushers me in. Jack is putting Madden into his stroller where Siarra awaits patiently. He takes one look at me and knows better than to give me a smartass comment. Instead he says, "I'll take them for a ride, so they can nap."

"I'm sorry, Jack."

"Don't worry about it." He kisses his wife and heads out with the twins.

Leila shrugs, "I told him you were very upset. It was his idea to leave."

"Thanks, Lei."

I sit heavily on the couch, and she sits beside me. She waits for me to speak first. I pull out the note and hand it to her.

"What's this?"

"I found it in his jeans. I was about to do laundry and there it was."

She frowns and shakes her head, "So?"

"Leila, I can't handle him cheating on me."

She shakes her head again, "Don't jump to conclusions."

"What if he is? What if he is simply incapable of being monogamous?"

"Lori, you can't assume all this from one little name and number. There could be a ton of reasons for this."

"Yeah? Like what?"

"It happens to Jack all the time. Someone could have slipped it to him. Doesn't mean he intended to call her."

"Jack's not a cheater, and that's Matt's handwriting."

She stubbornly shakes her head, sighing impatiently. "You need to stop. Before you speculate, you need to ask him."

"No way. There is no way I'm setting myself up for that."

She rolls her eyes, clearly losing her patience with me. "Where is he now?"

"He is supposed to be at Logan's helping him with house stuff."

"You don't believe he is?"

I let out a short, sarcastic laugh. "Not any more."

"Text him."

"No." She pulls the phone out of my hands and starts typing out a text. "Lei." I reach for it and she swats me away.

"I am not going to have you assuming the worst until you have just cause to."

I read the text she just sent and wait for a response. She asked him how it was going with Logan and how much more did they have to do.

When my phone bings with a response, I'm afraid to look.

*It's going great. We're almost done. I'll be home in a few hours.*

Leila picks up my phone and says, "Call Lis."

This is all so foreign to me. This insecurity, feeling completely unsure of myself, it's not who I am. I avoid. I run. I ignore. I've already proven that when it comes to Matt. I warned him. I told him over and over, I would kill him if he ever did this to me. How arrogant can he be to not have taken me seriously? More importantly, how stupid?

I reluctantly dial Alisa's number, hoping she doesn't answer. When she does, I get right to the chase. "Lis, is Matt there?"

"Hey, Lor. No, he left a while ago. Are you ok?"

"Yeah, don't worry, hon. I'm fine."

Alisa starts talking to Logan in the background and he gets on the phone. "What's wrong?"

"He's not answering his cell," I lie. There is a silence on the other end. "Do you know where he is?"

"Um…ah, he had a stop to make."

"For you?"

A short pause tells me Logan is covering for his brother. "No, um..." Logan fumbles with his words and adds, "Car trouble."

"Yeah, ok. Well, if he calls, tell him I called."

"Sure, Lori. I will."

Leila watches as I end the call and stare at the phone. "Ok, he's not there, his brother is covering for him. He's lying."

A few minutes later, Matt calls my cell.

"Answer it," she commands forcefully. I shake my head like a child. "Answer. It."

"Hello."

"You ok? Logan said you were looking for me?"

"Where are you?"

"I'll be home soon." He avoids my question and adds, "Love you."

I end the call without a response. Tears prick my eyes, causing my blood to boil in my veins. He doesn't deserve my tears.

"He didn't answer my question."

Leila shakes her head. “There’s got to be a logical explanation to this nonsense.”

Three seconds later and he sends a text, which I choose to ignore.

*Lori, what’s going on?*

The logical explanation keeps repeating itself over and over in my thoughts. He’s done with you. Matt doesn’t do break-ups. Matt cheats. This is his cowardly way of ending it.

Prick.

My practical side takes control. I’ll give him one shot to explain. I’ll know instantly if he’s lying. Then he gets two days to get the fuck out of my life. There’s no way I can continue to work with the band. I’m not that strong enough of a person. Jen will set me up with something else. She’ll help me.

Leila sits quietly, watching me, lost as to what she should do or say. She opens her mouth to speak and then chooses not to. I sit stone still on her couch for twenty minutes. My inner monologue completely occupies my attention. When her cell buzzes with a text, she silently reads it and responds quickly.

“What?”

“Nothing. It was Jack.”

I realize I once again barged in to their lives with my fucking drama. “I’m sorry. I’ve been sitting here forever. Did you guys have plans?”

“They can wait.”

“Lei?” Her cell buzzes again and she frowns while reading the text. “Leila?”

“What?”

“Tell Jack to come back. I’ll go home and figure out what I want to do.”

“Matt’s downstairs…with Jack. He wants to talk to you.”

“No. Tell him no.”

"Lori, you need to hear him out. Stop being so selfish."

"You of all people should know how I'm feeling right now."

"It's not the same." She sighs when I throw her a look. "It's not. You have no proof and I walked in on him. There's a big difference." She types out a text and waits. A few seconds later, Jack walks into the apartment, pulling the stroller through the door. Matt is right on his heels.

"What the fuck is going on, Lor?"

"Thanks," I snip at Leila.

"We'll give you some privacy," she ignores my sarcastic comment and stands.

"No," I grab her wrist, pulling her back onto the couch.

"Lori, can we go home and discuss this?"

"Nope. Whatever you have to say, you can say here." He looks at me like I've completely lost my mind. I have to hand it to him, he's very good at this. Leila was right.

"I'm a little lost as to what it is I'm supposed to say. You are acting like a nut again, and I have no idea why."

"You're slick. Think hard, it may come back to you…you prick."

"Nice. So this is how you want to play this?" he has the gall to get visibly angry with me.

"Play what? You want me to cut to the chase?" I slap the note on the table. "Who the fuck is Lily?"

He looks stunned before confusion takes over. "Where did you get that?"

"You first. Who. Is. Lily?"

"Can we go home to talk about this?" he pleads, as if he's talking to a child.

"Last chance," I fold my arms and wait.

His facial expression goes from impatience to anger. He actually has the nerve to stand before me right now and continue to seethe with anger.

"Fine. You want to be a difficult bitch?" He slams a little black box on the table before me.

Leila walks away, towing Jack and the kids with her. I sit stupidly, not knowing what to do.

"Go ahead, open it. You want to know who Lily is? She's a jeweler. She's the fucking jeweler I used to buy your goddamn engagement ring! Do you want to know where I've been? I've been at the Marina, on my buddy's boat, making it all nice and special for you. Do you want to know why I was making it special? Because I was going to take you there tonight and ask you to fucking marry me!"

I can't believe I lost faith in him so quickly. There's something sincerely wrong with me. He doesn't deserve me, or my huge ego…and I don't deserve to be happy. I am an untrusting, self-centered bitch.

He sits heavily beside me, continuously shaking his head. I've ruined it for him. The lump in my throat makes it hard for me to speak. Even if I were able to say the words, I'm sorry doesn't begin to excuse my behavior.

I need him to understand what caused this. Matt only responds when I'm completely honest with him. "I know this will sound like a pathetic excuse, but I love you so much, and the thought of you ever cheating on me or leaving me, causes me to act ridiculously. That's the only way I can describe what happened today."

"So, every time you assume something, I can expect this nonsense? Lori, I can't live with you mistrusting me at every turn. I made mistakes, but I was young and stupid. My cock controlled everything I did back then. You can't continue to hold my past against me. You need to trust me. We've discussed this before. You were very clear in explaining to me you wouldn't tolerate unfaithfulness. I made it very clear to you I wouldn't do that to you. I'm not that person anymore. I love you more than anything on this goddamn planet…but I can't live like this."

He scrubs his hands over his face, leaving them covering his eyes. My heart splinters, yet again, from the anguish I'm causing him. I really don't deserve to be happy. We sit, side by side silently, for the longest time. We're at a crossroads. We clearly still have issues that we need to resolve before we can commit to forever.

Hearing the twins crying is only adding to my anguish. I've screwed up Leila's day. I've fucked up my relationship, once again. I don't deserve any goodness in my goddamn life.

He turns to me and waits until I meet his gaze. "I had such high hopes for this day."

"You're making me feel worse than I already do." I lift the box, slowly lifting the top. A beautiful, classic engagement ring sits ominously inside. A dangling promise that I'm not sure either one of us can keep. "It's beautiful."

He doesn't respond and sits brooding while staring at the ring.

"I want to accept this. I want to say yes and without a doubt I'll marry you. I'm afraid you no longer want me to, or will believe me if I say so." He remains quiet, not helping me out at all. His eyes focused on the ring sitting in my hands, and not on me. "Matt, the only thing I can say is I do want to. I do want to marry you, but I know we have issues that are still lying beneath the surface. Actually, I have issues. It wouldn't be fair to accept until I work out my shit. But I do love you. I would rather be alone than be without you. I'm asking you to hold onto this and not give up on me." I wait to continue until he lifts his eyes from the ring to mine. "I'm asking for you to wait for me." After a few seconds pass, I take his hand and add, "Please?"

I hold out the box, and he takes it in his other hand. The tears that I've kept at bay, all day, finally spill. Once they start, there's no stopping them. He doesn't comfort me with his words. Knowing my boyfriend, he's completely baffled at the moment. A small sign of hope ignites when he finally pulls me into his embrace and holds me tightly.

After a few very long minutes, he quietly says, "I'll wait."

I tilt my head to look into his eyes. His face is still pained, but his expression softens. He wipes away my tears, palming my face in his hand. I lean into his touch, closing my eyes to stop the tears from flowing. When I open them, I quietly ask, "Can we go home now?"

"Yeah, let's go home."

# Chapter 28 – Jack

It's the twenty-fourth of May…Memorial Day weekend, and my son and daughter's six-month birthday. Six months? That's insane. It's just a blip of time. And yet, so much has happened. They develop so quickly. The first year is a miracle to watch. They go from two tiny helpless babies, and slowly, over each week that passes, something monumental occurs. The first time they belly laughed. The first time they slept through the night. The first time they recognized us. The first time Madden got frustrated, or Siarra got angry. They're people. They are two tiny, perfect, beautiful people.

They have us wrapped around their little fingers…and I wouldn't want it any other way. Everything and everyone in our lives have graciously taken a back seat to Madden and Siarra.

Juggling two kids, very demanding careers, and a bunch of nuts that we call friends and family, hasn't been easy. There have been near break-ups, weddings, engagements, and pregnancies all vying for our attention.

Anthony and Barb finally became husband and wife. It only took them twenty years to get to that point. Barb has taken Anthony's name, and my wife constantly busts Evan's chops that he should do the same.

Evan and Lizzy not only got married, but they announced upon the return from their honeymoon that they are expecting this fall. It was a surprise for them, as well as for us. Liz found out the day before their wedding. Leila is so excited that our kids will have a cousin their age. My brother-in-law is almost as bad as I was when Leila was pregnant…almost.

They both officiated as godparents to the twins. We had a simple ceremony and later celebrated at a quiet restaurant with our immediate families. Neither Leila nor I are very religious and purposefully kept it low key.

Hunter and Mandi set a date for their wedding. Trey tried to talk him and Scott into having a double ceremony / shared party to spare him being tortured twice. Trey said he's officially done with weddings and to please stop inviting him.

Lori and Matt are almost engaged. She was presumptuous in assuming he was cheating, when in fact he was planning their engagement. Afterwards, they both took a step back to regroup. They've enrolled in couples' therapy to help with her trust issues. She has made it very clear that when and if he asks again, she'll be ready.

Matt's brother Logan and his wife Alisa are doing well. Their daughter Michelle is walking now. Joe and Nina are going very strong. They are perfect together. It's only a matter of time before they join the rest of us happily married couples. Her ex-boyfriend came sniffing around, wanting to get back together, until Joe showed up at his place and pretty much scared the crap out of him.

L.R.V. Media have officially signed Cliffhangers. They are headlining their own tour next spring. They all have Lori to thank, as well as our agent. Jen is teaching Lori the ropes, and it's paying off ten-fold. Lori is more tenacious than Jen is. The only difference is Lori has an engaging personality and Jen does not.

Jen and Malcolm are getting a divorce. Malcolm reached out to Leila. Actually, he groveled, hoping this doesn't affect their working relationship now, or in the future. Leila assured him that nothing has changed, as far as her plan for her career. As long as he is ok with it and doesn't nag her, all is good.

With all the positive going on in our group and all the life events occurring, it has done nothing to change Trey. He's been seeing Tara for months now. He's included her when we hang out casually, but has never invited her to any major events. Leila and Tara have become good friends. She vents to my wife about her feelings for him and how she has no clue what he feels for her. I repeatedly tell Leila to stay out of it. She insists Trey has feelings for Tara and just needs help figuring it out.

Trey is unaware of all that Leila knows. I fear if he finds out, the shit will hit the fan. We are having a huge half-year birthday party for the twins at the beach house today. All our friends and families are coming, including Tara. Leila invited her, claiming she's our friend and has every right to be there. In fact, she had Tara come early to help with the preparations.

The weather is cooperating, and my wife is off the wall excited. She insisted on doing all the party prep herself, and I must say, she's done an awesome job. The deck is decorated with brightly colored balloons. She made all the appetizers and sides and has three chefs grilling a variety of main course choices. She's brilliant.

The twins are fed, bathed, dressed, and ready to host their first official party. My little bud, Madden, looks like a mini rock star in his jeans and black t-shirt. Princess girl is in a pink tutu. I keep snapping pictures of them. I can't stand it. They are so fucking cute. Madden has my coloring and dimples. His eyes are all Leila's. Siarra has Leila's coloring and my eyes.

"Ok, we're all set," Leila says, joining me on the deck. I have Madden on my lap, and Tara is holding Siarra. Madden smiles wide when he sees his mommy. She grabs the camera, snapping away. "Show mommy your dimples, Madden," she croons, and he giggles. He bounces his legs and arms, reacting to her voice.

"You two don't need both of them, do you? I'd be happy to take one off your hands," Tara says only half jokingly.

"Nope, we are kind of attached to both of them. Right, bud?" I ask Madden, and he grabs my nose. He reaches for Leila, and she lifts him out of my arms.

"Where are my babies?" my mom shouts from inside the house. She beelines right out onto the deck and right over to Madden, hitches him on one hip and places Siarra on her other. She doesn't even bother to ask for permission.

I shrug and apologize to Tara for my mother's behavior.

"It's ok. I expected it."

Every time one of our guests arrive, Tara's eyes fly to the door. Leila introduces her to anyone she doesn't know, proudly singing her praises. Tara is a very talented writer and our feature articles were awesome. She received all sorts of accolades from *Rolling Stone* and several freelance job offers from other prestigious magazines. The only problem was Trey's issue. Her editor wasn't happy with the word count or the content. From what Tara told us, he was actually furious and threatened to pull the recap article. Trey proved to be a very difficult subject to interview, and Tara did the best she could. She went above the editor's head and secured the publication with the Editor in Chief.

She said she may have burned that bridge, but she felt she was being bullied and wouldn't bow down to his demands.

"Lei?" Lori calls from the kitchen.

"Out here."

She walks out onto the deck with her hand thrust out in front of her.

"Lori, it's beautiful." Leila takes her hand as they both squeal. Patti, Lizzy, and Mandi all come rushing over to investigate. The girls are so loud that they practically clear the deck. The males all run to grab a beer and then down to the beach.

An hour into the start of the party, Trey still hasn't shown. "He said he was coming," Leila whispered to me. "She looks upset."

"Babe, don't get involved." She pins me with her eyes and then sticks out her tongue. "The day Madden or Siarra does that, I'm putting you over my knee."

"Is that a threat?"

I lean into her, close enough for my bottom lip to be touching hers. "It's a promise." Instantly, we forget the few dozen guests mulling around and lock lips like we are in our bedroom.

Hunter comes up beside us, "Keep going. In fact, if you slip away, I'll cover for you," he murmurs directly into my ear.

"What the fuuuu…gggge?"

"That was impressive. You switched gears mid fuck."

I push his chest, "Get lost. Why are you bothering me?"

Scott joins us next and says, "He bet me a hundred bucks that Leila will get pregnant by the time the twins are a year old."

Leila and I both level Hunter with our glares. "Really? You're betting on my wife?"

"Whatever. So are you going to slip out?"

"Who's slipping out?" Trey saunters over, his helmet tucked under his arm without a care in the world. "Lair, you're having slipping problems? Sorry, dude." He kisses Leila on the cheek and adds, "Actually, I should say sorry to you."

She shoves him, "You're late."

"No, I'm not. It's still the twenty-fourth."

"You rode your bike here?"

"No, I walked the seventy miles." He lifts the helmet and adds, "This is just in case I got hit while walking the shoulder on the parkway."

She releases a heavy sigh, just as Trey focuses on Tara. He looks down at Leila, not at all amused.

"She's my friend. What's the problem?"

"She's upset with me. So, thanks." He walks to Tara, they exchange a quick kiss, and he motions for her to follow him off the deck and down to the beach.

"You did it now, Little Lair," Hunter assumes the role of Trey.

She looks worried for all of three seconds and shrugs before moving on to mingle with our guests.

"She's on a mission," Hunter notices.

"It's been her one and only goal."

"Her one and only?" Hunter looks visibly upset. "Damn it! Her one and only goal should be your cock."

"You're a fucking sicko." I remember the twins and lower my voice, "And stop making me curse."

The party is in full swing and based on how much my friends are drinking, I predict a bunch of houseguests tonight. I haven't held my kids all day. They've been passed around between all four grandparents, never leaving a human lap the entire time. These two are going to be spoiled beyond reason.

Leila pulls out the cake, anticipating one or both of the twins don't have much longer before they crash. Madden has been rubbing his eyes, and Siarra has her - I'm about to lose it – look.

With much luck, they participate in the pictures without freaking out. Madden is happy as a pig in shit, sucking on his cake-covered fist with much gusto. Siarra wants no part of it, and after the fiftieth picture, she puckers her adorable face and loses it.

"Ok, party's over for these two," Leila announces. We each grab a twin, parade them around for their goodbye kisses, and retreat with them for their bedtime routines. This is my favorite part of the day.

"I'll throw *Cake Boss* in the tub."

She bends over and kisses his cake-covered cheek, "Yummy."

We have bedtime down to a science, and we are back with our guests in no time. Most of them have moved down to the beach. Leila and I join their huge circle with baby monitor in tow. Hunter is telling tour stories while everyone laughs at his expense.

Leila sits on my lap, snuggling close for warmth. "Where's Trey and Tara?" she asks, scanning the circle.

"With any luck, he's getting some." She shoves my shoulder and I chuckle.

"You have a one track mind."

I press my lips against her ear and admit, "You love my one track."

"I sure do," she whispers while wiggling on my lap.

"When are these people leaving?"

She laughs out loud and some of our friends look over at us. Hunter quips, "Tick…tick…tick."

"I may kill him before the twins' one year birthday," she mumbles so only I can hear her.

"I'll pay you a hundred bucks if you do."

As our party dwindles, we're left with Joe, Nina, Hunter, Mandi, Scott, and Patti. Trey and Tara never resurfaced. Our parents were the first ones to leave, pretty much minutes after Madden and Siarra made their exits…it's a good thing Leila and I don't take it personally. Evan and Liz left because she was exhausted. We offered for them to stay, but they had plans in the morning. Lori and Matt had some celebrating to do, Logan and Alisa needed to get home to relieve the babysitter.

Such has become our lives…

Fireworks are lighting the sky in the distance. "This place is my favorite place to be," Leila says while nuzzling my neck.

"Me, too."

She lifts her face so I can capture her lips with mine. As the kiss intensifies my fingers grip her hips. She's stirring me up, and I only want to take her upstairs and make slow, sweet love to her. The love I feel for her is so strong, so powerful, and even after all this time, it still scares me to death.

She's the first to pull away, sucking in a deep breath as she does. "How do you do that?"

"What?"

"You suck the life out of me. You make it so I forget to breathe, to think." She kisses my neck, adding, "Every kiss is like our first one. Remember, on the balcony during your party? I've never had a kiss as powerful as that one. You made me weak in the knees. I fell in love with you after that kiss."

"I did, too. I kept denying it, but it couldn't be stopped. You took my heart hostage that day, and never let it go." I place a gentle kiss to her soft lips, lingering for a few seconds before pulling away. "Baby, every kiss feels like the first one. Every time I take you, it feels like the first time. Every single time I do, my heart squeezes with the same emotions, just like it did the first time."

"Jack, you've made me so happy," she wipes away a single tear, never looking away from my eyes.

"Baby, I can't put into words how happy you've made me. There isn't a word that's adequate enough. I remember thinking this before. I tried. I came up with a few, but not that one single, all-encompassing word that could describe what you've done to me."

She nods, understanding my point.

"Leila, I do know that we were meant to be. You were made for me, and I for you. You've left an indelible mark on my heart. I know without a doubt, as you were growing up in New Jersey and setting yourself on the path that you did, I was on my side of the river waiting for you. The day you stepped into that studio, you became my **destiny**. ***Fate*** had you walking into that studio two years ago. I had no idea what ***love*** was, what love was capable of doing. It suffocates and debilitates and strips you raw, and I would do it all over again. You rocked my world to the core, you've altered every cell in my body, and you've secured my ***destiny***."

I sink my fingers in her hair, pulling her closer. Our lips dancing together, warming us both toward that crescendo we achieve so easily together. She smiles after she attempts to control her breathing. A quick look behind her clues her to the fact that we are now alone. The others slipped away, no doubt to get some privacy.

"Where did everyone go?"

"Don't know, but it's about time." I stand with her in my arms, "I have a hot woman to make love to."

"Lucky woman."

## Epilogue – Trey

We're at an impasse. She sits across from me, probing me with her big brown eyes. It's not her fault, but it is. All that I carefully planned is being threatened because I got involved with her. All that I purposefully changed and altered in my life is about to come crashing down around me, because of her. And none of this would have happened, if I had never met her.

There was a time I thought it could happen. A time when I worried it was just a matter of time before I would have to deal with all this fucking shit that I've been running from. But then it never did. Even with the success, the bottom never fell out. I fucked up, and the bottom is about to fall out. Unfortunately, somewhere along the way I lost focus. I got complacent. I started to feel.

"Do you feel anything? After all these months, do you feel anything for me, at all?" she asks, tears swelling in her eyes.

*If she only knew.*

If she only could read my thoughts to know how I can't stop feeling for her. I wish I could shut it off, turn it the fuck off. Sometimes I wish I never met her. How fucked up is that? How damaged and broken am I? I finally find someone I can't breathe without, and I rather it had never happened?

With this comes shit. Tons and tons of fucking shit that I don't want to deal with. I never wanted to deal with it again. And here I am, knee deep in all the shit that comes with a relationship…all the shit that comes from being accountable to someone…all the shit that is making it hard for me to not reach out, pull her into my arms, and tell her how I really feel.

But I can't.

I can't tell anyone how I really feel. I've become a master at hiding my feelings. Not even those closest to me have a clue who I am. And I like it that way, because that way I can't get hurt. One other time, I allowed a hot chick I was fucking to mess with me. Lori started infiltrating my thoughts. I saw the signs and ended it, never looking back. I moved on. I've done it before. I can do it again.

We left Jack and Leila's without a word to anyone. Tara actually was so upset, she stormed off and I stupidly followed. Why? Why can't I just let it be? We ended up back at my place, my plan to do what I'm good at...to deflect and distract. For the first time in my goddamn life, it's not working.

"I'm going," she says when several long minutes pass, and I still haven't said a word. She stands at my door, one hand on the knob. She's waiting for me to stop her, and I can't.

She pulls in an audible, ragged breath, turns to meet my gaze and says, "I'll say it. I'm not a coward. I love you." With that, she walks out the door, never turning back.

And still, I can't.

The End?

Want to know Trey Taylor's story?

Coming soon in Backstage, Book 4 of The Back-Up Series.

## Acknowledgements

Three books? I can't believe I have now published three books. The process may have gotten easier, my knowledge of the self-published indie world may have increased, but my neglect towards my family has remained the same throughout. So, for all the missed meals, and missed sporting events, and constantly having my face buried in my laptop, I'm sorry. You guys mean the world to me, and I appreciate you letting me have this time to do my thing. Your support during these past ten months has been unwavering, and I adore the three of you. To my three kings, you rule my world. I Love you J.D., A.M., and R.J.

I want to thank my immediate family. My parents, sister, brother, sister-in-laws, brother-in-laws, nieces and nephews, you are the best cheerleaders a new, insecure author can ask for. I love you and thank you for your support.

My Get-together Club. You all know who you are. I miss seeing your faces every day, but more importantly, I love you all.

I have met so many Bloggers, and I am privileged to call many of them my friends. Thank you for your love of The Back-Up Series, and of Jack, Leila and the gang. Thank you for the many contests, and raffles and never-ending pimps. You guys have most definitely contributed to the success I've achieved so far. I appreciate each and every one of you.

To Trish ~ I love you even more now than I did yesterday. Your ability to talk me off the ledge, to curb my FB crack addiction, and to cheer me on at every turn keeps me grounded and sane. I am super lucky to have you in my life.

C.D. I love you. That is all.

To my Beta Readers ~ thank you…thank you…thank you!!! I couldn't have found a better team to work with. You guys have no idea how much I loved hearing your comments regarding Encore. You had my back, helped me release a book I can be proud of, and showed your love and support the entire time. I hope and pray I can rely on you to beta read my future books.

To my original ten Madd Chicks – Trisha H, Jessica B, Stephanie F, Kimberly T, Rachel H, Marina M, Alexis B, Cheryl F, Kathleen DM, Desiree G. I am honored to now call you my friends. You guys have been with me since day one, and I couldn't ask for a better team to back me up.

To my muse, Pedro Soltz. Thank you for allowing me to use your gorgeous face as my Jack Lair. My fans have embraced you, and adopted you as their rock star. I appreciate you letting us indulge in our fantasy.

To my cover artist, Sarah, @ Sprinkles on Top Studios, thank you. To Alicia and Peanut, @ AVC Proofreading, I'm so glad I found you. I love you girl.

To my Sinners Sistahs ~ Christine Davison, Ann Vaughn, L.L. Collins, J.M.Witt, Ren Alexander, Tricia Daniels, A.D. Justice, & Skye Turner~ I'm still hoping for that Sinners girl weekend getaway with champagne glass hot tubs and tacky furnished rooms. Love you girls.

#Teamsuckit forever. #HeadSuckitBitch, #CaptainSuckit, #TheMadSucker, and #QueenSuckithashtag. Bahahahahahahahaaaa !

To all the fellow authors who I can now call friends, I love you gals so much. Some of you I will meet soon, some I hope to meet some day. You are all very talented, and I am working my way through your books. You make the romance genre better with your talents. To Joanne Schwehm, your writing sprints motivated my ass on more than one occasion. Te amo. Joanne

Schwehm is the author of My Chance, Unexpected Chance, and her new release Ryker. You can find Joanne's books at Amazon.com.

To Ann Vaughn for lending me Mike and Lainey Casiano, and for Aubrey, Keeley and Trevor's © remarkable story. I can't wait to read more of it in Tempting Trouble. Ann Vaughn is the author of Long Way Home, Finding Home, A Home for Christmas and Finally Home. You can find Ann's books at Amazon.com.

To Skye Turner for lending me Bayou Stix©, thank you. My rock stars are lucky to have your rocks stars as friends. Skye is the author of Alluring Turmoil, Alluring Seduction, Alluring Ties and Alluring Temptation. You can find Skye's books at Amazon.com.

To my girl, my self-proclaimed President of the Jack Lair Stalker Club, my therapist, my partner in crime, my creator of My Dom, I love you so much and so hard. Thank you for lending me The Steele Security Men. Those gorgeous hunks can guard my ass any day. A.d. Justice is the author of Crazy Maybe, Wicked Games, and Wicked Ties. You can find A.d.'s books at Amazon.com.

To my Devil's Lair Groupies. You guys are the best fans on Facebook earth. I wish I could name all one hundred twenty something of you. Thank you for supplying the name discussion, countless teasers, tireless pimping. For recognizing I needed a writing break by giving me many screen lick-worthy moments. But, by also cracking the whip, policing my crack addiction, and sending me back to the cave to resume my writing and get serious. Your pimping is second to none. Your support is immeasurable. I love you guys so much. If Devil's Lair were real, I would have you all in a front row seat, with backstage passes to a personal meet and greet with the guys.

To my teaser queens - Karen L , Janette G, Amber W, Stephanie F, Kimberly T, Christine D, Kathleen M-D, Nicole H, Miranda, Jesey N, If I forgot anyone, I apologize. But I added each and every hot and steamy teaser on my Pinterest board proudly.

To Stephanie F. – for telling me my "perfect Trey" doesn't exist and suggesting I give him a damn haircut. To Amber W. for Jack's kick-ass tattoo design.

To Tiffany Reed, Whitney Baer @ Readers Candy, April Nightingale Cestaro @Your Cup Says What , Lindsay Sparkes @ Cover Sparkle; my swag is awesome, many thanks to you gals.

Thank you to Kimberly Twedt for naming Jack and Leila's baby boy Madden Jackson Lair, for supplying Trey with his endless, tasteless, God-awful one liners found on Dirtyoneliners.com, and for those heart-breaking sad puppies. You made me cry way too many times with those damn puppies. I love you and am so happy I found you.

To my Devil's Lair Ho's, your "voices" cause a commotion wherever you go. For your protection, I will conceal your identities. You have become rock stars in your own right, and I am so proud and happy to have you in my corner. Love you guys!

Finally, to my readers. Each email, message, and review has touched me in one way or another. For those I haven't heard from, I thank you for #1clicking on my books and taking the journey with me. I hope you enjoyed the ride, and will accompany me on any future rides I may take.

Are you interested in becoming a Devil's Lair Groupie? Contact me at am.madden@aol.com. I'd love to have you.

## The Back-up Series Playlist ~

Reason I Am is an original song created for The Back-up Series. Lyrics - A.M. Madden, music - Mike Martone, vocals - Tyler Cohen, guitar - Randy Newberry, and recording engineer - Dennis Arcano. The song Reason I Am is available for download on Reverbnation and iTunes.

The songs listed below are both personal favorites and inspirational tracks that I played on a constant loop while writing The Back-up Series. I'm sure it's not a revelation to hear that I adore music, especially classic and modern rock. I did write a book about a rock band, after all. These songs helped set my tone, helped create my moods, helped inspire me. Every Avenue has a special place in my heart. If Devil's Lair were real, this is what they would sound like. I never tire of hearing them, which I feel makes the mark of a true masterpiece. Follow A.M. Madden on Spotify.com to find all The Back-up Series playlists.

Encore Playlist

Reason I Am ~ A.M. Madden
Dream On ~ Aerosmith
I Can't Not Love You ~ Every Avenue
Tie Me Down ~ Every Avenue
Burn it Down ~ Linkin Park
Come Undone ~ My Darkest Days
Mindset ~ Every Avenue
Only Place I Call Home ~ Every Avenue
A Story To Tell Your Friends ~ Every Avenue
A Thousand Years ~ Christina Perri
Better Days ~ Bruce Springsteen
Don't Stop Believin' ~ Journey
Dreams ~ Fleetwood Mac
F**kin' Perfect ~ Pink
Feels Like The First Time ~ Foreigner
Growin' Up ~ Bruce Springsteen
Here I Am ~ UB40

Layla ~ Eric Clapton
Think I'm in Love ~ Eddie Money
We Belong ~ Pat Benatar
Witchy Woman ~ Eagles
I Can't Help Falling in Love ~ UB40

# Follow A.M. Madden



Please support all Indie-authors and leave a review at point of purchase. Indie-authors depend on reviews and book recommendations to help potential readers decide to take the time and read their story. This Indie-author would greatly appreciate it.

Xo

A.M. Madden

You can contact A.M. Madden at:

www.ammadden.com

https://www.facebook.com/pages/AM-Madden-Author/584346794950765

https://twitter.com/ammadden1

https://www.goodreads.com/author/show/7203641.A_M_Madden

You can contact Jack Lair at:

https://www.facebook.com/jackhlair

https://twitter.com/jacklair1

Made in the USA
Columbia, SC
14 May 2018